# SEAL
## TEAM SIX
## OUTCASTS

# SEAL
## TEAM SIX
# OUTCASTS

A NOVEL

# HOWARD E. WASDIN
# & STEPHEN TEMPLIN

GALLERY BOOKS

New York   London   Toronto   Sydney   New Delhi

# G

Gallery Books
A Division of Simon & Schuster, Inc.
1230 Avenue of the Americas
New York, NY 10020

Copyright © 2012 by Stephen Templin and Howard E. Wasdin

First Gallery Books hardcover edition May 2012

GALLERY BOOKS and colophon are registered trademarks of Simon & Schuster, Inc.

For information about special discounts for bulk purchases, please contact Simon & Schuster Special Sales at 1-866-506-1949 or business@simonandschuster.com.

The Simon & Schuster Speakers Bureau can bring authors to your live event. For more information or to book an event, contact the Simon & Schuster Speakers Bureau at 1-866-248-3049 or visit our website at www.simonspeakers.com.

Designed by Renato Stanisic

Manufactured in the United States of America

10  9  8  7  6  5  4  3  2  1

Library of Congress Cataloging-in-Publication Data

Templin, Stephen.
    SEAL Team Six outcasts / by Stephen Templin & Howard Wasdin.—1st Gallery Books hardcover ed.
        p.   cm.
    1. United States. Navy. SEALs—Fiction.   2. War on Terrorism, 2001–2009—Fiction.
3. Commando troops—United States—Fiction.   I. Wasdin, Howard E.   II. Title.
PS3620.E53S43   2012
813'.6—dc23                                                                    2011048769

ISBN 978-1-4516-7566-5
ISBN 978-1-4516-7568-9 (ebook)

# PART ONE

*Courage can't see around corners, but goes around them anyway.*
—Mignon McLaughlin

# 1

*Acquire the target. Verify the target. Get authorization for the shot. Terminate the target.* Alex bared his teeth in something approximating a grin. This was going to be a good day.

In the darkness of 0530, SEAL Team Six sniper package code-named Ambassador and comprising Chief Petty Officer Alexander Brandenburg and fellow team member and spotter Petty Officer Second Class Theodore "Smiley" Lonkowski slow-crawled across the rocks of an Afghanistan mountain overlooking the border with Pakistan. They maintained separation so they didn't look like a huge blob to anyone scanning the mountainside. They were headed for an alcove ten feet below the peak of the mountain with a clear view of a nondescript goat path that crossed between the two countries. Alex wasn't worried about the Pakistani border guards. They weren't on the target list, at least, as long as they didn't interfere.

"Home, sweet home," Smiley whispered, sliding into the alcove and stretching out flat. Smiley got his nickname from the permanent grin on his face. Guys said that in Basic Underwater Demolition/ SEAL Training his smile drove the instructors nuts. Even during Hell Week, he smiled—it got knocked a little crooked, but he smiled.

"You're a trusting soul," Alex said, gingerly easing himself in beside him, all the while scanning the dirt and rocks for creepy crawlies. The men could be holed up here for hours, maybe days. He didn't want to be sharing dirt with something that could crawl into his clothes.

They wore their ghillie suits and ghillie boonie hats—handmade camouflage clothing that looked like part of the tan mountain they hid in. The cloth was even coated with a chemical that was designed to fool infrared, although Alex wasn't sure he trusted that. Best to stay as hidden as possible so that no one could see them, not even the RQ-170 Sentinel drone covering their area of operation from somewhere north of sixty thousand feet.

Where dark shadows normally fell on the skin around their eyes and other depressions on their faces they wore light, sand-colored paint. On their foreheads, cheeks, and other prominent features of their faces that normally shined, they wore dark gray-green face paint. They looked like shadowy ghouls, and Alex was entirely okay with that.

Alex cleared his mind and became one with the earth. He carried the .300 Winchester Magnum (Win Mag), a customized Remington 700 sniper rifle wrapped with an olive drab cravat and tied off with a square knot to break up the weapon's outline and contrast where the scope attached to the weapon. Olive drab and tan burlap straps broke up the cravat's solid green color, making it look like so much scrub and debris and not the deadly weapon it was. Firing a 190-grain match bullet designed to be perfectly symmetrical around its circumference, the Win Mag could reach out and touch anyone.

Alex remembered the look of bored indifference that other soldiers—nonsnipers—got when he talked about the various pluses and minuses of equipment makers and specifications, but then snipers were a special breed. Crazy, as Alex would be the first to admit, but crazy in a very, very purposeful way. The obsession with equipment spilled over into less critical areas of a SEAL's life, like having the right trousers or sunglasses—sometimes a guy needs enough pockets for his working tools and doesn't want to be blinded by the sun while he's working—occasionally, a guy just wants to look cool. Making the right equipment choice led to survival. Making the wrong equipment choice could lead to becoming a terrorist's new plaything.

Once in the alcove, Alex and Smiley lay close so Smiley could point out something to Alex on their map. Close enough so Smiley could watch the vapor trail of Alex's bullet splash into the target. If needed, Smiley could whisper feedback.

Smiley lasered the distances to prominent features: bend in a trail, boulder, clump of shrubs, abandoned house, etc. The boulder rested near the border between Afghanistan and Pakistan. Alex squeezed the two-pound trigger, dry firing while listening for the firing pin's proper operation. Then he simulated reloading: smoothly manipulating the rifle bolt with minimum movement and without taking his eyes out of the scope. In case their target ran, Alex practiced an ambush, holding his sight at a point ahead of the target's path and waiting until the dirtbag ran into Alex's crosshairs, then pulling the trigger.

The sun inched up the gray sky behind the thousand-foot-high, charcoal-colored mountains a couple of miles in front of the two SEALs. The long shadows, cast by scattered trees and shrubs, retracted. A light film of dirt powdered Alex's face. Except for the whisper of a slight wind, it was eerily quiet.

Through Alex's Leupold 10-power sniper scope, he spotted three specks in the distance. Smiley saw them, too. They came closer. Three bearded men appeared out of the gloom and walked across the border from Pakistan. They wore the traditional tribal *salwar kameez* combination of loose-fitting trousers and tunic and the distinctive *pakol* hats that reminded Alex of muffin tops. Each had an AK-47 slung across his shoulders. Alex paused. It was possible the weapons were AK-74s, the smaller 5.45mm version of Kalashnikov's original gift of terror to the world, but in the end it shouldn't matter.

As long as Alex and Smiley did their jobs, the terrorists would never get a shot off. Still, Alex reminded himself never to assume. It might make an ass out of you, but it could get him killed.

The men stopped four hundred yards in front of the SEALs at an abandoned house made out of mud. It was nestled among Afghan government buildings and a few empty shells that were once people's homes. The man in the middle was their target: Abu al-Zubaydi, one of the Taliban's leading bomb makers in Afghanistan. Al-Zubaydi first learned his trade in a Taliban training camp in Afghanistan. Recently, he had bombed the Red Cross, Afghan police, Afghan government, and others in order to destabilize the country—so he and his comrades could step in and take control. A lot of innocent men, women, and children had died because of him. The SEALs gave him the codename *Half-ass* because he had only one hand—the right. Even a terrorist needs both hands to be a complete asshole. On his right side stood his bodyguard, a native of Yemen according to the intel, and on his left was Half-ass's old friend from Tunisia: Hannibal. The three men wore olive drab Chinese AK-47 chest pouches.

"Zeus, this is Ambassador," Alex called on the radio. *Zeus* was the call sign for Patrick, Alex's boss. Patrick was a SEAL officer, but he wasn't much of a leader. He was simply a manager with no vision, reacting to events around him. Patrick maintained the status quo or whichever way the wind blew. He liked to take credit for things his men did well but blame them for things that went wrong. Patrick spent more time planning operations than operating. He preferred what looked good to what actually worked. Patrick had little vision of what the future could be. Even if he could envision the future, it was doubtful he could take his men there.

Static crackled in his earpiece. He tried again. "Zeus, this is Ambassador, over." More static. He looked over at Smiley.

"Wiggle the little doohickey on the top," Smiley said.

Alex shook his head. *Little doohickey?* This was a precision piece of electronic equipment. Still, Alex tapped the top of the radio and gave it a little shake.

"Zeus, this is Ambassador. Primary target in sight," Alex said.

Alex and Smiley's asset was supposed to meet with Half-ass and signal the sniper team, verifying it was indeed their target. Unfortunately, the asset was nowhere in sight. Maybe he'd decided he didn't need the money so much after all. Maybe he'd been captured. That thought gave Alex pause. Maybe the terrorists knew there was a SEAL Team out there. Alex banished the thought. One of Half-ass's bodyguards went inside the abandoned house, then came out a minute later. He said something before Half-ass disappeared into the house.

"Ambassador, Zeus. Confirm main target is Half-ass, over."

Smiley grunted. Alex took his eye away from the scope long enough to shake his head at Smiley. "Negative. Asset is a no-show."

Alex and Smiley waited—and waited. Half-ass stepped outside. He and the bodyguards looked around, fidgeting. Still, the asset was nowhere in sight. The terrorists seemed ready to bug out.

"Confirm target is Half-ass, over."

Alex cursed under his breath. "Asset is not available for confirmation ID, but I'm sure this is Half-ass," he whispered into his radio.

"Did the asset give positive ID, over?" Zeus asked. Alex knew it was Officer-in-Charge (OIC) Patrick.

"Zeus, I say again, the asset is a no-show, but I can verify that the primary target is Half-ass."

Zeus wasn't having it. "Not good enough, Ambassador. We need positive confirmation from the asset."

*For Pete's sake!* "I've memorized Half-ass's photos. Missing appendage, scar dissecting left eyebrow. I'm looking at him right now through my scope."

"We need asset confirmation of primary target, Ambassador."

Alex would have stood up and screamed into the morning sky if it wouldn't have gotten him and Smiley killed. "I say again, Zeus, the asset is a no-show."

"You know the parameters, Ambassador. No asset, no confirmation signal—no shot!"

*The asset is nowhere in sight.* Half-ass and his bodyguards began walking toward Pakistan. "It's him. Half-ass is moving toward Pakistan. If he walks fifty more yards, we lose him."

"Understood, Ambassador, but it doesn't matter. Without confirmation we don't engage."

"But he'll be inside Pakistan in another minute. That's why we have to take him out now."

"Negative, Ambassador, negative! We need asset confirmation, first."

Alex felt Smiley's hand resting on his shoulder. "Easy, tiger."

Alex clenched his teeth. "He meant to blow up those Red Cross nurses, Smiley. He targeted children. He's a sick killer."

"I know it and you know it and dollars to doughnuts, Zeus knows it, but that doesn't change things. The asset didn't show, so we don't shoot. This is not worth throwing away your career for . . ."

Alex couldn't believe his ears. He had one of the most evil men on the planet in his sights and he was being told not to shoot. It felt like he was choking.

Half-ass continued to walk back toward the border. He was now twenty-five yards away from safe haven.

"I understand your frustration, Ambassador," Zeus said, his voice taking on a sympathetic tone, "but our orders are clear: do not take out the target without direct confirmation from our asset."

"We'll never get another chance like this," Alex said to Smiley. "That's what I know."

"Let it go," Smiley said.

"I can't let him cross the border into Pakistan."

"I am telling you one last time: do not take out the target without asset confirmation."

Half-ass approached the border and began to walk faster.

"Request compromise authority, Zeus," Alex asked, going for the final fallback position.

"Permission denied."

"I can't accept that, Zeus."

"It doesn't matter what you can accept, it's an order."

Alex eased his face away from the scope and looked over at Smiley. "I can't accept it."

"What other choice do we have?"

The radio crackled. "Ambassador, confirm that you understand and will obey mission protocol. I want confirmation of that, now, or you will be finished!"

"Alex," Smiley whispered calmly. "He's in Pakistan now."

Through his scope, Alex saw Half-ass walking quickly beyond the boulder at the border. *All the months of work leading up to this moment . . . The sweat of my Teammates . . . Blood of the innocent . . .* He felt numb lying there in the dirt.

Then a single thought shone in Alex's mind. The way became clear.

"Zeus, we've been spotted. We're taking fire, we're tak—" Alex said before driving the SATCOM communications radio down onto a rock and smashing it.

"Half-ass is still in range. We're taking him out."

"You sure about this?" Smiley asked.

Alex reacquired Half-ass and focused on his breathing. "Always and forever."

"You're going to get us court-martialed," Smiley said, but he kept the laser range finder pointed on the terrorists.

Alex's rear elbow gave him balance. The rifle butt rested firmly in his right shoulder pocket. His shooting hand calmly held the small of the stock, finger on the trigger.

"Four hundred seventeen yards. Send . . . if you're sure," Smiley said.

Cheek touching his thumb on the small of the stock, Alex inhaled. He aligned his crosshairs in the center of Half-ass's back. *Exhale.* After purging the carbon dioxide from his lungs, he held the natural pause between his exhale and inhale—long enough to keep the crosshairs steady but not so long as to cause muscular tension and blurred vision. Even though the terrorists were walking away from him, he took his time. This first shot was the cold shot. The barrel wouldn't be as accurate because it hadn't warmed up yet from firing. His finger gently squeezed the trigger until he heard the shot and felt the recoil. Half-ass tumbled forward into the dirt.

Alex pulled the bolt back and removed the spent shell. With a smooth movement of his wrist and fingers that he'd practiced thousands of times, he moved the bolt forward, chambering a new one.

The bodyguards hugged the ground next to Half-ass. The one from Yemen was experienced enough for his eyes to follow the sound of the shot and the sound of the projectile flying through the air that took out his leader. He aimed his assault rifle—definitely an AK-47 by the sound—in the SEALs' direction and sprayed, but his shots weren't even close. He was shooting at ghosts.

Alex capped him in the forehead. The man's pakol popped into the air like a muffin flung from a baking pan.

Half-ass squirmed, his one hand flailing at the air. *Bastard's still alive.* Hannibal, the third terrorist, hopped to his feet and sprinted toward cover. If Hannibal hooked up with his comrades, they'd come looking for Alex and Smiley. Their evac route was a long hump up and down two mountain valleys crawling with Taliban. Hannibal couldn't get away.

Alex aimed at the middle of his back. As he squeezed the trigger, Hannibal tripped and fell. The shot missed. *Damn.* Alex had only two more shots in his Win Mag. He put a new round in the chamber. Hannibal stood and ran, but before he could gain speed, Alex caught him in the back, dropping him to his knees. The terrorist crawled, trying to get up again. Alex chambered the last round and put a bullet into the base of Hannibal's skull.

Smiley handed Alex a new round.

Alex calmly chambered the round in his empty Win Mag.

"Main target at four hundred eighteen feet. Send," Smiley said.

Alex reacquired the fallen terrorist and shot. He didn't pause, he didn't think of a cool line to say, he just shot. Three bodies lay still. Birds, scared by the gunfire, continued to fly north.

Although Half-ass wouldn't be terrorizing anyone anymore, Alex would have to face the consequences of disobeying a direct order. The enormity of what he had just done came crashing down on him.

"I enjoyed Team Six while it lasted," Smiley said.

"My call, my fall."

"I could have stopped you," Smiley said.

Alex blinked and lifted his face off the stock of his rifle. "No, you couldn't."


When Alex returned to their Afghanistan base, the shit didn't so much hit the fan as pile up all around it. Smiley, his grin never wavering, described in colorful detail the appearance of a group of Taliban that proceeded to open fire on them. Alex nodded and verified everything Smiley said.

Patrick didn't believe them. Alex knew damn well their mission had probably been monitored from at least two different platforms high in the sky, but he also knew there was enough truth in their story that it would be hard to disprove. And whatever else, three terrorists were dead.

Finally, Smiley was dismissed with no charges. Patrick waited until Smiley was out the door and then he walked right up to Alex.

"You think I don't know what you did? You failed to follow the protocol and you disobeyed a direct order." The words were clear, but Alex heard the wariness in Patrick's voice. *He's not 100 percent sure. He can't prove it.*

Alex knew enough to say nothing. Patrick barked for another ten minutes. If he thought Alex might break and admit everything, he didn't understand shit. From the first day of BUD/S, Alex had been prepared to go black. It happened when they made them swim and perform tasks under the water with no oxygen tanks. Your lungs would start to burn, then your vision would start to get gray at the edges before finally going all black and you went unconscious. It was terrifying, but it was also the only way. If you weren't prepared to go black, why the hell were you there?

Finally realizing the futility of haranguing Alex, Patrick ordered him to pack his bags and return to Dam Neck, Virginia, home of Team Six. Shit. He knew his days were numbered. Administrative duty if he was lucky, maybe even transfer him out of the Teams altogether. *What if they kick me out of the navy? If I can't hunt terrorists, what can I do?*

# 2

Two days later, at precisely 0855, wearing his best pressed khaki uniform, Alex knocked on the skipper's office door at SEAL Team Six in Dam Neck, Virginia. His biological clock was still on Afghanistan time—1555. Even though he'd arrived the previous evening, he couldn't sleep. Alex could take a cut in pay, getting busted in rank, and a variety of psychological and physical abuses, but getting kicked out of Team Six was the worst thing that could happen to him—the closest second would be getting kicked out of the SEAL Teams altogether. He hoped for the best, but his mind continued to spin around worst-case scenarios.

"Come in," called a deep voice.

Alex opened the door, walked in smartly across the navy blue carpet, and stood at attention in front of the skipper's desk. Like nearly 50 percent of SEAL officers, a high percentage in the military, Captain Kevin Eversmann was a maverick, going from the bottom of the enlisted ranks to becoming an officer, the equivalent of a full bird colonel—and he'd seen his fair share of combat as he climbed the promotion ladder. Although it was difficult to judge while Eversmann sat, he seemed nearly the same height as Alex, six feet tall, but his salt-white hair contrasted with Alex's—dark brown or black, depending on the lighting. The skipper had a reputation as a man who didn't suffer fools and Alex didn't want to find out why. Of course, the skipper didn't offer him a seat, and Alex didn't ask for one. A stack of four personnel files rested on the skipper's desk. Alex noticed his name on the top.

"At ease," he said. "I've called you in here because I've noticed something about your character. I've known counterterrorism operators from around the world, but for you the job seems more . . . What's the word I'm looking for? Personal."

"Yes, sir."

"Your personal enthusiasm seems to have served you well in the past, but this time it got you in some trouble with your OIC," the skipper said.

"Yes, sir."

"I understand that you were supposed to wait for asset confirmation before taking out a terrorist, codenamed 'Half-ass.' Also, the rules of engagement were not to fire upon enemies in Pakistan unless fired upon first. But somehow, three terrorists well inside Pakistan were killed, the asset never appeared, which means no confirmation was received, and your commanding officer expressly ordered you not to engage. Is my understanding of the information correct? Oh, and you were attacked by a group of wandering Taliban that somehow never showed up on any sat-tracking, intel reports, or recon patrols by units in the area."

Alex felt as if the world had begun to slip out from under his feet. In the heat of the moment, he knew he'd made the right decision. Even lying to Patrick had felt right. He had rid the world of three sick bastards, yet here and now, facing the skipper, the idea of telling the lie ate at his stomach like battery acid.

"Yes, sir."

"Yes, sir?"

Alex drew in a breath and kissed his career in Team Six goodbye. "I mean no, sir. I knew it was Half-ass with or without confirmation and so I took the shot. My spotter didn't know I was going to do it, and even if he had, he couldn't have stopped me."

Eversmann leaned back in his chair and studied Alex. Alex held his gaze, knowing he was done and wishing he could go black and end this.

"I think you understand why we have these rules in place."

To Alex's surprise, the skipper didn't yell. "Because of political objectives, sir."

"Well, yes. You also disobeyed a direct order from Patrick to stand down."

"Yes, sir."

"I think you can imagine what would happen if we all disobeyed orders."

"Chaos, sir."

"Something like that. You know Patrick is sensitive about his leadership effectiveness, and he wants to hang you from the nearest mast for what you did. Of course, he has to be able to prove it, and at the moment, your admission is just between you and me . . . and no doubt your spotter. If you had shot the wrong person and added more political pressures on our tactical operations in Afghanistan—or if Pakistan found out about your little shootout on their soil, you know how touchy they are after the bin Laden raid, and if it damaged our progress in rooting out terrorists there . . ." He paused for a moment. "As it turned out, you whacked the right person and his buddies, and I'm not too broken up about three less terrorists in the world."

Alex couldn't believe what he was hearing. The skipper agreed with him! He couldn't help himself. A smile started to creep across his face.

"Of course," Eversmann continued, "you're out of Team Six. Right or wrong, you broke the chain and that can't be tolerated."

Alex's smile melted. The joy of a second ago crashed into an abyss of darkness.

"But, sir, you said—"

"That I understand? I do, but tell me something, sailor, do you really think a cowboy can swim with a Team? What officer is going to trust you? What Team is going to trust you?"

Alex got the point, and it might as well have been a knife in his heart. "So that's it, I'm out?"

"Of Team Six, yes. Effective immediately you are on a six-month administrative leave to deal with personal issues."

"I understand," Alex said, his voice cracking. Being a SEAL was everything to him. There was nothing else.

The skipper shook his head. "Son, you really don't. I, however, do. You had a choice out there, and knowing that you risked your career you made the call that terminated some bad elements. That kind of independent action just won't wash in the current Teams and so you had to go."

Alex started to nod, then stopped. "Current Teams, sir?" Maybe the skipper had gone a little off the reservation himself when he'd been in Vietnam.

For the first time since Alex walked into the office, the skipper smiled. It made Alex think of a shark five feet below a surfboard.

"Do you know my story?"

"Yes, sir. Maverick, rose up through the ranks, three tours in Vietnam, awarded the Navy Cross in 1971 for actions against an NVA company when you were part of a search-and-rescue mission for an F-105 Thunderchief pilot shot down in the north. Recommended for the Medal of Honor on another mission in 1972 when—"

The skipper waved him to silence. "That's the official record, and all true, I might add. But like you, it isn't the whole story."

Alex held his breath.

"What do you know about the Phoenix Program?"

Alex had read about the Vietnam War in college. "Targeted capture and/or assassination of Viet Cong and other high-ranking North Vietnamese agents conducted by the CIA and U.S. forces during the war. It ran from 1968 to 1972. It was deemed successful, but also very controversial."

"Close enough," the skipper said. "Now, what do you know about the Bitter Ash Program?"

Alex shook his head. "Never heard of it."

The skipper stared hard at Alex as if weighing what to say next.

"When the Phoenix Program was shut down in 1972 and American forces left Vietnam, it was realized in certain circles that the South Vietnamese government would likely last six months at the most on its own."

"But it hung in there until 1975," Alex said.

"Thanks to Bitter Ash."

The light finally dawned for Alex. "From the ashes of the Phoenix, a new program rose."

"You're not stupid, I'll give you that. Yes, smaller, quieter, and even more precise than before. We went in, found who we were looking for, recycled them, and then vanished."

"When did they finally shut it down?" Alex asked, knowing the information the skipper was giving was beyond classified.

"It wasn't."

It took a moment for that to sink in. "You mean . . ."

The skipper nodded. "Codenames, people, protocols . . . they've changed many times since then, but the core mission hasn't. Doesn't matter when, doesn't matter where. There's always going to be terrorists of one kind or another trying to blow up the system and kill a lot of innocent souls in the process. In World War II the bad guys literally wore black. Now, hell, six-year-old kids and eighty-five-year-old grandmothers are strapping on bombs and blowing themselves up. Good as our military is, you can't train some eighteen-year-old recruit fresh from the farm to deal with that kind of threat."

Alex decided to take his shot. "So what does that mean for me? If I'm no longer a SEAL, what am I?"

The skipper slammed his fist down on his desk. "You're no longer a SEAL when I tell you, and not before." He took a breath and continued. "I've been tasked with putting together a new operational unit, Tier 1, same level of proficiency as SEAL Team Six and Delta but with an asterisk. I'm forming a new SEAL Team. It will operate, however, under Bitter Ash protocols. It'll be smaller, quieter, and tasked with targeted solutions to . . . thorny problems."

Alex fought the urge to scream with joy. He knew what he was being offered, and now that it was before him it was a dream come true. There was no way he was going to say no. He was still a SEAL, and a SEAL with a green light to do what he'd been trained to do.

"I have some problems that need your kind of enthusiasm. You're going to help me solve these problems, and I'm going to smooth things over with Patrick."

"Thank you, sir."

"Hang on for just a minute." Eversmann stood up, walked out of his office, and returned with two SEALs and a woman. The three stopped at attention in front of his desk. None of them looked over at Alex. Unlike Alex, each wore pressed camouflage utilities.

The skipper sat down behind his desk and told the three standing at attention to stand at ease.

"I've now had the same conversation with all four of you, well, as it pertains to your particular situation, and now it's time you meet." He gestured toward a charismatic brown-skinned guy in his mid to late twenties who was taller and heavier than Alex and built like a tank. "This is Petty Officer First Class Francisco 'Pancho' Rodriguez," he said.

The skipper turned to the second man, a handsome black guy with dark eyes who stood a couple of inches shorter than Alex. He had the physique of a triathlete, lean and ropey with that starving look about him. "Petty Officer First Class John Landry. He and Pancho served together in SEAL Team One, Echo Platoon."

Alex nodded, but Landry simply stared at him. Next to them stood a slender gal who was only a couple of inches shy of six feet.

Her skin was ivory white and she had a regal face—blond hair parted over her forehead to the left. "And last and by no means least, Petty Officer Catherine Fares. She worked for naval intelligence before joining us."

To the outside world it might have seemed shocking to see a woman with a SEAL Team, but many were already working with Team Six providing logistical support, intelligence, and cover stories in some very hot spots of the globe. Technically, the women weren't SEALs, but posing with a SEAL as husband and wife caused less suspicion at customs than a lone SEAL.

"Everyone, this is Chief Alexander Brandenburg. The chief is team leader, but make no mistake, I run this show. Now, let's get down to business. You're all here because you screwed up."

The three SEALs and Fares stiffened. Alex's elation of a moment ago bled away. He knew what he'd done to get here, and even though he was certain he was about to have his darkest desires granted to go after evil and kill it where he found it, he couldn't escape the fact that he'd screwed up. *So what the hell have the other three done to get assigned here?*

Landry started to speak, but the skipper cut him off with a stare. "If anyone here wants to dispute my assessment you can turn around and march your ass right out of my office and go back to whatever is left of your career." He waited. No one budged.

"Now, Fares, to be fair, you didn't so much screw up as piss everyone off."

Alex looked at her again with growing admiration. *What in the hell had she done?*

"Two admirals, an assistant secretary of defense, and, though no one has yet been able to prove it, the vice president," Eversmann said, a sense of awe clear in his voice.

Alex couldn't believe it. There was no way she could have been with all those men, could there? He took another glance. Sure, she was pretty, but no way.

Eversmann seemed pleased with himself and gave the group a nod. "Screwed up or the biggest pain in the ass of the free world, you're all here now. I know you all want to make amends, which is why you've all volunteered for a new Tier 1 counterterrorist unit."

This time Fares spoke. "We did?"

"And your country thanks you. If you follow orders and work as a team and complete the mission as defined your slate will be wiped clean and you will, if you wish, be able to resume your careers as before."

Alex had a suspicion that it wasn't going to be nearly as simple as that, but he held his tongue.

The skipper leaned forward in his chair. "President Kincaid is a former Vietnam SEAL. I served with the tough son of a bitch before he went all soft and got into politics," the skipper said, but his voice was filled with obvious affection. "Still, the salty bugger knows how the world works. He saw evil close up and didn't flinch. He expects the same from you four."

A chorus of "yes, sir" rang out.

"Feeding bin Laden to the fishes settled a big score, but it also set off a power struggle for the top slot in al Qaeda. The Five Families in New York didn't have this much trouble choosing a new don. It's a damn mess, which, while it's prevented them from launching large, coordinated attacks, has made them difficult to track as they splinter."

"Something's changed, sir?" Alex asked.

Captain Eversmann nodded. "We caught a major break with an asset deep in ISI."

Alex nodded. ISI, Inter-Services Intelligence, was Pakistan's largest intelligence service and reputed benefactor and ally of the Taliban in Afghanistan. With the Taliban and al Qaeda in bed together, it made sense one would know what the other was up to.

"We've ascertained the identities of seven candidates vying to take bin Laden's place. The president wants to finish off this Medusa, but he's under intense political pressure to stop large-scale incursions and drone attacks. In order to hit al Qaeda, we need a small team that can fly under the radar and accomplish the mission. Such a team will probably have to . . . finesse some of the United Nations' finer distinctions on national sovereignty and what constitutes an act of war."

The skipper paused and let that sink in. Alex looked out of the corner of his eye at the other three. They gave nothing away, but he knew they had to be thinking the same thing. This was black ops in the darkest of shadows.

"To the world at large you are little more than a support adjunct to the United States Navy. Mid-level sailors that once had promising careers and now are putting in time hoping to make it to a pension and an honorable discharge. The reality is far different. Your mission is simple—seven terrorists, seven terminations. You will hunt them down, you will kill them, and you will vanish. No one, beyond the five of us in this room and a handful of others, including the president, will ever know what you did."

Alex could live with that. It was a deal he'd already accepted when he joined SEAL Team Six.

"Should your team be compromised, the cavalry won't be coming to save your asses. You will have every intelligence asset and the entire United States military in your corner, but the moment you step on foreign soil 911 won't be in service. To put it bluntly, since the four of you have prior issues you're expendable."

Alex expected Fares to object. Whatever her training, she was a woman, and they weren't, well, the same as guys. There's no way she signed up for something like this. The skipper gave each one of them a long stare, but she never blinked. *Guess I'm a bit of a chauvinist.*

"Good." The skipper stood up and opened a file that was lying on his desk. He spun it around so the four members of the newly minted team could see its contents. Alex saw seven faces. They could have been doctors, mechanics, teachers, or accountants, and maybe they were, but they were also terrorists, and they were now their prey.

"This is Operation Black Flag. The first two of the seven insects are in Indonesia. Arif Setiawan, codename 'Cockroach,' and Rachmad Budi, codename 'Stinkbug.' The remaining five are in that searing piece of hell on earth we call the Middle East: Jamsheed 'Beetle' Jamshed; Khaled Qurei, aka 'Spider'; Lieutenant Commander Abdul-Nur Issa, or 'Lice'; Damien Guevara, 'Mantis'; and Kazim Halabi, who took the moniker the Red Sheik during the fighting against the Soviets in Afghanistan in the eighties. His codename is 'Mosquito.' There's conflicting thought on how these seven rank. Mantis is Mosquito's right-hand man, but at least one ISI report suggests he's being groomed for bigger things. Don't worry," he said, waving away their raised hands. "You will begin a series of thorough briefings so that you'll know what these men had for lunch when they're still eating breakfast."

The skipper looked at each in turn. "Any questions?"

Alex had a million of them, but he knew enough to wait for the briefing. He was being given a chance to save his career and take the fight to the bad guys in a way that finally made sense. Pancho, however, didn't seem to have the same restraint.

"Are we part of one of the color Teams or are we going to get our own color?" Pancho asked.

Alex started to open his mouth to tell the sailor to shut it, but the skipper smiled. "That's what you're worried about?"

Pancho's cheeks turned red, but he didn't lower his head. "No offense, sir, but you just told us we're going after some of the nastiest snakes in the jungle, in some of the darkest shitholes on the planet, and that if we're compromised, we're screwed."

"Go on."

"Well, sir, I'm still a SEAL, and you said we were still part of the Teams. I don't mind risking my life, but I want to do it under a color."

"Seems entirely fair," the skipper replied. "Gold, red, blue, and silver are already taken. So are black, gray, and green."

"Purple is a good color," Pancho offered.

John coughed, making his irritation with Pancho clear.

"It is," the skipper replied dismissively. "I was sitting on the toilet when I had an epiphany—you four are hereby designated Brown Team."

The Mexican giant nodded and held his tongue.

"Well, I've taken up enough of your valuable time. You have some briefings to get to. But be advised, you're mine now. The moment you step out that door you represent me. Mess up like you did before, and you are finished. Dismissed."

Alex came to attention and the others followed suit. Then they exited the office. Alex turned to have a word with Pancho, but before he could, two naval intelligence officers appeared and motioned them into an adjoining room.

For better or worse, the newest SEAL Team was now active.

# 3

Damien Guevara liked to carry a Russian OTs-38 Stechkin revolver in a customized KYDEX holster clipped inside the waistband of his trousers. Similar to a small .38, the double-action revolver held only five shots, but that was still four shots more than he usually needed. The 7.62 x 41.5mm SP-4 bullets made less noise and produced less flash than most sound-suppressed pistols, making for a quiet kill.

Quiet mattered to Damien. He understood the psychological power of something as audacious as the September 11 attacks against America, but the aftereffects of that one glorious day were still being felt. Wherever possible, he preferred a subtler, more elegant approach. A single bullet to the base of the skull, when applied to the right skull, could achieve more than a thousand jihadists strapped with bombs.

Stepping out of a Silver Bird taxi in Surakarta, Indonesia, Damien paid his driver a fifty-thousand-rupiah banknote and opened his umbrella. He used the umbrella to conceal his face as much as he used it to protect himself from the pouring rain. His sandaled feet stepped in puddles as he walked through a crowded maze of concrete buildings.

Damien could blend in like a chameleon in most places, and Indonesia was no exception. A native of Bolivia, his skin was naturally brown, blending with the Indonesian locals. For added measure he wore a casual brown Javanese shirt and dark green sarong.

Although in his early forties, he looked and moved like he was in his twenties. His diet was strict, and though he prayed five times a day, he did so not out of religious fervor, but because it was expected. He was no believer. He was a hunter. If he had to kneel toward Mecca in order to work with the jihadists, then so be it. Among mules, he would be the wolf.

Damien walked with purpose, deliberately going past the apartment building that was his destination. He circled the block, carefully observing the area and charting possible escape routes. Still walking at a steady pace, he approached the apartment building with dirty, faded white paint and cracks in the concrete and then turned and walked down an alley and came to the back of the building. He paused and bent down to adjust his sandal, all the while watching the alleyway he had just come down. No one followed him.

He looked up at the building and at each window. No one was looking out. That made him angry. There should be at least three men watching at all times. He debated to himself about turning around, leaving, and never looking back, but he'd come here for a purpose, and no matter the risk, he must see it through.

Damien walked into the back entrance and climbed four flights of steps to the top. The building did have an elevator, but Damien distrusted the things. Too easily trapped.

He stepped into the fourth-floor hallway and paused again. Not a watcher anywhere, not even children playing that could act as lookouts. He made a mental note and walked to the apartment at the far end of the hall.

He knocked three times, then after a beat, twice more.

Footsteps sounded from behind the door and a moment later a light appeared in the peephole, then the peephole turned black. Two locks were released and the door opened. He walked into a three-bedroom apartment, ignoring the man who opened the door. He was in the scorpion den now.

Arif Setiawan stood in the kitchen next to a dark-skinned guard, who held a pistol down at his side. Another guard and Setiawan's right-hand man, Rachmad Budi, sat at the table, but got up when Damien entered.

Damien pointed his nose at the pistol in the hand of the dark-skinned guard. "You might want to put that away—unless you're going to shoot me."

The guard looked at Setiawan, who translated Damien's English into Indonesian. The guard hesitated. Setiawan looked at Damien's eyes for a moment. Setiawan motioned for his guard to obey. The dark-skinned guard put his pistol in his shoulder holster, concealed by an open shirt over his T-shirt.

"I need you to stand guard outside and make sure we don't have any surprise visits while I'm here," Damien said.

Setiawan translated. Again, the dark-skinned guard hesitated. Setiawan looked at Damien again like he was trying to read him. Setiawan ordered the guard to leave. After he walked outside, Damien locked the door behind him.

Damien gestured for the three men to sit at the table. "Please, sit down."

When Setiawan sat, the other two followed.

Damien took a chair and joined them. "How is everything?"

"Everything?" Setiawan asked. "Everything is fine."

"Fine?"

"Yes."

"You must understand, the Red Sheik is hearing rumors that you want to become the new head of al Qaeda."

Setiawan paled. "Who said that? I never said that."

"And you've been running your own little secret moneymaking operation."

"We're not."

"A senior American diplomat said that you're making money off the sale of drugs and that you have aspirations for a higher leadership position."

"We were going to tell the Red Sheik about our efforts to increase funds. I'm sorry. It won't happen again."

"The Americans, however foolish and blundering they might be, have been at war with drugs for far longer than they have been at war with us. It is an obsession with them. They devote many men and much treasure to tracking the sale of drugs across the globe. By so brazenly engaging in this activity you have jeopardized our entire organization."

Setiawan stood up. "As you are a most honored guest in this house I am sure you will feel better about things after some refreshment and a chance to think longer on your . . . observations. I have served holy jihad far longer than you, my friend, and I assure you, I know what I'm doing."

"Perhaps you are right," Damien said, smiling and raising his hands in a gesture of peace. Setiawan lowered himself back into his chair. "My journey was long, and not without incident. Tell me, Budi, do you agree with my host? Am I, as he suggests, in need of some time to reflect on the soundness of your new ventures?"

Budi shifted in his chair. "Please, we are all friends here."

"Indeed we are," Damien said, still smiling as he lowered his hands. "And as my friend, I ask you, am I overreacting? Do you believe your moneymaking efforts are suitably quiet that they will not bring unwanted attention?"

Budi looked at Setiawan and then back at Damien. "Yes, they are."

Damien sighed. "Ah, then I owe you both an apology." Damien drew his OTs-38 Stechkin revolver. Setiawan's eyes grew wide just before the shot struck between them. Setiawan's upper body tipped forward until he gently collapsed on the table, a pool of dark red blood oozing out from the wound.

The guard at the table reached to his shoulder holster. Damien twisted in his chair and shot him in the head, knocking him backward as his arms flailed and his pistol clattered to the floor. Damien put another shot into the guard's heart, then turned and aimed at Budi, who had not moved.

"Please."

The guard outside pounded on the door, speaking loudly in Indonesian. Then he pounded harder. He was trying to break inside.

"Tell him everything is okay," Damien said.

Budi stared at the barrel of Damien's Stechkin. Budi called in Indonesian to the guard outside.

The door bowed and then shot open as parts of the frame splintered and flew into the room. The guard stumbled, his right hand, in which he was holding his pistol, slamming to the floor as he tried to keep from falling down. Damien shook his head. *Amateur.* The man didn't even have the sense to drop all the way down to his stomach and raise his weapon. Not yet realizing he was already dead, the guard pushed himself up, his pistol flopping around in his injured hand.

Damien let him stand straight up before firing a single shot into his upper chest, just to the left of his sternum. The guard opened his mouth, but no sound came out. The second shot caught the guard under the right eye, drilling a tiny black hole in his face.

The guard twisted as he dropped, landing on his side. His body twitched.

Damien reacquired Budi in his sights.

"I told the guard everything was okay," Budi pleaded. "Just like you said."

"I trust you don't have ambitions for taking over al Qaeda."

"Yes, of course. I mean no, no ambitions."

"Tell me, do you still believe Setiawan's drug venture is a smart one?" Damien asked.

Budi's eyes darted as he looked at the bodies around him. "It ends today. All ties will be cut. No more drugs."

Damien smiled and lowered his pistol. "And the Red Sheik said I would likely have to kill you, too. I am so happy that is not the case. Tell your followers that Arif Setiawan is dead. They belong to you now. And you belong to the Red Sheik. Congratulations."

Budi's lips quivered. He tried to smile, but his eyes kept going back to the pool of blood now dripping from the table edge onto the kitchen floor.

# 4

The briefings blurred into one another over the next six days. Alex and his new Team learned to distinguish the linguistic tics of each target. Facial recognition software ran multiple variations of what they might look like depending on diet, health, facial hair, at various distances, and even plastic surgery, although that was considered a low probability. Through it all Alex marveled that all this study was for but one purpose—to kill these seven men.

While the team studied the seven bugs, as the terrorists came to be called, there was little time for them to actually bond. It bothered Alex, but time was not on their side. The intelligence they had was actionable for a short period. There wasn't time to get surveillance assets in place to track them as had been done with bin Laden at his compound in Abbottabad. This was being done very much on the fly.

And then there were the weapons. SEALs trained with all the major weapons types used around the world, everything from the ubiquitous AK variants to the more cutting-edge near-future weapons like the ultracompact KRISS Super V submachine gun firing the heavy .45 ACP round and the Israeli-designed CornerShot, which, as the name suggested, allowed the shooter to shoot a full 90 degrees from center. It dawned on Alex that his days of being a sniper might be few and far between. They were training almost exclusively on short-range weapons.

Finally, the briefings ended. It was 0230 hours and the strain was showing on everyone. Alex knew they couldn't embark on a mission like this. He still knew next to nothing about any of them. Captain Eversmann could call them a Team, but until they bonded, they were just four highly trained individuals sharing the same geographic location.

There was a knock on the briefing room door. Pancho groaned. "Are you kidding me? If they try to cram one more fact into my head I think my brain is going to start leaking out my ears."

Alex got up from his chair and walked across the room and opened the door. He paid the petty officer and returned carrying three large pizzas and a blue plastic cooler. He set the pizzas down on the table and put the cooler on the floor. Three sets of eyes followed his every move as he flipped open the top to reveal twelve glistening bottles of beer and several Cokes awash in a frosty blanket of ice.

"Chief! You just restored my faith in humanity!" Pancho said, leaping out of his chair and diving into the cooler. John and Cat followed suit, Cat grabbing a beer, while John snatched a Coke. Cat pulled out a second beer and handed it to Alex.

"Nice surprise, Chief."

"I have my moments," Alex said, twisting off the top of his beer and taking a long pull. The cold beer slid down his throat like a jolt of icy lightning. His whole body tingled for a moment and then oozed into one long sigh of contentment.

John popped the lids on the pizza boxes. "Any anchovies?"

Alex shrugged. "I asked them to give me a bit of everything. Don't really know what everyone likes, so we've got one super veggie, one death by sausage, and one everything but the kitchen sink."

For the next twenty minutes there was relative silence as the team ate and drank. Alex watched them, trying to get a better sense of who they were. Cat, as Catherine had quickly become known, ate nothing like her domestic namesake. She chugged her beer and tore off chunks of her pizza like a lion on the savannah. It was . . . attractive.

*Stow it, sailor*, he told himself. That was the last thing any of them needed! Alex quickly turned to study the other two. Pancho, in spite of his immense size, ate as if he were tasting pizza for the first time. Each bite was small, and he chewed slowly and carefully, his eyes often closing as he made low, guttural sounds.

"Hey, Pancho," John said, wiping a hand across his mouth as he emptied his soda. "You eating that zaa or making love to it?"

"Both," Pancho said, his grin reminding Alex of Smiley. "Food, like making love, should be savored. Every moment is precious. Why would you want to rush?"

Alex grabbed a second beer and twisted off the cap. They were about to go on a mission that none of them might return from. The ramifications of what they were doing, and what might happen if they were caught, started to make him feel dizzy. He shook his head and took a long pull from the bottle.

The rest of the team were now slouched in their chairs, the effects of pizza, beer, and too many long nights clearly evident. Alex knew this was his chance.

"Listen up, I've got something to say," he said, wiping his mouth with the back of his hand.

Pancho groaned. "Chief, seriously, I think I speak for all of us when I say I don't think I can learn one more thing about these bugs. All I want to do now is kill the bastards so I can get some sleep."

"That's not it. We are ready, at least, from a technical standpoint. But we're not a Team yet."

That got everyone's attention. They all sat up in their chairs.

"I might be old-fashioned, but I want to know you, and I want you to know me. Maybe in time that would happen, but we don't have time right now. Each of us knows why we're here, but none of us know why the others are here. That just won't cut it."

He paused to take another drink. No one tried to interrupt, so he continued. "I was part of a two-man sniper package in Afghanistan on a mission to take out a high-value target. We found him, but the asset that was supposed to confirm his identity never showed. No asset confirmation, no shot."

"Damn lawyers are taking all the fun out of war," Pancho said.

"What did you do?" Cat asked.

"He's here, isn't he?" John said, pointing his Coke can at Alex. "He disobeyed orders and took the shot."

Alex nodded.

"Did you get him?" Cat asked, ignoring John's look.

"He's here, isn't he?" Pancho echoed John's words, smiling. "No way the skipper would have a sniper who couldn't shoot straight leading this band of rebels."

"No, just one who couldn't think straight," John said, upending his can. Some of the soda spilled out the side of his mouth and onto his shirt.

Alex pivoted in his chair to look straight at John. "Maybe, but I'm not here to apologize, and I sure as hell don't need your approval."

John slammed his can down a little too hard. "You understand we're disposable, right? That the only reason they put us together is that if it all goes to hell they just write us off as some kind of training accident. Meanwhile, their precious SEAL Teams don't get their hands dirty."

The bitterness in John's voice surprised Alex. This team-building chat wasn't going at all the way he hoped, but there was no turning back now.

"I don't see it that way," Cat said. "Sure, the skipper talked a good game, but at the end of the day, look at what he's asking us to do. They need people like us."

John laughed. "Really? And what is it you bring to the table? We did Hell Week. We've been in combat. You, apparently, have been screwing around with every politician and government official you could find."

Alex was halfway across the floor when Pancho intercepted him in a bear hug. "Easy! Easy!" Pancho shouted, pushing Alex back. "John, you stupid ass. And you wonder why you're here?"

Alex was still glaring at John when Cat's voice cut through the tension. "It's true, I was involved with all those men, but it's not what you think. I confronted each and every one of them about the fact that women are still denied access to all combat roles in the military."

Alex looked past Pancho. "Confronted?"

Cat's face grew red. "I kicked one senator in the nuts after he called me sweetie."

Pancho let Alex go. "What did you do to the VP?"

Cat put her hands on her hips. "Nothing! I met him at a private fund-raiser in D.C. and tried to explain why women should be allowed in combat."

"And?" Alex asked.

"I crushed a couple of nuts," Cat said. "Walnuts. We were talking, he wasn't listening, and I just reached into the bowl on the table, grabbed the nuts, and smashed them. The Secret Service deemed me a threat."

Pancho was chuckling. "And I thought John was going to be the hothead in our group."

Alex instinctively backed up a pace. "Well, let's agree right now that no one calls Cat anything other than Cat."

"So what did you do?" Cat asked Pancho, pointedly ignoring John.

Pancho shrugged. "We were down in Mexico training some of their naval counterterrorist forces," he said, looking over at John. "While we were there, three of the Mexican sailors' families were kidnapped and murdered by one of the drug cartels. Kids, too—

the sick scumbags even killed the kids." Pancho stopped, his voice breaking.

Cat got out of her chair and walked over to him, putting a hand on his shoulder.

"I was there, too," John said, apparently deciding to rejoin the conversation in a more civil manner. "No way we should have been burned for it."

Alex looked over at John. "You two got the blame for that?"

Pancho shook his head. "No, it was what happened after. Two days later the local drug baron for that cartel was killed by a car bomb along with three of his men."

Alex understood. "But they couldn't prove who did it, even though they suspected."

"Wasn't right," John said. "They butchered those people. Animals, just sick animals."

Alex wondered if he sounded like that. He hoped not. He couldn't afford to let his emotions get the better of him, even if that's what got him here. He had to use his head. The fine line he was walking just got a little thinner.

"Look, there's nothing any of us can do about the past. What happened, happened. What is in our power, however, is what we do now. Whether you look at this as some kind of punishment or reward, the bottom line is we have a chance to do some good. There are more terrorists out there eager to wreak havoc and we've been given the green light to terminate them. I don't know about the rest of you, but that's what I live for."

As speeches go, Alex figured it wouldn't crack the top one million in history, but he'd never been much for that long-winded crap.

"I said it before, and I'll say it again," Pancho said, holding out his hand palm down. "I'm in, all the way."

Cat put her hand on Pancho's. "I'll add my ovaries to your balls. I'm in, too."

Alex looked at John, waiting. They were only a team if everyone bought in. John looked at each of them and then placed his hand on top of Cat's. "I'm still in, I just have my opinion about stuff."

*Good enough.* Alex clamped his hand down on John's. "All for one, and one for all. We might be outcasts, but here, now, we're all part of the same team. Now let's go change the world one dead terrorist at a time."


AFTER FAR LESS SLEEP than he needed, Alex awoke feeling better than he expected. His attempt at team-building wasn't going to be studied as one of the more brilliant examples of how to get a group of people to work well together, but on the other hand, no one had a broken nose, or was waiting to make bail. He allowed himself a little smile. Not bad.

He walked into the team room after a quick shower and found the other three going over their gear as they prepped and bagged it. Everything was tagged so it was clear whose was whose. Alex was pleased he didn't have to explain his methods. You trained hard so you fought easy, and that meant making damn sure all your kit got where it was going. It was pointless to send a Team halfway around the world only to discover its gear and weapons were being unloaded at a weather station in the Antarctic.

There was no need for trying to disguise their weapons and other gear as everything for the mission was traveling with Pancho and John on an Air Mobility Command (AMC) flight going to Yokota Air Base in Japan. Cat and Alex, however, would travel undercover as a newlywed couple. He wasn't entirely sure if he'd won or lost. He was a soldier, not a spy. Sure, he'd let his hair grow long and had infiltrated more than one country in civilian garb, but he'd never enjoyed it.

"Anyone seen my Dramamine?" John asked, digging through his bag. "Figures Pancho and I would get stuck having to transfer to a Greyhound and lay over on a bloody boat."

Cat looked up from her bag. "They're putting you on a bus?"

Pancho sighed. "No, a C-2 COD. They're staging us from the *George Washington* somewhere in the Indian Ocean. After that we'll insert into Indonesia with the kit and rendezvous with you two lovebirds at your honeymoon suite."

"Not without my Dramamine," John said.

"It's like babysitting sometimes," Pancho said, holding out a small plastic bottle and tossing it to John. "How he made it through Hell Week I don't know. Only SEAL I know who gets airsick, seasick, carsick, and probably hot air balloon–sick if we ever have to fly in one."

"Ha, bloody, ha," John said, putting the bottle in his pocket.

Alex stayed out of it, concentrating on his own kit while keeping an eye on theirs. He was the team leader. It was his job to make sure everyone was ready. He remembered thinking babysitting was a girl's job when he was younger. Now, hell, he wished he'd done it a few times so he'd have some experience.

AFTER SAYING THEIR GOODBYES, Cat and Alex flew on a civilian flight from Virginia to Vermont, then chartered a van that took them across the Canadian border and up to Montreal. There they disappeared into the crowd and made sure they were "clean." Their cover was that of a married Canadian couple from Calgary on vacation. Alex carried an Alberta driver's license, Canadian Tire Visa credit card, library card, video store membership card, and Safeway supermarket card, all in his alias. The pièce de résistance, however, was his Tim Hortons card. America might have Dunkin' Donuts, but north of the border, Tim Hortons reigned supreme.

"Aren't you worried about traveling unarmed?" Cat asked.

"No," Alex said. He thought for a moment, then showed her a flat black Columbia River Knife and Tool (CRKT) Tao pen. "I have this as a backup."

It didn't look like a tactical pen. "A pen?" she asked.

"Yes. But this pen is made of 6061 aluminum, aircraft aluminum—so it won't break when you use the cap as a blunt striking or raking weapon. The butt can be applied to pressure points. And in a more serious scenario, the pen point won't break off when you stick it in your opponent."

"Oh. Does it write?" she joked.

"Even in the rain."

Cat seemed impressed.

From Montreal, they flew Air Canada to Toronto. Next, they flew from Toronto to Hong Kong, where they caught a Cathay Pacific flight to Soekarno-Hatta International Airport in Indonesia.

Cat and Alex stood in a slow-moving line at the airport until they reached the customs inspector. They handed him their passports: navy blue, CANADA written at the top, and marked with the Royal Arms.

The middle-aged inspector asked, "What is the purpose of your stay, Mr. and Mrs. Brown?"

They told him that they were on vacation for their honeymoon.

"And where will you be staying?" he asked.

"The Grand Hyatt Jakarta," Alex said.

Cat's eyes lit up. "We want to see the temples. With the tall pointed roofs."

"And the lights at night and the Ramayana dancing," Alex added with as much enthusiasm as he could muster, which wasn't a lot, but played perfectly for a new husband acquiescing to his wife's wishes. "They have such beautiful costumes and look so sophisticated the way they hold their hands . . ." The line of passengers behind Alex and Cat became longer as the pair eagerly described their travel plans.

The inspector quickly became bored. He stamped their passports and waved them through. Even if he had searched them, he wouldn't have found anything beyond a laptop, a Canadian paperback edition of the *Lord of the Rings* trilogy, clothes, a guidebook for Indonesia, and the usual tourist items.

When they got outside the terminal, a wave of humidity and smog hit the couple. Chaotic clusters of people scampered about as two cabdrivers solicited them to use their taxis. Alex ignored them and hailed a Silver Bird taxi—a black Mercedes. Their drivers were known for being able to speak English.

"Where go?" asked the driver. His face red with acne, he looked like a young man in his early teens, not old enough to drive.

Alex liked to ask the price beforehand so he wouldn't be surprised later. "How much to the Grand Hyatt Jakarta?"

"One hundred forty thousand rupiahs," the driver said.

It sounded like a lot, but when Alex dropped off the zeroes, fourteen dollars seemed reasonable for a Mercedes with a driver who spoke English. "Okay."

The driver helped them put their luggage in the trunk. They stepped into the taxi, sat, and locked the doors—Alex and Cat didn't want any surprise visitors. The driver probably got the message, too. He sped out onto Tol Prof. Sedyatmo Street. People drove like maniacs—including Alex and Cat's driver.

Cat smiled. "The adventure begins."

"Or ends," Alex said.

The driver passed a vehicle and almost collided head-on with a honking truck. The rules of the road seemed to be *there are no rules*. Alex couldn't see any evidence of town planning: old buildings, glass skyscrapers, slums—all were clumped together. Later, traffic jammed up, and the taxi crawled past Park Royale. After nearly forty minutes of riding the stop-and-go roller coaster southwest they'd covered about seventeen miles. The driver whipped around a roundabout and slammed on the brakes in front of the Plaza Indonesia, from which the Grand Hyatt Jakarta rose up. The Hyatt stood like a long bird staring up at the sky with its wings spread open. People arrived and departed in a casual rhythm that disturbed Alex.

Although Alex hadn't been present during the 2002 Marriott hotel bombing in Jakarta, he'd read the intelligence reports. A twenty-eight-year-old man drove a Toyota Kijang minivan loaded with explosives to the front of the Marriott lobby and stopped. No one there except the suicide bomber could've known what was about to happen. Civilians were going about their daily lives when the vehicle exploded, killing eight Indonesians, a Dutch businessman, one Dane, and two Chinese tourists. One hundred and fifty people were wounded. The suicide bomber's head flew into the air and landed on a fifth-floor balcony. If someone could've killed the suicide bomber before he detonated the explosives, those people would still be alive, and their families could continue with their daily lives without all the grief.

Alex paid the driver, then stepped out. He was two steps away from the car when he remembered his "wife" and turned around to help her out.

Cat smiled at him and blew him a kiss before grabbing his hand and walking to the hotel. Alex kept telling himself this was the cover and to just go with it. He knew the real reason he was here. Cold-blooded murderers were going to die.

"Ouch, too hard," Cat said, batting at his arm with her free hand.

"Sorry," Alex said, loosening his grip.

Inside the lobby, everything except the small waterfall and palm trees was colored in gold: marble staircase, ceiling, and walls. After checking in at the reception counter, they took the elevator up to the sixth floor, where they found their Grand Twin room. The gold color extended to the walls and trim inside their room. Even the marble in the bathroom was gold—subdued, but still gold.

Cat crossed the room with the grace of a feline. Halfway across, she hesitated, as if she was unsure of herself—or carefully stalking her prey. Then she continued walking until she reached the window. "Check out the view," she said, her back facing Alex.

"I am."

"Just because we're married doesn't mean you're entitled."

Alex joined her at the window. Below was a large free-form pool surrounded by a magnificent garden. "I was talking about the garden."

"Uh-huh."

"Think I need to take a swim."

She wrinkled her nose. "Not smelling like that, you don't."

Alex detected an odor, too. It had been about two days since they'd left Virginia. "You're developing a bit of a fragrance yourself."

"You want to shower first, or shall I?"

"I think you need it more."

She smiled. "I was hoping you'd say that." Cat headed into the bathroom.

Alex sat at a table and fired up his laptop. The laptop had covert software installed. Even if customs had checked it, they wouldn't have found the hidden programs. Briefly Alex sent a message to Joint Special Operations Command (JSOC) saying that they'd arrived without incident. Their team couldn't begin their mission without checking in.

After sending the message, Alex stood, stretched his legs, and stared out the window at the pool. Growing up, his family had a pool. The Brandenburgs' forty-acre gated estate was nestled along the waterfront in Annapolis, Maryland. From the street, a security gate led to a driveway that circled around to the three-story main residence. The main residence had an elevator, six bedrooms, six fireplaces, eight bathrooms, eight garages, and multiple balconies.

Inside the front door, a chandelier dangled from a ten-foot ceiling. French doors opened up to the rest of the house, lit during the day by the sunlight entering through the French windows. Grandpa lived in the in-law suite. The maid resided in her quarters.

Outside, to the right of the estate sat a guesthouse. Behind the main residence, a cabana with indoor and outdoor kitchens adjoined the in-ground pool and hot tub. Beyond the pool the Brandenburgs had their own deepwater pier on the waterfront.

When Alex's sister, Sarah, was eight years old, he sat with her beside the pool petting their dog, a Labrador that had strayed to their house and joined the family. Alex named him Rocky because he liked to retrieve the rocks Alex threw. Mom looked on from inside the enclosed glass porch.

Alex was eleven. "Why don't you go play with friends?" he asked.

"Why don't you?"

"Because I'm always playing with friends. I need a break."

"I wish I could be like you. So many friends."

"You could make more friends if you spent a little less time with Grandpa wandering around in the woods and more time with kids your age."

"You sound like Dad."

"You say that like it's such a bad thing."

"I like it better when you sound like you." She was quiet for a minute. Others feel uncomfortable after the first few seconds of silence, but Sarah was comfortable with silence. Alex let her feel comfortable. "People scare me," she said.

Alex almost laughed, but when he noticed she wasn't joking, he stopped himself. "You're serious."

She nodded. "I know what animals are going to do, but I don't know what people are going to do."

Alex put an arm around her.

# 5

**A**knock sounded at the hotel room door. Unarmed, Alex looked around for weapons of convenience. *Chair? Maybe, but too far away from the door. Plus it wouldn't be the easiest thing to swing around in a confined space.* He'd be better off breaking the chair into pieces and using a leg as a stabbing weapon, but he was pretty certain terrorists wouldn't knock and he didn't want to get kicked out for trashing the room. He took a breath, calmed himself, and pulled out his pen and walked to the door. *Better be the hotel staff.*

He looked out the peephole. Pancho was making faces on the other side.

Alex shook his head in relief and opened the door.

Pancho walked in smoking a cigar.

Alex looked out into the hallway and counted to ten. No one appeared. He let the door swing shut, counted to twenty, then swung it open and stepped outside like he was going somewhere in a hurry. The hallway was empty. He came back into the room and shut the door.

"Don't try that with the windows," Pancho said. "You don't look like you bounce."

Alex ignored his humor. "What happened to the coded knock?"

"Forgot it," Pancho said, his booming voice a shock after having

Cat's softer tones as company. "Want me to go out and try again?" He handed Alex a cigar.

Alex was tempted to say yes, but shook his head and took the cigar. The clear plastic container said jalapeño flavored, from Texas. "Thanks." Alex put it in his shirt pocket.

"You ready to come over and pick up your stuff?" Pancho and John's room was next door.

Cat stepped out of the bathroom wearing only shorts and a T-shirt, wrapping her hair in a towel.

"Whoa," Pancho said. "Didn't mean to interrupt."

"You weren't interrupting," she said.

Pancho sat down on the sofa.

Alex looked at Pancho and said, "I thought we were leaving."

"I like your room better."

"That's why we're going to your room."

"Aw." He reluctantly stood up and walked toward the door. On his way, Pancho stopped and quietly told Cat, "If the marriage doesn't work out, you know where to find me."

She grinned. Her reaction only seemed to encourage him. Alex practically had to pull Pancho out the door.

Walking in the hallway, Pancho asked, "Can I borrow two hundred thousand rupiahs?" Alex did the math. Twenty bucks give or take.

Alex started to ask him what it was for, then realized he wasn't his father and this wasn't an allowance. He dug the money out of his wallet and gave it to him.

"Thanks." Pancho swept his card through the reader mounted on the wall. The door unlocked, he opened it, and the two walked in.

On the couch sat John, reading a Bible and sipping a can of the local Country Choice guava juice. Alex knew John was religious—his file had told him just about everything he'd ever want to know about John except for the reason he was out of the Teams—but his little bonding exercise had explained that.

Pancho walked over to the air-conditioning control and lowered the temperature. "John's daddy was a preacher," he sang. Pancho half-danced and half-walked to the bedroom, singing: "John L. was a preacher's son, and when his daddy would visit he'd come along . . ."

"If Pancho said I puked on the aircraft carrier he's full of crap," John said.

"Good to see you, too, John," Alex said.

"You'd think a ship that big would be stable."

"Okay," Alex said, not rising to the bait.

Apparently satisfied, John changed the subject. "And if Pancho asks to borrow money, just say, 'no.' "

*Now you tell me.*

John stood, walked over to the air-conditioning control, turned the temperature up, and returned to the couch.

Pancho came out with a large black duffel bag and put it on the floor in front of Alex.

Alex unzipped it and found his and Cat's holsters, SIG SAUER P226 Navy 9mm pistols, and ammo magazines. Next, Alex checked to make sure the SIG was loaded, then he concealed it on his hip under his shirt. When Alex finished, he zipped the bag and took it.

"Thanks. Cat and I are going to dinner before our appointment. You guys okay for chow?"

"Fridge is full, and we got room service." Pancho turned the AC control down.

"Okay, see you."

"Later," Pancho said.

John didn't look up from his Bible or say goodbye. Alex was beginning to understand why John didn't win popularity contests.

Back in his room, Alex took a much-needed shower and shave.

Thirty minutes later, Cat and Alex stepped out of the hotel and into the night air. They took a taxi to an upscale restaurant for dinner. They looked just like any other tourist couple except that they carried concealed SIG SAUER P226 Navy 9mm pistols.

In the restaurant, Cat started with *bakso*, a meatball soup, while Alex chose the *gado gado*, thinking it was some kind of pasta. Turned out to be peanut dressing on a salad of blanched cabbage, bitter melon, tofu, and egg. *You've eaten worse*, he told himself, shoveling in the salad and doing his best to keep it down.

The restaurant continued its busy, noisy pace, leaving the two to eat and talk in their own private world. Unlike back in the States during their briefings, Cat ate slowly now—either out of caution or wanting to savor it.

"This is delicious," she said.

Alex nodded, his mouth full. It was actually growing on him.

"Can I try yours?" she asked.

"Sure," Alex said, quickly pushing his plate toward her.

With her fork, she stabbed some salad off his plate and took a small bite. Then she spooned one of her meatballs onto his plate.

"We've been together all this time, and I still feel like I hardly know you," Cat said. She smiled brightly at him, even reaching across the table to gently stroke the back of his hand with her fingers.

Alex grinned. "What's to know?"

"The ski—, I mean, Skippy, that old family friend, said your grandfather was in the service in England. Did he make a career out of it?"

Alex fought the urge to turn around to see if anyone noticed Cat's slip. *Damn, this undercover stuff isn't easy.* He was enjoying her company way more than he should be. Maybe she was, too.

"No, he got out after the war and became a gamekeeper on an estate, protecting the wildlife from poachers and animal predators, that sort of thing. He took the owners, their relatives, and friends on hunting expeditions. My grandma's parents owned the estate. Grandpa and Grandma were both in their late twenties when they met. When Grandma's parents found out, the estate owners fired him, but that didn't keep them apart. They ended up eloping to the U.S. Big surprise, her parents disowned her."

Cat patted his hand. "That must've been hard for her."

Alex had never really thought about it. "Her parents never really forgave Grandpa, but eventually they forgave Grandma. She was an only child. When she gave birth to a boy, the family mellowed even more. Mom was born second. My uncle inherited over half of the estate. My mother and her two sisters inherited the rest."

"So does that mean you're in line for the throne?"

"Good grief, for the sake of the empire I hope not," he said. "I still can't tell one fork from another, let alone how to curtsey."

Cat giggled. "Men don't curtsey, only women do."

Alex wiped his brow with obvious relief. "Whew! You just saved me from a big embarrassment. Now I know why I married you."

The waiter brought their meals. Cat ate *nasi goring*, rice fried with garlic, egg, and prawns and spiced with chili pepper and tamarind. Alex had *satay*, beef skewered with bamboo, wrapped in fat and grilled on charcoal. The waiter served the skewered beef in sweet soy sauce and pepper. Alex drank a martini garnished with a pick stabbed through three olives. Cat wasn't sure which wine to drink, so Alex ordered a glass of white wine—pinot gris. She sipped. Islamic dietary restrictions forbade liquor, but this was one of the restaurants that served it anyway.

"Your grandfather must mean a lot to you," she said.

"What makes you say that?"

"You seem excited when you talk about him."

"You're the first person to notice."

"He sounds like a wonderful man."

"Mom thought so. Dad always seemed embarrassed by Grandpa— the money and always saying the right things were a part of Dad's identity but money and society meant little to Grandpa. More than anything, Grandpa loved the land. And Grandma. When Grandma died, Mom let Grandpa live with us. He and my sister, Sarah, became close, which irritated the hell out of Dad. Sarah thought the world of Grandpa."

"And you?"

Alex glanced at his wristwatch. "It's getting close to eight-thirty."

"Sometimes I talk too much."

"No need to apologize. I've enjoyed your company. And the dinner." He paid for the meal, and the two stepped outside, where taxi drivers solicited them for rides. Alex chose the man wearing a blue baseball cap with the bill turned around to the rear—their first contact. His taxi looked like any other Silver Bird taxi, but his was owned by Uncle Sam.

Alex and Cat sat in the backseat. Next to the driver sat a Caucasian male in the passenger seat. They exchanged bona fides.

"The scenic route to the Plaza Indonesia," Alex said.

"Wouldn't you like a less expensive route?" the taxi driver said.

"I'm Alex."

"Felix," the passenger said.

"Nice name."

"You, too."

"Mine is real," Alex said.

"So is mine."

Alex smiled, not knowing whether to believe him or not. "The driver, is he cool?"

"He's one of us," Felix said.

"Good."

"It appears you made it here without any trouble."

"Knock on wood."

"There's been a slight change in plans."

"Oh?"

"Your first target is already dead."

"Dead?" He looked over at Cat, who shook her head.

"Shot. The news media suspect that Budi had Setiawan killed in a violent takeover. That's what the intelligence services are reporting, too." Felix's voice lacked conviction.

"But you don't believe it."

"Budi and his followers are ambitious, but not that ambitious. And they're afraid of making a move without the Red Sheik's approval. Setiawan, on the other hand, was ambitious. I think the Red Sheik put an end to any hopes Setiawan had of taking control over al Qaeda."

"Interesting theory."

"A few hundred American dollars got me a peek at the coroner's report. The bullet that killed Setiawan was a 7.62 by 41.5 millimeter. The same caliber that killed Setiawan's bodyguards. The police interviewed people in the neighborhood and nobody saw or heard anything suspicious—not even gunshots. I only know of one kind of weapon like that. Mantis uses a gun like that."

Damien Guevara, Alex realized. So, one of the bugs was making a power grab.

"Are we still on for tomorrow?"

"Yeah, Budi is still scheduled to check in to the Hotel Mulia Senayan tomorrow."

"One down, six to go," Cat said, her voice a purr that made Alex's skin tingle. Cat was definitely a predator.

# 6

That same evening, Damien and his son, Mohammed, sat on a bench like tourists in a part of Jakarta popular with Western visitors. The rain had subsided, giving the air a cool and refreshing tang. Both dressed like Western tourists, but they didn't look like father and son. Mohammed's blond hair, blue eyes, and fair skin contrasted starkly with his father's browner complexion. At twenty years old, Mohammed was nearly half his father's age, but in addition to the very different ethnic look of the two men, Damien's youthful appearance made it seem unlikely that they were father and son.

Sitting on the bench they could see a dance club a hundred yards away. Mohammed mounted a small portable digital camera on the bench between them and pointed it at the club. As they waited, he said, "You never talk about Mother."

"Nothing to talk about."

"There must be something."

"I told you not to ask," Damien said, annoyed his son chose now to discuss it.

"Would it hurt so much to tell me?"

Damien turned to look at his son. "Why are you so curious now?"

"I'm not a child anymore. You must know something. I know nothing."

"If you must know—we didn't have a relationship."

"You had me."

"It was years after your birth that I found out you existed. I didn't know what to think at first. The more I thought about it, the more I realized what a great opportunity it would be. I could give you all the training my parents never gave me. You could become greater than me—my legacy. So I took you from her."

"What'd she say when you took me?"

"She wasn't happy. Your mother was a Swedish beauty, but her anger in that moment—and her sadness when she realized she couldn't stop me—made her so beautiful—more beautiful than ever."

"What happened to her?"

"She disappeared."

"Did you try to find her?"

"That's enough. I've told you enough for now."

Mohammed let it rest. It was the first time Damien had talked about his mother, and he seemed satisfied for the moment.

An Indonesian man carrying a blue backpack walked toward the club. "This is similar to how it was done in Bali," Damien said. "You can start recording."

Mohammed pressed *record* on the camera, aiming it at the club.

The man with the blue backpack passed a white van parked outside and walked into the club. Within a few minutes a large explosion rocked the club. After a moment of silence came screams, then people, some bloodied and some blackened, stumbling out of the front door. Thick, roiling smoke poured out of doorways and shattered windows.

Damien looked at his watch. "One has to time the fuse to get the most effect. One can use a timer, but I prefer to keep things simple. Now make sure the white van is in the center of the camera."

People from inside the club helped the seriously wounded exit. Pedestrians and others passing stopped to look. Others from the neighborhood came to see what was going on. Minutes later, police and paramedics arrived with their sirens blasting. More people packed the area around the club. There were those who seemed frozen in a state of shock; some wandered in circles, and others sobbed.

Keeping an eye on his watch, Damien ducked behind the low wall between him and the club. Mohammed took the hint and ducked, too. A blast ten times more powerful than that in the club pounded the air and rippled through the ground.

Damien and Mohammed rose from behind the low wall and observed the carnage. The charred remains of the van resembled nothing of the original. All over the area lay scattered parts: twisted vehicles, demolished buildings, and body parts.

Damien looked over at Mohammed. He wanted to share this moment with his son. This child he had fought for, and raised to be his heir. He turned away before Mohammed was aware of him staring. Damien forced himself to remain calm, but inside his heart burned with joy.

"Come, my son, we must go. Remember the camera, and please, smile."

# 7

The taxi stopped near the Plaza Indonesia. Alex and Cat thanked Felix and got out. "Good luck," he said. "You're going to need it." Alex stepped into a large mud puddle. He frowned.

As they walked toward the hotel, Cat leaned into him and held on to his arm. "Let's shop for souvenirs, darling. You know Aunt Ida will be expecting something."

She was right, but Alex was in the hunting mood, not the shopping mood. "Shopping now?"

"Can we? I promise to make it worth your while," she said, looking up at him and batting her eyelashes.

Alex groaned. "You're too good at this, you know?"

"Thank you, honey," Cat said, lifting her head to give him a quick peck on the cheek.

They walked past the hotel and down the next street, where a group of high-end shops were grouped. Alex let Cat lead the way. She obviously knew what she was doing. He kept scanning around and looking for trouble, but nothing looked promising.

They stepped into a store with Indonesian clothes that to Alex looked a lot like bedsheets hung from metal bars. Souvenirs filled the spaces between. The quality seemed good, but the prices weren't cheap. The store clerk busily rang up a young female customer as two men in their early twenties walked in and began jabbering away as they discussed the various cloths.

A couple maybe, Alex wondered, noticing that they stood very close to each other. Good for them, he decided, turning back to check on Cat. She was captivated by colorful scarves. Aunt Ida was going to get a very nice gift by the look of it.

Alex stopped at the end of an aisle, where he found a dagger. *Keris*, he remembered from one of the briefings, with its distinctive curvy blade like a snake's body. He hefted one in his hand. He didn't get it. It wasn't balanced worth a damn and would likely get stuck between ribs the first time you used it. He ran a finger along the blade. Duller than Sunday school. Still, it was a chunk of steel, and if worse came to worst, it could do the job.

"Sweetheart?"

Alex looked up. Cat had enough scarves in her arms to wrap a mummy.

"Yes, dear?" It was easy to play the role of her husband. He stamped on the thought before it went any further.

"Chahaya here, oh, I'm sorry, did I pronounce that right?" she asked, turning to the clerk standing beside her.

The man beamed and nodded. His name could be George, Alex figured, but he was about to sell a lot of scarves, so Cat could call him whatever she liked.

"Chahaya says there is a store just one block over that has the most gorgeous bolts of emerald silk. They're planning to make scarves out of it, but not until next week when we'll be gone."

Alex was already shaking his head before she finished.

"Be a dear and go around and buy a yard of it. Tell them Chahaya sent you. They'll know which fabric."

"Why can't he go get it himself?" Alex asked, hoping he didn't sound too annoyed.

Cat started to pout. "He can't leave the store, darling, not with customers," she said, motioning her head toward the gay couple still browsing.

Alex started to open his mouth again and then stopped. He could have a public argument about how incredibly idiotic this was, or he could simply walk one block, buy the damn silk, and be back, their cover intact and a fight with his "wife" averted.

"Fine, but don't go anywhere. If I'm not back in five minutes, call my nephews," Alex said, alluding to Pancho and John.

Cat smiled. "You could already be halfway there by now. Go out, turn left, then left on the main street, then left again. It's called the Bali Flower. You can't miss it."

Alex stifled a groan and turned on his heel and left the store. It wasn't raining, but the streets glistened with water from the streetlights. He heard a noise behind him and turned. The gay couple had come out of the store behind him. As soon as they realized they'd been spotted they bowed their heads.

"We do not mean to intrude, but the emerald fabric sounds divine."

Alex shrugged. *Damn, I miss the days of freezing my ass off on a mountainside waiting to drill a hole in someone's head.*

"The more the merrier," Alex said, turning and heading off again.

He expected the men to walk beside him, but they kept a few paces back, talking softly and nodding and smiling whenever he looked over his shoulder at them. Alex got to the main street and turned left, heading for the next block. Foot traffic was light, but that suited him just fine. He'd once spent a rainy weekend in New York City dodging umbrella-wielding pedestrians and almost lost an eye.

He got to the end of the block and started down the street. This one wasn't as well lit and many of the stores were already closed for the night.

Alex felt goose bumps crawl up his arms. He'd walked another two steps before he realized the couple behind him had gone silent. *You stupid jerk!*

He spun around as he took a step back, the knife blade of his attacker just missing his cheek. The "gay" couple stood a yard apart, each with a six-inch knife in his hand. Alex noted that neither one carried a keris. Both were crouched low and moving toward him from the sides.

"You've done this before," Alex said, recognizing the move. He put up his left hand as a sign of surrender while pointing down toward the wallet in his pants. The attacker to his right looked down where Alex's wallet was. *Bingo.* Alex knew it would be a simple matter to pull out his SIG and finish these two, but the noise would attract unwanted attention. "Look, I don't want any trouble. Let me—" he started to say, then charged the man.

All the training came back in a rush. He ducked low, then drove up with the flat of his palm, catching the man under the chin. Teeth exploded out the attacker's mouth as a shock of pain traveled up Alex's arm.

The second man yelled something and lunged, but Alex was already pivoting and caught the second assailant's blade hand at the elbow. Instead of pushing back, Alex let the man's momentum bring him closer as Alex lowered his head and rammed it into his face. There was a loud crack and Alex stumbled back a step, the top of his head suddenly feeling numb and tingly.

The attacker clutched his broken nose with one hand while still swinging his knife with the other. Alex glanced quickly to the first assailant and saw he was curled up on the ground moaning. With that threat neutralized, he focused on the one still standing.

Whether out of the need for vengeance or simple stupidity the attacker came at Alex again. Alex drove straight at him this time, catching the man square in the crotch with a knee that felt like it broke his pelvis. Knife and attacker fell to the ground. Alex looked around, ready for more, but no one appeared.

He looked down at the two men and tried to decide what to do next. His hand went toward the SIG SAUER tucked under his shirt. Was this just a random mugging, or did they know who he was? If they did, that meant—Cat!

He'd left Cat alone! Alex left the men where they lay and tore up the street. *Dammit!* He wasn't this stupid, was he?

He rounded the corner onto the main street and picked up his pace, dodging through a scattering of pedestrians like a running back going for the Heisman. He got to the street and rounded the corner, slipped in a puddle, and stumbled to his knees before getting up and charging into the store.

Cat and the clerk looked up from a collection of beads.

"Damn, Alex, what happened?" Cat asked.

Alex scanned the store. Everything appeared fine. He focused on his breathing, calming himself as he stepped farther inside and made an attempt to brush his hair into place. "You're okay?"

"I'm fine," Cat said, looking far from it. The fear on her face made Alex all the more angry with himself. "What happened to you?"

"What, oh, I forgot, we have dinner reservations and we're going to be late. We'll have to get the silk another time. C'mon," he said, reaching out and grabbing her by the wrist.

"I have to pay for all this," Cat said, motioning to the pile of scarves and other souvenirs she'd amassed.

Alex started to protest, then thought better of it. He'd already drawn enough attention to himself. "Yes, of course." He reached into his wallet and pulled out a large wad of cash. He plunked it down on the glass counter. "Will that cover it?"

"That's too much," Cat said, looking at Alex with obvious concern.

"It's fine. We're on our honeymoon and Chachi here has been a real sport keeping you company. Bag it up, Chachi, we're late."

Smiling and nodding, the clerk hustled to put Cat's purchases in a bag while Alex kept one eye on the street. Scenario after scenario raced through his mind and in each one he screwed up.

"Okay, we're out of here," he said as the last scarf went in the bag. Cat barely had time to grab it before Alex had pulled her out the door.

"You want to tell me what the hell is going on?"

"Keep walking and smiling," Alex said, steering her to the inside of the sidewalk and away from the street. "Those two guys in the store that followed me out jumped me. Might have been just looking for an easy buck from a tourist, or . . ."

Cat's eyes grew wider. "How could anyone know we're here?"

Alex shook his head. "I don't know, but we'll regroup at the hotel and figure out our next move. Just keep walking and smiling," he said, forgetting the second half of his instruction himself.


THEY WALKED AS QUICKLY as they could through the hotel lobby, past the elevator bank, and up the stairs. Cat was gasping by the time they reached their room. Although she was in excellent physical condition, she was no match for Alex. Alex picked up the hotel phone and called Pancho and John's room and got Pancho. He kept it light.

"Wondered where you two lovebirds got to," Pancho said, his words garbled as he was clearly eating something.

"Bit of excitement," Alex said, sitting down on the edge of the bed and refocusing his breathing. "Couple of guys tried to mug me."

There was silence on the other end of the line for several seconds. When Pancho spoke again, his voice was crystal clear. "Is the party still on?"

Now that Alex had a moment to breathe and to think, he could step back and look at it with more perspective. "Yes. It's our honeymoon after all. They were just a couple of thugs looking to score quick cash from a lost tourist."

"You sure about that?" Pancho asked.

Alex nodded, then realized Pancho couldn't see the gesture. "Yes, absolutely. Just a case of being at the wrong place at the wrong time. The party is still on. See you later." He hung up the phone.

Later, while Cat changed clothes in the bathroom, Alex went to the bedroom, stripped down to his black silk boxer shorts, and went to bed.

He couldn't sleep—his adrenaline was still pumping. An hour passed. His eyes were closed, but he heard Cat enter the room. She slipped into her bed. Even though he'd convinced himself that the attack really had been a random event, he wanted to put Cat on the next flight out, but it'd probably raise eyebrows if his "wife" left and he stayed. Killing Budi would raise more eyebrows. Alex needed her to maintain his cover for the hit. *Tomorrow we hunt.*

"I guess the honeymoon is over," she said from her bed.

"But at least you got the scarves."

For the next fifteen minutes, the two of them laughed as the tension slowly bled away. Alex drifted off to sleep still smiling.

# 8

Damien drove a small red ten-year-old Suzuki Alto through an affluent neighborhood in Islamabad, Pakistan. Next to him in the passenger seat, Mohammed kept his head down. They passed upscale condominiums and five-star hotels before coming to a halt behind a truck at a stop sign.

"We could buy a bigger car," Mohammed said. "We have more than enough money."

Damien silently cursed. Did the boy still not understand? "And draw attention to ourselves?" As if to prove his point, a black BMW idling behind them honked its horn. "You see, the driver of the car behind us swells with arrogance because he drives a large automobile while we putter around in this. To him, we are poor, ignorant workers."

"But we're not, Father. We are the blade of Allah."

Again Damien silently cursed. His son was a religious fool, but it served Damien well among the jihadists, so he did his best to tolerate it.

"We are power and strength a thousand times more valuable than money. We should not be ashamed to show it."

The truck pulled ahead but Damien kept his foot on the brake. Youth did not understand. The BMW honked again.

If not for the stream of cars coming from the opposite direction, the BMW probably would've passed by now. Mohammed shifted in his seat and shook his fist at the driver behind them. This only elicited more honking.

"He needs to be taught a lesson," Mohammed said, his face flushed with anger.

Damien calmly put the car in gear and eased forward, then suddenly slammed on the brakes. A moment later the car shook and jumped forward as the BMW slammed into it. Damien let out the clutch and made a quick turn down a narrow alley between two buildings. The BMW followed.

"Father, what are you doing?" Mohammed asked, his voice not as angry as before.

Damien came to a stop, put the car in park, turned off the ignition, and opened his door. "Come, my son, and let the lesson be taught."

A fat man in his forties in a suit sat behind the wheel of the German car. Damien placed his hands together in front of him in a sign of apology and bowed his head as he walked toward the car. He stopped by the driver's door and motioned to Mohammed to join him.

The fat man looked at Mohammed with obvious surprise, but his anger was still in full fury. He swung his car door open hard, forcing Damien to back away.

"You should be back on the farm driving an ox, you fool," the man said, stomping past Damien to the front of his car. While the bumper of Damien's car now hung by one rusty bolt, the bumper of the BMW looked barely scratched. This only seemed to infuriate the man more.

"And how will you pay for this?"

For an answer, Damien pulled out a four-inch blade from beneath his shirt and drove his right hand forward, stabbing the man just below the heart.

"Father!" Mohammed shouted, spinning around to see who was

watching. The bustle of traffic on the street masked the noise of the man gasping for breath as he crumpled to his knees. Damien eased the knife out of the man's chest, wiped the blade on the lapel of his suit, then turned to his son.

"Slit his throat." He spun the knife in his hand so that the handle faced Mohammed.

Mohammed backed away until he bumped into their car. "Father, we have to get out of here. If someone sees . . ."

Damien spun the blade in his hand again, turned, and stabbed the man again, this time in his stomach.

"By Allah, mercy!" the man cried, clutching at his wounds. He would have fallen all the way to the ground, but Damien grabbed him by his shoulder and pushed him against the wheel of the BMW. He pulled the knife out again, cleaned it once more on the man's suit, and held the blade out to his son.

"This is the lesson. You wanted to show this pig who you were. Now you can. Do you shrink from the opportunity to prove yourself?"

Mohammed looked from his father to the man. "I've never . . . I mean, not like this. He's not an infidel."

Damien shook his head. "But you are the blade of Allah. Isn't this what jihad demands?"

Mohammed shook his head.

Damien smiled. "You see, your beliefs will let you down at the most inopportune moments. That is why it is better to be cold and strong. Rely on yourself, not a power you know nothing of. Now slit his throat and let us be gone."

He thrust the blade toward Mohammed. Slowly, Mohammed reached forward and grasped the handle. Damien let go and grabbed Mohammed's wrist and pulled him forward until he stood above the man.

"Do it," Damien said, forcing Mohammed's hand toward the man's throat. In response, the man tried to cower, but Damien kicked him in the stomach and with his free hand grabbed his hair and pulled his head up and back, exposing his neck.

"This is the way, my son. Blood of my blood, do this."

Mohammed brought his hand forward so that the blade touched the man's throat. The man cried, and tried to move his head, but Damien slammed his head back against the car and kept it still. When Mohammed brought the blade no closer, Damien gripped his son's wrist harder and thrust. The blade plunged into the man's throat. Dark red blood trickled forth from the wound, splattering their hands.

Mohammed retched, but Damien remained calm, studying the blood flow. With a practiced skill he drew the blade across the throat, severing the carotid artery. Now the blood gushed as the man gurgled and thrashed.

Mohammed pulled his hand free and more blood flowed out as Damien finally released the man's head and let his body slump against the wheel. Damien carefully wiped the blade one last time on the man's suit, looked in both directions on the narrow street, and, grabbing Mohammed by the arm, walked him back to the car.

He sat Mohammed in the passenger seat, shut his door, then walked around to the driver's side. He started up the car, put it in gear, and drove away, never once looking in the rearview mirror.

They drove in silence, father and son. Damien was aware of Mohammed's stare, but he ignored it and kept his concentration on the road. The boy would learn, or the boy would die.

Twenty minutes later they pulled up at the French-Pakistani fusion nightclub that acted as the Red Sheik's headquarters. The smell of blood lingered in the car. It made Damien hungry. He finally looked over at his son.

"Take this car and burn it, then buy something else. I trust you'll make a suitable choice."

He didn't wait for his son to respond. He stepped out of the car and walked into the nightclub. He whispered to the hostess, who seated him at a reddish-brown table covered with a crimson linen tablecloth. Like the table, the chairs and paneled walls were made of mahogany wood. Long silk drapes parted to reveal the city lights. An international mix of dance music pulsated as couples gyrated on the dance floor.

Thirty minutes later, the Pakistani marine, Lieutenant Commander Abdul-Nur Issa, marched in, the shortly cut hairs on his head standing at attention. "You're early," Issa said with obvious disappointment in his voice.

Damien watched him carefully. "So are you."

Issa watched Damien carefully, too. "But you're earlier."

"I wouldn't want to show you a weakness," Damien said. "I know that you are more capable than anyone of exploiting it."

"I don't know whether to take that as a compliment or an insult."

"You can take it as a warning not to arrive earlier than me, or I might think you've prepared an ambush," Damien said, growing tired of their verbal sparring.

Issa laughed, but it was a nervous laugh.

Next Jamsheed Jamshed strolled in. Damien frowned. The man was too Western. His nickname was Freddie, chosen by Jamsheed himself because he worshipped Freddie Mercury from the music group Queen. He even dressed like him in flamboyant clothes. More than a few heads in the club turned to watch his theatrical entrance.

"How's public relations, Freddie?" Issa asked.

Freddie sat down. "In your bombings on the Pakistan navy, you killed twelve—killing the female naval officer was a nice touch. Then the attack on the Mehran naval aviation base that killed eighteen and wounded sixteen. Impressive."

"It was our revenge for the martyrdom of Osama bin Laden. We are still strong. But you're avoiding my question."

"Not good. The Red Sheik's brother, Ahmed, continues to cause us trouble. On top of that, the death of bin Laden has caused others to lose interest in us. But we're planning on a recruitment animation aimed at kids: adventure, killing Westerners, the prophet—*Aladdin* for al Qaeda."

Issa nodded. "Same. Recruitment for the militia is down. Somebody should take care of Ahmed. New recruits are avoiding us to become pacifists. We've run out of adults, so we have to use children for jihad."

Khaled Qurei walked in briskly, looking neither to the left or right. With his thick glasses and dark banker's suit, he displayed his cold authority as the man in charge of the money. The birthmark under his left eye made him easy to distinguish from others. He sat down and breathed a sigh.

Freddie smiled. "You having problems, too?"

"Yes," Khaled said. "Donations are down. People donate when we kill infidels, not when infidels kill us. More of our bank accounts have been frozen. But it seems donations have risen for Ahmed."

Damien caught himself before he snorted his disgust. The jihadists' constant talk of religion was trying on his nerves.

"Where is the Red Sheik?" Freddie asked.

Issa looked at his watch. "He's already five minutes late."

Freddie used the downtime to send text messages on his cell phone.

Seven minutes later, the Red Sheik arrived, with a dark-skinned brunette in her twenties to his left and a fair-skinned blonde in her twenties to his right. He was twice their age. Money might not buy love or happiness, but it bought them—at least for the evening. The Sheik's beard was well trimmed, but his stomach extended over his belt. He wore a red silk shirt with a dark suit, probably French. "I have some business to take care of," the Red Sheik told the girls. "Go have a drink at the bar." He handed them a wad of money.

The blonde kissed him on the cheek. Not to be outdone, the brunette did, too. They giggled, their eyes flirting with Damien and Freddie.

Damien ignored them but Freddie winked. Damien enjoyed women, but not when he had business to conduct. Freddie wasn't as particular about when, and he wasn't particular about gender.

The two women headed to the bar.

"It's finished," Damien said. "Setiawan is gone. Budi has control."

The Red Sheik smiled.

"Are you coming with me to climb the Matterhorn?" Freddie asked the Sheik.

"A mountain! Snow and wind and the danger of falling to one's death. Why?"

"It's a good excuse to see friends nearby," Freddie said.

"You're crazy," the Red Sheik said. "And even if your idea was sane, which it isn't, I have a dinner engagement with the Sultan."

"I didn't tell you when I was going," Freddie said.

The Red Sheik looked at Damien before responding. "Trust me, I will most definitely be busy no matter when you plan to climb your mountain."

Seeing the Red Sheik and Freddie interact reinforced Damien's belief that Islam was a sham, just like Christianity, Judaism, and all the other religions. Muslim law applied only to those without power, while powerful people like the Red Sheik and Freddie could do as they pleased. The Red Sheik and Freddie merely gave the appearance of being Muslim. Even so, for Freddie to truly have a good time, he had to leave the prying eyes of Pakistan and go to some faraway place like the Alps.

The Red Sheik looked around the table. "What I've asked each of you here for is because we need to plan a new operation. Something big to strike at the heart of America in response to killing our leader. Something to rival September Eleventh. We must replenish our recruits and fill our coffers." As the Red Sheik talked, his brother Ahmed entered the restaurant wearing a white *thawb*, an ankle-length garment, and white keffiyeh, a traditional headdress.

The brother's clothing contrasted with the Westernized high fashion of most of the other club patrons.

The Red Sheik let out a quiet groan. "Why can't he leave me alone?"

"He is your brother," Damien said simply.

The Red Sheik said nothing.

Ahmed approached their table.

"*Salaam*," the Red Sheik greeted. *Peace*.

"*Salaam*," his brother replied.

"Do you always have to dress this way?"

Ahmed stepped back a pace. "Is there something wrong with the way I dress?"

"You make people feel uncomfortable," the Red Sheik said.

"Why should they feel uncomfortable?"

"How are our brothers?" the Red Sheik asked, changing what was becoming a frustrating conversation.

"They have some questions."

"They should worry more about providing support for our cause."

Ahmed ignored this. "How many more innocent people have to die in the name of al Qaeda?"

No one at the table spoke. Damien waited. He knew what must be done, but it was not his decision to make. Ahmed was a dangerous fool. He did not understand the way of things.

The Red Sheik finally spoke. "That is what's troubling them—the innocent people?"

"Yes."

"Troubling them or troubling you?"

"Both," Ahmed said, standing his ground.

"They are the poor and the uneducated. Your followers."

"The killing must not continue," Ahmed said, his voice as steady as Setiawan's had been nervous.

"We are at war, little brother."

"Because you choose to be. You may also choose not to be. On this, I must raise my concern. Bloodletting serves no one," he said, turning to look at Damien.

The Red Sheik bowed his head. "Ah, brother, you are wise. Perhaps that is why you became imam."

If Ahmed was flattered he didn't show it. "I'm only trying to do what's right."

The Red Sheik didn't try to hide the pain creeping into his voice. "I never claimed to be a caliph. I've always looked to you for spiritual guidance."

"I do Allah's will, as I understand it. This jihad with the infidels is not the future for Islam he envisioned."

"You always heard Allah better than me. He never tells me his will."

Ahmed leaned forward and placed a hand on his brother's shoulder. "One just has to want to listen."

"I will do what I can, brother, we all will. It will not be easy, but you have always been a voice of reason in this storm."

"Thank you, brother," Ahmed said, kissing his brother on both cheeks. "Your reward will be eternal."

The Red Sheik smiled. "Enough. Let us celebrate our new path. Brother, join us."

Ahmed looked around the table. Damien could read his thoughts as if he'd spoken them aloud. The imam would sit down with a pack of hungry wolves before he sat with them.

"Thank you, but I must see to other matters. Goodbye, my brother. Be well."

Ahmed left as he came, looking straight ahead. People hurried to get out of his way.

The Red Sheik watched him go, then turned back to the table. "Now, we need a plan that will make the infidels' blood flow like rivers to the sea."

# 9

Alex didn't fall asleep until about 0230. Rain sprayed the glass doors of the hotel room. He knew that water can be your enemy or your friend. His first real taste of the water as an enemy came in Basic Underwater Demolition/SEAL (BUD/S) training. Alex's boat crew valiantly paddled their black Inflatable Boat, Small (IBS) out to sea, but the Pacific Ocean didn't welcome them with open arms. Instead, she formed a mighty wall to keep them out. Alex's coxswain tried to keep them united: "Stroke, stroke!" The wall rose higher. Alex felt his adrenaline surge as he dug his paddle deep and pulled hard with his shoulders. The guy in front of him panicked, rapidly slapping the top of the water with his paddle—out of synch and ineffective in technique, he accomplished little to help them row over that wall. Moments later, the wall picked them up and slammed them down—with the ocean below and the IBS above, they were sandwiched in between. Alex tasted rubber boat, boots, salt water, and wooden paddles. He had no idea which way was up or down, but eventually he washed up onshore.

Later in training, the water became Alex's friend. When his feet were tied together, hands tied behind his back, and he hopped into the deep end of a pool, he quickly understood what it meant to have no fear but fear itself—*be calm or die*. The water became his friend.

Fear became his enemy. The water protected him from the taunts of the instructors.

Alex woke up at 0430, half an hour before his watch alarm. Being in a different time zone had thrown off his biological clock, and his anxiousness about the day's mission wouldn't let him sleep anymore. Rather than fight it he decided to embrace it. After taking a shower, Alex dressed in white Bermuda shorts and a pink polo shirt, then stepped out of the bathroom. Cat was already awake and dressed.

"You're not going to shower?" Alex asked.

"I shower in the evening."

Alex made his bed as neatly as it was when they first arrived.

"So I guess that means we slept in my bed?" she said.

Alex nodded.

She pulled the sheets out on both sides of her bed to make it look like they were a happily married couple. Such details might seem small, but taking care of the small details often prevented big problems, especially when local eyes began to investigate.

Alex sat down on the couch and relaxed for a moment. He played the upcoming hit over and over in his mind so many times that he didn't need to play it anymore.

Wearing matching white Bermuda shorts and a light green polo shirt, Cat sat in a chair. "Is everything okay?" she asked.

"Yes. Why?"

"You're so quiet."

"I'm just relaxing."

"Your eyes. They're different," Cat said. It wasn't worry in her voice, not exactly.

"My eyes?"

"They look so distant."

Alex wasn't about to attempt to explain what he was feeling. He wasn't sure he could. "You ready for this?"

"Ready as always."

Alex glanced at his watch: 0550. "Shall we go?"

# 10

Cat and Alex put on their backpacks, went downstairs, and took a taxi to a restaurant. After breakfast, they made sure they weren't being tailed and walked to a side entrance of a nearby hotel, where they split up to use the restrooms.

The men's restroom was empty. Alex entered the last stall and locked the door. Then he hung his backpack on the door hook, unzipped it, and pulled out a satchel. From the satchel, Alex pulled out a dark suit similar to the suits the staff at Budi's hotel would be wearing and put it on over his shorts and polo shirt. In a pancake holster, he holstered his SIG SAUER on his hip, concealed by the suit jacket. To complete the disguise, Alex pasted on a fake mustache and put on black horn-rimmed glasses.

Heavy footsteps echoed in the restroom—Pancho sat down in the stall next to Alex, who tapped his foot three times, paused, then tapped two times. Pancho tapped his foot four times. Alex expected to hear him changing into his disguise, but instead, Pancho dropped a deuce. Consistent with Pancho, it was loud. The smell was inhuman—not even a courtesy flush.

Alex put the empty backpack into his satchel, opened his stall, and checked himself in the restroom mirror—everything looked all right. Out of the restroom, Alex joined John sitting on a bench in the lobby. John, drinking a can of mango juice, wore a suit similar to Alex's.

After a few minutes of silence, Alex said, "You ready for this?"

"Always."

"Stay sharp," Alex said.

"You just worry about your part of the game, Chief, and I'll worry about mine."

Cat exited the restroom wearing a dress suit similar in color and style to Alex and John's. Her wig transformed her from blonde to brunette. She sat down in the chair farthest from them, ignoring them.

Pancho exited the restroom dressed like the others.

Alex and John stood up, headed out the back door, and caught a taxi that took them to the forty-story Hotel Mulia Senayan, a high-class hotel. They took an elevator to the twenty-fifth floor. If anyone saw them they'd assume that's where they got off, but the pair walked down several flights of steps to the twenty-first floor, where Budi was staying. The Agency guys stayed in Room 2110, on the same floor as Budi's room so the Agency could keep it under surveillance. Alex gave the proper knock on room 2110, and the door opened. A thin Indonesian with a missing tooth opened the door and said, "Toilet is broke."

"Let's see if we can fix it," Alex said.

Toothless let them in. After the door closed, Toothless took a post spying through the peephole.

A bald Felix and a poker-faced Indonesian stood and greeted Alex and John. Felix and the Indonesians wore suits similar to theirs. "Budi is still in Room 2117," Felix said. "He's got a bodyguard with him."

"Only one?" Alex asked.

"Only one so far, but there's been a change. A courier is going to meet them. We don't know what it's about, but he's coming from Pakistan. Your orders are to wait until the meet with the courier and then to take them out when they return."

Alex kept from cursing, but just barely. It was starting to sound like Afghanistan all over again. "How do we know he'll come back to his room after the meet?"

Felix shrugged. "We don't. This all happened in the last twelve hours. Budi is booked here for another night, so we're betting on him coming back."

Alex felt John's hand on his shoulder. "Easy, Chief. We're not charging up San Juan Hill. We've got to let this play out."

Alex nodded, and turned back to Felix.

"Are you really bald, or is that makeup?" Alex asked.

Felix smiled.

Alex and John handed their satchels containing the empty backpacks to Felix, who put them in an overnight suitcase.

Soon, Cat and Pancho joined them. Poker Face took his turn doing surveillance through the peephole while the rest sat and waited. Alex updated them on events.

"How do we know he's coming back?" Pancho asked.

Alex massaged his temples with the tips of his fingers. "We don't, but a wise old SEAL told me we have to let it play out, so that's what we're going to do."

Felix broke out a deck of cards and asked, "Poker?"

Alex and John looked at each other and then at Pancho.

"Deal," Pancho said.

They sat at the table and Felix dealt the cards.

"John, can I borrow twenty bucks?" Pancho asked.

"What for?" John asked.

"Because I'm broke, and I'll pay you back."

"Where have I heard that before?"

"Maybe you imagined it. This time is for real."

"I think last time was for real, but this time I'm imagining."

"Why don't we bet a little money to make the poker game interesting," Felix said.

"No!" Alex and John snapped.

"Okay," Felix apologized. "Just an idea."

Cat giggled. Alex liked the way it sounded.

After an hour and a half, Poker Face whispered, "They go. Budi and bodyguard go."

Felix motioned to Poker Face. "Go."

Poker Face put his radio earpiece in and walked out the door, followed by Toothless and Cat, who also wore earpieces. Toothless and Cat would watch the elevator and stairs on the target's floor while Poker Face went downstairs to keep an eye on the lobby below. The others inserted their earpieces.

When the all-clear signal came, Alex, Pancho, and John went to Room 2117. John wielded a modified VingCard pocket PC Lock-Link that was no bigger than a cell phone. Pancho and Alex stood guard while John plugged the LockLink into the hotel door card reader and turned it on. The Windows logo flashed on the monitor as the operating system came on. John clicked open the software application, then clicked *Run*, hacking into the hotel's lock system. The LockLink unlocked Room 2117. John opened the door, and Alex and Pancho entered with pistols drawn. The two of them searched the bathroom and the rest of the hotel room. Meanwhile, Alex knew John was reprogramming the card reader to lock. When finished, John joined them inside.

The three Outcasts attached sound suppressors to their SIG SAUERs and took up positions hiding in the room. Pancho stood behind a corner out of view from the hallway. John lay between the beds with his head at the foot, and Alex lay between the bed and the window with his head at the head. Alex listened to the flesh-colored earpiece in his ear canal—silence.

They'd waited for fifteen minutes when Alex heard a faint sound—it seemed like snoring. The sound stopped. Then Alex heard it again. "What is that?" he whispered.

John laughed, sucking air through his nose. "Pancho."

"Wake him up," Alex said.

"I'm awake." Pancho defended himself.

"You were asleep."

"I wasn't asleep," Pancho said.

"You were snoring."

"I was relaxing."

"I don't care what you call it," Alex whispered back, not quite believing he was having this conversation.

"He calls it his *combat sleep*," John interjected.

Alex could feel his pulse rise. "No more relaxing, no more combat sleep. These guys are armed, and they won't be happy when they see us."

"Budi won't know what hit him," John said.

"The way it should be."

"Good."

Pancho chomped on something. Then he passed a handful to John, who started eating. Pancho offered a handful to Alex, but he pushed Pancho's hand away.

"What is that?" Alex asked.

"Banana chips," they said.

Alex shook his head. "Where'd you get banana chips?"

"They're everywhere," Pancho said. "Sure you don't want some?"

"I'm busy. We've got two armed bad guys about to arrive any moment, and I'm stuck here with Sleepy and Dopey. I'm just imagining how I'm going to take them both by myself."

"We're going to help you," Pancho said. "Well, John will probably finish before you and I get a chance."

"Pancho, just what is it that you contribute to on this mission?" Alex asked.

"I brought the banana chips."

"Pancho is strong as a mule," John added.

"Great," Alex said. "I'll let you know when I need to plow a field."

After waiting in the room for three hours, Alex had calmed down when he heard a voice in his earpiece: "Package and two suitcases in lobby." Budi now had two bodyguards with him. Or perhaps the courier had joined them. Damn, there was no time to find out. They weren't set up for a snatch and grab.

Alex felt his heart rate speed up. Taking long, deep breaths, he calmed his heart down. Earlier in his SEAL career, he would try to imagine something calm to relax himself. Later, he could just skip the mental imaging and will his heart rate to slow down.

"Going up," the voice said.

Forty-five seconds later, Cat said over the radio, "Good afternoon, gentlemen." That was her planned greeting to the terrorists. So far, so good.

Budi and his bodyguards' voices became audible in the hall. They inserted their card in the card reader. Alex hoped the lock opened and that John hadn't broken it. The door opened and the three men walked inside. The door slammed shut, but Alex still couldn't see them as he lay hidden. Pancho initiated shooting. John and Alex popped up and opened fire. Alex caught Budi high in his chest, punching two holes above his sternum. Budi gurgled and reached for his chest. Alex fired twice more, once through Budi's hands and the final shot into his forehead. Budi dropped to the floor.

John popped rounds so fast that it sounded like he was praying and spraying, but the two other men fell. The Outcasts moved toward the targets with their pistols aimed. As they proceeded, they put holes in the skull holes. Budi and his bodyguards' pistols were still in their holsters. Holes and blood spatter marked the door and walls. Even though the Outcasts had used sound suppressors, their ambush sounded like strings of muffled firecrackers. Hopefully, the local authorities would continue to believe there was a power struggle among the terrorists, but the Outcasts weren't going to stick around to find out. "Two down, five to go," Alex said.

All three began searching the bodies. "Grab anything—paper, memory stick, anything at all. Check waistbands, ass cracks, inside their shoes—"

"Ain't our first rodeo, Chief," Pancho said, methodically patting down one of the bodies.

"Okay, time's up, let's go," Alex said, taking his small stash of personal items from Budi and jamming them into the inner pocket of his jacket.

The three holstered their pistols and hurried out of the room. Felix was already walking away, heading toward the elevator, pulling his overnight suitcase behind him. Not to be left behind, the Outcasts quickened their pace—*it pays to be a winner*.

Alex turned the corner to find Cat and Toothless waiting for them with two open elevators. Alex got into the elevator with Felix while Toothless rode with the others.

"No problems?" Felix asked.

"Just a couple of dead batteries in the remote," Alex said, pulling Budi's personal effects out of his pocket and handing them to Felix, who deftly pocketed them.

"Souvenirs?"

"Could be. If there's anything interesting, please let me know."

They rode the rest of the way down in silence.

The Outcasts stopped on the restaurant floor and took the stairs down to the lobby. Cat and Pancho headed through a side door to the outside while Alex and John exited the back. A siren blared—Alex didn't know if it was from an ambulance, a police car, or what. Cars honked—*is anyone honking for us?* His hearing picked up footsteps that weren't even close to him. The rush of adrenaline had heightened his senses—an asset in the wide-open desert, but now a problem in the crowded city of Jakarta. His eyesight became keen. People seemed to be everywhere: cars, sidewalks, reflections in windows, standing on verandas upstairs—*are they looking at us?* Alex could see each tiny hole in the asphalt and people far away. Smells of spicy food mixed with humidity and the smog—not only did he smell it, he could taste it. Adrenaline sped up his brain, and the world seemed to slow down. Alex struggled to sift through all the sensory information flooding his brain. Thinking, no matter how simple, became a burden. It would be easier to limit his eyes to tunnel vision, but Alex had to maintain sight of the big picture. His body operated on automatic muscle memory developed from the thousands of hours of training.

John and Alex hailed a taxi back to a different hotel from where he'd changed earlier. Once inside the men's restroom stall, Alex stripped off his suit, exposing his Bermuda shorts and polo shirt. He pulled a plastic shopping bag out of the pocket of his Bermuda shorts. Then he put the suit in the bag along with his glasses and fake mustache. Finally Alex washed his face and hands with soap in the sink.

As he stepped out of the restroom he looked for Cat. *Is she okay?* Then Alex walked over to a nearby bench and sat down. *Breathe.* The long, deep breaths helped dilute the effects of the adrenaline. His racing heart rate slowed. He remembered the first time he killed an enemy—how unnatural to see someone full of life one moment and dead the next—it gave him a queasy feeling in his gut. The second time felt more natural, and his stomach felt less nauseated. After that, part of him looked forward to killing while part of him resisted such emotion. Alex never wanted to enjoy killing. One had to have the conviction of a madman to take out his target and the rationale of a sane man to get away. It was a difficult balancing act, but Alex had his justifications.

Cat stepped out of the women's restroom carrying her things in plastic shopping bags. She flashed a nervous smile.

"Breathe," Alex said. "Slow and deep."

She did.

They returned to their hotel, packed their bags, and checked out of the Grand Hyatt Jakarta. Once again, Alex was without a firearm. If worse came to worst and he found himself in a shootout, he could always run. They took a taxi to Soekarno-Hatta International Airport. Inside the terminal, passing through security made him nervous, but he didn't show it. Passing through immigration raised his anxiety again: *Did the police send out a report looking for us? Are our Canadian passports still good?* Each government official was a potential snag. Quickly Alex willed himself to be calm: *Even if someone spotted us during the hit, we changed appearances. Our passports are the best.* In spite of the pressure, Cat remained cool. They crossed over into the lounge. Alex could hardly wait to board the plane, but he put his anxieties away. After they boarded the Cathay Pacific plane, they sat parked on the tarmac for what seemed an hour, although it had probably been only minutes. Police could try to stop them as they taxied down the runway—it was unlikely, but Alex and Cat weren't out of danger yet.

"Ladies and gentlemen, this is your head steward. We apologize for the delay, but we've been asked to go back to the terminal."

Cat looked at Alex with wide eyes. "They know."

Alex shook his head. "Just keep breathing. We're on our honeymoon."

Once they pulled up to the skyway the cabin door opened and two police officers followed by a customs official boarded the plane. Alex squeezed Cat's hand. He'd never felt so helpless in his life.

The police talked with the steward, who pointed down the aisle toward Alex. *Oh, no!*

The police started to walk toward him. Both were armed although their pistols remained in their holsters. The police came to Alex's row and kept walking. Alex heard Cat catch her breath.

They stopped two rows down and asked a young man in his twenties to come with them. Alex risked a glance back. By the look of the sweat beading on the man's face, someone had just failed Smuggling 101.

After the man was escorted from the plane there was an audible sigh of relief from the passengers. Conversation buzzed to life as people speculated on what the poor man might have done.

"I didn't enjoy that," Cat said.

"Still want to get into combat?"

Cat punched him in the arm. Hard. "They serve nuts on planes, don't they."

Alex kept his mouth shut as they took off and climbed to altitude.

He felt the weight of the mission lift from him, relieving his mind and body. Exhausted and wanting to rest, Alex closed his eyes.

Before Alex drifted to sleep, he thought he felt Cat put her hand on his.

# 11

Alex had entered junior high school while Sarah was still in elementary school. That was when Grandpa taught Sarah and him how to track ants. Alex and Sarah could follow the insects across the dirt, but when the ants crossed a boulder, the tracks vanished. After an hour, Alex and Sarah gave up. Grandpa's eyebrows frowned. "You know why you didn't find them?"

Alex heard the lecture before. "Because we gave up too soon."

"Yes," Grandpa said. "When you stop believing, you stop putting forth the effort, focusing, and persisting. You lose sight of the goal, and you fail. And what are you left with?"

Alex and Sarah looked at each other. They didn't know.

"Regret," Grandpa said. "If you stop believing now, later you'll wonder, 'What if I'd tried a little harder? Maybe I could've done it.' If you do it too many times, you'll feel like you're drowning."

"Do you have any regrets, Grandpa?" Sarah asked.

He thought for a moment. "No. But I see so many people my age with regrets: the girl he didn't date, the college degree she didn't apply for, the job he didn't seek, the skill she didn't develop—it never goes away. Those regrets lead to depression, and the depression drowns their spirit."

"What if we fail?" Alex asked.

"If you truly fail having given it your all, you realize it wasn't meant to be. You can move on with your life. But many don't even know what their all is. They float between failure and success having tasted neither. We're capable of so much more than we realize. I've failed many things many times, and I've succeeded a few times, too. But I don't have regrets."

Sarah tried again, putting her head close to the ground, so she could see the sunlight reflect off the rocks. "There's dust on the rocks!" Sarah exclaimed.

Alex saw it, too. The ants had flattened a trail through the dust on the boulder.

# 12

After the sunset and sunset prayer, Damien and the Red Sheik walked from their parked car to the Sultan's gate. "Is it nature or nurture?" the Red Sheik asked.

"What do you mean?"

"I mean, why do you act the way you do? As for me, I'm like my mother. My little brother acts like my father. When we were growing up, I spent all my free time with militants, while my little brother associated with imams. So in our case it's both nature and nurture."

"Neither," Damien said. "My parents were good people—raised me in a wholesome environment. My grandfather and grandmother were good people, too, and they said their parents were good people. But I chose a different path. People can choose."

Inside the Sultan's gate, a servant carrying a lantern greeted them and led them across the grounds.

"The police authorities say Budi's death was part of an inner struggle for power, but I don't believe it," Damien said. "Not after I just sent his people such a clear message to behave." He'd been shot in a hotel room. That sounded like the Israelis.

The Red Sheik seemed to have other worries. "The Sultan doesn't invite me to see him unless there's a problem. In the years I've known him, he hasn't asked to see me once unless there was a problem. It's about the money. We're not sending him enough money."

"We should've arrived earlier," Damien said.

"We couldn't impose on him by coming earlier."

"Feels like an ambush."

"Are you armed?"

"Of course."

The servant opened the front door to the sitting room (*majlis*). Leaving their shoes outside with nine other pairs of shoes, Damien and the Red Sheik entered. Inside, a silk-woven, cream-colored Tabriz carpet covered the floor. In the center of the carpet, symbols of fish broke the water's surface to see the reflection of the moon. Weeping willows, symbols of love, lined the outer edges of the carpet. From sitting on cushions on the floor, the Sultan and his nine other guests rose. *"As-salamu alaykumu."* Peace be upon you, Damien and the Red Sheik formally greeted the Sultan and his guests.

The Sultan lightly kissed them on the cheeks and shook their hands. *"As-salamu alaykuma."* Peace be upon you, too. He offered Damien and the Red Sheik a seat at the place of honor.

"We are fine," the Red Sheik said. "We can sit at the other end."

"I insist."

The Red Sheik and Damien sat at the place of honor. The Sultan helped them set up their cushioned armrests while a servant brought them each a small bell-shaped Arabic cup filled with a few table-spoons of spicy hot black Turkish coffee. As was customary, the Red Sheik and Damien slurped until their cups were empty. Immediately, from a shiny brass coffeepot, the servant refilled their cups.

The Red Sheik and Damien complimented the Sultan on his coffee.

The Sultan thanked them. "The infidels grow increasingly bold. Look what they did in Libya. Their planes bombed Ghadhafi to death."

Damien chose not to correct the Sultan that it was, in fact, Ghadhafi's own people that had killed him.

"Now, in Syria," the Sultan continued, "that fool Assad gives them yet another reason to defile our lands. And the Persians, ah, the Persians. They provoke the Jews like a blind dog barking at a lion. Do they not see that is not the way?"

"We must retaliate. We're thinking about the U.S. Bank Tower in Los Angeles, the Willis Tower in Chicago, or the Empire State Building in New York."

"We still have a cell in New York. New York would be good."

"Yes."

The Sultan asked, "How is your brother, Ahmed? He chose a different path."

"My brother," the Red Sheik said. "My brother, he's doing well."

The Sultan looked at Damien. "And how is your son? Mohammed? It is good that you chose to honor the Prophet this way."

Damien nodded, but kept from smiling. Naming his son Mohammed had been a stroke of brilliance. The jihadis ate it up. "Very well, thank you."

"Good. I am told that you personally took care of that embarrassing problem in Indonesia."

Damien nodded. "It was an honor to do so."

"I am distressed, however, to hear that the successor did not survive long. Perhaps he was the wrong choice?"

Damien could read tea leaves as well as the next man. "It was no mistake. I believe the Jews got to him."

The Sultan nodded. "Ah, I wondered. They are resourceful in that way. They have done us a favor. Let them go after the slow and the stupid while those swift of foot and thought prepare for the next blow."

The Red Sheik and Damien finished their second cup of coffee. When the servant offered them a refill, the Red Sheik shook his cup and said, *"Bass."* Enough. Damien did the same, followed by the other guests.

After collecting their cups, the servant brought them thick glasses and from high above poured mint tea into them, creating foam at the top of the glasses. As the Sultan spoke with his guests, they drank three glasses. "In Morocco," the Sultan said, "it is said that the first glass is as bitter as life, the second glass is as strong as love, and the third glass is as gentle as death."

The servant announced, "Dinner is ready."

The Sultan, Red Sheik, Damien, and others walked outside, put on their shoes, strolled across the courtyard, and entered a large room filled with food but no furniture. They sat on the floor on oilcloths covering the carpet. Trays were filled with roast lamb on rice and roasted chicken on top of sumac, onions, and pepper on flat-bread. Eggplant, meat, and cauliflower made up an upside-down casserole (*maqluba*). On another tray were white cheeses: some smooth and salty and others sweet. There was a tray covered with dates, figs, olives, pistachios, almonds, and walnuts. Balls of spiced fried hummus, falafel, were stacked on another tray. Tomato salad (*salatat al-bundura*) was served with fried slices of pita. Servants brought coffee, tea, apricot juice, tamarind juice, and carob juice.

As the Red Sheik looked at the feast, his eyes and shoulders appeared to relax. It occurred to Damien that killing someone in such a setting would be easy to clean up—one could just wrap the deceased in the oil carpet and dispose of him.

Before eating, the Sultan and his guests said, *"Bismillah."* In God's name. The Red Sheik and the other guests complimented the Sultan on his feast. They ate with their right hands. During the meal, there was little conversation. Such a feast was meant to be eaten. Damien ate sparingly, hating to feel bloated. In contrast, the Red Sheik ate his way to ecstasy.

As the Red Sheik and the guests stopped their feeding orgy (the leftovers would be given to the poor), the Sultan whispered to one of his servants. Recorded music played from speakers and into the room came two Turkish belly dancers.

Both were in their twenties and wearing dancing costumes, *bedlah*—fitted plunging bras and hip belts that sparkled. The beads on the fringes of their bedlah rattled as the girls danced. Slits in their skirts rose high up their legs to their low-riding, curved hip belts. The Turkish dancers showed skin—cleavage, bellies, and legs—and they flirted with their eyes and their hands.

One dancer's bedlah was gold colored while the other's was red. The gold-colored dancer entertained guests at the far end of the room. The red dancer's eyes made contact with the Red Sheik's; she locked on to him, smiling and dancing closer. She had an oval face with a perfectly straight nose. Her brown hair curled and flowed to her lightly tanned shoulders.

The Red Dancer seemed to move inside herself, one part at a time. Small and lithe, she flowed like liquid. Her shoulders shimmied, causing the metal ornaments on her bra to jingle. The shimmy eased down her stomach, and as she turned, her back shivered—down went the movement until it reached her hips, which pounded harder to the rhythm of the music—hips jingling. Each beat of the song seemed to resonate inside her from the top of her head down to her high heels. Red Dancer's whole body appeared to move inside itself—up, down, and side to side.

As the Red Dancer moved closer, Damien watched the Red Sheik's reaction. The Red Sheik's head moved back and forth with her rhythm. His mouth hung slightly open, and his eyes glazed.

She moved closer. He reached out to touch her hip, but his hand glanced off as her hips beat out the increasing tempo of the music. Red Dancer rose up and down as if riding a camel.

The Red Sheik trembled as if his chest were on the edge of bursting.

The few sets of eyes in the room still watching the gold belly dancer shifted to watch Red Dancer.

As Red Dancer's face neared the Red Sheik's, he said, "Tell me what you want, and I'll give it to you—anything."

She danced over to the Sultan and leaned over.

The Sultan whispered in her ear.

Red Dancer shimmied back to the Red Sheik and asked him, "You will do anything for me?"

"Yes, I'll do anything for you," he boasted. "Just tell me what you want."

"Execute your brother," she said aloud, her smile remaining steady.

His face filled with a mix of amazement and horror. He looked at the Sultan.

The Sultan nodded.

The Red Sheik probably regretted his promise to the young woman, but it would shame him to renege. Killing his brother was necessary for his own survival and the survival of his people. On top of it all, the girl continued to mesmerize the Red Sheik. He looked over at Damien and said, "Make it happen."

"You want me to kill your brother?" Damien asked.

The Red Sheik nodded.

After the performance, the guests said, "Thanks be to God."

The belly dancer left with the Red Sheik and Damien. Outside, servants held brass containers of warm water, soap, and towels. The Red Sheik, Red Dancer, and Damien washed their hands with soap as a servant poured the warm water over them. The three wiped their hands on towels.

The Sultan and his guests returned to the majlis and had coffee and tea again with some conversation. A servant brought in a bottle of perfume to the Sultan. He put a couple of drops on his hands and rubbed them. Another servant waved a wooden urn containing smoldering sandalwood in front of the Sultan. He lowered his face into the smoke. The Red Sheik and the others also took their turn applying the perfume and putting their faces in the sandalwood incense.

The Red Sheik knew the party was over, and he requested permission to leave.

"Are you sure you must leave?" the Sultan asked.

"Yes, it is getting late."

"Take good care of her." The Sultan stood.

The Red Sheik rose to his feet and shook the Sultan's hand. "It was an excellent feast and you were a very gracious and hospitable host."

Damien and the others rose to their feet and complimented their host.

"It was my pleasure," the Sultan said. He led them outside into the courtyard and walked them out the front gate. Beyond the gate lay darkness. *"Fi aman illah."* Go in God's keeping.

# 13

After killing Budi in Indonesia, the Outcasts returned to Dam Neck. Alex met with the Outcasts in a secure room at SEAL Team Six. He took a moment before jumping right in. They'd done it. They'd come together as a team and taken out three terrorists without being discovered.

He opened a manila file folder and held up a color photo. "Our next target is Jamsheed Jamshed, the spokesman and public relations man nicknamed 'Freddie.'"

"He looks like Freddie Mercury," Pancho said.

Alex huffed. "Freddie Mercury was one of the greatest singers of all time, but this terrorist is one of the greatest shits of all time. SIGINT have been able to track him thanks to the intel received from ISI. They intercepted a call that Freddie and a couple of his terrorist buddies have booked an excursion to climb the Matterhorn. We're going to help them with their descent."

John raised his hand as if he were in a classroom. "Terrorists are taking vacations now?"

Alex started to tell John to stow it, but then he stopped. Why wouldn't terrorists take vacations? No one could be twisted and sick 24/7 their whole lives, except maybe a psychopath. It was convenient to think of terrorists like psychos, but Alex knew the reality was far different. It was something worth keeping in mind.

"So it seems," Alex said, "which means we're heading to the Alps. Cat and I will assume new Canadian identities as boyfriend and girlfriend, keeping our first names."

"Wait, how come you two are always the married couple?" Pancho asked.

"You and John could be married," Cat said, her voice a purr. "It's a brave new world out there."

Alex saw John's upper lip quivering and decided to cut off the fun before someone got hurt. "All right, next time we can all be married. We'll tell them we're hippies. Now, Cat and I fly civvy, you two fly to Aviano Air Base in sunny Italy, pick up your car, and drive north, well, northwest."

"Not exactly the middle of nowhere. The Alps, I mean," John said.

"Neither was Jakarta, but we did it, and we'll do this."


ALEX AND CAT FLEW from Montreal to Malpensa Airport in Milan, Italy. They took a taxi from the airport to the Central Railroad Station. In the same city stood modern skyscrapers and architecture dating back hundreds of years: towers, monuments, galleries, cathedrals, and basilicas.

From Milan, they rode an electric train north. Riding out of Milan, gradually the man-made architecture gave way to natural lush forests spreading over majestic mountains. They crossed an iron bridge—vehicles rode on the level above them while the cool blue Ticino River flowed below.

Alex drifted off to sleep.

Sarah started junior high school when Alex began high school. One day, they played chess in the game room of their mansion. The chess table was made from black marble and white onyx, as were the chess pieces.

Sarah played the white pieces, so she moved first. She advanced her queen's pawn forward two spaces. "When I grow up, I want a lot of kids."

Alex thought about moving his chess pieces to the useful squares, where they could have the most influence on winning. He defended against white advancing farther by moving his black queen's pawn forward two spaces. "Don't you want a career?"

She moved her left bishop's pawn forward two spaces. "My family will be my career."

He captured her pawn. "I'm going to be a businessman. Like Dad."

She moved her queen's pawn forward one space, freeing her bishop to move. "You can be anything you want. And our families will live near each other."

He knew he couldn't save his pawn and later win the game, so he sacrificed it and moved his knight to f6. "That'd be cool."

Sarah's bishop took his pawn. Now they had both lost one pawn, but Sarah had better control of the board's center. "What kind of girl do you want to marry?"

"One who's kind to me."

"And beautiful."

Alex chuckled. "What kind of guy do you want to marry?"

"Someone who's kind to me and handsome. Like you."

Alex smiled.

"But you're older," she said. "So you have to get married first. Don't wait too long."

"Why do you say that?"

"Sometimes you get too focused on water polo. You forget about everything else. Like Dad gets with work. I just don't want you to be lonely."

"Okay. I won't wait too long."

# 14

Alex and Cat passed the shore of Lake Maggiore. Wind rippled the water's surface, and light sparkled across its face. Their train took them through Simplon Tunnel and crossed the Italian-Swiss border. Later, inside the car, over the door leading to the next car, a digital monitor displayed the next stop: *Brig*. A female voice announced in German, Italian, French, and English that they would stop at that village. The train came to a halt. Cat and Alex got off, walked to the Matterhorn-Gotthard-Bahn line, and sat on a bench waiting for their next train. As they sat, a thin woman wearing a yellow beret and carrying a large gray duffel bag sat down next to Cat. The thin woman's bag caught Cat's and Alex's eyes.

"The weather has been beautiful," the thin woman said.

"Nice bag," Cat said.

"It's Swiss."

"I can tell," Cat said, keeping up the pleasantries.

Their harmless chitchat was actually an exchange of bona fides. The thin woman's yellow beret helped identify her as a contact. She laid her bag on the bench next to Cat. The thin woman was a U.S. diplomatic courier who had picked up the bag with diplomatic markings from an Agency officer in Geneva. Just before meeting Alex and Cat, the thin woman removed the diplomatic markings.

"Would you mind taking care of it?" the thin woman asked.

"No problem," Cat said.

A small train stopped at their station. Cat picked up the gray bag and boarded the train with Alex. Their journey ended at Zermatt, Switzerland. There, Cat and Alex stepped off the train and left the station. Outside, the air was cool, crisp, quiet, and clean. Gas vehicles were mostly outlawed in the city, so most of the cars were electric. The couple caught their hotel taxi from the station. The ride was peaceful.

"This isn't Jakarta," Cat said.

Alex smiled.

A church bell chimed on the hour. In the distance, Alex spotted the Matterhorn. At over fourteen thousand feet high, the lone black pyramid rose above the glaciers. The Matterhorn's beauty was deceptive—hundreds had died trying to climb it: the unlucky and the foolish. It occurred to Alex that he could be numbered among them, but he chose not to dwell on it. Climbing the mountain and taking out Freddie would be enough of a challenge without having to fight self-doubt, too. Clouds gathered around the Matterhorn's two snowcapped peaks. In the window's reflection, Alex could see Cat was looking his way. He couldn't tell if she was looking at the Matterhorn or him. When he turned to see her eyes, she turned away.

# 15

Alex and Cat's taxi stopped at the Omnia Hotel—part tradition, part nature, and part modern. It resembled a traditional wooden Swiss chalet, with its long, sloping roof. The chalet extended into the mountain. Numerous large glass windows covered its face. Cat paid the taxi driver.

The couple entered a tunnel that led to an elevator they rode up through the rock to the lobby. From the lobby, Alex could see the city of Zermatt below. They checked in at the front desk, then rode the elevator up to their room. Instead of room numbers, the rooms had letters of the alphabet. White oak and black granite decorated the interior. Between the bed and the balcony sat a black, egg-shaped fireplace with stacks of firewood on an open container on the hardwood floor. Alex opened the sliding glass doors, stepped out onto the balcony, and gazed at the Matterhorn rising above them in the distance.

"Nice view," Cat said.

Alex turned to look at her.

Her eyes rested on his. "We've spent all this time together, and you haven't tried to—you know . . . get to know me better."

"I think that would be crossing all kinds of lines," he said.

"Not that kind of get to know you better."

"Pancho and John might start thinking I was favoring you on this mission."

"I think you can be covert when you want to."

"Are you saying you want me to get to know you better?"

Cat paused. "I'm saying you haven't answered my question yet."

"Which question was that?" he asked.

"Why haven't you tried to get to know me better?"

"Oh, that question," Alex said, stalling for time.

"Sometimes you look but don't say anything."

Alex wasn't ready for this. "Look, we've got a mission to prepare for. Can we talk about this when we're back in the States?"

For an answer Cat walked into the bathroom and shut the door. She didn't slam it, but Alex would have preferred that. He could handle emotions when they were raw and on the surface. All the yelling made sense to him. It was the quiet hurt and the way she looked at him that set him adrift.

"So maybe?" he said softly to the closed door.

# 16

Damien watched the Red Sheik, looking for a sign the man would change his mind about killing his brother. *Does he know if he does I'll kill them both?* Damien wondered.

After the sunset prayer, Damien, Commander Issa, and the Red Sheik sat on cushions on a thick, ornately designed carpet in the Red Sheik's majlis, waiting in silence. Although Damien normally enjoyed silence, the Red Sheik liked to talk.

The servant opened the front door. The imam left his shoes outside and entered. Damien, Commander Issa, and the Red Sheik rose. The Red Sheik's brother greeted them.

The Red Sheik returned his brother's greeting, lightly kissing him on the cheeks and shaking his hand. Then he offered his brother a seat at the place of honor.

"Who else is coming?"

"Only us."

"Only us?" Ahmed asked.

"I insist." The Red Sheik pointed to the seat of honor.

His brother refused, sitting in the nearest open space.

"As you wish," the Red Sheik said. He helped his brother set up cushioned armrests while the servant brought them Arabic cups filled with coffee. The men slurped, and the servant refilled their cups from a shiny brass coffeepot.

"I understand that you have a shepherd in your custody," Ahmed said without preamble.

The Red Sheik laughed nervously. "We have many people in our custody: murderers, thieves, and so on."

"This one is innocent. His parents died when he was a child, and he has no relatives to help him. No friends with any power. He's mentally slow."

"Oh, that shepherd. He confessed to crimes against Islam—engaging in extramarital sex with belly dancers . . . sodomy. Neighbors have joined him in the orgies with the belly dancers."

Ahmed laughed. "Belly dancers? There are more reports of these so-called transgressions than there are belly dancers. I checked. Even if there were, the shepherd is not a man of charisma to entice such women. He is too poor to pay for one dancer let alone for all that is claimed."

"These are confessions out of his own mouth. Signed by his own hand."

"He has no family who will attack you out of revenge. You assert your power over him as an example to others so you can control them through fear. You've destroyed the honor of his village by these confessions."

"We may have influenced him to tell the truth, but truth it is."

"Why are these so-called transgressions always with belly dancers?"

The Red Sheik became silent.

"Do you get some kind of perverted satisfaction from hearing such confessions?" his brother asked.

"That is enough. This is not the time for such discussions," the Red Sheik said.

"You think you can do anything you want because of your power and claim that you're acting in the name of Islam? It is blasphemous."

The Red Sheik's body sagged. "You're right. You always have been. I'm a slave to my passions, but I always tolerated you. And you always tolerated me. No one else have I showed one-hundredth as much patience to. We're brothers in flesh, but our spirits are strangers."

"The shepherd. He's an innocent man."

"Yes, I'll let him go. And I'll destroy the confessions. Leave his village alone."

"Thank you."

"Now can we enjoy ourselves?"

"Yes."

The servant collected the coffee cups, then brought thick glasses and poured tea in them. After three rounds of tea, the servant announced, "Dinner is ready."

The Red Sheik, Ahmed, Damien, and Commander Issa walked outside, put on their shoes, walked across the courtyard, and entered a large room filled with food but no furniture. Damien experienced déjà vu. They sat on the floor on oilcloths protecting the carpet. A variety of meats and vegetables formed mountains on the trays. There were fruits, nuts, salads, and pita. Servants brought coffee, tea, and fruit juices.

Damien was relieved to see that even the Red Sheik's brother was seduced by the food. It would make killing him easier.

The Red Sheik and his guests said, *"Bismillah."* In God's name. No one spoke; the only sound came from their eating.

Damien whispered in the servant's ear, sending him out of the room. Damien rose to his feet and calmly strode behind Ahmed as if to approach a tray for more food. Damien stopped, drew his sound-suppressed pistol, and fired into the back of Ahmed's head, blasting it forward. His neck stopped the forward momentum. The Red Sheik's younger brother was probably brain-dead before he landed face-first on the floor.

The Red Sheik stopped eating and turned away. Damien had

never seen him stop eating before. He always attacked his meals from start to finish. The Red Sheik choked in a garbled way that made it sound like he might vomit. Damien saw his reaction as a sign of weakness. In fact, Ahmed had been a constant source of weakness in the Red Sheik's life. Damien had no siblings, but if his son ever became such a source of weakness, Damien would have no qualms about getting rid of him.

Damien wrapped the body in oilcloths. Commander Issa helped. The Red Sheik, pale, didn't resume eating. He mumbled something and stumbled out of the room without any *Thanks be to God*. Damien was relieved not to hear the Islamic babble.

# 17

In the Swiss hotel room, Alex fired up his laptop and found a message waiting for him from JSOC: target Jamsheed "Freddie" Jamshed will be arriving with two Albanian terrorists. The first terrorist, known only by his nickname, "Rock," had dark hair shaved to stubble on his head, dark eyes, and brown skin. His neck and shoulders appeared strong. Rock was a boxer who wasn't quite talented enough to make it professionally. The second terrorist, Burim Haliti, at six feet five inches, had the good looks and charisma of a movie star.

Rock and Haliti joined the Kosovo Liberation Army (KLA) to rebel against the government in hopes of making Kosovo independent from what was left of Yugoslavia. They helped the KLA harass, intimidate, kidnap, torture, and murder hundreds of people opposing them, including their own ethnic group of Albanians. The KLA bombed police stations, cafés, bus stations, and other places, killing many innocent civilians as well. The KLA recruited children as young as thirteen years old, who made up 10 percent of their terrorists.

In 1999, Rock and Haliti joined the Liberation Army of Presevo, which was similar to the KLA in mission and structure. They operated until 2001, when the group disbanded. Then they went to work for the Kosovo mafia, trafficking prostitutes, drugs, and human organs. The mafia took Serbians and others hostage, ages twenty-five to fifty, and held the healthiest ones in a special prison until the surgeons were in place so the mafia could shoot them in the heads and the surgeons could take their livers and kidneys. The organs were then sold for forty-five thousand U.S. dollars per body in Istanbul, where they were transplanted.

*You keep some sleazy company, Freddie. Now where are you and your friends?* Alex logged on to Facebook using an alias courtesy of JSOC: a wealthy young Swiss playboy. As the playboy, Alex checked the posts of one of his "friends," who also happened to be one of Freddie's friends: Heidi Andress. By train, she lived only a couple of hours away from Alex's hotel. One of Heidi's friends posted a message about getting together at the Broken Bar Disco in the Hotel Post in Zermatt.

Sitting in a stuffed chair, Cat looked up from a local brochure she'd been reading. "Anything interesting?"

"Would you like to go dancing tonight?"

"Is this business or R and R?"

"Freddie might show up at the Broken Bar Disco," Alex said.

"What time?"

"They don't open until twenty-two hundred hours."

"Okay."

At a little after 2200, Cat and Alex took a taxi to the train station, split up, made sure they weren't being followed, and took separate taxis to the Hotel Post on the main street in the heart of Zermatt. From the outside, the Hotel Post looked like a large mountain lodge. Alex knew the Matterhorn could be seen from the hotel, but he couldn't see the mountain in the darkness. Alex entered the hotel first. He passed through the lobby, where a fireplace glowed, and music pulsated from what sounded like the Broken Bar Disco below. He walked down the stairs that led them beneath an old vaulted cellar.

At the reception desk of the Broken Bar Disco hung pictures of patrons, probably famous, who looked like athletes and models. The interior resembled a cave with its rocky walls and ceiling. Techno music pulsated out of speakers hanging from the low overhead. Most of the patrons were in their twenties and upper-class, dancing and mingling. The place was less than half full, but people continued to trickle in, their body heat warming up the air. Alex unzipped his gray fleece jacket. Under it he wore a simple white T-shirt, standing out among the autumn-colored sweaters and jackets that dominated the place. He sat down at the bar and ordered a martini. The bartender had a solid upper body and arms that looked like they could chop trees, but she also had pretty green eyes. She put three green olives in Alex's drink and smiled as she handed it to him. Alex smiled back.

Cat arrived and sat two bar stools away, pretending not to know Alex. Her head made a slight swaying motion in rhythm with the music. When she glanced his way, he raised his eyebrows at her. She rolled her eyes to show disinterest.

Scanning the room, Alex saw no sign of Freddie or his friend Heidi. He chatted with the bartender in English, asking her if she knew Heidi.

"Oh, yes," the bartender said. "Beautiful girl. Come here many times last year but not this year."

Alex didn't ask about Freddie. If Freddie found out that Alex was asking around about him, it might blow the whole mission—or worse, get the Outcasts killed.

A tall, stocky guy missing a tooth, who wore a long-sleeved green rugby shirt with black stripes, sat down next to Cat and started talking to her. He didn't look like the sharpest knife in the drawer. The more he talked, the less she talked, and the more he looked at her, the less she looked at him. Rugby finally gave up and went to sit with his noisy friends at one of the tables fashioned from a large keg.

An hour and a half later, as Alex was feeling all dressed up for nothing, the bartender came over and spoke quietly, "There she is."

The bartender pointed her chin in the direction of a brunette walking at the head of a female entourage.

"Are you sure?" Alex asked. "Heidi is a blonde."

"Those are her friends, and that's her with them. Looks like she dyed her hair."

"Thanks."

Heidi surveyed the room and spotted Alex checking her out but didn't lose a step as she led her entourage to an empty table. Alex could see he'd have to work for this one, and seeing how guys' heads were turning, Alex knew he'd better move quickly before someone else did. *It pays to be a winner.*

Alex picked up his drink and went straight to her table. "Heidi, it's me, Alex."

She grinned, but Alex could tell by the blank look in her eyes that she didn't remember him.

"Alex from Facebook. You said you want to ride on my yacht someday."

"Oh." Her eyes sparkled. "Did you bring your yacht?"

Heidi's friends laughed.

"Not tonight," Alex said. "Is this seat taken?" Alex asked.

She motioned for him to sit.

Alex overheard one of Heidi's friends tell her in German that she thought Alex was hot. Heidi agreed.

Alex wanted her to keep speaking and think he didn't understand. Also, he didn't want to risk his cover by letting her know he could speak her language. His watch chimed.

One of the girls asked to look at it.

He showed her.

"What kind of watch is it?" Heidi asked.

"It's German—a Lange."

"Can I see?"

"Sure." She was too far across the table to reach, so he took it off and passed it to her. Alex hoped she didn't break it because JSOC had been extremely clear in which they wanted their watch back in the same pristine condition in which they lent it to him. If Alex showed anxiety about the possibility of the watch getting damaged, it would detract from his rich-playboy image, so he acted calm. It was an interesting-looking watch, with jumping numerals and crocodile wristband, but not something Alex would ever buy. Even though the chimes could be turned off for stealth, it couldn't survive even a shallow swim.

"It makes a high-pitched chime every fifteen minutes and a low-pitched chime on the hour. If you fast-forward the chimes, they play Beethoven's Fifth Symphony."

"What brings you to Zermatt?" Heidi asked.

"Climbing the Matterhorn," Alex said. He shrugged as if it were no big deal.

"Oh, I have a friend who is doing that," Heidi said.

"When?"

"I don't know yet. Soon, I think."

"Are you climbing, too?" Alex asked.

She giggled. "No. I might be wild, but I'm not crazy. My friend Freddie, he's crazy."

*Jackpot*, Alex thought. "Do you dance?"

"Of course." She hesitated. "Are you asking?" Her Swiss accent was a turn-on.

"Yes," Alex said.

As Alex and Heidi headed out to the crowded floor to dance, he noticed Cat sitting alone at a table watching him. Cat had stopped swaying her head to the music and stopped smiling. She stood and headed to the bar.

"Do you know her?" Heidi asked.

"Well." He tried to think what he should say. If he said yes, it might hurt his chances of getting information about Freddie, but if he said no, Heidi might catch him in a lie, also hurting his chances of getting information about Freddie. "I'm not sure."

"She should join us."

Alex had to think quickly. If Heidi lost interest in him because she thought he was taken, he might lose his only lead to Freddie. "She looks like she's waiting for a friend."

"If her friend doesn't show, she can join us."

*In spite of appearing like a diva*, Alex thought, *Heidi seems like a nice person*. They danced.

Alex couldn't see Cat, but he could feel her eyes on him. He tried to block out all thoughts of her.

"Are you climbing the Matterhorn alone?" Heidi raised her voice to be heard above the music.

"No, but my friends and I are looking for someone to climb with. Never done it before and figured a few extra people would be smart."

Heidi nodded. "I haven't heard from Freddie, but I'll message you on Facebook if I do."

Heidi's full hips popped and dropped to the beat of the music. When she turned, the music seemed to flow through her shoulder-length brown hair in waves. Alex stayed in close, almost like he was bodysurfing her.

He knew he was using her to get to Freddie, but he was also attracted to her. The more they danced, the more the line between the mission and his interest in Heidi blurred.

"More than anything in the world, I want to live someplace warm," Heidi said.

"Why don't you?"

"Too scared, I guess."

"You don't look like the scared type," he said.

"Here, I'm not scared. My friends and family give me power."

They danced some more before taking a break. When they took their seats at her table, she sat next to Alex. He ordered drinks for Heidi and her friends.

Meanwhile, a guy with olive-colored skin, dark hair, and dark eyes walked with Cat out onto the dance floor. She laughed and seemed to enjoy herself. Alex should've been happy that she was enjoying herself, but he wasn't.

The waitress brought their drinks. Heidi took her margarita and sipped. "What brought you here tonight?" Heidi asked.

"I don't know."

"What do you want more than anything in the world?"

"I don't know."

"You already said that."

"What do I want?" Alex thought for a moment: *I want to throw Freddie off the top of the Matterhorn. What do I want more than that? Throw his buddies off the Matterhorn with him—not just Damien and the Red Sheik but every single terrorist on the planet. Then there would be no more terrorism.*

"Yes, what do you want?"

"Peace," he said.

As they talked, Heidi moved closer, touching his shoulder. He didn't know if it was the dancing, the margarita, or what, but her cheeks had turned a light shade of rosy red. He also noticed that Cat's friend had disappeared and she was alone at the bar.

Heidi's friends finished their drinks and hit the dance floor. Heidi playfully blew in Alex's ear, feeding oxygen to the flame.

Meanwhile, a new guy hit on Cat, but Rugby cut in and chased him away. Cat tried to shrug him off, but he persisted. She left the bar counter, but no tables were open, so she stood next to a wall.

"You've been looking at her all night," Heidi said, removing her hand from Alex's shoulder.

"Her friend hasn't shown, and I was wondering if she's okay."

"Maybe you should ask her."

Now Rugby cornered Cat and started to get all touchy-feely. Alex felt his anger start to burn. She struggled to get away from him, but he stopped her. With all the people and noise, no one seemed to notice her trouble. Cat was a tough woman, but this guy looked like more than she could handle. She broke loose and headed for the exit. Rugby followed her. Then his two friends followed.

"Damn," Alex blurted.

Heidi looked at him with disappointment in her eyes.

"I'm sorry," he said, then stood up and hurried for the exit.

# 18

Alex ran up the stairs and rushed into the hotel lobby to find Cat resisting Rugby's attempt to take her upstairs where the rooms were. The desk receptionist stood paralyzed behind the counter. A couple sitting on the couch near the fireplace stared at Cat and Rugby. The key to a good ambush is surprise, speed, and violence of action. Since Rugby still had his back to him, Alex didn't let the opportunity go to waste. Cupping both of his hands, Alex clapped Rugby's ears as hard as he could: *pop*. With his eardrums busted, Rugby couldn't maintain his equilibrium. He toppled forward. Cat stepped out of the way, breaking from his grip just before he fell. His face hit the floor. Blood trickled out of his left ear. He probably had a perforated eardrum.

Alex turned to face Rugby's two buddies as one bent low and charged as if to tackle him. Taking a step forward, Alex thrust his right knee up and nailed the charger in the chest—stopping him cold before he crumpled to the ground. He gasped for air and his hands clutched his ribs. The remaining friend looked at Alex for a moment before taking a step back. He didn't want the same fate as his friends.

Alex took Cat by the hand. As they headed outside, Rugby tried to stand but fell down like a drunken sailor.

Outside, the pair found separate taxis, headed to the train station, made sure they weren't being followed, and shared a taxi returning to their hotel.

Inside the hotel room Cat said, "You seemed to enjoy being with her."

"What?" Alex said.

"Heidi. You seemed to like her."

"Are you serious?" Alex asked. He'd just saved Cat from being raped and she was pissed at him?

"I'm sorry I ruined your night with her."

"You're welcome."

"You seem upset about it."

"I was just doing my job," Alex said, feeling slightly guilty now because he had enjoyed dancing with Heidi. A lot.

"Well, you certainly love your work," Cat said, her eyes flashing with obvious anger.

"You didn't seem to mind dancing with that one guy."

"I was acting."

"I aborted the surveillance to rescue you from Rugby and his buddies, and that's the best thanks you can give?"

"Thanks," she said, turning and walking into the bathroom again. This time, she did slam the door.

Alex stood dumbfounded. Their surveillance at the Broken Bar Disco was blown, and they still didn't know where Freddie was. He wanted to punch the wall, but he was worried he'd put a hole in it. If he kicked the table, it'd probably break. Going for a walk might get him noticed by the police.

Too pissed off to sleep, he took some time to message Heidi on Facebook, apologizing for his running out on her. Part of the reason for his apology was to maintain a relationship so he could get to Freddie. The other part of his apology was real. She probably wouldn't reply—he knew he wouldn't if he were her. He checked his personal email and saw the coded message from Pancho and John saying they were here and would check out the Broken Bar tomorrow night.

The next morning, Alex and Cat checked out the sports shops. The sun shone brightly, reflecting off the snow-sprinkled rooftops, streets, and walkways. Some of the buildings looked like chalets, with their wide, sloping roofs and overhanging eaves. Green shrubs and flowers decorated the balconies. Most of the signs to the shops were in German. Among the pedestrians, one man skied down the street.

To Alex's left, a beautiful chestnut-colored draft horse with a flaxen mane and tail pulled people on a red carriage through the street. Cat pulled Alex's arm. She pointed her nose to the right. There he was—Freddie—stepping out of a shop called Matterhorn Sports. Two Albanian men, Rock and Haliti, caught up to their friend from behind. They linked arms with Freddie, one on each side. Then they walked away chattering, oblivious to Alex and Cat.

Alex and Cat crossed to the far side of the street and followed them. They made sure to take turns watching so that only one had eyes on the terrorists at any one time while the other window-shopped. Alex also looked for escape routes—if needed, they could bug out via a side street or duck into a store. Earlier in his training at Team Six, Alex learned surveillance and countersurveillance from the experts: the CIA at Langley, Virginia. Except for some specialized classes that legally differentiated them from the CIA spooks, Alex had received his training right along with the spy trainees. Cat had undergone the training, too.

Freddie shopping with his two friends was easier to follow than just Freddie. Visually, it was easier to spot the three of them than if Freddie were alone. In addition, his friends drew Freddie's attention away from his surroundings. Also, they probably slowed him down from his normal walking speed.

In addition to conducting surveillance on Freddie, Alex kept a lookout for countersurveillance. Though it seemed unlikely, it was still possible someone was protecting Freddie by looking out for people like Alex and Cat—maybe standing on a balcony with a wide view of Freddie's route.

Freddie and his friends turned into a jewelry store.

"Let's watch from inside there," Alex said, pointing at a Victorinox store. They entered the store. While Alex looked at Swiss Army knives near the window, he kept his eye on the jewelry shop.

Cat picked up a blue bottle. "Look, Swiss Army perfume."

"Sounds romantic," Alex said sarcastically.

"This one's called 'Mountain Water.' "

"Swell."

A clerk asked in German, "Can I help you?"

"Could I smell a sample of this Mountain Water?" Cat asked in English.

The clerk switched to English. "Yes." He went behind the counter, returned with a scented strip of paper, and handed it to Cat.

While Cat tried each of the perfumes, Alex unfolded each blade on each of the knives. Before they moved on to the clothing, Freddie and his friends had exited the jewelry shop, Rock carrying a shopping bag, and headed up the street opposite Alex and Cat's direction. The two Outcasts thanked the clerk and left without buying anything.

Staying on their side of the street the two followed Freddie and his friends until they turned off onto a side street. Alex and Cat picked up their pace until they reached the same street and turned. Freddie and his buddies continued on their merry way with Alex and Cat on their tail.

Suddenly, the terrorist trio stopped and turned around, catching their pursuers in a bad spot. There were still enough pedestrians between the trio and the two Outcasts to prevent Freddie and his friends from getting a good look at Alex and Cat, but now Freddie's group was walking toward them. Alex and Cat were caught between shops. They could walk forward to the nearest shop to enter, but that would put them too close to the terrorists for comfort. If Alex and Cat turned around to visit the shop behind them, Freddie might pick up on the change of direction and suspect a surveillance team. Alex hurriedly pulled Cat into the alley between the two shops.

The alley was clean and had no odor, but it was a dead end. Now they were trapped.

"If they spot us here, we'll stand out like two rubies in a toilet bowl," Cat said.

"If we walk out of here, they'll spot us as surveillance."

"What'll we do?"

"Improvise." Alex put his arms around Cat.

Her eyes widened as if to say, *What are you doing?* Before she could mouth the words, Alex kissed her. It happened so fast that he almost knocked her over. She took a step back to catch her balance. He put his right hand out straight to steady them on the wall behind her. Then she closed her eyes. Her mouth was soft and warm. Her lips reciprocated and her arms tightened around him. In the minutes that followed, he forgot about the mission, the Swiss Alps, the past, and the future. The more they kissed, the more he forgot, and the more he forgot, the more he wanted to forget. There was only them, and nothing else mattered. Alex stopped thinking about thinking or not thinking. Snowflakes drifted down from the sky, melting into the ground like time.

The two paused for air. "Did you kiss me for cover, or did you kiss me because you wanted to?" she whispered.

He kissed her again.

She kissed him back.

They continued until the cold air made their bodies shiver.

Alex pulled away from Cat. "I'm sure he's gone now," he said.

"What should we do?"

"Are you hungry?"

Cat kissed him once. "Are you?"

Alex returned her kiss. "Starving."

"We could go to dinner."

"Now?" he asked as she nibbled on his ear.

"Whenever you want."

"I want to check on something first."

"Now?" She brushed her nose across his cheek.

"Yes. Before they close." She leaned forward as if to kiss him, or hoping he would kiss her, but Alex withdrew from her. "Let's check the Matterhorn Guide store that we saw Freddie and his friends come out of," he said.

"Do we have to?" she asked.

"Yes." Alex walked to the mouth of the alley. Cat followed. He looked along the street to the left, then right—no sign of Freddie.

They walked to the Matterhorn Guide store. As they entered, Alex spotted the clerk, an elderly man, and Alex told Cat, "Maybe you should ask. He might respond better to you."

She approached the clerk and spoke English. "A friend of mine came in here earlier—a colorful Pakistani man with two handsome friends. He's going to climb the Matterhorn, and we want to surprise him."

The clerk hesitated.

"It's his birthday," she said.

The clerk sighed.

"We'd like to join him." She pulled out her wallet and asked, "How much?"

"Three hundred Swiss Francs each," he said. "The climbers already finished some smaller climbs to acclimate themselves. Some of the group already dropped out, but not your friends. I have some openings now. Are you sure you are a strong climber?"

"Yes," Alex said.

Cat gave the clerk a credit card in her alias. "I won't be climbing," she said. "I'll be watching."

The clerk seemed confused as he held out his clipboard with the name list for Cat to sign.

Alex took the clipboard and looked at the list of climbers. At the bottom were three names. Alex didn't recognize the other two names, but he recognized one: Freddie. Alex signed up for Pancho, John, and himself. After registering, the Outcasts thanked the clerk and left.

# 19

Alex and Cat returned to the Omnia Hotel. Alex emailed Pancho and John with the good news. They were going climbing with their targets. Now that things were set, Alex felt at ease. He escorted Cat to the downstairs restaurant. Sitting next to a crackling fire, they ate Wiener schnitzel with mountain cranberries and hot potato salad. After the meal, they sampled the restaurant's chocolates.

"Are you okay?" Cat asked.

"Why do you ask?"

"You don't seem okay," she said.

"Just trying to enjoy the evening," Alex said.

"Trying?"

"Here I am, eating delicious hot food next to a warm fire with a beautiful woman, but tomorrow and the next day I'll be sucking on cold energy gel in the freezing snow with John and Pancho. Not to mention getting kicked in the nuts by the Matterhorn. Part of me wants to stay here and live like a normal person."

They sat in silence for the next several minutes until Cat finally asked a question. "There's something I don't understand. Why'd you graduate Harvard to become an enlisted SEAL?"

He swallowed hard. "I went there to study business management because I thought I wanted to be a CEO."

"So why didn't you?"

"I realized I didn't want to become a businessman."

"I still don't understand."

The conversation was starting to feel like an interrogation to Alex. "Because I realized that more than anything in the world, I wanted to kill terrorists. I went to each of the military recruiters and asked about their Special Ops units. Then I went to the Widener Library to begin checking each of them out. I knew before graduation that I wanted to become a SEAL."

"Let me guess—you became an enlisted SEAL instead of an officer SEAL because you thought you could kill more terrorists that way?"

"The enlisted guys spend more time operating and less time pushing papers. Officers may start out operating about the same, but over time, the officers end up farther away from the killing than the enlisted men."

Cat chuckled.

Her reaction surprised him.

"I'm sorry," she said. "I don't mean to be rude."

"I'm baring my soul, and you're laughing."

"I'm sorry, but I don't see you as the terrorist-killing type."

"How did you see me in Jakarta?"

"That's what I can't figure out. You come from a wealthy family, and you could've become almost anything in the world. You're intelligent and a gentleman—I mean SEALs are an intelligent group, but why you? That's what I can't understand."

"It's just what I wanted to do."

"Kill terrorists? Before 9/11? Back when the U.S. hardly knew what a terrorist was? It doesn't make sense. Does it have something to do with your grandfather? I can't figure out what else it could be."

"Yes."

"Maybe he taught you some things, but I don't see how that connects to killing terrorists."

"Grandpa taught Sarah more than me."

"Sarah—your sister?"

"Yes. Grandpa taught her to spend hours observing something. Sarah would use a deer's foot and make four prints in the dirt—side by side. The first print would be a half-inch deep and she'd make the next ones deeper and deeper until the fourth print was an inch deep. Then she'd take a picture and record the time and weather conditions. Six hours later she'd do the same thing again—make a new print and record the data. She'd take a picture of the first prints and compare them to the new ones. Sarah did that for twenty-four hours. Later, she'd record the data every half hour. She tried it in different soil and under different weather conditions until she became an expert at determining the age of a track. Meanwhile, I was busy playing water polo and hanging out with my friends. I didn't always have the patience for Grandpa's ways, and Grandpa didn't always have the patience for mine. Sarah was his apprentice."

Cat remained silent—waiting for more.

"It was my senior year in high school. Started out as a great year. As the goalie, I led my water polo team and we were headed for the Maryland State Championship. One day after school, I drove Grandpa and Sarah in my car to the post office so they could mail a package. I don't even know what was in the package or who they were mailing it to. Grandpa insisted on paying for it, and Sarah insisted on carrying it. Those two were inseparable. I parked the car and kept the engine running while I listened to music on the radio. It was some pop song I didn't like, so I changed to the classical music station. I remember Grieg's music, 'The Death of Ase.' People entered and exited the parking lot.

"There was a loud bang. For a moment I couldn't process what had happened, but when I saw the smoke and the chaos, I knew.

"Later, we found out who did it—some unemployed guy blew

up the post office to fight what he called the 'tyranny of government.' Later, when the police closed in on his apartment, he shot himself. I wish he would've shot himself before he blew up the post office. Why do they have to kill innocent people before they kill themselves—why don't they just kill themselves first?

"I didn't cry at the funeral. I loved her and missed her, and I missed Grandpa, but I had to play goalie at a water polo game. We won the state championship that year. After the game, I went home. I cried all night until I slept. I really missed Sarah. Still do."

Cat's eyes filled with tears, but she kept them from falling.

Alex didn't know why she was crying. He should've been crying. Maybe he had shed all the tears he could for Sarah, but he hadn't whacked all the terrorists he could—not even close.

They finished eating, paid for their meal, and strolled out arm in arm. On their way to the elevator, they bumped into Pancho.

"You two look quite cozy together," Pancho said.

"We're boyfriend and girlfriend," Cat explained.

"For real?"

"You know what I mean," she said.

"I liked it better when you two were married."

Alex and Cat told Pancho good night and returned to their room.

Inside, Alex locked the extra latch on the door. As he turned, Cat's arms wrapped around his neck and pulled his lips to hers. He tasted the chocolate on her mouth.

When Alex came up for air, he reminded her, "I have to climb the Matterhorn tomorrow."

"I know."

Alex walked across the room, and she walked with him, her hand on his shoulder. Alex picked up the phone. "I have to make a wake-up call before I forget." He kissed her.

"Yes, of course," she said between kisses.

Alex broke away and made the call.

"Front desk, may I help you?" the clerk said.

"Yes, I'd like to get a wake-up call," Alex said.

Cat kissed him.

"What time, sir?" the clerk asked.

Alex separated his lips from Cat's. "Nine o'clock. Room M." Then he kissed her.

"Nine o'clock wake-up call, Room M," the front desk clerk confirmed. "Is there anything else, sir?"

Alex's lips were locked on Cat's.

"Sir?" the front desk clerk asked.

Alex couldn't stop kissing her and hung up the phone. Then he realized he almost forgot something. He drew his pistol, took it outside, and put it in the plant pot nearest the sliding glass door. When he returned, Cat asked, "Why'd you put it outside?"

"After about two hours, I'll lubricate it with graphite, then leave it out there until tomorrow morning."

"So it's acclimated for tomorrow's cold weather op?"

"Yep."

"What'll we do while we wait for you to lubricate your pistol?"

Alex kissed her and slowly unzipped her jacket. She unzipped his. He lifted off her heavyweight long undershirt—exposing her naked ivory skin. Her perfume smelled like apricots. Cat took off his undershirt. They embraced. He felt the heat of her breath and skin burn against his skin. Alex held her hand and led her to the bed. They lay down and wrapped themselves around each other.


GOLDEN MORNING LIGHT FLOATED in through the open curtains and filled their room with its warmth. The sun glowed on Cat's skin and sparkled through her hair as she lay next to Alex in bed. Thoughts about chasing terrorists had disappeared—in place of the thoughts he felt peace. He stepped out of bed and walked to the sliding glass door leading to the balcony. His eyes followed the jagged mountains high into the air—the Matterhorn. Rather than going out to wrestle with it, he could enjoy its majesty from where he stood. It looked so tranquil. *But I have a mission to complete*, he thought.

While Cat slept, he made sure all his climbing gear was ready to go: backpack, zero-degree sleeping bag, headlamp, two one-liter wide-mouth water bottles (water bladders were too prone to freezing), a 65cm ice axe with a leash for glacier climbing, crampons with "cookie cutter" frame rails (heel bail/toe strap), forty feet of soft 6mm cord, and collapsible trekking poles.

Then Alex made sure Pancho and John were good to go. Inside their room, he reminded them of the critical component. "We have to get them alone. We're not going to kill an innocent bystander because they see what happens."

Alex returned to his room to find Cat awake. They went downstairs for lunch. During the meal, Alex drank as much water as he could without throwing up—just in case their mountain climb lasted longer than he expected, his water-saturated cells would keep him hydrated longer. After lunch, Alex and Cat returned to the room.

Alex put his climbing gear on. First, he donned heavyweight long underwear—tops and bottoms. Cotton kills because it retains sweat and water instead of wicking it away from the skin, so he wore polypropylene. He put thin wool socks on his feet to protect them from blisters. Over the socks he wore soft heavyweight wool socks.

Next, he wore cargo pants and a soft-shell jacket with a zipper, which could ventilate better and was easier to put on than a pullover.

Over that he wore an insulated synthetic jacket and pants. For the pants, he had full side zippers, so he could ventilate or take them off without taking off his boots. In the right thigh pocket, he carried his blowout kit: four-inch-square gauze bandage with tie straps, a cravat, and a Vaseline-coated dressing for a sucking chest wound—all vacuum-sealed in plastic to be compact and waterproof—not the greatest first-aid kit but good enough for gunshot wound/bleeding trauma. In the left thigh pocket he carried his escape and evasion kit: three hundred Swiss Francs, pencil flare, waterproof matches, compass, map, red-lens flashlight, space blanket, and tube of energy gel.

He went onto the balcony and retrieved his SIG SAUER 9mm pistol, which he had taken a time-out from Cat to lubricate. The magazine was loaded. After returning inside, he holstered the pistol on his belt, which held three more magazines in pouches. On top of all that, he put on a hard-shell jacket, waterproof and breathable, with a hood. It had underarm zippers for ventilation. Alex also wore hard-shell pants with full-length zippers on the sides so he could take them off easily. The purpose of the hard shell was to protect against wind and water.

Alex cinched tight a climbing harness with two pear-shaped locking carabiners attached. For his feet, he slipped on plastic boots, then a plastic shell over the boots. Over that he wore gaiters.

After protecting himself with sunscreen and lipscreen, Alex wore dark wraparound goggles to protect him from snow blindness. He put a balaclava on his head with a wool hat that covered his ears. On his hands, he wore mitts over his synthetic gloves with string attaching them to his wrists—losing a mitt off the summit would make for a cold climb down.

"Think I'm ready," Alex said.

"See you in a couple days." Cat kissed him.

Alex headed over to Pancho and John's room. They were all bundled up and ready to go. "Can I borrow a twenty?" Pancho asked.

"What for?" Alex asked.

"I'll keep your money dry if you fall off the mountain."

"I'm not going to fall off."

From their hotel, they took a taxi southwest several miles to a cable car. Snow continued to fall. After half an hour on the cable car, they arrived at the foot of the Matterhorn. Then they hiked on a marked trail that snaked its way to Hörnli Hut.

Pancho led them up the trail. "Doesn't this feel great? I love this weather."

John brought up the rear. "Great that I don't have to chaperone you anymore at the Broken Bar Disco. Maybe I can get some sleep tonight."

Pancho turned to Alex and smiled. "Heidi liked to yodel."

Alex marched in line between the two of them. "I don't want to hear about it."

"Really?" Pancho said. "Heidi seemed like your type."

"What's my type?" Alex asked.

"I don't know—classy, I guess."

"If she was so classy, why was she with you?"

"That hurts, amigo. She was classy until her clothes came off . . ."

"I said I don't want to hear about it."

"Aah, so she *was* your type." He paused. "Okay, maybe you don't want to hear about Heidi, but I know you'll want to hear about the twins. Well, they weren't really twins, but they looked like twins. When the three of us got to rolling around in bed, it all got a little confusing: arms, legs, and *tetas*."

"Hey!" John raised his voice. "We don't want to hear about it!"

Actually, Alex did want to hear about the *twins* but he let it go.

After two hours of hiking, they reached the Hörnli Hut, on the northeastern ridge of the Matterhorn. Inside, nearly everything was made of light brown hardwood: walls, pillars, rafters, tables, and chairs. There were about one hundred sleeping places and a kitchen with a gas stove. There was no drinking water, but the snow could be melted and boiled for drinking and cooking.

There were already about twenty-five climbers in the hut. Some were women, and they were already eyeing the SEALs like girls in a Baskin-Robbins eyeing the thirty-one flavors. Some of the men appeared irritated while others appeared to be contemplating damage control.

Most of the climbers seemed in good physical shape, but a few looked like they weren't going to summit. The SEALs probably should've done some climbs to acclimate themselves, but they had been too busy searching for Freddie. He and his friends were nowhere in sight. The guides hadn't arrived yet, either.

"Hope he shows," Pancho said. He strolled over to the ladies and chatted them up, irritating their boyfriends and husbands. Alex secured sleeping places for Pancho, John, and himself. Then Alex joined John outside to gather snow to boil for drinking water.

They spotted the guides coming up to the hut. A group of three men followed close behind and Alex recognized Freddie and the two Albanians. Haliti looked in good physical shape, but Rock looked stronger. Alex waited until they passed by and watched them go into the hut. He scanned the trail to see if anyone was watching, but if they were, he couldn't see them. He looked over at John, who shook his head.

"Here we go," Alex said, walking back to the hut with John following. Once inside they went to the opposite side of the room from the targets.

As the hut began to fill up with people, the air became stale. Alex stepped back outside to catch some fresh air. The snowfall had become so heavy that it hid the trail leading down the mountain. About ten minutes later, Freddie came outside, too. Alex wanted to go back inside, but he didn't want to look like he was avoiding Freddie, so he stayed.

"You climb much?" Freddie asked.

"A little. You?"

"A lot. The Matterhorn is an easy one."

Alex wondered if he was boasting or if it really was an easy climb for him. "Your friends look like they're in pretty good shape."

"Tomorrow they'll both summit. Personally, I'd rather climb something bigger than the Matterhorn, but not this time."

"Why not?"

"Work."

"What kind of work do you do?"

"Public relations. How about you?"

"Did okay on Wall Street, so now I play."

He smiled. "Wish I could play full-time."

"You don't enjoy public relations?" Alex asked.

"I enjoy being seen—worshipped. Doesn't everyone? If you feed people a story enough times, they'll worship anything—even dog shit."

After dinner, Alex went to bed. He wore his clothes to sleep in. The three SEALs took turns staying awake, just in case things started to go south. When it was Alex's turn to sleep, he was so jacked up on adrenaline and worried about their mission that the little rest he got was light. At 0400 they woke up and ate breakfast. Again, Alex drank as much water as he could.

One of the guides approached Freddie and said, "We can't guide you up today. The weather is starting to close in. We'll have to try another time."

"I don't need a guide." He and his friends put on their crampons, then roped themselves to each other.

A muscular climber told Freddie, "You should listen to the guide. He knows what he's talking about."

"You should shut up," Freddie said. "You don't know what you're talking about."

Alex, Pancho, and John clipped their crampons on their feet. Then they roped themselves to each other.

The guide tried to reason with them, saying, "It's dangerous up there. You could get killed." He was right. But it wasn't the first time Alex had risked his life to kill a terrorist.

The muscular climber warned them, "Don't follow that guy. He's crazy."

Freddie and his friends switched on their headlamps and headed out the door. Likewise, Alex's crew switched on theirs and followed the terrorists into the darkness: Pancho first, Alex second, and John third.

Outside, snow plummeted to the earth like mini asteroids and the wind stirred up snow from below. Alex couldn't see much of anything except Pancho's headlamp and the faint lights of Freddie and his friends. If Pancho led them off a cliff, Alex probably wouldn't know until it was too late. *Maybe this is a dumb idea.*

Alex asked the obvious question: "Do you know where you're going, Pancho?"

"Trust me."

*This is a dumb idea.*

# 20

The three Outcasts continued to trudge painfully slowly up the Matterhorn. In John's backpack he carried a couple of hundred thin, three-foot-long green wooden dowels that he used to grow tomatoes with, but instead of using these to grow tomatoes, he had attached red tape like flags on the tips to use them as visual markers—about every five yards, he stuck one in the ground so the SEALs could see them on their way back down the mountain.

Alex tried to look behind him every so often so he could see what things would look like on their way down, but it was too dark and snowing too heavily to see much of anything. Likewise, he couldn't see the summit—on the positive side, he couldn't see how high they'd have to climb—ignorance was bliss. He just kept forcing one foot in front of the other and he wouldn't stop until he reached the top. Stopping would only make the climb mentally and physically harder.

Pancho plowed forward at a good pace. Alex followed, breathing heavily. Normally, he could outrun Pancho, but climbing uphill in the snow, he had a hard time keeping up. His thighs and lungs burned. Gradually, Alex's body got so hot that he unzipped the zipper under his armpits to let some cool air in.

Although the Outcasts moved at a good pace, they hadn't passed

Freddie, which meant that Freddie's crew was moving at a good pace, too. Alex's hope of catching them partway up looked unlikely.

Gradually, the sun came out. The wind still blew and snow kept the mountain obscured, but visibility was better. After two hours, they reached the halfway point, the Solvay emergency bivouac hut. It was about one-tenth the size of the Hörnli Hut.

Freddie and friends had stopped.

"Do we do them here?" John asked.

Alex shook his head. "I'd like to, but everyone saw us leave with them. If they find three dead terrorists in a hut we're screwed. We'll have to wait for someplace better."

Alex waited until Freddie and his friends exited the hut, then went in for a brief rest before heading out and following them again.

Every so often now a gap in the snow-blanketed sky appeared, allowing the sun to reflect off the snow bright enough that Alex put on his goggles to protect his eyes. One would think the sky had dropped enough snow that there wouldn't be any left, but soon it was snowing harder. Because the sun made the snow wet, sometimes chunks built up under Alex's crampons, threatening to make him stumble. With the shaft of his ice axe, he hit the side of his crampons, knocking the chunks off. Repeatedly cleaning snow off his crampons, struggling with the lack of oxygen at high altitude, and straining to put one foot in front of the other tired him.

After an hour, they were climbing in snow up to their knees. Alex's whole body seemed to move in slow motion. Even his brain became lethargic. *Pick up your feet and put them down. Pick 'em up and put 'em down.* Soon that became too much effort, so he simplified: *Pick 'em up, pick 'em up.* Gravity would take care of the rest.

Suddenly, the sky cleared, and the summit came into view. They followed fixed ropes on the mountain, taking them to the top. At the peak, Freddie stood proudly with his friends. "What took you so long?" Freddie said. "We've been waiting for you to take our pictures."

"We were enjoying the scenery," Pancho said.

Freddie held out his camera. "Well, hurry up and take our picture while the sky is clear."

Alex wanted a moment to rest, but Pancho and John pressed upward, so Alex followed.

"Come on. You climb like old ladies." Freddie snickered and poked his camera into John's stomach. "Photo," he spoke slowly and loudly, like John was both dim-witted and hard of hearing.

Pancho pulled John aside and said, "Let me."

Freddie offered Pancho his camera. Pancho took it and motioned for the three men to stand close together. He started taking photos.

"The sun's getting in the lens," Pancho said, taking the camera from his eye and flicking through the shots he'd just taken. "Yup, too much glare. Try moving a bit over to your left."

"Just take photo," Rock said, his voice gruff.

Alex looked back down the trail behind him. Unsurprisingly, there was no one in sight.

"I want to get this just right for you," Pancho said, crouching down and snapping a few photos like he was a fashion photographer. "Keep smiling. I'm going to take a few head shots now."

Alex and John drew their pistols at the same time. Alex took Freddie, putting two shots into his forehead. John caught Rock just above the right eye with his first shot and Haliti on the bridge of his nose. Freddie and Haliti went down face-first while Rock sagged to his knees and tipped over onto his back.

"Say cheese, assholes," Pancho said, snapping one more photo.

John walked up and put one more bullet in each skull for good measure.

Alex looked down the trail again, but it remained empty. No one had followed.

John started to rifle through the pockets of the terrorists, careful to put items back again.

Alex holstered his pistol and undid his jacket, then took it off.

He shivered in the wind. Pancho followed suit. Alex bent down and picked up Freddie's ice axe.

"Okay, let's get this over with," he said, lifting the axe above his head and bringing it down with all his might on Freddie's head.

The skull split open on the first hit, cracking along the fracture line created by the double impact of the bullets. When the bodies were discovered, and they would be, it had to look like an accident, at least for as long as possible. Pancho and Alex proceeded to pulverize the men's skulls for the next minute until all three were shattered.

"A lot of blood and brain matter," John said, critiquing their work.

Alex looked up at the sky. "More snow coming. We'll scrape off this mess and then let Mother Nature take care of the rest."

Grabbing each terrorist by the ankles and shoulders, Pancho and Alex heaved them over the side and watched them tumble down until the snow obscured them from sight.

As the last body went over the side, Pancho suddenly swore. "Aw, damn it!"

Alex looked around them but saw nothing. "What?"

"We should have asked them to take our picture first!"

They took one last look around the summit, then started their descent. The sunlight faded as they climbed down the mountain. Soon they found themselves in a maze of paths leading down. One led safely down to Hörnli Hut and others led off various cliffs—but which was which? They followed John's red flags on the green tomato stakes. The Outcasts proceeded down the mountain until they couldn't find the next stake.

Pancho stopped in front of Alex. "Something funny about this snow," Pancho said. He squatted, pulled out his ice axe, and started digging a hole.

Alex stood there with a dumb look on his face. While Alex wondered what Pancho was doing, the snowy ground beneath them slid. With the ground pulled out from underneath Alex, he lost his balance and fell, riding the white blanket straight toward the cliff of a thousand-foot drop-off. Alex flipped ass over head, passing Pancho, who had anchored himself into the ground with his ice axe in the hole he'd dug. As Alex headed for the cliff, his rope, tied to Pancho, jerked him to a stop. Then John slid past Alex until the rope that connected them to each other jerked John to a stop. A wall of snow pushed over them. There was so much of the white stuff that it enveloped them in darkness. Pancho was strong, but Alex didn't know how long he could hold him and John if they kept pulling on Pancho. Alex grabbed his ice axe and chopped through the snow to anchor himself. The enveloping darkness slid over the edge of the cliff, but the Outcasts held on to the Matterhorn. The snow beneath Alex stopped sliding and the world became white again: white sky, white air, and white ground.

The three amigos recovered and backtracked to the last red flag. "I take back everything bad I thought about you, Pancho," Alex said.

Pancho's eyes smiled.

They searched around until they found the next flag. After that, the other flags were easier to find. Pancho blasted past Hörnli Hut, and they caught the lift back to Zermatt. They didn't want to run into any of the people who had seen them before. Alex knew that the guides would have reported six men going up the summit. When they didn't check in, a search would begin. He wanted to be long gone before any of the bodies were found.

At the hotel, Alex and Cat packed their bags, and the next morning they left town on the first train. This time they rode to Germany, and then flew back to Canada. From there they took another flight to Virginia Beach.

# 21

When Damien walked into the Red Sheik's office, the Sheik sat up in his chair behind the desk in the center of the room. His eyes were red and puffy. Closed curtains kept most of the light out of the room.

"We have a problem," Damien said.

"I don't want to hear about it," the Red Sheik said.

"Freddie is dead."

"How?"

"The Swiss authorities are still investigating. He went mountain climbing with two associates and it appears all three fell to their deaths. There was a huge storm and they were apparently warned not to summit, but they did anyway."

The Red Sheik groaned. "He was a fool."

Damien shook his head. "There's more. The news is reporting that there was a second party of three men that went up the mountain at the same time. Their bodies haven't been found."

The Red Sheik looked at Damien. "What, you think the Jews got him? No," the Red Sheik said, "no, I know what this is. It's him."

"Him?" Damien asked.

"My little brother."

"Ahmed?"

"He wants justice. We killed an imam and now he seeks revenge."

"Ahmed is dead," Damien said, wondering if he would have to kill him next.

The Red Sheik began to rock back and forth. "He has come back from the grave, and now he's coming for me."

"Whoever it is, he shouldn't have killed Budi. And I shouldn't have let him kill Freddie. But now I'm going to kill him."

"You can't kill a ghost."

"I can kill a ghost. I can kill a hundred ghosts."

"Let Commander Issa handle it. I need you to do something more important."

"More important than your safety?"

"My legacy. I want you to see to it that our cell stops dragging their feet in New York."

# PART TWO

*Only the dead have seen the end of war.*

—Plato

# 22

lex and Cat's plane descended on Lebanon. To the west lay the
Mediterranean Sea and to the south, Israel. Syria bordered the
country to the east and north. Except for the western coastal
region, mountains covered much of Lebanon.

They landed at the Beirut–Rafic Hariri International Airport,
named after a wealthy businessman who became prime minister
of Lebanon. After the Lebanese civil war, Rafic Hariri helped re-
build Beirut. When he opposed Syria's moves to control the Lebanese government, Hezbollah terrorists blasted him in his motorcade
with 2,200 pounds of TNT. Outraged, the Lebanese demanded that
Syrian supporters leave their government and Syrian troops depart
their land. Later, the Lebanese named the airport and a hospital
after Hariri.

Alex let his beard start to grow out. Cat dyed her hair black and
wore brown contact lenses. Speaking fluent Arabic, she hailed a taxi
that took them out of southern Beirut. They passed bombed-out
buildings dotted with bullet holes. Many of the people looked bat-
tered in their ragged clothes. Lebanon had been at war and civil war
for years and much of the fighting took place in the south, where
Hezbollah reigned supreme.

The taxi took them farther north, where they stopped at an

outdoor food market in a large parking lot. They stepped out and strolled past the stalls.

"This used to just be a farmers' market, but it has grown to be a lot more," Cat said. "They have everything here. Old style, new style, from the mountains, the sea, north, south. Everything, all natural."

The exotic smells made Alex hungry. His eyes took in the variety: multicolored lettuce, radishes, olives, tomatoes, pomegranates, apples, pickled vegetables and fruits, breads, jams, cheese, breads, tofu, cookies, pastries, and foods he didn't recognize.

"What is this place called?" he asked.

"Souk el Tayeb," she said. "*Tayeb* means good." She gave him a sample of pastry.

Alex ate it. "Yes, good."

"*Tayeb* also means to be alive." Cat sampled one. She started to say something more but stopped.

"What?" Alex said.

"Nothing."

"It must be something."

"You make me feel alive."

Alex didn't know what to say. He'd led men to their deaths. Of course, he never wanted them to die, but sometimes it happened. In the end, everyone dies. He wanted to make her feel alive, but he knew he was leading her into danger.

They loaded up the taxi with food, almost half of it for Pancho— Alex and Cat didn't know how long their upcoming surveillance would last, so they stocked up. Inside they sat. The taxi driver shifted the vehicle into gear. They passed fashionable people strolling the sidewalks in front of modern buildings. The taxi driver continued to a marina in St. George Bay. Palm trees lined the coast and people walked, jogged, and biked along the waterfront. Mount Lebanon, grayish green in color, rose in the east. If it hadn't been for all the wars, Lebanon was paradise.

As they drove, Cat spoke on her cell phone in Arabic. Alex couldn't understand, but he guessed she was confirming their yacht rental. When she finished, Alex remarked, "You really seem at home here."

"This is my grandmother's home. So I guess that makes it my home, too."

The taxi driver parked at the marina and waited for Alex and Cat to secure their yacht before he helped them carry their luggage and plastic bags of food onto the boat.

After paying the driver, they boarded their yacht and launched. Alex steered them straight out to sea. Occasionally he looked behind. The land became smaller and smaller until he could barely see it anymore. From the shore, no one would be able to see their yacht with the naked eye. He stopped the yacht.

The sun dropped low in the sky, landing on top of lemon-colored clouds. Above the sun, vanilla and strawberry colors streaked across a tangerine canvas. At sea, the sky and ocean were enormous, free from Mother Nature's trees and mountains—free from man-made telephone poles and buildings. The couple ate pastries stuffed with white cheese and nuts while easing it down their throats with cinnamon tea. Alex didn't think about what had happened or what would happen. Dwelling too much on that could wear a person down. He didn't think about how his face now neared Cat's and hers neared his. It felt natural—their lips touched.


AT 2400, THEY'D BEEN floating in the darkness with no lights on. Cat switched their red port light on and off two times, signaling in the darkness. In the distance, a red light flashed back at them. It was Pancho and John. Alex watched aft until they emerged from the darkness. With Pancho and John in a black rubber Zodiac boat rode a crew of about five SEALs with darkened faces and wetsuits. Pancho, John, and the other SEALs lay prone, hugging the Zodiac and keeping a low profile. As they neared, one of the men in front threw the bowline up to Alex. He wrapped the line around the fittings on their boat and pulled out the slack before securing it. Then he helped transfer several large black duffel bags of gear to their yacht. Finally, Alex gave Pancho and John a hand climbing on board and cast off the bowline. The Zodiac disappeared back into the darkness.

Alex started up the yacht and piloted north for fifteen minutes before he turned 90 degrees to the right and headed toward land. Meanwhile, Pancho and John stored their gear. Alex stopped their yacht within binocular range of the beach estate of the Red Sheik's banker, Khaled Qurei.

The Outcasts drew straws to see who had to stand watch first. Cat drew the shortest straw. Until 0400, she would keep an eye on the Banker's estate to see if he showed. Also, she would make sure no ships were on a collision course with them, and would look out for anything suspicious. Alex, Pancho, and John tried to get some sleep in their separate cabins. John would take the morning watch from 0400 to 0800. Then Pancho would stand the forenoon watch, beginning at 0800. Soon after Alex's head hit the pillow, he fell asleep.

Alex awoke at 0830 to the smell of food cooking in the kitchen. He opened his eyes and followed the aroma to the kitchen, where Cat was making breakfast for the crew. Alex was surprised that he'd slept so quickly and so soundly—*must've been more tired than I'd realized*. John seemed to follow the smell of the food, too, joining them in the kitchen. Cat had made Lebanese pizzas topped with ground meat, cheese, and thyme.

Pancho sat down with them around a table while maintaining surveillance on the Banker's resort.

Cat placed the food on the table. The Outcasts took turns serving slices of Lebanese pizza on their plates. After filling their plates, the Outcasts began eating, except for John, who said a silent prayer before eating.

"All three of you were in the Iraq War, right?" Cat asked.

Pancho kept eating, but Alex and John paused.

"Do you think we should've gone to war or not?" Cat asked.

"Yes," John said. "We went in to get WMDs." WMDs were weapons of mass destruction—chemical, biological, radiological, or nuclear weapons that can kill many people.

"How many did we find?" Pancho asked.

John didn't reply.

Pancho continued: "You see, John acts like he's concerned about whether we capture or kill tangos, but deep down inside he's looking for any excuse to kill them all. Killing is what he does best."

"Most of the news reported that there were no WMDs," Cat said.

"We found some chemical weapons, but they were low in quantity and quality," Alex said. "Not capable of mass destruction."

"Do you think we should've gone to war?" Cat asked.

"I supported the president, just like most of the nation did in the beginning," Alex said. "When the nation stopped supporting him, I still had a job to do."

"Two bodyguards," Pancho said, stopping the discussion. "One inside and one out."

"Probably not guarding an empty house," Alex said. "If the Banker isn't already there now, he should be arriving soon."

After breakfast, Pancho continued surveillance on the Banker's estate and Alex cleaned up while Cat and John rested. It was important to sleep whenever and wherever possible because when the shit started flying, there might not be an opportunity to sleep for days.

Alex took the afternoon watch beginning at 1200. At 1537, through his binoculars, he saw a black BMW pull up beside the beach estate. Out stepped a man wearing a black banker suit and thick glasses. A birthmark colored the skin below his left eye. "It's him," Alex said.

"Are you sure?" John asked.

"Check it out." Alex offered the binoculars.

John looked through them. "It's him."

"John, call for the extraction to stand by. Tonight we take out the Banker."

AT 0130, DRESSED IN camouflage with camouflaged faces, Alex, Pancho, and John carried HK416 assault rifles made by the German maker Heckler & Koch (HK). Each HK416 had adjustable six-position telescopic butt stocks that had space inside to store items. The HK416 held 30 rounds in the magazine (with options for 20-round or 100-round magazines) and could fire .223 (5.56 x 45mm) ammunition at a rate of 700–900 rounds per minute. Its short-stroke gas piston operating system had fewer malfunctions, lasted longer, and was easier to clean than the M4 assault rifle. Also, SEALs could come out of the water and shoot the HK416 without having to drain it first. On the barrel, Alex and the guys had fixed a Knight's Armament Company sound suppressor to each. SEALs carry whatever weapon is most appropriate for the mission. Alex often preferred his men to carry similar weapons so the ammo could be exchanged when a Teammate ran low.

Attached to the rifle was a Picatinny rail, named after the Picatinny Arsenal in New Jersey, where it was originally tested. The rail served as a bracket to mount accessories. On the Picatinny rail, Alex, Pancho, and John had each mounted a Trijicon Advanced Combat Optical Gunsight (ACOG). The ACOG 1.5x magnified images to 1.5 times their normal size. Its aiming reticle glowed in low-light conditions without a battery. In addition, the ACOG was waterproof to five hundred feet.

The three SEALs slipped off the back of the yacht and into the black ocean. Alex hoped their luck wouldn't run out on this hit. Wearing black swim fins on their feet, they did the sidestroke, which didn't make splashes in the water. Rather than use his hands to swim, Alex mostly used his legs—long, strong kicks. With each kick of his fins, the anxieties dissipated. Going with the tide into shore, they swam quickly. When they reached water shallow enough to stand in, they crouched low and watched the shore. No late-night lovers lay on the beach. Alex could see that no lights were on in the Banker's residence. Everything seemed calm. The three took off their fins and attached them to bungee cords strapped across their backs. Alex and John spread apart and low-crawled from the water. Lying down in the sand, they pushed with their legs, pulling with their arms and moving sand with their faces. Eventually, they reached the bushes surrounding the estate and used them for concealment. The bushes would help hide them from the enemy's eyes, but Alex held no illusions; if shooting broke out, the bushes wouldn't protect the SEALs from bullets. Alex and John peeked over the bushes; they looked for any danger. Clear. Alex hand-signaled back to Pancho in the water that everything was clear. Then Pancho low-crawled to join them.

The three crept past the bushes and reached a thick glass wall on the balcony. John slipped over the wall and checked the sliding glass door leading into the back of the house—locked. If there had been a lock on the outside, John could've picked it, but there was none. With the curtains drawn, they couldn't see inside, but that also meant that the inside guard couldn't see outside.

Alex signaled for them to go up to the second floor. The three took turns standing on the metal frame of the glass wall, jumping up to the second-floor balcony and pulling themselves up and over the thick glass balcony wall. While one SEAL moved, the others covered the surrounding area with their sound-suppressed HK416 assault rifles.

When they all reached the second floor, John checked and found there was no outside lock on the sliding door. However, the curtain was wide open. The Banker was sleeping in his bed, with his glasses on the nightstand.

From his backpack John pulled out a thin plastic rope filled with compressed powdered explosive, pentaerythritol tetranitrate—

detonating (det) cord. While Alex and Pancho stood guard, John taped the det cord in a door shape around the edges of the glass. Then he attached the blasting cap, fuse, and handheld detonator. John stepped to the side of the window and nodded.

*Boom!* White appeared in the center followed by a ring of yellow and then orange and red. Alex rushed in first through the blown-out glass. The Banker opened his eyes—disoriented. Alex knew Pancho was right behind him and covering the other side of the room. "Clear!" Pancho called.

Before the Banker understood what was happening or could even think about negotiating a deal for his life, Alex put two rounds in his face. "Four down, three to go," Alex mumbled.

As he glanced at the Banker's glasses on his nightstand, Alex noticed a USB stick next to them. He picked it up and put it in a waterproof pouch.

"I'm taking us out!" Alex called.

Alex headed out onto the balcony, climbed over the wall, hung down, dropped from the second floor to the ground, and covered the area while Pancho descended. Meanwhile, John stood on the second floor, covering with his HK416.

On the ground, from around the corner of the building, a massive bodyguard with an AK-47 came at a fast hobble toward Alex. Alex quickly aimed at the bodyguard's chest and rapid-fired three shots, stopping him. The bodyguard's feet slid out from underneath him and he landed on his back.

John lowered himself from the second floor to the ground.

"John, take us home," Alex said.

John walked point toward Mother Ocean with Alex behind him, and Pancho brought up the rear by keeping an eye out for anyone trying to follow them. They'd already made enough noise that they weren't worried about being quiet now—they just wanted to get the hell out of Dodge.

"Contact rear!" Pancho shouted. He fired his HK416.

*Shit.* Alex and John dropped to the ground and turned to their rear.

From the Banker's bedroom, a bodyguard's AK-47 flashed in the night, illuminating him in a strobe of light and sound. The bodyguard sprayed and prayed at the ocean. He didn't seem to know what he was shooting at because none of his shots hit close to the SEALs.

Alex and John assisted Pancho in returning fire at the bodyguard. The bodyguard's flashes and noise stopped.

John raced ahead of them, changing magazines as he went, and took point, leading them to the ocean. In the shallow water, they took their fins off their bungee cords, put them on their feet, and swam out to sea. The swim out was more difficult than the swim in had been because now they were swimming against the waves. Fortunately, the waves were small and the SEALs' adrenaline was high.

Soon the three reached their yacht and climbed aboard. Cat brought in the anchor, and Alex piloted them out to sea. John and Pancho stood lookout. The cloud cover had cleared, and the sea glimmered in the moonlight. Minutes later, John called, "We got company, rear!"

"Who is it?" Alex asked.

"Don't know," John said.

"Great," Alex said. Was it the Banker's men? How could they respond so fast? Was it the police? *This can't be good, whoever it is.* Alex cut off the engine and called, "Cat, I need you to take the wheel. Tell them you have engine problems. If they ask to come aboard, or they want you to go aboard, tell them in English that it's okay."

"Okay." She took Alex's place at the wheel.

The silhouette of a patrol boat approached from the starboard side, sweeping the ocean with a spotlight. Alex grabbed Pancho and John and hid with them on the port side. Alex could hear the engine coming closer. He readied his HK416. *Maybe they won't see us.*

The spotlight stopped in the direction of their yacht. The light became brighter and the engine became louder. The patrol boat stopped nearby and a male voice shouted in Arabic.

Cat replied in Arabic.

The conversation went back and forth between them. Then she said, "Yes, I'll be happy to go aboard your boat."

*Not good.* Alex and Pancho appeared from the bow—Alex crouched low so Pancho could shoot over his head. On the other boat's bow an unkempt man in a wrinkled camouflaged uniform stood behind a 7.62 mounted machine gun. Midship stood what looked like the leader, holding a pistol in his hand and wearing a different camouflage uniform with some colorful rank insignia on it. Aft stood a bearded man in black carrying an AK-47, and a silhouette behind a floodlight. The men looked more like militia than police or military.

Because a metal shield protected the 7.62 gunner's upper body, Alex took an extra fraction of a second to aim at the gunner's head. The SEALs fired before the enemy got off a shot. The enemy fell to the deck.

Then John opened fire into the pilothouse. Alex spotted the silhouette of a pilot. Alex and Pancho fired, too. The pilot's body jerked before he fell out of sight.

Alex walked over to Cat. Her right hand gripped the wheel tight and her eyes were glazed.

"You okay?" Alex asked.

Her voice trembled. "Yes."

"Why don't you go below deck and sit down for a minute."

"Yes."

She stood still.

"Are you injured?" Alex asked.

"Yes—no. I don't think so."

Alex put his hand on her right hand, still gripping the wheel, and gently pulled her fingers away. "It's going to be fine," he said. "You did good. You saved us."

A tear flowed from her eye, and her voice still trembled. "I was so scared."

"It's finished. We're going home." He put his arm around her and led her below to the couch in the living room. Then he laid her down on a couch. "I'm going to drive us out of here."

"Yes."

As Alex ascended the steps to the outer deck, he heard a large boat engine. Worse, he heard the roar of a .50-caliber machine gun, then the sound of baseball bats whacking their yacht.

"Alex, sail us out of here!" yelled John.

As Alex stepped out on deck, he saw a large patrol gunboat, over a hundred feet long. The size of it in comparison to their yacht took his breath away. It made a run past them and was circling around to come back.

Alex started the engine and pulled down on the throttle—full speed away from the gunboat. "Where'd these guys come from?!" he yelled. Alex looked aft. The gunboat was gaining on them.

"Can't you go any faster?!" John yelled.

"I'm giving it full throttle! Can't you shoot them?!"

"It's an armored gunboat!"

"Where the hell is Pancho?!"

John shot at the gunboat. "He isn't with you?!"

"Pancho!" Alex screamed.

As the gunboat neared them, Alex turned hard to starboard. The .50-caliber machine gun rattled the air. A round punched through the pilothouse. Alex ducked. Then the pilothouse windows imploded and chunks of bulkhead whizzed over his head.

The yacht's engine stopped. Alex tried to start it a few times—nothing. The fuel gauge needle had dropped to empty. "Damn!"

The gunboat passed, then turned around to make another run at the Outcasts. Alex aimed his HK416 at it, but the gunboat was so heavily armored from top to bottom that it was like shooting spitballs at a rhinoceros. He aimed for the .50 gunner. Adrenaline pumping, firing at night with the bow of the yacht pitching up and down, and the sides rolling left and right, Alex couldn't hit the .50 gunner on the speeding boat. Although Alex's HK416 suppressed much of the muzzle flash, it still gave off enough light to make Alex a target. "Pancho!" Alex shouted.

Pancho emerged with a disposable antitank rocket for close spaces (AT-4 CS). Salt water could absorb much of the back blast, so it could be fired from a closed area without incinerating buddies nearby. Pancho removed the safety pin, popped up the iron sights, cocked the AT-4 CS, and placed the launcher on his shoulder to aim.

The gunboat's .50-caliber rounds smacked the air around Alex with frightening sonic booms that came closer and closer. He hugged the ground as the rounds shredded the pilothouse. Glass and metal rained down on him.

Then Alex heard the pop of the AT-4 CS, a swoosh, and the resulting explosion. He stuck his head out to see a flaming gunboat pass. It crashed into the patrol boat sitting dead in the water. The patrol boat caught on fire, too.

"You're the man!" Alex shouted.

"Yeah!" John yelled. "Now let's get out of here!"

"Engine is dead," Alex said. "And both our main tank and reserve are reading empty."

Cat came up from below and said, "We're sinking."

All four of them hurried downstairs and found themselves in water up to their ankles.

"I tried to jam everything I could find in the holes, but it didn't stop the water from coming in," Cat said. "Seems like more water is coming in from somewhere else, but I can't find it."

"We need to abandon ship," Alex said. "Take what you need and meet me at the rowboat."

John held up a mangled wet hunk of metal—it was a portable satellite dish for secure communication. "Won't be needing this anymore."

Alex grabbed his bag, rushed upstairs to the stern of the yacht, and lowered the rowboat from the mounted davits. The rowboat looked like it could comfortably carry eight people, so it was big enough for the four of them and their gear.

The others joined Alex with their bags. Pancho chomped on a mouthful of food.

"What's the plan, Chief?" John asked.

Alex assumed their covers were blown, so he and Cat couldn't count on using their passports to get through immigration and customs then out on a commercial flight. They could travel over land to Syria to the north or east, but Syria, with its ties to Hezbollah terrorists, probably wouldn't be too eager to help the Outcasts. Another option would be to go south to Israel, but anyone suspecting Israeli involvement in the hit would be waiting to intercept them trying to sneak back across the border, and there were hordes of Hezbollah between Alex's crew and Israel. "Since we missed our primary extraction, we go back to Lebanon, get a boat, and sail to Cyprus," Alex said. "Just like our E-and-E plan." Alex finished lowering the rowboat into the water. The Outcasts piled in, and Pancho rowed. Using the digital compass on his Casio Pathfinder watch, Alex helped navigate. Pancho rowed over large swells. They were lucky the weather was calm. Gradually, the dark sky in front of them became lighter as city lights on the coast emerged—land. As they neared Lebanon, they followed the coast looking for a marina to dock at. When they found one, they prepared to insert.

Alex studied the waves in the surf zone in front of them in order to time the low sets. He didn't want to get wiped out and have to play fish-for-gear. When the waves calmed, Pancho rowed them in. Since Alex was in the rear of the boat, he watched their flank.

A patrol boat scanned the water between the coast and the surf zone with a searchlight. "Pancho, if you can row faster, now would be a good time," Alex said.

# 23

The Outcasts looked back and saw the patrol boat. "Uh-oh," Cat said. Pancho dug the oars deeper into the ocean and pulled longer, causing the rowboat to go faster.

The patrol boat turned toward the Outcasts, scanning the ocean with its searchlight.

As the Outcasts neared the rows of boats moored at the marina, Alex told Pancho, "Hide us between the boats."

He did. They waited in a narrow space between two yachts berthed to the pier.

From the direction of the patrol boat, a voice spoke Arabic through a megaphone.

"What's he saying?" Alex asked Cat.

" 'Come out now. We don't want to hurt you.' "

"Sure," Alex said.

The patrol boat motored toward the marina flashing its light. It headed straight for the Outcasts.

They could move to a more concealed position, but their movement might give them away. Alex and his crew crouched as low as they could.

The light passed over them and a voice called in English over a megaphone: "Come out now. We don't want to hurt you."

*Did they see us?* Alex thought.

The light returned, stopping directly on the Outcasts. A 7.62 machine gun unleashed its fury in their direction. Shots ricocheted off the yachts.

Pancho rowed them under the pier to the other side. "Leave what you can't carry in the boat," Alex said. But he didn't want the enemy to get their stuff—more out of pride than secrecy. "John, booby-trap the rowboat." Alex, Pancho, and Cat used the pier to pull themselves out of the rowboat without capsizing it. They lowered themselves into the water. Because Alex carried extra gear, he blew some air into his gray inflatable life vest to help him stay afloat while he treaded water. Then Alex heard the pop of a fuse being lit and could smell the cordite burn. John joined them in the water under the pier. "How much time on the fuse?" Alex asked.

"Five minutes," he said. "About."

Now Alex was more worried about getting blown up than he was about getting shot. They swam quickly under the pier toward shore.

The patrol boat came around to the side where the rowboat floated, and lit it up with the patrol boat's searchlight and machine-gun fire.

The Outcasts continued under the pier until they reached where it connected to land. They didn't want to leave the water just yet. The patrol boat didn't know where they were, and Alex wanted to keep it that way.

From the patrol boat, someone had lowered a ladder over the side and sent some poor bastard down to investigate. The poor bastard rummaged around in the rowboat, then held up a satchel. His comrades in the patrol boat yelled at him. He dropped the satchel and clambered to get up the ladder.

"Any moment now," John whispered.

The satchel exploded, enveloping the poor bastard in a ball of flame and knocking his comrades off the patrol boat, which rolled violently onto its side. One of the yachts adjacent to the rowboat burst into flames.

The Outcasts took the explosion as their cue to haul ass. The four crept onto land, then ran across the marina parking lot. Some parking lot lights kept the area partially illuminated.

When the Outcasts reached the middle of the parking lot, two small 4x4 pickup trucks, one white and one black, with half a dozen militia in the back of each, screeched into the marina. The Outcasts took cover behind two parked cars, Alex and Cat behind one and Pancho and John behind the other—but it was too late, the militia had already spotted them. The trucks zeroed in on their position while the militiamen fired their AK-47s.

Alex shot a three-round burst through the front windshield in the white truck and it slowed to a halt. Militiamen jumped out of the vehicle and came after them on foot. Cat fired her HK416, hitting a baggy pants militiaman in the upper body and taking him out of the fight. John tossed a fragmentation grenade into the middle of them. The resulting explosion took out three militiamen and wounded several others. Then Alex shot the one tango dumb enough to remain standing.

After making one firing run past the Outcasts, the driver of the black truck, not learning a lesson from his colleague in the white truck, turned around and came at them again. Pancho, wielding an AT-4 CS, unleashed a rocket that slammed into the front of the speeding black truck, stopping it dead and catapulting bodies. With some dead and others having the fight knocked out of them, their assault came to a halt. The shooting stopped.

"How many of those AT-4s you got?" Alex asked.

"That was the last one."

"We need to get out of here before the main party arrives."

Pancho eyed the bodies and the white 4x4. "Looks like we got a vehicle."

Minutes later they rode off in the 4x4. Alex drove with Cat in the passenger seat while Pancho and John rode in the truck bed.

"I need you to give directions," Alex said.

"Where do you want to go?" Cat asked.

"Where no one is shooting at me."

"Where is that?"

A shot punched through the back window between them. In the side-view mirror Alex saw a green sedan followed by a black one. "Not here."

Alex turned right down a narrow street, speeding into the turn. The green and black sedans followed with AK-47s hanging out the windows, the shooters firing at them. Alex hung a left—in the back, Pancho and John rolled from one side of the truck bed to the other.

"You trying to kill us?" Pancho shouted.

"They are!" Alex shouted.

"I'd rather take my chances with them!"

Alex whipped the steering wheel right, and drove down a busted-up street. Bumps and potholes bounced Pancho and John up and down.

The black sedan was nowhere in sight, but the green sedan caught up with them. More gunshots followed.

"Let us out!" Pancho's voice rattled.

"Stop whining and start shooting!" Alex yelled.

"We are shooting!"

"How can you shoot when you're whining?!"

Between bumps and potholes, John cut loose on full auto into the engine and windshield of the green sedan, stopping it.

"Get us off this street!" Pancho yelled.

Alex turned left. The road widened and became smooth, but Alex almost hit an oncoming car. Both vehicles swerved, missing each other. Alex picked up speed. Then a large truck, carrying men waving AKs out the windows, emerged twenty yards up the road and headed straight for them. Cat braced her feet against the floor, pressed her HK416 muzzle against the windshield, and fired at the large truck. Alex grabbed the handbrake and pulled hard, locking their back wheels as he turned left, sending them into a controlled skid that took them from the right lane to the left lane heading away from the truck. But Alex's truck lost all momentum and came to a complete stop. Looking in the rearview mirror, Pancho crawled off from on top of John, whose face looked filled with pain.

Alex stomped on the accelerator. The wheels spun as they struggled to gain traction. Alex eased off the accelerator enough for the wheels to slow down and catch a bite of the street. The Outcasts' truck took off.

The large truck pulled up beside the Outcasts and broadsided Alex's door, knocking them into a building on Cat's side, which caused her side-view mirror to break off. Her metal door spit sparks as it scraped against concrete. Cat aimed her HK416 in their direction, but seemed hesitant to fire with her muzzle so close to Alex's face.

Pancho and John took shots into the large truck, taking out two of the AK-waving tangos. Then Pancho landed on top of John again.

Alex broadsided the large truck, but the enemy truck was too massive to budge. The large truck countered by ramming Alex's vehicle against the wall again. The passenger aimed his AK-47. Alex and Cat leaned back as Alex stomped on the brakes. An AK-47 round passed in front of their faces, popping the air with its mini sonic boom. The large truck sped in front of them. Cat fired through the front windshield at the large truck while Pancho and John rose and fired, too. They must've hit something, because the large truck came to a halt. Alex ran into the large truck from behind, knocking Pancho and John off their feet again.

*"Aidez-moi!"* John wailed. Help me!

Alex passed the immobilized truck and breathed a sigh of relief, but the enemy gave him no rest as a black sedan from behind sped toward them.

Up ahead, Alex saw palm trees lining the coast. He turned right. With the ocean on his left, he headed north, hoping the straight-away would give the guys some relief from being bounced around, and, more importantly, a better opportunity to shoot their pursuers. Alex stomped the gas pedal to the floor.

The black sedan began closing the gap, its occupants firing AKs in the Outcasts' direction.

Pancho and John aimed and fired in rapid succession. Suddenly, the black sedan veered right until a concrete building stopped the vehicle.

Alex drove north as fast as he could so they could get more dis-tance between them and the mess they'd left behind. The sky became lighter. They needed a place to hide out before sunrise.

John moaned. "I'm going to puke."

Police sirens blared in the distance. "Are those behind us or in front of us?" Alex asked.

"Not sure," Cat said.

Alex kept going north, hoping the police weren't in front of them. After several minutes, the sirens quieted down.

"Turn right here," Cat said. "This village is abandoned."

Alex slowed down and turned right. "Where are we?" he asked.

"Up ahead is the village of Bjarine, abandoned during World War I. We're in the northern part of Amsheet, mostly a Christian town."

"There's no more road."

She pointed. "Just follow that trail."

Alex followed the trail inland. A village of old stone houses and what looked like a church emerged. Sheep and goats populated the area. "We need a place to hide the vehicle," Alex said. He drove to the outskirts of the village and stopped behind some bushes.

The Outcasts exited the truck. John hadn't staggered more than a couple of steps before he vomited.

Pancho told John, "You look how I feel."

The Outcasts gathered some leafy branches, then used them to camouflage their truck. Next, they entered an old stone house, chased out some sleeping sheep, and lay down for the night. Because of all the danger they'd encountered, instead of keeping one person on watch and letting three sleep, Cat and Alex kept watch while Pancho and John slept. With half of them already awake, they'd be able to react more effectively if trouble arose.

As Pancho and John slept, their breathing became heavier and slower.

"They were all over us," Alex said. "Like they knew we were coming."

"Do you think there was a leak?" Cat asked.

"I can't imagine anyone on our team . . ."

"I don't know the right way to say this."

"Say it anyway."

"When that big gunboat attacked us, Pancho was below deck—safe from the .50-caliber fire while you were getting shot at."

"You were below deck, too."

"I was in shock."

"Pancho was getting the AT-4."

"Well, I guess what I'm asking is—how much do you trust him?"

Alex looked at the Mexican giant sleeping soundly on the ground. "Pancho is a lot of things, but I trust him. Simple to the ways of the world. Living at his own pace." He tried to think of a point of reference. "Like Sarah was."

# 24

I t was still nighttime. In the middle sedan of a three-car motorcade, Commander Issa and Lieutenant Garza sat behind Commander Issa's driver and an elite soldier from the commander's
Special Guard. Lieutenant Garza wore a green baseball cap turned
backward on his head.

The four men listened to a radio scanner to monitor law enforcement and militia communications, but they heard no new news.
Behind them rode several small trucks with armed militia riding
in back. The caravan rode over bumps and potholes in a busted-up
street. They passed a green sedan and a large white truck dotted
with bullet holes—the occupants appeared dead.

"I thought you had an ambush waiting for the infidels at Khaled's
beach estate," Commander Issa said.

"Most of my men were on land," Lieutenant Garza explained.
"Your goal was to use Khaled as bait, not save him."

"You succeeded in giving the infidels the bait."

"We'll find them."

The caravan turned right. Palm trees lining the coast came into
view. The motorcade turned right. With the ocean on their left,
they proceeded north until they came upon a black sedan smashed
into a concrete building.

"Slow down," Commander Issa said.

A survivor sat in the dirt next to the vehicle.

"Stop! Stop here!"

The caravan stopped just past the wreck and Commander Issa ordered his vehicle to back up. After it stopped next to the survivor, Commander Issa and Lieutenant Garza hopped out.

"Where are they?" Lieutenant Garza asked the survivor.

The survivor's nose hung as if broken, blood staining his mouth and the front of his neck. Both of his legs appeared broken. His right arm seemed okay as he used it to point north.

Lieutenant Garza turned to his vehicle when Commander Issa said, "He failed. Is this how you punish failure?"

"Am I giving him a ride to the hospital?" Lieutenant Garza asked.

"I don't know. Will you?"

"Certainly not."

"I thought failure of such an important task would result in more serious consequences."

"If I did that to each of my men for failure, I'd have no one left."

They returned to their vehicle and proceeded north with their caravan. The motorcade continued through Amsheet and passed an abandoned village, Bjarine.

"This village is Christian," Commander Issa said. "I hate Christians. They stink like hamburger meat. Every living one of them nauseates me. If I had the resources to blow up this village, I'd do it now. They have the nerve to call themselves Arabs, but they aren't even human."

# 25

The sun rose, and the Outcasts took turns lying in watch, two on and two off. If they could wait for the darkness to give them cover, they could look for a marina with a boat they could acquire to get out of Lebanon.

Late in the afternoon, they heard the voices of children playing, possibly a hundred yards away, between the Outcasts and the ocean. An uneasy feeling turned Alex's stomach—maybe the children would discover them. He woke up Pancho and John.

The voices came to within about fifty yards and stopped, but the footsteps of one or two children came closer.

The Outcasts had hid themselves on the side of the house farthest from the entrance, under the leafy branches they'd collected.

Two whispering boys came inside the Outcasts' stone house. The boys walked closer. Then they tugged at the branches concealing Alex. He tried to hold his in place. As the boys wrestled with the branches, the smaller boy spotted them and jumped back, startling his friend. The Outcasts threw aside their branches, lunged forward, and grabbed the two boys. They screamed.

"We're not going to hurt you," Alex said.

The boys trembled.

Alex turned to Cat. "Tell them we're not going to hurt them."

She spoke to them in Arabic.

"We can't kill them," Alex said.

Cat started to translate but stopped.

John picked at his shirt sleeve as if there were lint on it, but there was none.

"What is it, John?" Alex asked.

"If we let them go, they'll tell their parents, and they'll call the local authorities to apprehend us," John said.

Pancho nodded. "Maybe we could tie them up until their parents send out a search party and find them."

"I think we should get out of here right now and take the kids with us," Alex said. "When we get far enough away, we'll let them go so they have a chance to get home just after dark. By then we should have a big enough lead away from them."

"We'll have to lead them in a false direction until we let them go so they won't be able to tell people the real direction we're heading," John said.

The voices of playing children became louder. They were coming nearer.

"Can't we just leave them here and tell them to count to two thousand?" Cat said. "And make them promise not to tell their parents about us?"

John nodded. "That'll save us the time of creating a false direction."

Pancho also nodded.

The sound of children came closer.

"That's assuming we can trust them," Alex whispered.

"I don't trust them," John said, "but I think it's our best option to buy some time without hurting the boys."

Pancho and Cat agreed.

"Okay," Alex said. "Let's do it."

Cat told the boys and they started counting.

The Outcasts stepped out of their stone house and peeked

around. The other children had gone off in the opposite direction. The Outcasts hurried to their white truck and loaded into it. When Alex turned the ignition, it didn't start.

Although the two boys remained quiet in the stone house, the other children called out to each other, nearing the Outcasts again. Although the bushes between the Outcasts and the children blocked their view, the children were coming closer to compromising the Outcasts' position.

"Truck's dead," John said. "Let's hoof it. We've already wasted enough time."

They unassed the truck and patrolled east, away from the ocean and heading into the mountains.

# 26

On their radio scanner, Commander Issa and Lieutenant Garza heard police communicating about children running into armed men hiding in a stone house. Commander Issa ordered their driver to turn around and head south in their three-vehicle motorcade, leading four trucks loaded with militia.

His caravan entered the village of Bjarine and followed a road leading away from the ocean. Even though the road ended, they continued driving along a small trail until a cluster of old stone houses appeared. When they reached the end of them, they stopped next to a local police car.

Commander Issa and Lieutenant Garza exited their sedan and walked past some bushes to find a policeman standing next to a small white pickup truck with leafy branches on the ground next to it.

"Were those branches covering the vehicle when you arrived?" Commander Issa asked the policeman.

"Who are you?" the policeman asked.

"Friends of Khaled Qurei."

"You're al Qaeda." The policeman frowned. He didn't seem to like al Qaeda.

"Khaled Qurei was murdered."

"This is a police matter. I'm waiting for backup officers and the senior investigator to arrive."

"While you're waiting, I don't suppose you noticed that clue."

"What clue?"

"That one."

"Where?"

Commander Issa pointed. "Under the truck."

As the policeman bent down to see the clue, Commander Issa drew his pistol and shot him in the back of the head. Commander Issa looked at four sets of footprints in the ground. The wind hadn't rounded off the edges of the prints yet. "These are fresh." Also, the strides were long. "They're running." Commander Issa followed the prints at a jog while Lieutenant Garza and the others followed.

# 27

Daylight faded. Cat pointed south. "Ibrahim River is less than ten kilometers south of here. We could use it to get back to the ocean, find a boat, and get out of here."

"Let's do it," Alex said. "Pancho, take us south."

Pancho looked at the compass on his watch then jogged south at point, followed by Alex, then Cat, with John bringing up the rear. Pancho's eyes covered everything in front of them, Alex watched right, Cat scanned left, and John handled rear security, periodically stopping to turn around and make sure no one snuck up behind them. Each member of the patrol had to pay attention to the person near them.

As Alex patrolled forward with his team, not only did he have to cover his area of responsibility to the right, but he also had to pay attention to Pancho in front of him. If Pancho gave a hand signal that he spotted the enemy, Alex would repeat the signal back to Cat so she could pass it behind to John. Likewise, Alex periodically looked back at Cat for hand signals, including those she relayed from John.

After five kilometers, they snaked around trees and boulders. Alex looked back at Cat as usual, but this time instead of nothing to report, she signaled that the bad guys were coming up on their left flank. She pointed to where roughly thirty men thrashed through the woods in the distance, heading toward the Outcasts. Alex stopped and dropped to a crouch and signaled for her to do the same. Alex pivoted around to the front. Pancho continued forward a little before turning. When Pancho saw Alex and the others stopping and crouching, as well as Alex's signal, Pancho did likewise.

Alex didn't have to think much about the situation. The enemy was tracking his team at a fast pace. It was only a matter of time before the booger eaters caught up with the Outcasts, possibly before they reached the river—if there was a river. With contact imminent, better to use surprise in the Outcasts' favor.

Alex signaled the team to organize a hasty ambush. The Outcasts lay down and prepared their weapons. In the bushes Alex concealed two olive drab claymore mines: the horizontally convex plastic cases, containing C-4 explosive and seven hundred steel balls in epoxy resin, sat on top of four legs. On the front of the mine was written FRONT TOWARD ENEMY. He placed the claymores far enough apart to spread their 60-degree arcs of death over a wide area. Alex used detonator wire to daisy-chain the two mines so he could fire them simultaneously. Then he connected another detonator wire between one mine and a plastic trigger (clacker) that he took to his ambush position. Alex laid the clacker on the ground in front of him.

Next to the clacker, he laid a fragmentation (frag) grenade and a thirty-round magazine of .223-caliber bullets for his HK416.

Pancho and John would wait for Alex to initiate the ambush before firing, unless they saw a dangerous situation that necessitated one of them initiating the ambush, such as a bad guy spotting one of them.

Alex whispered in Cat's ear, "Just wait for me or one of the guys to initiate the attack, then you join in shooting."

Cat nodded.

Alex painted Cat's skin—hands, neck, ears, and face— transforming her into something other than human. The shadows on her face became light, and her light became shadows. Alex used dark green on her forehead, brow, cheeks, nose, and chin. He colored her skin light green where her eyes sank in, below her nose, under her lower lip, and the places that weren't colored dark. Cat touched up Alex's face paint, too.

Alex had applied face paint to his buddies many times before and they had applied face paint to him, but when he did it with Cat, the mundane task became sexual. Because this wasn't the time or place for such feelings, he hid them in a box where he hid all of his feelings that didn't belong.

Then the Outcasts waited. Maybe the enemy would pass without seeing them. Maybe the enemy would turn around and head home before nightfall.

Unfortunately for the enemy, they did neither.

A tracker led his comrades toward Alex's position. Next to the tracker, a man wore a green baseball cap on backward. Baseball Cap noticed something in the bushes and hurried out ahead of the tracker. Soon his buddies and others joined him. They had spotted the claymore mine.

Alex focused on his HK416 sight instead of Baseball Cap. This way, the target's sixth sense wouldn't be alerted that someone was watching him. The target had neared the claymore, but Alex wanted to save the claymore for later. Alex had already squeezed his HK416 trigger partway, and he held his breath as he squeezed it some more. He knew about where the trigger would cause the weapon to fire, but he tried not to anticipate it. *Pop.* The shot hit the man in the chest. *Pop.* The second shot hit him again near the same bullet hole. Although both were separate controlled shots, they sounded like one pair. Baseball Cap dropped his AK-47, standing there in shock.

Pancho, John, and Cat joined in shooting before the enemy could respond. The Outcasts' sound suppressors masked their location from the militia. Four enemy fell. The surviving militia answered the Outcasts by shooting chaotically. The Outcasts took five more of the enemy out of the fight. Shots popped the bushes, trees, and air around Alex. The Outcasts fired back, taking out more militia. But now the enemy was pinpointing the Outcasts' position. Alex had fired all thirty of the rounds in his HK416 magazine. Rather than reload, he laid his weapon on the ground and grabbed a grenade. Alex pulled the pin and let the spoon fly. He had five seconds before the grenade exploded. Alex cooked off two seconds before throwing it. "Frag out!" He hugged the ground. Pancho, John, and Cat hugged the ground, too.

*Boom.* The grenade blasted everything on the enemy side for a radius of fifty feet; its steel fragments struck farther. A scream pierced the air.

Alex ejected the empty magazine from his HK416 and loaded a new one.

Although the group of thirty militiamen had been nearly cut in half, they grouped together and charged the Outcasts' position, firing and screaming.

"Grenade!" shouted Pancho. He picked up the enemy's thrown grenade and threw it back. *Boom!*

Alex squeezed the clacker, detonating the claymores. *BOOM!* Fourteen hundred steel balls shredded bushes, trees, and militiamen. The Outcasts shot at anyone still bold enough or dumb enough to remain upright.

One of the militiamen shouted what sounded like a command, then he repeated it. Five militiamen rose to their feet, turned their backs, and ran. The Outcasts fired, taking out two of them before the other three disappeared.

Alex didn't wait for the enemy to bring back reinforcements. "Pancho, take us south."

Pancho headed south, followed by Alex, Cat, then John. After they separated from the ambush area, Alex signaled for them to stop and form a defensive perimeter. They formed a box, with the four of them facing outward. "How are we doing?" Alex asked.

Each gave their name and status. "Pancho okay, three magazines."

"Alex okay, four magazines."

"Cat okay, three magazines."

"John okay, two magazines."

Alex was relieved to hear that no one was injured. He tossed John one of his thirty-round magazines of .223 ammo. "Pancho, take us out," Alex said.

The Outcasts resumed their patrol south for a few minutes when John said, "We got company."

Alex looked back and saw a mob of reinforcements coming. "Let's pick up the pace."

Pancho sped up.

"Faster," Alex said.

Then the militia behind them began to light up the woods. Bullets cracked the air around the Outcasts.

"John, drop smoke!" Alex yelled without looking back.

"Already dropped!" John called.

Alex looked back to see the smoke beginning to cloud the area between them and the militia. The Outcasts ran faster and faster. Tree branches snapped above before falling. The Outcasts ran faster still. "Where's that damn river, Cat?!" Alex demanded. He looked back to see that the smoke grenade had saturated the air behind them, but it wouldn't be long before the militia broke through.

Before Cat answered Alex's question, they reached a river flowing west to the sea. Pancho slid on the riverbank and fell into the water. Cat jumped in. Alex followed, dropping below the river's surface and swallowing a mouthful of water as it swept him away.

Alex had always thought drowning would be one of the worst ways to die—fighting the water while it suffocated him to a torturous death. Memories from BUD/S flashed in his mind. The pool stretched impossibly long in front of him. The pain that small body of water could inflict was legendary. He knew the drill, somersault into the pool like a rock. No diving like they did in a swim meet.

Twenty-five meters one way, touch the wall, then twenty-five meters back. All underwater. Going up for air even once, even for a millisecond, was a total fail. Guys who stayed near the surface were doomed. It was better to swim deep, letting the increased pressure help a guy hold his breath a little longer.

"Go for the blackout" was the chant. It sounded macabre, but they weren't training to become pastry chefs. Everything they did was meant to push to the very limit because one day, they would likely have to do that and more when the instructors were long gone and it was just a SEAL Team alone in a foreign land surrounded by the enemy.

Alex remembered that swim. It was seared into his mind. His lungs burned with the need for oxygen, but all he focused on was the chant—*go for the blackout*. His vision began to gray around the edges and his limbs barely responded. Each arm and leg felt like five hundred pounds of lead. Gray turned to black and he knew it was about to end.

With one last thrust that he wasn't sure translated from his brain to his arm, he reached out with his hand and groped for the wall. His fingertips brushed the side of the pool and he knew he'd made it. Before he could slip completely into unconsciousness, an instructor pulled him out. He gulped down air as his entire body shook.

He'd done it. He passed. Some didn't.

And now Alex was actually drowning in a Lebanese river with no instructor to pull him out—lungs burning for air, throat convulsing. His gray vision became a black tunnel. The light at the end of the tunnel shrank to the size of a pinhole. He felt calm. *So this is how it ends.* Then he realized he hadn't inflated his life vest. His hand moved in slow motion to the cord on his vest and pulled it. The vest inflated and floated him to the surface. He sucked a shot of oxygen straight to the lungs. His head felt light and his body tingled. Alex took another bite of air. As his head bobbed on the surface, taking in oxygen, he gradually returned to normal.

Now that Alex wasn't fighting for his life he realized, *Shit, this river is cold.* The river knocked him downstream, bouncing him off a mud bank. A low-hanging branch whacked him on top of the head, and he drank a gulp from the river.

After some more mouthfuls of water, bruises, and cuts, the river spit Alex and his team out into the ocean. They crawled onto the beach then walked south until they found an old station wagon with the door unlocked. John used the butt of his HK416 to break off the ignition lock before he hotwired it. The Outcasts loaded up in the station wagon and Alex drove south until they hit the first marina. There they commandeered a small yacht and sailed to Cyprus, where they refueled in a civilian port, then continued on to the U.S. Naval Support Activity Souda Bay in Crete. Next, the Outcasts boarded a navy flight to Sigonella, Italy, where they booked their next flight before cleaning up at a hotel.

"Where should we eat?" Alex asked the others.

"Anywhere," Cat said.

"Italian," Pancho said.

"Anywhere but Italian," John said.

"We could eat some fast food on base," Alex offered.

"I hate fast food," John complained.

"What about Popeyes?" Alex asked.

"Yes," Pancho said.

John smiled. It was fast food, but it was Cajun fast food.

Alex took them to Popeyes on base, where they ate combination meals of Cajun fried chicken, Cajun fries, soda, and biscuits. Pancho ate two meals.

After eating, the Outcasts boarded another navy plane, which flew them to the States. On the transatlantic flight, there were few passengers. Pancho sat in the aisle closest to the stewardesses forward of the plane. John sat next to a window, away from Pancho—on a plane, usually the window was the safest place to be during a hijacking. Alex and Cat sat by themselves farther aft, on the starboard side.

"We almost didn't get out of that last one," Cat said.

"Things got a little hairy."

"A little?" Cat shook her head. "There were a couple times I thought we were finished."

Alex thought so, too, but he couldn't say it. Maybe he was too proud or maybe he thought he'd jinx himself if he verbalized it.

"You seemed so calm," she said.

"I was scared."

"You didn't look scared."

"Everyone gets scared unless they're stupid. What's important is knowing how to deal with being scared. That's where our training comes in. The thing that people get wrong about combat is that you don't so much rise to the occasion as you fall to the level of your training. And you know the SEAL motto, the only easy day was yesterday."

Cat tried to smile, but Alex could tell she wasn't entirely convinced. "Do you ever think that next time you might not survive?"

"Try not to. The missions don't get easier. Next time will be harder. They'll be expecting us—more than they expected us before."

"How do you know when a mission is too dangerous?"

Alex shrugged. "The missions are always too dangerous. That's why they call us. You seem concerned."

"I'm worried," she said.

"You'll be okay."

"About you."

That gave Alex pause. He was used to command worrying about the success of the mission, not someone worrying about him personally. "No need to worry about me."

"I feel so alive when I'm with you. Don't know what I'd do if something happened."

"Nothing is going to happen to me."

"How can you be sure?"

"Because I have to," he said, wishing she'd let it go.

"You have to."

"Yes, I have to," Alex said. She looked like something was still troubling her. "What?"

"Nothing."

"Nothing what?"

"Just nothing," she said.

Alex debated leaving things at that, but decided he had to know. "You're thinking about something."

"Let's just forget about it."

"Something's wrong. How can I forget about it?"

Cat took a deep breath before continuing. "Would it be so bad? To try something else? You have more talents than you know."

"It isn't so easy," he said.

"It could be easy."

They both became silent. She was right—becoming a frogman was voluntary. It was his choice to endure the constant training: hypothermia, heat exhaustion, sweat, sore muscles, bruises, blood, and broken bones. He could've refused any mission he'd undertaken, but he didn't. He survived when friends died, not because they were less able than him, just less lucky. Guilt and stress added to the challenges. Alex knew more than one guy who tried to drown his troubles in alcohol. Long-term relations were difficult to maintain. Divorces were common. It could be a lonely business. The Team consumed Alex's body and mind—even his soul. He knew frogs who stayed in the game until they were too broken or too old. Like Matthew, who'd been a star operator in his earlier years, but later in life struggled to keep up. He began to blame anything and anyone around him to explain his shortcomings, until no Team guys wanted to work with him. Lacking enough talent for currency to buy into new missions, Matthew sold his integrity to manipulate the system in his favor, taking on assignments he wasn't qualified for and putting the success and safety of others at risk. It was tragic. Would

Alex become like that—too old? Or too dead? Or would he get out before then? Cat was right, *there must be other things in life*.

"Maybe there are other things in life," Alex said. "But I'm not doing this just for me."

"That was a long time ago. I think you've done more than enough since then. I'm sure Sarah would want you to move on with your life."

"I can't."

"You can, but you're too much like Pancho and John. As for me, I can leave this anytime I want."

Alex turned away from her and closed his eyes. He felt tired in his mind and in his bones. Gradually, he fell asleep.


HE WOKE UP. A blanket covered him. Cat must've done it. He looked over at her, sleeping. Maybe this time it wouldn't have to end. She was kind—and beautiful. That first kiss in Switzerland never seemed to end—he didn't want it to end—even after their lips parted, he was still kissing her in his mind. He'd known a number of women, but Cat affected him like no other. Outside their window, high above cumulus clouds, the starboard wing glistened in the sunlight. Cat rested peacefully. Her skin radiated. She was the type of girl he could imagine marrying.

The cabin lights switched off. Alex stared into the darkness for a moment. Then he closed his eyes again and slept.

He awoke just before their plane touched down at Norfolk, Virginia, and a gray navy van took them home to Dam Neck. When they arrived, Alex began thinking about leaving the Outcasts, the Teams, and the navy—and taking Cat with him.

# 28

I n Nuevo Laredo, Mexico, near the U.S. border, Damien entered a broken-down old hotel. He knocked on the door of the room at the end of the hall. Soon the door opened and he walked in. An elderly man, middle-aged man, pregnant woman, and her teenage son and daughter waited as a man wearing a black cowboy hat greeted Damien.

The man in the black cowboy hat was a coyote—one who helped people illegally cross from Mexico to the United States. He seemed to have an eye for the teenage girl in the group. "Let's go," he said.

They headed outside and loaded into a dust-covered truck that took them off-road to an area near the border fence. The truck stopped, they stepped out, and Coyote directed them to take two ladders out of the truck. The driver and the others propped one ladder against the wall, and Coyote climbed up. "Hand me the other ladder," he said. They did. Coyote lowered it onto the other side and crossed into Texas. The others followed. Finally the driver, at the top of the fence, pulled the ladder from the U.S. side and lowered it onto Mexican soil. He disappeared behind the wall on the Mexican side.

Damien didn't hike in front of the group or lag behind—he stayed quiet in the middle—watching. The group continued their evening trek across the desert.

The old man was the first to wear down, complaining of a sore leg. Coyote gave him an "aspirin" to help with the pain, but it was probably an amphetamine to speed him up. He did speed up for a mile or so, but then he lagged again.

Damien looked over his shoulder. The old man was almost out of sight.

"I'm worried about the old man," Damien said.

"Don't waste your time with him," Coyote said.

"I'll catch up," Damien said. He jogged back to the old man and found him lying on the ground clutching his chest. From the old man's position, Damien could barely see the group. "Let me help you," Damien said. From behind, he lifted the old man's head up and wrapped his left arm around the front, with the old man's trachea in the crook of his elbow, and grabbed his own right bicep. His right hand touched the back of the old man's head. Damien squeezed his left bicep and radius bone on the old man's carotid arteries, cutting off the blood circulation to his brain. After three seconds, the old man's body became limp. Damien continued strangling him for almost three minutes as he watched the group get farther and farther away. Now there would be no chance that he'd give Damien's identity to any law enforcement authorities who might find him. Damien dropped the old man in the sand and jogged away.

Coyote looked surprised when Damien caught up with them.

"I couldn't help him," Damien said.

"Told you," Coyote said.

As they walked, Coyote kept looking at the teenage girl. After an hour, Coyote stopped in front of her and said, "Come with me."

The mother protested, but Coyote grabbed the girl by the hand and pulled her away from the group. Damien and the middle-aged man just stood watching. The teenage boy confronted Coyote, but Coyote punched him in the face, dropping him in the dirt. The mother screamed.

"Shuttup!" Coyote yelled at the mother.

Still wobbly on his feet, the boy stood and charged forward.

"No!" the mother screamed.

Coyote stepped to the side, and the boy tumbled past him and landed on his stomach in the dirt. Coyote pulled out a .357 pistol and shot the boy in the back before he could stand. The kid lay still in the dirt. His mother, hysterical, hurried to the kid and tried to revive him. Damien wondered what prevented Coyote from killing all of them. Maybe if Coyote delivered them to someone for slave labor, he received a payment for each illegal immigrant.

"Let's go," Coyote said.

Damien slipped in behind him, drew his OTs-38 Stechkin revolver, and popped Coyote once in the back of the head. Coyote dropped to the earth like a bag of rocks. The others looked at Damien with surprise. Then their faces brightened at their savior. Damien holstered his pistol, picked up Coyote's .357, and searched his body. He took a wallet full of cash, pistol holster, and a pocketful of bullets. None of the survivors posed a serious threat, but the teenage girl seemed the most likely to succeed in running away, so Damien shot her with the .357. The pregnant woman wasn't going anywhere fast, but she would be more likely to resist. *Bang!* The sole survivor was the middle-aged man.

"You didn't budge to defend anyone or run," Damien said. "You're not much of a man. Even an animal would at least try to flee. You've probably lived your whole life the same way, just sitting there like a potted plant." Damien slowly aimed the .357 above the bridge of his nose. Damien wasn't surprised when the potted plant closed his eyes. He was so predictable that he made Damien laugh just before he shot him.

# 29

In Alex's hand, he held the black USB stick he'd recovered from the Banker. He walked across the Team Six compound in Dam Neck, Virginia. Alex entered the Intel Shed, passed a clerk, and strolled into Miss Pettigrew's office. The intelligence lieutenant with short brown hair looked up from the paperwork on her desk. "Alex!" she exclaimed.

He smiled. "Miss Pettigrew."

"Did you bring me something from Lebanon?" She ran out of breath as she spoke.

"Yes, I brought you this." He handed her the black USB stick.

Miss Pettigrew frowned without accepting the stick. "I was hoping for something with a fragrance. Or sweet tasting."

"You know how fraternization between female officers and enlisted men is against navy rules and regulations."

"Yes, you're always so careful to obey rules and regulations."

"Would you mind taking a look at the stick?"

She seemed to hold back a smile. "Is your computer down?"

"This is security-encrypted."

"How soon do you need it?"

"Now would be great."

"Always in such a rush. I'm really busy now . . ."

Alex looked discouraged.

"But I'll make time for you," she said sweetly.

He grinned. "You're a sweetheart."

"Flattery will get you nowhere, but do continue." She inserted the stick in a USB port on her PC. Then Miss Pettigrew clicked her mouse several times. After a moment, she said, "My Arabic isn't perfect, but there are documents about bomb-making and a U.S. building."

"Does it give any more details, like which building or when?"

"I'll need more time."

"We don't have more time."

"I'll have our translator look at it."

"Could you update the skipper?"

"Will do."

"You're awesome."

Miss Pettigrew sighed. "If you only knew . . ."


THAT EVENING IN THE Ready Room restaurant in Virginia Beach, Alex ate a small pizza with everything on it. He thought: *What could I do outside of the navy?* He had little interest in wearing a suit and managing a business. As he contemplated his future, he noticed an army staff sergeant at the bar drinking a beer. On the soldier's shoulder was a Special Forces tab—he was a Green Beret—kind of gutsy wearing his uniform so openly in SEAL territory. Maybe he was looking for a fight.

A navy guy in camouflage fatigues with a black trident above his breast pocket—a SEAL—sat down at the bar and ordered a drink. The trident consisted of an eagle clutching a U.S. Navy anchor, trident, and flintlock pistol.

The Green Beret faced the SEAL. "You're a SEAL?" the Green Beret asked in a northeastern accent.

"Can I help you?" the SEAL said.

"You guys did a great job getting UBL." UBL was the government designation for Usama bin Laden.

"Wasn't me but thanks."

The Green Beret called to the waiter, "His drink is on me."

"That's okay," the SEAL politely refused.

"Lost a lot of good friends hunting that piece of shit. I don't know which of your brothers did the assault, but I have to thank someone. Please." His eyes watered.

The SEAL nodded.

Alex began to have difficulty swallowing his pizza. He didn't know exactly why, but he had a vague idea. "Waitress."

The waitress came over. "Yes?"

"Can I have the check and a doggy bag?"

"Sure. I'll be right back."

After she brought the check and a box, Alex boxed his pizza, paid the cashier, and left.

Driving his SUV through the night, he didn't know why, but he wanted to cry. Pedestrians, cars, and lights seemed in a distant background. His body became numb.

He arrived at his house in less than thirty minutes. The house was a gift from his mother. With four bedrooms, it was more than he needed, but it was the smallest he could find that looked nice inside and out with a fireplace and pool—in a good neighborhood. More importantly, it was close to the SEAL Team Six compound. While on standby, when his beeper went off, Alex had only one hour to get his ass to base ready to go. His mother wanted to give him a nicer place, but Alex talked her out of it.

Inside, Alex passed through the living room in the dark and flicked on the light in the kitchen. He put the pizza in the refrigerator. Returning to the living room, the telephone answering machine light flashed, but he ignored it. He trudged over to the stereo to find

**194**   Howard E. Wasdin & Stephen Templin

something to listen to. Tired of the same CDs, he reached for an older one. He found a disc he'd burned without labeling. Alex stuck it in and pressed *play*. Then he sat down on the couch.

Classical music played: Grieg. He remembered. When the stereo came to the track "The Death of Ase," his body became heavy. After the song finished, he played it again and pressed *repeat* on his remote control. Over and over he listened until he was exhausted. Eventually he lay down and closed his eyes.

Alex remembered his junior year at Harvard. He had returned home for the summer. During a Saturday evening dinner at home, it was just him and his parents. "Michelle's father mentioned something strange to me," Alex's father said. "He told me that Michelle is breaking up with you because you're going to join the navy."

"Yes," Alex said.

"She's a beautiful girl—smart. Her family is well respected. Why?"

"To fight terrorists."

"For what?"

He felt puzzled that his father had to ask for what. "For Sarah."

"Sarah?"

"I've thought about it a lot. It's what I want to do."

"I thought you wanted to work with me."

"I apologize."

"Apologize?"

"I'm sorry."

"Why? Sarah's killer is dead. You can't fight him."

"But I can prevent what happened to her from happening to others."

"You're breaking my heart, Alex."

"I'm sorry."

"Please reconsider."

"I did. Many times."

His father looked at the ceiling. "That day, when my secretary told me there'd been an explosion at the post office, I was afraid it was you. I didn't know what I'd do if I lost you. When I heard it was Sarah . . . I was just . . . relieved you were okay."

Alex stared at him in disbelief.

"Think about what you're doing," his father said. "I don't want to lose you."

"Screw you." Alex hadn't really said those words because those words were his grandfather's, and Alex wasn't his grandfather. But now Alex had become more like his grandfather than his father—even in his dreams.

In the morning, at the Team Six compound, Alex and Cat greeted each other.

"I'm sorry, Alex," Cat said. "I shouldn't have . . ."

"Don't know if I changed to be where I am, or if not changing is why I am where I am," Alex said. "But I can't change now."

"I know," she said.

"The insertion on the next hit will be a little tricky."

"I can do tricky."

"You've done a great job . . ."

She seemed to be reading his mind. "But not this time."

"I wanted you to hear it from me first."

"It's okay," she said, but her eyes said it wasn't okay.

Alex looked down. "I've got to go get ready."

She stood stoically, but he couldn't look at her eyes because he didn't want to see what she was feeling. Alex was on a mission, and he didn't need feelings that might compromise it. He put those feelings in a box and walked away.

# 30

**D**amien, sporting a backpack and wearing his dusty and sweat-stained clothes, strolled into a Greyhound bus station in Laredo, Texas. He purchased a Discovery Pass, allowing him to travel anywhere in the United States without informing anyone of his final destination. After purchasing the ticket, he went into the restroom, washed up, and shaved in the sink.

Damien caught his bus and rode it for thirty-one-and-a-half hours, stopping every three to four hours for breaks to stretch or eat. Damien transferred buses at San Antonio, Houston, Atlanta, and Fayetteville, North Carolina, before arriving in Charlotte in the afternoon.

Damien stepped out of the bus station and looked for a taxi, but there were none. He walked around the block when he noticed three disreputable-looking men standing twenty yards away. When they saw Damien they began walking toward him. Damien glanced around for others, but, except for a car that passed, they were the only ones in the immediate area. Damien continued walking. The thugs followed him, quickening their pace.

Damien stopped walking and turned around. As the men neared him, he asked, "Can I help you?"

"Can you help us?" the one with big ears said. "Yeah, you can help us." He pulled out a knife. "Empty your pockets."

Damien raised his hands in surrender.

They moved closer: Big Ears faced Damien while the other two flanked Damien on each side. "Empty your pockets, bitch!" Big Ears ordered.

Damien held out his left hand, gesturing for the men to wait. Smoothly his right hand drew his Stechkin revolver from its KYDEX holster clipped inside the waistband of his trousers and fired a sound-suppressed round into Big Ears' chest. Damien put another hole in the chest of the man next to him, then took a fraction of a second longer to shoot the third man in the face. Damien returned his aim to the second guy and gave him a coup de grâce to the head. When Damien aimed again at the first guy, Big Ears, Big Ears wheezed, "No hard feelings, man. "

Damien smiled and shot him in the face. Then he reloaded his revolver while nonchalantly walking away from the three men lying dead on the sidewalk.

Damien found a taxi, flagged it down, and took a seat inside. "Take me to the Frito-Lay distributor," he told the driver. When the taxi neared within a block of Frito-Lay, Damien told him, "Stop here."

"We're not at the distributor yet," the driver said.

"Just stop here."

After the taxi driver dropped him off, Damien walked toward Frito-Lay. People wouldn't be walking around carrying backpacks there, and he had to blend in, so halfway to Frito-Lay, he looked around to make sure no one was watching and stashed his backpack in some bushes next to a light pole.

With no security at the Frito-Lay entrance, Damien walked onto the property and to the loading dock, where employees loaded and unloaded trucks. Damien studied the area and saw boxes of Lays chips stacked near a wall. He picked up a couple of boxes, concealing his upper body, and walked into the back of the warehouse. He continued forward, his head facing straight ahead while his eyes searched the perimeter. Damien spotted a restroom/changing room with a large metal bin in front to deposit uniforms for dry cleaning. He stopped in front of the bin, put down his boxes, and pulled out two pairs of overalls. Then Damien went inside the restroom/changing room. The first uniform was too small, and the second too big. He put on the big one and rolled under the sleeves and trouser legs, shortening them.

Damien headed out of the restroom/changing room and dumped the small uniform in the cleaning bin. After picking up the boxes of Lays chips, he exited the warehouse and headed toward the aluminum walk-in trucks painted white with red banners with *Lays* written on them. Damien chose a vehicle near the end but not on the end. He wanted to be out of everyone's general sight but not so out of sight that he drew suspicion. From the truck next to his, a driver stepped out.

Damien could try to avoid eye contact and risk attention or greet him and hope he didn't blow his cover. "Hi," Damien greeted the truck driver.

"Hi," the driver said.

Damien, fumbling in his pocket, proceeded to the driver's side of his truck.

"Hey," the driver said.

"Yes?" Damien asked.

"You must be new here. I'm Freddy. I'm new here, too."

Damien looked down at his name patch. "Bob."

"Welcome. We've got another Bob here, too. You're a little shorter than him."

"Small world."

"Yep."

"Nice meeting you."

"You too." The driver headed into the warehouse.

Damien checked the truck door—locked. He pulled a pick and tension tool out of his pocket and used them on the door. Then Damien jiggled the pick in the lock until he depressed the tumblers, adding tension with the tension tool until he could turn the lock. It opened.

Inside the truck, Damien pulled out a hammer and a flathead screwdriver. He pounded the flathead screwdriver into the ignition key slot, then turned it, starting the vehicle.

Although his heart raced with anxiety, his face remained calm as he drove off the Frito-Lay property. Damien stopped for a moment to retrieve his backpack.

Then he drove northeast through Virginia, Maryland, Delaware, Pennsylvania, New Jersey, and New York until he reached a safe house in the woods of the Adirondack region of New York. He parked the Frito-Lay truck in the driveway.

Inside the safe house, some men greeted him. Among them was Damien's son, Mohammed.

"Who is in charge of this cell?" Damien asked.

"I am," the one with a gold tooth quickly answered.

Damien shot him in the forehead. The cell leader slumped to the floor, blood leaking from the hole in his skull. "Who is in charge here?" Damien repeated the question.

The others hesitated, glancing at the pistol in Damien's hand.

"Who is in charge here?" Damien repeated.

"You are," Mohammed said.

"Does everyone agree?" Damien said.

They nodded.

"Good. We'll get along just fine," Damien predicted.

# 31

Naval Station Norfolk, in Norfolk, Virginia, was the world's largest naval station, controlling the movement of more than 3,100 ships. The USS *Humpback* (SSBN-650), a ballistic missile submarine, remained docked at pier 24. At 0600, Alex strolled up the gangplank wearing his khaki chief's uniform. Instead of his gold SEAL trident insignia (nicknamed *Budweiser* for its similarity to the old Budweiser beer symbol), he wore a submariner's insignia. His eyes studied the petty officer of the watch (POOW), who looked to be in his early twenties, then glanced at the Colt .45 pistol on his belt. "Do you know how to shoot that thing?"

"Yes, Chief."

"Make sure you shoot every terrorist that comes across this quarterdeck, but don't shoot me."

"Yes, Chief."

The messenger of the watch (MOW), who appeared younger than the POOW, smiled.

"Where in the hell did you learn to iron that uniform?" Alex growled.

"Well—I—I'm . . ."

"Probably the same place you learned to talk. Don't be screwing up my navy, hear?"

"Yes, sir."

"And don't call me sir. I work for a living."

After his grand entrance, Alex disappeared below deck. He knew that John would arrive next wearing his navy working uniform and carrying his olive drab seabag, blending in with a group of submarine crew members. Following him, Pancho would amble across the gangplank wearing shit-kickers, blue jeans, rodeo belt buckle, and cowboy hat with a plug of Red Man tobacco in his cheek. Four other SEALs would clandestinely arrive with them.

At 0930, some of the *Humpback*'s submariners brought "food" boxes below to the SEAL quarters. Alex, Pancho, and John opened the boxes and removed their weapons, ammo, explosives, satellite communications, and other gear. Their grenade pins were taped with black tape to prevent anything from snagging one and pulling the pin. After stowing the gear, Alex heard over a speaker the announcement that the submarine had left the pier and was under way.

Alex went topside to watch from the bridge. The submarine passed between buoys that guided them through the Norfolk Harbor Reach. As they passed under the Chesapeake Bay Bridge-Tunnel, sunshine shimmered off the tips of the ocean's waves. Alex loved the scent of salt in the air. When he was on land, he wanted to be at sea, and when he was at sea, he wanted to be on land. They were both his home, yet there were times when neither felt like his home. The gentle rocking of the waves soothed his mind, and he thought of Cat.

"Lookouts, clear the bridge," the captain said.

Alex and the other sailors cleared the bridge and went below. At noon, Alex, Pancho, and John ate lunch with the crew. After dinner, some of the crew remained and played Texas Hold'em with poker chips instead of money. The three SEALs joined them.

Pancho cleaned everyone out.

"I thought you sucked at poker," Alex said.

"You thought wrong. Mama raised all six of us boys by herself, but she couldn't make enough money to feed us. After school, my older brother had to work to help out. He offered to quit school and work full-time, but Mama wouldn't let him. I took the money my brother made and tripled it by playing Texas Hold'em."

"Pancho wins more than he loses," John said. "His problem is that after he wins, he thinks he's rich, so he spends it all."

"Navy feeds me and gives me a place to sleep without holes in the roof," Pancho said. "What else do I need money for?"

"Rig for ultraquiet," a voice came over the loudspeaker. Maybe a submarine was trying to follow them.


Grandpa always told Alex and Sarah, "Believe." Alex thought about how Grandpa's advice helped him play water polo in high school. Alex was the goalkeeper and played with six other first-string members. Water polo required a lot of stamina: treading water, short-and-quick front crawl, modified backstroke, throwing the ball, and shooting it. At seven minutes per period for four periods, twenty-eight minutes total (which didn't include the clock being stopped for fouls and time before scoring and restarting) seemed like a long time. It wasn't unusual to swim two kilometers during a game. Players held and pushed opponents, and water polo resembled something like a combination of wrestling and handball played in a pool. Because of the aggressiveness of the sport, fouls were common: elbowing, kicking, punching, or even drowning others. Guys tried to rip off swim trunks, so Alex wore tight-fitting ones with extra stitching. Heads, shoulders, and fingers often got injured—especially goalies'. Alex got a bloody nose from a fast ball more than once. Sun burned the skin if not protected with sunscreen and no goggles were allowed, so chlorine was a constant irritation to the eyes.

As the goalie, Alex had the most challenging job. Players would pump-fake, bounce the ball off the water, sidearm a heavy backspin, or shoot it in a vertical arc. He often had to quickly jump high and tread water while holding his position to block shots. Anticipation and tracking the ball's movement were key, as was quick movement. He also led the team by calling offensive plays. After graduating from high school, Alex played water polo on the team at Harvard.

Of all the men who showed up at Basic Underwater Demolition/ SEAL (BUD/S) training, water polo athletes succeeded more than anyone else. For water polo athletes who played chess, their success tripled.

When Alex tested for BUD/S, he and forty-nine others passed, out of five thousand total. Of those fifty men, twenty-five dropped out, mostly during Hell Week—the week when Alex's understanding of "believing" grew exponentially.

Hell Week began on Sunday night, nicknamed "Breakout." For the next five and a half days Alex and his classmates trained with only four to six total hours of sleep. Reality overlapped dreams and dreams overlapped reality until the distinction between them blurred. Hallucinations became common.

Alex experienced his first hallucination one evening in the middle of Hell Week during an evolution called "Around-the-World." His class launched from the Naval Special Warfare Center in San Diego. As Alex's boat crew paddled north, they passed a boat crew. They rowed past the Hotel del Coronado, whose lights shone on the rocks they'd cracked with their bodies earlier.

In the dark sea, Alex saw someone walking across the water. He nearly jumped out of the boat, but Sanchez, the Ecuadoran Special Operations exchange student, and the others in his crew didn't seem concerned. "Did you see that?" he asked, pointing to the silhouette.

Then Alex saw that there were three women. The black musical trio shook their act on the water.

"See what?" Sanchez asked.

"Never mind." Alex realized he was hallucinating, but he enjoyed the dance while it lasted.

His boat crew passed another boat. They looked like half of them were asleep. Minutes later someone said, "Stop. We've got to stop for the stoplight." Then he realized there couldn't possibly be a traffic light in the middle of the ocean. Even if there was, why would they stop for it? He laughed.

The night ocean lay quiet and peaceful. In the boat, Alex and his crew stayed dry and no instructors harassed them. They sailed through the magical waters between consciousness and sleep. *Bloop.* Sanchez suddenly disappeared. He had fallen asleep and toppled into the ocean. The cold splash quickly woke him.

"Man overboard," Alex said. The boat crew's response was slow, but they maneuvered the boat to Sanchez and helped him back aboard.

As they paddled near the northern part of Coronado, Alex fell in and out of a light sleep. Suddenly Danny sat straight up and screamed. Everyone sat upright and looked at Danny for a moment before they busted out laughing. Danny laughed, too. No one asked him what he saw—talking was a burden.

They paddled south in San Diego Bay along the eastern coast of Coronado. Alex saw his next hallucination: a navy destroyer lit up like Christmas. The ship stretched more than five hundred feet in length and displaced over eight thousand tons. It made Alex feel smaller than an ant on a buffalo turd. The destroyer's foghorn let out a deep, long belch that almost knocked Alex and his crew off their floating turd. It was not a hallucination! The destroyer had just started moving in their direction as they attempted to pass in front of it. They snapped to hyperawake and paddled for their lives. The monstrous ship sailed for the boat crew's starboard side. They paddled faster and faster until they cleared its path. Even then, they continued to paddle fast.

Physical challenges persisted throughout the torturous week, day and night: doing calisthenics until their limbs felt like useless rubber; swimming; running; running the obstacle course; running with rubber boats on their heads; paddling the boats; other events—

over and over again. Alex hated running on land with his boat crew carrying the Inflatable Boat, Small (IBS) on their heads. His legs felt the ground pounding upward and the boat pounding downward—both ends seemed to intersect in his knees.

If someone wanted to quit, all he had to do was ring the bell that the instructors carried around with them and it was over. Many of Alex's classmates did.

Wednesday night, SEAL instructor Robert Evans, who was one of the tougher instructors, gathered Alex's class near a bonfire on the beach. "I'm proud of you guys," he began. "You made it to Wednesday night of Hell Week. You'll make it all the way." He joked and told SEAL stories. "I was doing a parachute jump when I got tangled up and landed headfirst, breaking my neck. The doctor put me in a halo brace. Attached it to my skull with screws, and the halo was connected to a plastic vest . . ."

Sanchez and Alex stayed close to the fire but far from the SEAL instructor. They sat so close to the fire that their wet clothing smoldered. All the time, Alex repeated to himself: *I want to get in the ocean. The ocean is so warm and peaceful. I want to get in the ocean, I want to get in the ocean* . . . Alex noticed Petty Officer Park, the Army Ranger combat vet, standing away from the fire, shivering. Park had been halfway through Hell Week before when he got pulled for stage 3 hypothermia. Now, even though his approach was different, he was expecting the same thing that Alex and Sanchez expected. Alex knew the body experiences less shock going from cold to very cold; however, it takes longer for the body temperature to drop from steaming hot to very cold.

One of Alex's classmates said to Sanchez and Alex, "You guys are catching on fire."

Sanchez and Alex remained in place—smoldering. "Thanks," Alex replied. When his front got too hot, he turned around to heat up his back. He popped open the packet of peanut butter he saved from lunch and kept telling himself how much he wanted to get in the water.

The joking and stories continued until Instructor Benelli joined the party, relieving the other instructor. Alex and his classmates liked the Italian Stallion. On weekends, with his leather jacket, thick black mustache, and Harley-Davidson motorcycle, he looked like a Hells Angel. Benelli's laughter was infectious.

*"Hooya, Instructor Benelli!"* the class cheered.

"What are you people doing?!" he screamed. "This is Hell Week! Get in the water! *Now!*"

The class was shocked to see this other side of Benelli, but Alex convinced himself he was happy to be heading back into the surf. It was just what he'd been hoping for. As he rolled around in his Pacific hot tub, he tried to remember every girl he'd ever kissed— the innocent first-grade kiss of Christina on the playground, the not-so-innocent high school kiss in the backseat of a car on Friday night, and the others . . . While he sat in his hot tub reminiscing of good times, he shut out everything around him. A blur of guys rang the bell—if Alex focused on them, it might've broken his heart. He might've realized how cold he was. He might've started feeling sorry for himself. It was demoralizing to realize some of his toughest brothers were gone. The good-cop, bad-cop routine had taken a sizable chunk out of the class. And those who stuck it out were freezing their petunias off.

After the bell-ringing died, Alex, Sanchez, Park, and their classmates came out of the water. The survivors stood together shivering on the beach—except for Park. He stood away from everyone, not shivering, staring off into the sand berm. He'd "hyped out," stage 3 hypothermia. Although sleep deprivation and the constant physical challenges were tough, the cold was tougher. The instructors kept them wet constantly, which meant being cold constantly—especially at night—and experiencing hypothermia throughout the week.

Most people have experienced stage 1 hypothermia, when the body shivers. At stage 2, the body shakes violently and the mind begins to numb. Alex and his classmates experienced stage 2 often, bumbling around like idiots. The instructors measured the windspeed, air temperature, and ocean temperature to see how long they could keep Alex and his classmates at stage 2 without escalating to stage 3. The instructors didn't want the students to reach stage 3, when the shivering stops and the brain becomes irrational. There is no stage 4, only death.

"Get back in formation!" Instructor Benelli called.

Instead of getting in formation, Park staggered back toward the ocean. Instructor Benelli speedily cut him off before Park reached the water. Benelli led Park to the green ambulance. Alex and some others started to follow Park to help him, but Benelli barked, "Stay in formation!"

The ambulance sped away with Petty Officer Park, taking him to Medical. The vehicle's lights flashed and its siren wailed. Fortunately, Park would survive.

Thursday morning, the SEAL instructors' concerns of weeding out the weak shifted to preserving the Hell Week survivors—Alex and his classmates were the ones who had to be killed before they would give up.

Friday afternoon, Alex's class stood at attention, like a platoon of the walking dead, facing the Naval Special Warfare Center. The commanding officer gave a short speech: "This week, you made the impossible possible. You did something few people can. In the future, if you ever start to feel sorry for yourself—stop. Remember this great achievement, and know that you can achieve more. Congratulations, men. I'm securing Hell Week."

"*Hooyah!*" the class cheered. Some guys hugged each other, some cried, and others cheered. Those like Alex stood there in a stupid daze. *If Hell Week is finished, why am I standing here?*

When he touched his arm, water oozed out like water from a

sponge. He'd already started to shed his skin like a molting snake. He looked down at his combat boots. They had been almost new before Hell Week. Now they looked as if he'd worn them his whole life.

Medical screened Alex and his classmates. Guys had cellulitis—infection had traveled from cuts to deep inside their skin. Others had iliotibial band syndrome—they'd damaged the bands of tissue over their pelvises, hips, and knees. The docs checked for flesh-eating bacteria—actually bacteria that release toxins that destroy skin and muscle. Because trauma covered their bodies from head to toe, Alex and his classmates were meals on wheels for the killer bacteria. Everyone was swollen from head to foot and had to hobble because they couldn't walk.

Hell Week had changed Alex forever. He felt like a new dimension to the universe had opened up to him. He'd accomplished so much more than he imagined ever possible. Now he could clearly see what Grandpa had been telling him. *Believing* engaged Alex's effort, focus, and persistence—and that fueled him with challenging goals. To accomplish the goals, he broke them down into smaller objectives, and to accomplish the objectives, he created strategies. Alex had even developed Grandpa's sense of black humor for dealing with tough times.

As THE SUB NEARED Pakistan, the three Outcasts, four SEALs, and two divers sat in the Special Operations Forces (SOF) compartment. The divers secured the hatches, sealing themselves and the others inside. One of the divers turned on the flood valve. Seawater rushed into the compartment and rose up their bodies. Alex, Pancho, John, and the four SEALs sucked on the air lines attached to the submarine's breathing rig before the water reached their mouths. The divers breathed off their SCUBA tanks.

Inside the submarine's SOF compartment, water covered Alex

and the others' heads, flooding the chamber. The inside water pressure equalized the pressure outside the submarine. Huge domed hatches opened hydraulically. Moonlight shone in and sparks of light flickered in the water.

The divers left the compartment to retrieve the collapsed black rubber Zodiac boat and buoy from the submarine locker. The divers would inflate the Zodiac with a low-pressure air hose attached to the submarine.

Pancho let go of his air line first and ascended. Alex followed, blowing out air as he ascended so the increase in pressure wouldn't cause his lungs to pop. The higher he ascended, the more the pressure pushed on his lungs. Alex continued to blow out air. He knew John would be right behind him.

As Alex's head broke the water's surface, he sucked in a shot of air. The sky was lighter than the ocean, but still dark. Rain pattered on his face. The Outcasts and four SEALs gathered together and loaded into the Zodiac. The coxswain SEAL tried to start up the Zodiac's engine, but it wouldn't start. He kept trying but no luck.

In the Teams, one is none, two is one. "Fire up the reserve," Alex said.

The coxswain fired up the reserve to no effect. Then it started the second time. The wind howled and rain dumped on them. The guys lay low in the boat as the quiet engine sped them about five miles toward the coast. Alex held on for dear life as huge ocean swells bullied them. The Zodiac caught air and came down hard, crunching his bones. Alex thought he'd toss cookies as the Zodiac kept jumping off swells and crashing down. He could barely hold on. The boat accelerated and hit one swell that almost knocked everyone out into the ocean. Alex crashed down on the boat and bounced. His legs landed in the water. He pulled himself back in.

The Zodiac motored east through a labyrinth of waterways south of Karachi. As they reached five hundred yards from their destination, everyone broke out their paddles and started paddling. Alex and the others dug their paddles slowly and deeply, propelling the boat more quickly than fast, shallow strokes. Near the shore, they stopped and put on their night-vision goggles (NVGs). The world became one color—green—and one-dimensional. Alex and his men examined the area for a moment. Alex signaled with an infrared (IR) light toward shore.

From the shore an IR light answered him.

"Let's do it," Alex said.

The Outcasts slipped over the side and swam the sidestroke to shore. The SEALs in the Zodiac would hang around until Alex's team rendezvoused with their contacts.

When Alex, Pancho, and John reached water shallow enough to stand in, they stopped swimming. The Outcasts exposed only enough of their heads to breathe through their noses as they surveyed the shore. Everything looked calm. The three took off their swim fins and attached them to bungee cords strapped across their backs. Pancho and John low-crawled to the left and right flanks while Alex covered them from the rear. Then Alex and Pancho moved forward while John covered. Alex and Pancho neared the two men. The Pakistanis' faces looked like the Greek masks: Tragic and Comic. The Pakistanis exchanged bona fides—Tragic and Comic folded their arms. Alex answered by bowing his head while maintaining eye contact. *Good.* Alex motioned for them to turn around. They did. He and Pancho handcuffed them. Tragic complained, "We your friends. Why you do us this?"

While Pancho trained his weapon on them, with John doing the same, Alex patted Tragic down for weapons, communications, or anything else that didn't belong. "Just a precaution."

"What mean precaution?" Tragic asked.

"Safety."

"We safety."

Alex patted down Comic. "Not your safety—ours."

After Tragic and Comic checked out okay, Alex cut off the cuffs. Tragic and Comic led the Outcasts through low brush and trees to a black-windowed white van parked in the dirt. The Outcasts loaded into the back while Tragic and Comic hopped in front. Tragic started the ignition, then put the van in drive. He drove off the uneven dirt and onto a smooth surface. Alex took out his GPS and tracked their movement. They headed northwest as planned.

Tragic turned on the air-conditioning, chilling Alex's wet skin. The Outcasts dug into their waterproof bags, fished out dry clothes, and changed. The frogmen knew that it wouldn't take long for a wet body to contract hypothermia and that hypothermia could lead to death.

Alex's GPS showed them winding through the streets of Karachi. Eventually, the van stopped. Tragic, Comic, and the Outcasts left the van and entered a two-story mansion on a hill facing Pakistan Naval Station Qasim, less than half a mile away—close enough for a sniper shot with Alex's Win Mag.

# 32

Damien parked his Frito-Lay truck in the garage of an auto body paint shop in Albany, New York. The owner, a Latina with an attractive face, touched a switch that lowered the garage door. As Damien stepped out of the vehicle, he smelled paint, but it didn't flame his nostrils. Either the ventilation in the ceiling was highly effective or her last job must've been a while ago. The ceiling, walls, and floor were colored white. The white fluorescent lights embedded in the walls and in the corners of the ceiling weren't so bright that he needed to wear sunglasses, but he kept them on anyway.

"Same deal we agreed to on the phone?" he asked in Spanish.

"Yes," she said in English.

He switched to English. "A bit pricey."

"The cost of discretion. A cost a movie production company should be able to afford."

He studied her face. "But you don't believe I'm producing a movie."

She smiled. "I believe you need discretion." Then she held out her hand. "Like we discussed, half now and half when I finish."

As he paid her, Damien looked at her paint-spattered coveralls, trying to imagine the shape of her body underneath. "You're a smart woman. Easy on the eyes, too. But I don't see a wedding ring."

"Not unusual for a painter."

"Which is not unusual, *easy on the eyes* or *no wedding ring*?"

She smiled. "Smart."

"It's nearing dinnertime. You know any good restaurants around here?"

"Some, but I don't usually eat dinner in this neighborhood."

"I'd like to eat with company."

She stared at his eyes. "I'd rather not—not tonight."

"Yolanda, I'm just asking for dinner."

"How do you know that name?"

"Do you think I'd trust this job to someone who I don't know anything about?"

"Your paint job will be ready when I told you."

"I'm just asking you about dinner."

"You need to leave."

"Why make this difficult?"

She reached over to a paint-splattered open metal box filled with what looked like her painting equipment and pulled out a .38 revolver. "Leave now," she said. "You can pick up your vehicle when I'm finished."

"Exciting. I like that."

"I know how to use this and I will." She aimed at him awkwardly.

Damien grinned. "No, I don't think you do know how. You don't hold it like you know. Adding to the difficulty, your palms will begin to sweat and muscles start to twitch. Maybe you'll get lucky at this close range, but I've been shot before, and it only made me angry. I don't think you want to make me angry. Then again, you might get even luckier still and kill me with the first shot. You could probably clean up the blood, but you have to get it out of the hard-to-reach places. Remove the residue. Then you'll have to dispose of my body. A dead body is heavy. And there's the problem of disposing of my vehicle."

"I'll claim self-defense."

"When the police start investigating, they'll find out about all the stolen cars you painted—won't help your credibility on the witness stand."

"Who are you?"

"Damien."

"I'm not going anywhere with you."

"Think of your family and friends."

"I don't have any."

"Mother, father?" He studied her for a reaction.

Nothing.

"Brother, sister?" he probed.

Her body stiffened.

"Brother?"

Same rigidity.

"Sister?"

Her body became so tight that she appeared about to snap.

"You care about your sister," Damien said. "Just spend some time with me tonight and I won't have time to think about her. You finish my truck tomorrow, and you'll never see me again."

She lowered her pistol.

"You'll have a good time. I'll treat you right just like I want you to treat my truck. I'll make you feel—so beautiful."

Her face became pale and her body swayed like she was about to pass out.

"You got to bend your legs at the knees," he said. "You're cutting off the blood circulation to your brain."

She did as he said.

# 33

The U.S. relationship with Pakistan ran hot and cold. In the 1980s, America and Pakistan were allies during the Soviet-Afghan War; however, in the 1990s, when Pakistan insisted on building nuclear weapons, the United States imposed sanctions and relations fell apart. Then Pakistan supported the Taliban in neighboring Afghanistan until the September 11, 2001, attacks on the United States. Since that time, Pakistan's leaders have walked a precarious line between appeasing Taliban supporters and helping the United States' war on terror. Even the Pakistani military felt strain within their ranks: Taliban supporters versus supporters of the United States.

The second floor of the Outcasts' two-story safe house faced Pakistan Naval Station Qasim, the main base for the Pakistan marines and related amphibious forces. Alex wore a two-tone light and medium gray battle dress uniform. The same-color helmet and bullet-resistant vest protected his head and upper body. Alex covered the window with gray cheesecloth while John, dressed the same, did the same to the back wall facing the window. A countersniper team would be able to see only gray on gray—nothing. Pancho, also dressed in gray and wearing a bullet-resistant vest, opened the window. Tragic and Comic left the sniper hide for the evening.

John unscrewed the lightbulb so no one could accidentally turn on the light and thereby blow the whole operation. Pancho moved a large desk off to the left side of the window—if someone started shooting through the window at Alex, he didn't want to be directly in the line of fire. John used his laser range finder to aim a laser beam at the parade ground reviewing stand on the naval base in the distance. Using the time-of-flight principle, the range finder measured the time it took for the laser pulse to reflect from the reviewing stand back to John: 812 yards. Alex dialed in his Leupold 10-power scope to 812 yards. John lasered the distance to surrounding objects and he and Alex marked them in their waterproof sniper notebooks. Finally, the three Outcasts took turns sleeping in their sniper hide until morning came.

The next day, late in the afternoon, Pancho guarded the building from downstairs and John looked through his spotter scope while he sat on a large desk. Alex rested his Win Mag on some bags of rice he'd put on a desk. He looked through his Leupold scope at the parade ground, which appeared ten times closer thanks to the lens. Some officials gathered to practice for a change-of-command ceremony. Among those at the practice was Lieutenant Commander Issa. Now he walked with a limp and his arm rested in a cast and sling. Alex waited until Commander Issa took his seat on the reviewing stand. The commanding officer and his executive officer were absent from the practice, but Alex wasn't concerned about them. Commander Issa was his target. Not only did Alex want to snuff Issa, but so did leaders in the Pakistani military and intelligence communities.

Alex's shot would be through the cold bore of his rifle. Because the first shot warms the barrel, the second and third shots are more accurate. However, after the first shot, Commander Issa probably wouldn't stick around for the second and third.

With the bullet chamber empty, Alex practiced acquiring his

target, aiming, and pulling the trigger—maintaining his breathing and following through after the shot. He practiced reloading and getting back into his scope for the next shot.

He used to have to imagine something calm to make his heart rate and breathing slow, but having done it so many times, he could skip the visualization and cut straight to willing that to happen.

Muscle memory took over. When one has driven to the supermarket many times, one doesn't have to think so much about each step in the process: open the vehicle door, sit, put the key in the ignition and turn, put the gear into drive, step on the gas, turn, stop, accelerate, etc.—and so, with little conscious thought, one arrives at the supermarket. Similarly, when one has fired a weapon many times, one doesn't have to think so much about each step in the process. Alex placed his left forearm on the desk for balance. He held the rifle butt tightly in his right shoulder pocket. His shooting hand, not too stiff and not too limp, firmly held the small of the stock. His trigger finger caressed the trigger. Cheek firmly against his thumb on the small of the stock, he inhaled. Then exhaled. Alex extended the natural pause between exhaling and inhaling—keeping his lungs still so they wouldn't throw his aim—long enough to take a shot but not so long as to cause his muscles to tense or his vision to blur. Breath holding was a skill that frogmen excel at.

Commander Issa sat down. Alex's scope was still dialed in—812 yards. He centered the crosshairs on Commander Issa's chest. Alex focused on the crosshairs and not his target because sometimes a person knows when he's being watched. Alex had to be careful not to alert Commander Issa.

Abruptly, Commander Issa stood up. Alex contemplated taking a hasty shot. Commander Issa and the officer next to him changed seats. Alex chose to be patient. As Commander Issa settled in his seat, Alex resumed his aim. He squeezed the trigger. The Win Mag fired and Alex felt the gratifying recoil pull into his shoulder. Commander Issa's body folded at the waist before he fell. "Five down, two to go."

Voices came from downstairs. Alex had been so focused on his target that he wasn't sure when the noise had started. Now there was shouting. Alex and John rushed downstairs to find Tragic and Comic arguing.

Comic said, "Tomorrow you shoot! Not today!"

"It not matter tomorrow or today," Tragic said. "It finished."

"You kill Commander Issa—not good!" Comic said.

"What?" Tragic asked.

"We die!"

AK-47 shots sounded from outside and bullets penetrated the second floor. Somebody had tipped off the terrorists. Before Alex could eliminate the traitor, John fired his HK416, executing Comic with a single shot to the head.

"Pancho, take us out," Alex said. Alex's body jacked adrenaline into his arteries. He gestured to Tragic and said, "Stay with me."

Tragic looked from the body of Comic to Alex. Alex tensed, waiting to see what his response would be. Tragic's eyes grew wide, wider than Alex thought humanly possible. *Okay, shock it is.*

"You, stay with me," Alex repeated, softening his voice like he was talking to a puppy. Tragic nodded slowly.

Pancho hurried out the side door and turned south, heading away from the Pakistan navy base. Next came Alex and Tragic. An AK-47 fired on automatic, and one of the bullets passed behind Alex's head. As the bullet flew, it split open the air. When the air closed shut again, it did so with a clap, like a mini sonic boom. Alex heard the clap and felt the vapor trail the bullet created behind his head. Rounds hit the house next to him and spit out pieces of concrete. *Shit.*

"Contact rear!" John shouted, firing back at the attackers to the north.

"Contact rear!" Alex echoed, ducking into a doorway and pulling Tragic in with him.

Pancho ducked into a side street with Arabic written on one of the white walls. A yellow gas-powered rickshaw nearly hit Pancho.

"Coming back!" John shouted. After firing one last round, John turned his tail toward the enemy and ran south past a woman fleeing on a bicycle.

As John passed, Alex leaned out of the doorway and fired over John's head at the attackers. Alex wasn't sure where the enemy was, so he fired in the general direction of the sound of their muzzle blasts, hoping to keep their heads down long enough for the Outcasts to get away. "Coming back!" Alex shouted. He slung his Win Mag across his chest, switched to his pistol, and took Tragic with him south. After passing Pancho, the three Outcasts turned onto another street. Men and women scattered everywhere. With so many bullets flying and so much adrenaline pumping, it took discipline not to shoot a civilian—something the terrorists didn't worry about.

A man with an AK-47 appeared in front of John. John aimed. The man with the AK raised his weapon and John shot him.

"John, take us out," Alex said.

John took the point, followed by Alex and Tragic, with Pancho bringing up the rear.

As the Outcasts proceeded, a terrorist in black popped up from behind an open window in Alex's field of fire. Alex shot him in the neck and the terrorist toppled out of sight. John and Pancho kept busy moving and shooting, too.

From a corrugated-tin rooftop, a fat man aimed his AK down at them and sprayed. Alex lined his sights on the terrorist's head and squeezed the trigger, pulling the terrorist down off the building. The terrorist hit the ground with a heavy thud. Alex busily covered his own field of fire, and he didn't have time to look too far ahead or behind; he trusted John and Pancho to take care of their areas.

As Alex reached another alley, to the left, he spotted a figure crouching low: a woman in black. Alex held his fire. She huddled near the ground as if to protect herself from all the shooting. Alex continued to follow John.

At a window with a busted-up wooden frame, a woman wearing white stood. Her hands were down, so she didn't pose an immediate threat, but her eyes showed more contempt for Alex than fear. Something was wrong. Alex aimed in her direction. A silhouette appeared from the side pointing an AK-47 at Alex and firing. One round hit Alex in the chest before he shot the terrorist in the eye. Even with his bullet-resistant vest on, the impact of the bullet stung. Alex kept his weapon aimed in her direction for other threats when she popped up with the AK. Alex shot her down. Blood splatter smeared the wall behind her.

Pancho and John continued shooting, but Alex didn't have time to see whom they shot.

John climbed through the window of a small, white concrete house. Alex joined him, followed by Pancho. They had climbed through the kitchen window. A young woman sat huddled in the corner. The furnishings were simple—table for two, bed that pulled down from the wall, small shelf with a little TV on it, and a small couch. Inside the house, the SEALs had some protection against enemy bullets, and they also had clear fields of fire at their enemies. Alex took a window that had a view to enemies on the rooftops about one hundred yards away.

He switched from his pistol to Win Mag. A man with an RPG ran across a flat concrete rooftop. Alex aimed at Mr. RPG and missed. When Mr. RPG stopped running, Alex fired again. Although Alex was aiming for his chest, Mr. RPG ducked, catching a round in the face. Quickly Alex scoped a man with an AK-47 and squeezed the trigger. The shot struck the man in the shoulder and spun him around. He dropped out of sight.

Pancho and John fired furiously. Tragic had picked up an AK-47 and was battling for his life. Fallen enemy lay on the ground, in buildings, and on rooftops. The enemy's shooting lulled, but reinforcements came, replacing each of the dead—and then some. The enemy's shooting picked up again. "We can't stay here all day!" shouted Alex. "Pancho, take us the hell out of here!"

The SEALs and Tragic squeezed off final shots before Pancho led them out through the front door—shooting and moving. Alex switched to his pistol again for close combat.

Pancho led them through another building, a small meat shop. Enemy combatants lay in a pool of blood on a black-and-white checkered linoleum floor. The blood hadn't had time to dry, and Alex had to move carefully to keep from slipping and falling. On the floor, one of the bodies lifted a pistol, but Tragic cut loose on full auto, laying the guy out flat.

They exited the shop through a window and found themselves on top of a building as the city sloped down a long hill. The buildings were a hodgepodge of sizes, shapes, and colors: white, brown, red, faded yellow, narrow, wide, short, and tall. The SEALs caught three terrorists below by surprise, raining death down on them.

Although there were fewer terrorists on the rooftops, the Outcasts had no cover to protect them from bullets. They ran across one rooftop until they reached the end and jumped several feet over to the next rooftop. When they ran out of that rooftop, they leapt to the next.

Pancho dropped off the roof of the one-story building, followed by Alex, Tragic, and John. Above the Outcasts, a roof they had cleared now had a terrorist wearing a red headdress and aiming an AK down at them. Alex fired a burst into his chest, dropping him. As Alex looked behind to make sure John was still with them, a door burst open and John filled the doorway with holes—an AK fell out into the street. About twenty feet above, smoke trailed through the air—Alex couldn't see the RPG shooter or what he was shooting at. Alex listened for the explosion, but it didn't come, or else the chaotic noise of the battle had dulled Alex's hearing.

A bullet grazed Alex's shoulder, cutting his flesh. He didn't know where it came from or if maybe it was a ricochet. One thing was clear: the enemy were all over the place. Three men rushed toward the Outcasts. Alex nearly capped them before he realized that they were unarmed—civilians. An AK-wielding terrorist flew out from the same area as the civilians, but the terrorist didn't see the Outcasts as he ran with his back to them. Pancho stitched him up the back with his HK416.

The Outcasts ducked into another alley, where the air heated up. Bullets coming from the sides, above, and a crisscross of angles popped all around Alex. Large pieces of ground and walls took flight. Smaller pieces sprayed. More AK-47s rattled the air and the rattling became louder as the enemy closed in. The Outcasts were trapped.

Alex didn't want it to end this way. He looked forward to seeing Sarah again, but not like this.

"RPG!" John shouted from the rear.

"RPG!" Alex repeated. As he glanced past John to see a bushy-haired tango standing behind the tango with the rocket-propelled grenade launcher, Alex pulled Tragic into an alley. The RPG's back blast must've fried the bushy-haired tango standing behind it. Alex covered his ears with his hands and opened his mouth so the blast wouldn't pop his eardrums. The rocket-propelled grenade skipped along the ground past Alex and Tragic, landing in John's direction.

No explosion. *Maybe it's a dud.* The RPG exploded: *Boom!*

Tragic's body became limp in Alex's arms. Blood soaked the side of Tragic's head. Alex lowered Tragic's body to the ground and felt the pulse in his neck—dead. Tragic's eyes remained open. Alex closed the Pakistani's eyes.

Alex peeked around the corner where the grenade went off. John had hidden in a doorway, avoiding the blast. Now John was engaged in a furious firefight with the terrorists to the east. On the opposite side, Pancho shot it out with the terrorists to the west. With terrorists to the east and west of them, they were trapped in the narrow alley. All the doors and windows in the alley were boarded up, offering no escape. Their situation was getting out of hand, and Alex felt hopeless.

"Cat," he said. He didn't know why he said her name. Maybe saying her name relaxed him. Maybe saying her name gave him hope.

Alex glanced down at the dusty street. The RPG explosion had tilted open the lid of a manhole in front of him.

"Pancho and John, drop smoke and come to me!" Alex said.

They each popped smoke grenades, then withdrew to Alex's position. The smoke clouds protected them from the terrorists' eyes, but the clouds didn't protect the SEALs from bullets. The Outcasts dropped to the ground as the air above them crackled and sparked with shots. Alex pushed the heavy metal water drainage lid to the side.

"Pancho," Alex said, pointing his nose at the manhole.

Pancho shook his head. "I don't know what's down there."

"You know what's up here," Alex warned.

Reluctantly, Pancho squeezed down into the hole. Alex followed, holding the outer rods of a metal ladder and sliding down. John came down partway, covered the hole above his head with the metal lid, and finished descending.

Above them, the gunfire and explosions increased in rate and noise. Men cried out in pain. It sounded like the terrorists were attacking each other through all the smoke. John made a nose snicker, sucking air through his nostrils.

In the concrete tunnel, it was too dark to see, so everyone went on their NVGs. There wasn't enough headroom to stand, so the Outcasts hunched over as they waddled through what smelled like dirty rainwater, which came up to their ankles. Even though they tried to proceed quietly, the sound of their feet moving through the water softly echoed in the tunnel. Alex whispered to Pancho, "Get us as close as you can to the Karachi train station."

"We're not going home yet?" Pancho checked his compass.

"Red Sheik," Alex answered, blanking on the bloody bug code-name they'd given the terrorist.

"Are you sure?" John asked. "After we took out Commander Issa, the Red Sheik is probably guarded in a fortress. Terrorists are out looking for us, and if you're planning on using the train, that sniper rifle of yours is going to stick out like a hairy mole. We don't have much ammo left, either."

"We've got to get to him and Damien before they reach the U.S. and launch their attack."

After thirty minutes of waddling underground like ducks, Pancho stopped beneath a ladder. "I think this is as close as we get."

Alex submerged his Win Mag under the water. "After all you've done for me over the years, I feel bad about leaving you, but I have no other choice."

Alex reached into his backpack and pulled out some indigenous clothing. Over his BDUs, Alex put on *shalwar kameez*—pajama-like clothing worn by both Pakistani men and women. The kameez shirt extended down to his thigh and had splits in the sides for freer movement. Next, Alex kept guard while Pancho and John dressed. They packed away their NVGs.

Pancho went up the ladder first, followed by Alex. When Alex came out of the manhole, he could see that darkness had fallen on Karachi, but the sky was still brighter than the inside of the tunnel. A donkey pulling a cart almost ran over him. Alex ducked back into the manhole until the cart passed. Then he came out and joined Pancho at the side of the road. John came out last, covered the manhole with the lid, and followed his buddies to Pakistan Railways' Karachi Station.

At the station, Alex stood near the middle while John went to the far end. After Pancho bought the tickets, he gave Alex and John theirs. Pancho strolled to the end of the station farthest from the guys. The Outcasts didn't want to be recognized grouping together. After the express train came to a stop at their station, Pancho boarded near the front. Seconds later, John boarded the rear of the train. Last, Alex stepped onto the middle of the train.

On the train, Alex walked to the first-class section, where he saw an attractive Pakistani woman with what appeared to be her teenage daughter, and who was almost as beautiful as her mother. Alex avoided eye contact and entered his compartment, where Pancho and John joined him. Fortunately, the compartment had air-conditioning and a private toilet.

"How long is the ride to Islamabad?" Alex asked.

"About two days," Pancho said.

John groaned.

# 34

Damien arrived at the safe house just before 0900. His Frito-Lay truck now had a new paint job, transforming it into a brown UPS truck. He parked it in the barn, walked past a group of cars sitting on the property, and entered the back door of the safe house using his own key.

Inside the house, four cell members enthusiastically greeted him. None wanted to be viewed as uncooperative.

Damien skipped the greeting and got down to business: "Here are my shopping lists. Have your girlfriends or female assistants go with you so we don't arouse suspicion." He handed out the first shopping list. "I need you to get the cannon fuse, barrels, plastic mixing buckets, weight scale, power drill, screws, plastic pipe, duct tape, brown spray paint, diesel fuel, and some other items. Spread out your purchases to different stores."

"Yes, sir," they said.

Damien faced his son and gave him a list. "The youth of this land are known for their reckless pursuits. You will pose as a drag racer. I need you to buy nitromethane. It is . . . unstable, but handled with care it poses no threat."

Mohammed nodded.

Damien gave the next man his list. "You're going to be a farmer buying some good ammonium nitrate fertilizer."

He saw the puzzled looks from his son and the man. He had no desire to explain himself, but he knew that giving them some insight into what they were doing would keep them motivated. "It is used to oxidize the nitromethane and shape the charge. Hire a female assistant to help you so people don't ask stupid questions."

"Yes, sir."

"I'm going to pick up our weapons and ammo," Damien said. "I'll need one man to help me."

Damien gave another man a list. "You'll need to sneak into a quarry to steal the spools of shock tube, blasting caps, and Tovex. The Tovex was a water-gel explosive that is more stable than dynamite. There's an address and map for the quarry on your list."

UNDER THE LIGHT OF a three-fourths moon, rolling north from Interstate 90 into New York's Adirondack Park in a green Chevy Tahoe, Damien sat in the front passenger seat wearing dark clothes and reading a handheld GPS. "Turn right at this next road," he said. With no entrance gates, the park was easy to gain access to.

The baby-faced driver, also dressed in dark clothes, turned right at the next road. "This sure is an out-of-the-way place to hide the weapons and ammo," Baby Face said.

"Could've just added a secret storage at the safe house," Damien pointed out. "When did your former leader cache everything?"

"Last month," Baby Face said.

"Well, your former leader was an idiot. I did the world a favor by getting rid of him." Damien continued to give directions, taking them on a dirt road, until they reached the spot nearest the point of the weapons and ammo cache. "Park here."

Baby Face stopped the SUV along the side of the road. Without being told what to do, he grabbed a shovel out of the back and followed Damien into the woods. The two had walked a few hundred yards into the woods when they heard a noise on the ground in front of them. Damien stopped and surveyed the area. Baby Face stopped, too.

A small mammal that looked like a cross between a mouse and a mole stopped to glance at them before running away. Damien and his partner passed the carcass of a fawn. The more they walked, the denser the forest became, and the denser the forest became, the less the moonlight shone. The area became darker and darker.

Fifty yards later, Damien halted. He looked around until he found the three fat trees with thicker trunks than the trees around them. Off to the side sat a clump of boulders. Damien oriented himself, then pointed to the ground. "Here."

Baby Face stuck his shovel in the dirt and dug. As he dug, it occurred to Damien that this would be a great way to kill someone. Make them dig their own grave in a remote location, then do the deed and bury them.

Three feet below the surface Baby Face hit something—a large rock. Baby Face dug next to it and hit another rock. He shoveled dirt from around the rocks, then removed them, exposing two large rectangular cases.

Baby Face pulled out the cases and set them next to the hole. Damien opened the first and examined inside: sixteen AKS rifles. He opened the second case: magazines filled with ammo totaling at least a thousand rounds. Damien said, "The magazine springs will weaken when loaded like this for a long period. It's good we're taking this stuff now." Before he closed the cases, he paused. Something wasn't right. He looked up at one of the trees. Six feet from the ground, the bark was stripped off like it had been scratched off or eaten.

"What?" Baby Face said.

A large, grunting black mass on two legs stood over six feet tall behind Baby Face. When Baby Face realized something was behind him, it was too late. The bear came down on Baby Face, knocking him down onto his shovel.

Damien's heart leapt in fear. The black bear mauled a shrieking Baby Face. Damien drew his pistol and fired it into the bear until he ran out of bullets.

The bear turned around and eyed Damien before charging him. Damien thought about the AKSs and ammo in the open cases. Not enough time to reach them before the bear reached Damien. Damien dodged the black monster. After it ran past, Damien went for an AKS and a magazine. He jacked the magazine into the weapon and jerked back the charging handle, loading a round into the chamber. As the bear turned around to return, Damien fired two shots into its torso. The bear finished its turn, then came at him again. Damien aimed for the head and squeezed the trigger—*pop!* The bear's momentum carried it forward as the beast landed on its lower jaw at Damien's feet. Damien took a step back as he tried to catch his heartbeat and breath.

*Woof!*

Damien spun around to the source of the noise. Another bear came galloping on all four legs at what must have been thirty miles per hour, straight at him. *"Mierda!"* Damien shouted in Spanish. Shit! He dove out of the way, the bear just missing him. No longer on his feet, Damien had trouble maneuvering. But he did have time for a shot—if he kept his cool. The bear turned and galloped toward him. Damien knelt on one knee and fired. Too quick—he missed. The bear quickly closed the space between them. Damien took an extra moment to aim, then squeezed the trigger, hitting the bear in the face. It went down.

Both of the bears remained still. Damien felt relief. Baby Face lay still, too. Now he would have to drag the weapons and ammo to the SUV by himself.

*Roar!* Damien turned to see a huge black bear standing six feet tall directly in front of him with its mouth wide open.

*"Mierda, Mierda!"* As the bear attacked Damien, he fired into its face. The bear and Damien crashed to the ground, with Damien landing on his back and the bear landing on top of him.

Damien struggled underneath the behemoth until he wiggled out from underneath it. His heart raced his breathing as he frantically spun around 360 degrees looking for more bears. There were none in the immediate area, but he couldn't be sure one wasn't hiding behind a bush or a tree. He checked out Baby Face's bloody body— dead. Damien searched his bloody pockets until he found the keys to the SUV and put them in his own pocket.

Soon a park ranger would come to investigate the gunshots. Time was ticking. Damien slung his AKS across his chest and closed the weapons case and the ammo case. He grabbed the handle of one case with his right hand and took the handle of the other case with his left hand. He dragged the two cases through the woods, his eyes alert for more bears. The cases were so heavy, he had to take breaks, but each break increased his fear of another attack.

The trek back to the SUV seemed infinitely longer than the trek into the woods had been. He didn't feel safe from the bears until he locked himself inside the vehicle and started the engine. Even then, he wondered what damage an American bear could do to his SUV.

# 35

Alex first became a SEAL at Team Two and the first time he killed was with Team Two. Alex's new platoon needed an additional sniper. The position appealed to Alex because he felt being a sniper was more of a thinking man's world—the more time he had to think, the more successful he'd be in combat. The platoon had a shooting competition and Alex won. He trained and became a sniper at the SEAL Sniper School. Later, he deployed with SEAL Team Two to Iraq.

While in Iraq, his red-haired chief told him and another SEAL, "You two will be one of my SR [special reconnaissance] teams to observe a highway where the enemy have been planting IEDs beside the road to kill U.S. troops or Iraqi police driving by. These bombs are now responsible for most of the U.S. deaths and casualties. Find out who is planting these and neutralize them."

Under the cover of darkness, Alex and Jabberwocky, so nick-named because he jabbered nonstop, flew in a Pave Low helicopter that hugged the desert, rising with the hills and falling with the valleys. "We're going to pop your cherry on this one!" Jabberwocky shouted above the rotor noise.

Alex kept quiet.

Jabberwocky chewed on his plug of tobacco. "I was scared my

first time, too! If you ain't scared, you're stupid! Some people let scared gobble them up! But I know you're going to swing that scared like a baseball bat and crack some insurgent ass!"

"Fifteen minutes!" In their headsets the air crewman's voice relayed information from the pilot.

"Ten minutes!" the air crewman called.

Alex was scared. He'd trained at shooting targets, but this time they'd be shooting back. He'd practiced against SEALs role-playing opposing forces, but this time the bullets coming at him would be for real.

"Five minutes!"

Jabberwocky spit on the helo floor.

"Three minutes!"

The helo slowed.

"One minute!"

The front nose of the helo flared as the pilot brought the bird to a stop in the air. Then the helo landed.

"Showtime!" Jabberwocky called with a grin so wide it looked like his face would crack. He really loved being a SEAL.

Alex and Jabberwocky hopped out. Jabberwocky spotted a gulley and lay down in it. Alex lay down behind him. Although days in the desert were hot, the evenings were cool.

The helo staged a fake insertion in the distance, then another, before disappearing from earshot. Alex and Jabberwocky lay there for thirty minutes listening and watching the area. When Jabberwocky was sure they didn't have visitors, he motioned to Alex, *Take us out.*

Alex led them out of the gully and east toward a main highway next to a city. The physical exertion of patrolling with the 150-pound pack on his back and the mental exertion of walking point through insurgent territory calmed him.

Alex watched the 180 degrees across their front while Jabberwocky covered the 180 degrees behind them. Periodically, Alex looked behind to make sure Jabberwocky was still with him and if

Jabberwocky had anything to communicate. When the two reached a large sand berm within three miles of the highway, Jabberwocky raised his fist, signaling Alex to stop. He did. Jabberwocky signaled to cache some of their equipment for emergency use later.

After caching part of their supplies, they traveled east for more than two miles, stopping within a few hundred yards of the highway. At a little before 0100 they began digging their reconnaissance hide: 6 x 6 feet wide and 5 feet deep. At the bottom, they dug a sump about 2 feet long, 1.5 feet wide, and 1 foot deep, sloped at 45 degrees to drain any rainwater or unwanted grenades. They filled sandbags to line the soft walls and the top rim. Finally, they extended metal rods shaped like an umbrella to cover the site. On the umbrella, they placed desert camouflage fabric, sealing them into their sniper hide. Jabberwocky radioed that they'd arrived safely. As the sun rose from behind the city, it shone on their hide, warming them.

The duo lived in their hole: eating, sleeping, relieving themselves, and taking turns tracking enemy movement. On the first day they spotted a middle-aged man who strutted around carrying an AK-47 slung over his shoulder and acting like he was the boss.

In the evening of the fourth day an old man came to the road and looked around. Alex woke Jabberwocky from a nap and told him. They both watched. The old man left.

Then a teenage boy arrived and lingered in the area, longer than the old man. Later, replacing the boy, a truck showed up. As the truck reached the area, it slowed down, then stopped.

Soon a car appeared on the scene and stopped behind the truck. In the front seat next to the driver sat the cocky man with the AK-47—the Boss.

The truck's driver and two passengers stepped out of their vehicle and dug a hole in the sand with their hands. One of them brought something out of the back and carried it to the hole.

"When I say execute, you cap Boss and I'll cap the bomb," Jabberwocky whispered. "Then we'll both get Boss's driver."

"Roger." Alex looked through his advanced combat optical gun-sight (ACOG), magnifying 1.5x, aiming for Boss's neck.

"Three, two, one, execute . . ."

Alex squeezed the trigger. When the bullet hit the windshield, its path shifted down and to the side, striking Boss on the side of his chest, his chin dropping on it.

A loud explosion sounded, but Alex couldn't think about it—Jabberwocky exploded the bomb and the tangos near it. Alex aimed at the Boss's driver and fired. Jabberwocky shot, too. Both bullets hit the driver before he knew what to do next.

One moment the Boss was strutting around town and the next moment he sat lifeless. It gave Alex a strange, uneasy feeling in his gut to extinguish a life. Alex alone had pulled the trigger and he alone felt the heavy responsibility. On the positive side, the Boss would no longer terrorize U.S. troops or Iraqi policemen. In addition, Alex felt that somehow he had achieved some justice for Sarah's death.

Later, Alex didn't have flashbacks or nightmares. Maybe it was because he'd been born for this work, or maybe it was because of the training—maybe both.

Alex received more missions. Each time he killed, the strange, uneasy emotions lessened and the natural emotions increased. Killing still placed a heavy responsibility on him but it had become a natural responsibility. Even so, the feeling of justice didn't last long, and he was itching to get the feeling again.

THE TRAIN CARRYING THEM through Pakistan clattered and rocked as if every screw and bolt were loose, which, Alex figured, they probably were. John squirmed and mumbled in the seat beside him before finally waking up and staring at Alex.

"What?" Alex asked.

"I had a dream," John said.

"So?"

Pancho lifted his head and rubbed his eyes. "What's going on?"

"Nothing," Alex said.

"I had a dream," John said.

"What kind?" Pancho asked.

"It was so real," John explained.

"It was just a dream," Alex said. He'd been on missions before when guys had had dreams. They were never good.

Pancho sat up. "Maybe it was, but after John has dreams, real things happen."

"I don't believe in that kind of thing," Alex said, hoping that would end the conversation.

John was still staring at him. "One of us died."

*Damn.* "I had a dream where we completed the mission successfully, got ice cream and cake, and all went home," Alex said.

"Which one?" Pancho questioned, ignoring Alex.

"Belay that," Alex said. "John, you even try to open your mouth I will jam my fist in it. You can believe whatever the hell you want, but I don't want to hear it, not here, not now. Is that clear?" He looked from John to Pancho.

"I wasn't going to say," John said, looking away.

"Glad we agree, then," Alex said, giving Pancho a warning look. "Now let's just relax and remember what we're here for."

The train rattled on for another fifteen minutes before the brakes screeched and it shook to a halt. Luggage fell from racks and there was much cursing and shouting throughout the train.

"Did we hit something?" John asked.

"Didn't feel like it," Alex said, although would they have felt it if they had?

"We're at some piddly little station, I think," John said, looking out the window. "And it looks like we're about to have company."

Alex leaned over to look out the window. A group of men in traditional tribal garb were boarding the train. Each carried a cloth bundle about the size of an AK-47.

"Damn it, this is the last thing we need," Alex said.

"What's the play, Chief?" Pancho asked. He'd already slid his HK416 onto the seat beside him.

Alex thought quickly. "Look, this isn't our fight. We lie low, don't do anything aggressive, and let a little larceny slide."

"And if they start something?" John asked.

"Then we take them out, every last one of them. There's no way they know we're here, so the advantage is ours. First sign of trouble we hit them fast and don't stop until every one of them is down."

"That's going to draw all kinds of attention," Pancho said, although he didn't sound disappointed at the prospect.

"So would our dead bodies."

A short burst from an AK-47 rang out, followed by wailing. Pancho clicked off the safety on his rifle. "Sounds like we weren't the intended target."

"Not yet," Alex said.

"They probably whacked the train cop," John added.

Alex poked his head out of their compartment. One of the suspicious men walked through the train carrying a large sack while his armed accomplices forced people at gunpoint to give up their money, cell phones, jewelry, and laptops. Alex ducked back into the compartment and warned his Teammates, "They're robbing the train."

"Uh, I don't have much money left to rob, so that works out good for me," Pancho said.

"So do we give them some money, or do we take them out?" John asked. "They started it, but it's still kind of calm."

Alex knew it was risky, but he wasn't dying here on this bloody train.

"We'll play it cool, give them some money, and hope they leave us alone," Alex said. "The moment they show any sign of aggression, though, we pop them. Hide your watches."

The SEALs waited, listening to the men working their way through the train, robbing its passengers. Footsteps neared their door just before it flew open. An angry man waved his AK-47 in the SEALs' faces and shouted out commands in what sounded like Urdu, the main language of Pakistan. Angry Man didn't know how close he was to being wasted. Bag Man extended his sack. An armed middle-aged, pimply-faced man looked over the two robbers' shoulders as if he was supervising. The SEALs acted scared and handed over some of their money.

Angry Man yelled at them again, waving his AK-47 at them. The SEALs gave him more money but kept the rest hidden.

Angry Man repeated his threats.

Pimple Face spoke English. "Give money and everything."

"We gave you everything," Alex said. "We have more at the hotel, but we gave you everything we have now."

"Watches!" Pimple Face demanded.

"Back at the hotel," Alex said, trying to sound scared, which actually wasn't that hard. "We were told not to bring any watches or valuables because of possible robberies. We only brought the money we needed."

Pimple Face had more people to rob and no patience to argue. He spoke to his men in Urdu, and they left the SEALs' compartment.

"Is that it?" John asked.

For an answer, a shouting match erupted in the cabin beside theirs.

A woman was arguing with Pimple Face.

"Just give him the money," Pancho thought aloud.

There was scuffling before the woman screamed. Silence followed. Another struggle began. This time a girl screamed.

Alex remembered the pretty Pakistani woman and her teenage daughter. "They're raping the girl."

"What girl?" Pancho asked.

Alex uncovered his pistol and hurried out of the cabin.

"Shit," Pancho said, getting up and following.

At the neighboring cabin, the door was closed. Alex threw it open. Inside, Bag Man held the sack of loot. Beside him stood Angry Man. The mother lay passed out on the floor. On the bed, Pimple Face was naked from the waist to his ankles, lying on top of the teenage girl, whose clothing was ripped. Angry Man seemed to pose the most immediate threat and Alex aimed at him first.

He put two shots into the man's left temple, knocking him backward against the train window.

Pancho slid his bulk into the cabin beside Alex, his HK416 held tight against his right shoulder in a shooting stance. He squeezed off a three-shot burst that caught Bag Man center of mass. The loot bag dropped to the floor and Bag Man crumpled on top of it.

Alex looked over his shoulder and breathed a sigh of relief. John stood in the hallway covering their backs.

"Get off her," Alex told Pimple Face.

Pimple Face looked at his AK-47 standing in the corner, then looked at his two dead compatriots. He nodded and got up. Pancho drilled him twice in the head and the rapist buckled at the knees and bent over backward, his now flaccid penis flopping around like a worm on a hook.

"How's the girl?" Pancho asked, keeping his rifle trained on the three bodies.

Alex went over to her. "Scared out of her mind, but okay. Looks like Mom is coming to as well. We've stepped in it now. Better haul ass."

Alex grabbed up the weapons and ammo from the robbers and started to toss them out the window, then decided to keep one AK for himself.

The woman on the floor regained consciousness and sat up

slowly. She went to her daughter and hugged her. Both women stared at the SEALs.

Alex tried to make a motion with his hands that everything was okay, but each hand held a weapon, which didn't help his cause.

"You two want to hurry up in there?" John said from the hallway. "A lot of heads are popping out of cabins to have a look."

"Any sign of the rest of their crew?" Alex asked.

Instead of answering, John opened fire, then slid into their cabin, which was now seriously crowded.

"I dropped two, but there's still more out there." He popped his head out, then back, then out again, swinging his rifle up and letting off another burst.

"I think I heard something on the roof of the train," Pancho said.

"You're kidding me," Alex said.

Pancho shook his head. "Wish I was. They all ride topside over here. Don't think anything of it."

*Great, just great.* "Fine," Alex said, climbing over the bodies to get to the window. "Pancho, you and John keep things tight here. I'll go topside."

"Don't fall off," John said from the doorway.

Alex frowned. "I wasn't planning to." Alex used the butt of his rifle to smash out the window. He stuck his head outside and looked up. No sign of anyone, but that didn't mean squat. Slinging his rifle, he pulled himself out through the window and grabbed hold of the metal ribs running along the side of the train.

The wind whipped at his hair; the train was traveling at some speed. He did his best to ignore the Pakistani countryside whizzing past. Cursing John for his damn dream, Alex took in a breath and pushed off of the windowsill while pulling himself hard up and onto the roof. He landed with a thud and had his newfound AK up and ready. Two robbers stood crouched twenty feet away, looking at him with obvious amazement. Both carried AK-47s, but neither had them in a firing position. They clearly hadn't expected anyone to join them.

Alex fired two quick bursts, traversing from left to right. The man on the left fell forward and tumbled off the side of the train. The one on the right, however, slumped down as if he were kneeling to pray. Alex put another round into him, but he still didn't fall off the train.

"Are you kidding me?" Alex shouted, firing two more bursts. Blood, flesh, and clothing flew through the air, with some of it spraying Alex. Finally, agonizingly slowly, the body began to slide off the roof and toward the edge. Alex was about to run forward and kick the corpse the rest of the way when it finally rolled over and was gone.

The sound of AK-47s came and went inside the train, punctuated by the concise staccato of Pancho's and John's HK416s.

Alex started to get up from his crouch when a head with orange-colored hair appeared at the far end of the car. The muzzle of an AK-47 materialized beside it.

Alex aimed and fired, but just then the train lurched and the shots went wide. The head vanished but then popped up again. The robber sprayed his AK on full auto, but his angle was bad and the shots went slicing up into the sky. Alex took aim again and fired, skipping a couple of shots off the train's roof and catching the robber in the neck. Blood geysered into the wind and the man was gone, his scream abruptly ending as he hit the earth.

Alex crouch-crawled to the front of the car and then slid on his stomach. He swung down the opposite side from where the guy with orange hair had appeared, then prepared to shoot whomever he found. The open space was empty.

He realized he hadn't heard any shots for the last minute. He eased open the door of the car and peeked inside. Two robbers lay on the carpet.

"Ambassador coming forward!" Alex shouted. He bent down and

picked up AK-47s as he went. By the time he got to the cabin he had five slung over his shoulder.

"Roger, Ambassador!" Pancho shouted back. The train smelled like a slaughterhouse.

"You guys okay?" Alex asked.

"If we'd known you were coming, we'd have saved some for you," Pancho said.

"Any bandits left alive?"

"If they are they aren't saying," John said.

Alex nodded. "They've got cell phones here. We've just created an international incident. We need to get off this train, now."

"You realize it's still moving?" Pancho asked.

"Think of it as parachuting, without the parachute."

Pancho smiled. "Okay, you lead the way, Chief."

The Outcasts policed up their gear, threw the extra AKs out the window, and hurried down to the end of the car.

The noise was loud, and judging by how fast the shrubbery was passing by, the train was still moving at a pretty good clip.

"We'll never survive a jump going this fast," John shouted.

"It slows down when it takes a curve. We just have to time it right," Alex said, hoping he wasn't imagining that fact. A few minutes later, the train began to lean to the left as it started to go around a bend. Yes, it was slowing, although not by much.

"This is our stop," he said, motioning with his hand to the open air. "Jump!"

Pancho went first, followed by John a split second later. Alex drew in a breath and went after them. His boots hit the ground and he managed two steps before momentum drove him into the ground and he rolled and slid the next fifteen feet.

He got up, spitting dirt out of his mouth to see Pancho and John jogging toward him. Thank God no one twisted an ankle.

"I saw a burned-out warehouse a few hundred yards back just

before we jumped," Pancho said. "Not much, but it'll give us a chance to hole up and get situated."

Alex nodded. "Lead the way."

As hides went, it wasn't much, but it would do. They crawled around the burnt timbers and crumbled masonry until they found a small hollow that would fit all three of them. They crawled inside and waited until it was completely dark out.

"Do you know where we are?" John asked.

Surprising himself, Alex did. "We're ten klicks from our target. We just have to follow the tracks for another six then angle due north."

"With half the Pakistani police and military looking for us," Pancho said.

"Maybe, maybe not," Alex said. "We're rough and ragged looking, the firefight was confusing as hell, and we saved the lives of those passengers. Maybe it'll go down as a fight between two sets of bandits."

Judging by the looks on their faces, Pancho and John weren't buying it. Alex didn't, either, but it didn't matter. They were getting the Red Sheik tonight.

When it was pitch dark and no sound from people or vehicles could be heard, Alex led them back out of the warehouse and onto the deserted dirt path. A beat-up taxi was parked thirty feet down the road, the driver leaning against it while having a smoke.

"We'll grab his ride, tie him up, and head for the Red Sheik's place," Alex said.

"We're really winging this now, aren't we," Pancho said.

"This place is going to get molten hot. If we don't move now, we won't get another chance," Alex said. He knew the prudent course would be to abort and get the hell out of Dodge, but then there was a reason he had been chosen to lead the Outcasts.

They used the cover of a ditch to approach the taxi driver unseen. Alex stepped onto the path first, scaring the man so much his cigarette dropped from his mouth and into the folds of his shirt.

"Easy, we just—" That was as far as Alex got when John appeared and cracked the driver on the side of the head with his rifle butt, dropping the man to the ground.

"No time to be nice," John said, leaning down and dragging the man off the path.

Alex sighed, but climbed into the taxi with the other two. Pancho got behind the wheel. After a couple of false starts, the tiny engine coughed to life and they rattled off.

They got to the outskirts of an affluent neighborhood outside of Islamabad. They ditched the taxi and moved into the brush, angling their way toward the Red Sheik's house.

His estate remained quiet. No lights shone, and there were no signs of security or other personnel. The grass had grown long and was burned out in one spot.

"Nobody's home," Pancho whispered.

"Maybe it's a trap," John said.

They put on their NVGs. Alex could see infrared lasers criss-crossing the backyard—an outdoor security system. "Let's go," Alex said.

The Outcasts proceeded, stepping over the lasers until they reached the back door. There Pancho and Alex held their weapons ready while John picked the first of two locks. The second was un-locked. John opened the door and Pancho slipped inside first. Alex went second, and he knew John was right behind them. In the front-door vestibule, mail piled up below the mail slot on the door. Pancho peeled right, Alex peeled left, and John had responsibility for the middle of the first room. They methodically searched the bottom floor. There seemed to be no inner alarm system. Then the Outcasts cleared the second floor. Nobody was home.

"You guys keep watch while I try to find out where he's gone to," Alex said.

Still on the second floor, John watched through a back window and Pancho kept an eye out through a front window.

In an office room, Alex searched through desk drawers. "These papers look like they're in Urdu—either of you guys know how to read Urdu?"

"Nope," John answered.

Pancho chuckled.

Alex continued searching for anything he could recognize.

"Let's just scoop up some stuff and take it to Miss Pettigrew," John said.

"Car coming," Pancho said.

"Is it him?" Alex asked.

"Can't see," Pancho replied.

"You guys come here, and let's ambush him in his bedroom."

As they waited to ambush the Red Sheik, the driver stepped out of a BMW. She was a woman.

"Now what?" Pancho asked.

"I'm thinking," Alex answered.

"Think faster," John said.

The woman was in her twenties and wore a hip belt that sparkled in the moonlight. Her plunging neckline showed cleavage—not the modesty of the average Pakistani woman. She had an oval face with a perfectly straight nose. Her brown hair curled and flowed to her shoulders.

The woman used the keys in her hand to open the front door. She walked in. Then she walked out with an expensive-looking vase and put it in her car. Next, the woman returned and took a painting out to her car. "We need the PC hard drive to find out where the Red Sheik and Damien are," Alex whispered. "We've got to stop her before she takes the PC."

Alex crept out of the bedroom and stood beside the wall next to the stairs. Pancho and John followed. Alex motioned for them to stand by.

The woman returned and picked up something. When she went outside, Alex descended the stairs with his partners. He pointed for Pancho and John to take positions next to the front door with him. The woman walked through the doorway. The Outcasts took her down and bound her hands and feet.

She pleaded in English, "I sorry. I give. I give. I sorry."

"Where is the Red Sheik?" Alex asked.

"He go Paris. He say want see Paris again before die. Red Sheik die Paris."

"Where in Paris?"

"Condo. Red Sheik has condo."

"What is the address?"

"I not know."

"He's planning an attack in the U.S."

"I not know."

"Where in the U.S.?"

"He not tell me."

"Who are you?"

"I Red Sheik girlfriend."

"Where are you taking his things?"

"I tell you. He go Paris. Die in Paris. He not need things."

"Did he tell you to take his things?"

"He die. Not need things. I take."

Alex grabbed her by the neck. "Did he tell you to take his things?"

"Not need things. I give you. I sorry. I give you. I sorry."

Alex released his grip. "Who are you?"

"I Ziynet. Ziynet Mehmet."

Alex looked at John and said, "Check her car for ID."

John left then came back with a purse. He opened it, looked in her wallet, and pulled out an ID card. "Ziynet Mehmet."

"What do we do with her?" Pancho asked.

"Let's check the PC notebook." Alex walked over to the PC notebook, turned it on, and searched the hard drive for *Paris*.

"Find anything?" John asked.

"Urdu and Arabic. I can't read hardly any of this," Alex said.

"Cat can read the Arabic," Pancho said.

"Well, she isn't here now," Alex snapped.

Pancho laughed, followed by John.

"Let's take the notebook and have this woman drive us to Commissioner Gordon's," John said. *Commissioner Gordon* was their code word for the CIA station chief's residence. The whole Batman theme for code words was fine until Alex became Batman. Neither Pancho nor John wanted to be Robin. So Alex stayed with the codename *Ambassador*.

"Yeah," Pancho agreed.

"Okay," Alex decided. He put the PC notebook in his backpack. "Ziynet, we need you to drive us to Diplomatic Enclave, Ramna 5." Using his pocket knife, he cut the flexicuffs off her wrists, pulled out a wad of Pakistani money, and gave it to her. "I'll give you the rest of the money when we arrive. Do you understand?"

She nodded.

Alex cut the flexicuffs off her ankles. "Let's go."

Ziynet and the three Outcasts left the house and loaded into her car. Ziynet drove. Pancho, who was more likely to pass for Pakistani than Alex or John, sat next to her. Alex rode behind Ziynet—if she gave them trouble, it was the Outcasts' understanding that Alex would kill her. Beside Alex sat John.

Without buckling up, she started the vehicle and put it in drive. The Outcasts put on their seat belts.

Pancho turned to her and said, "You can put on your headlights."

Startled, she did as he said.

Alex hoped she wouldn't have a nervous breakdown before they arrived at the embassy.

"You'll be okay. We just want to go to Ramna 5. After you drop us off, you'll have some extra money, and you'll be free."

Ziynet forced a smile.

Periodically, Alex glanced out the window behind him. They were the only ones on the road.

The first minutes of the ride remained quiet until Pancho broke the silence. "How'd you meet the Red Sheik?"

"The Sultan ask me dance. Red Sheik happy, so I go him."

"Do you like dancing?"

"Yes. But no like them."

"Why not."

"They scare me."

"Why dance for them?"

"The money is good."

"I understand."

"Why you do this?" she asked.

"This job?"

"Yes. Why this job?"

"The food. And a place to stay."

"Why not other job?"

"Because these two guys"—he pointed his head at Alex and John—"are my brothers."

"They don't look brothers."

"They're not really my brothers, but they are like my brothers."

"You have real brothers?"

He paused. "Yes. Do you?"

"No. Only sisters."

"There's a police car behind us," Alex said calmly.

# 36

Pancho and John turned around to look behind them.

"Everyone turn around at once," Alex said sarcastically. "We want to let them know we're worried about them."

Ziynet looked in her rearview mirror, then turned her head around to look at the police. She veered toward the middle of the road.

Alex shook his head.

Ziynet slowed down.

John picked at his clothing like he was removing lint.

Minutes later the police flashed their lights, sounded their siren, and called out over a loudspeaker. The Outcasts didn't have to understand the words to know that they were being pulled over.

"What do?" Ziynet asked.

"Just do what the police say," Alex said.

She pulled over to the side of the road, stopped, and turned off the engine.

A Pakistani policeman approached their car and spoke with Ziynet. As they spoke, the police officer glanced at Pancho. When the policeman looked in the backseat and saw Alex and John, his eyes stopped—staring.

Ziynet spoke. She seemed to be explaining her passengers.

The policeman frowned.

Alex handed him some money.

The policeman stopped frowning, but he wasn't smiling.

Alex gave him some more.

Now he smiled. The policeman said something and walked back to his car. The patrol car's engine started, then he drove away.

Ziynet's hands tightly gripped the steering wheel.

Pancho put his hand on hers. "It's okay. You did great."

"We need to get moving again," Alex said.

"Are you okay?" Pancho asked her.

She nodded. In what seemed to be an afterthought, Ziynet started the car. She sat staring straight ahead. She stepped on the accelerator while the vehicle was still in park. When she realized the car wasn't moving, she put the car into drive, spinning the tires and swerving out of control until Pancho reached over and stepped on the brake. He put it in park. "Maybe I should drive," Pancho said. He looked back to Alex for approval.

Alex nodded.

Pancho looked at Ziynet. He motioned that they should exchange seats. She nodded and they did.

Pancho buckled up and recommended Ziynet do the same. She followed his advice as he started the engine and drove confidently back onto the road.

Ziynet's hands trembled.

"It's okay." Pancho tried to reassure her. "You're doing okay."

She nodded as if she wanted to believe him.

"You said that the Red Sheik went to Paris. Why does he like Paris so much?"

"He like everything Paris—food, clothes—everything."

"What does he like the most?"

"Most?"

"You said he liked your dancing. Does he like any dancers in Paris?"

"Have you been to Paris?"

Pancho chuckled. "More than once."

"He talk Hustler Club and girl name Colette."

"I know the club," Pancho said. "But I don't know Colette. Is she a dancer?"

"Yes. He say Colette like men and women."

Ahead of them in the headlights two trucks blocked the road. Pancho slowed down. Two men armed with AK-47s stood between the trucks and the Outcasts while two more men remained in the trucks. "Alex?"

"Let's try to pay them off," Alex said.

Pancho stepped on the brake, stopping in front of the trucks. He left the engine running, just in case. The two men sauntered over to the Outcasts' vehicle.

Alex gave Pancho a handful of Pakistani money.

Pancho rolled down his window enough that he could fit the money through. The armed man stopped in front of Pancho's door and spoke with garlic breath. Pancho responded by pushing the money through the crack in the window. The armed man's anger dissipated as he took the money and counted it.

Meanwhile, his partner, who had a face full of craters, noticed Alex and John in the backseat and started shouting and pointing at them.

Garlic Breath stopped counting his money and looked. When he saw Alex and John, Garlic Breath raised his AK-47.

Alex put a 9mm round in Garlic Breath's forehead. John squeezed the trigger on his HK416, silencing Crater Face. Pancho shifted into low gear and accelerated, plowing a path between the two trucks. Ziynet screamed. The Outcasts passed the trucks and the men inside sprayed at them with their AKs. Pancho shifted into drive and floored the accelerator. Alex and John pressed the muzzles of their weapons against the back window and fired at the men in the trucks. The hot shell casings ejected from the Outcasts' weapons bounced around in the car. Ziynet screamed again when one of the hot shell casings hit her. The men in the trucks stopped shooting. Probably out of ammo, but maybe they were dead. Alex expected the former but hoped for the latter.

"Are they following us?" Pancho asked.

"Not yet," Alex said.

Pancho asked Ziynet, "Are you okay?"

She didn't reply.

"Are you injured?" Pancho continued.

She sobbed.

"Hurt?"

Ziynet shook her head.

A police siren went off. Instead of moving toward them, the sound of the siren moved away.

After about fifteen minutes, Ziynet began to calm down.

Alex asked, "Ziynet, have you heard anything about the Red Sheik planning a new terrorist attack?"

No answer.

Pancho repeated the question.

"No," she said slowly.

"Are you sure?" Pancho asked.

"Soon. Don't know where."

"Do you know how soon?"

Ziynet shook her head. "I sorry."

Pancho drove until they reached the German embassy, where he stopped the car. He thanked Ziynet as he and his buddies got out of the vehicle. Alex gave her more than enough money for her time and to buy new windows. The Outcasts stood beside the street and waved goodbye.

After Ziynet drove away, the Outcasts hoofed it to the local CIA compound. "I guess I know where we're going next," Pancho said.

Alex nodded.

"Are we going straight there, or are we going home first?" Pancho asked.

"Straight there."

"We could use Cat," John said.

Alex grunted. "Why?"

"I'm the only one who speaks French besides her. And it would look less suspicious to have a woman with us instead of only guys."

"I don't know."

"Not sure what's going on between you two, but you've got to put that aside and focus on the mission," John said.

"I thought that's what I'm doing."

Alex looked at Pancho for help.

"She did a good job, and we could use an extra hand," Pancho said.

*Thanks, buddy*, Alex thought with sarcasm.

The Outcasts met two guards at the CIA compound. After they exchanged bona fides, one of the guards made a call on his radio. He let the Outcasts inside the gate. A third guard appeared and escorted the Outcasts inside a two-story building. In the living room, a CIA operations officer greeted them cordially and offered them a seat. It was the middle of the night, but he looked wide awake. He was a handsome, slender Caucasian man with long brown hair that curled in the back as it reached his collar. "I'm Barry," he said.

The Outcasts introduced themselves.

"We need to go to Paris," Alex said.

"I think the quickest we can get you to Paris is on a civilian flight tomorrow: Pakistan International Airlines. You'll fly to Italy, then ride a train to Paris."

"We'll take it," Alex said.

Barry helped them get settled, then the Outcasts caught some sleep.

The next day, Barry ate breakfast with them at the CIA compound. "What kind of shampoo do you use?" Pancho asked.

"You're giving me a hard time about my hair," Barry said.

"No, I'm jealous," Pancho said. "I wish I had hair like that. Don't you Alex?"

"I don't think it'd suit me, but your hair is beautiful," Alex said.

John snickered, sucking air through his nose.

"So what brought you into this business in the first place?" Barry asked.

"Me?" John asked.

"Barry was looking at you, John," Pancho said.

John said nothing.

Barry's cell phone rang. He answered it, then told the Outcasts, "Sorry, guys, I'm going to take this call in the other room. I'll be right back." He stepped out of the room.

"Trouble with a girl," Pancho spoke for John. "To be more specific, a girl's boyfriend."

"You talk too much," John said.

"Ooh, a little fight in you," Pancho teased. "I like that."

"Nothing happened between us."

"That's the way you like to tell it."

"I was reading her poetry."

"While her parents were away."

John became quiet.

"But you hadn't counted on her boyfriend showing up," Pancho said.

John's eyes narrowed, glaring at Pancho.

"That's enough," Alex said.

"It's not enough," Pancho said. "You haven't had to put up with all his self-righteousness for as long as I have. This girl's boyfriend freaked out and went outside to his truck and grabbed a .38 revolver from the glove compartment. Then he returned inside his girlfriend's house, gun blazing. John even has a scar to show for it."

"Frankie was a control freak who never let her out of his sight," John said. "A control freak with a temper."

"So you killed Frankie with your bare hands. That's when you knew you had a gift—for killing."

"The official verdict was self-defense. Not a gift—more like a curse. I had to leave town, so I went to the armed forces recruiting offices. I went to the air force, but the recruiters weren't in, so I went to the navy recruiter. At boot camp, our company commander made us take the SEAL physical screen test, so we did. I was the only one who passed."

"That's when you began to imagine yourself becoming some kind of modern-day paladin."

"What was I supposed to imagine?"

"All for a girl. I'd like to meet her someday."

John didn't speak.

"Seriously, I've got to meet the woman who transformed you."

John's eyes became distant.

"Aren't you going to introduce her to me someday?" Pancho prodded.

"Not in this lifetime."

"Don't be like that."

"The first bullet struck her near the heart and killed her. The second went through my right thigh. Now you know the rest of the story."

Pancho stared blankly for a moment. "I didn't know. I'm sorry."

"You never know when to shut up, do you?"

Barry returned to the table smiling. "Did I miss anything?"

The Outcasts sat in silence.

In the afternoon, Barry gave them their plane tickets, then two security officers took the Outcasts shopping at a U.S. commissary for clothes and other items. That evening the bodyguards dropped the Outcasts off at Benazir Bhutto International Airport, the third-largest airport in Pakistan, located in Chaklala, Rawalpindi. The airport was named after the former prime minister of Pakistan, the first woman elected to preside over a Muslim country. She was assassinated by al Qaeda.

There were no door entrances to the airport building. Its face opened like a bazaar with a roof over it. Pancho stepped out of their parked vehicle and walked into the airport. The Outcasts would raise less suspicion if they appeared to travel separately.

Alex followed, staying as far away as possible while keeping Pancho within eyesight. Pancho casually looked over his shoulder to make sure Alex was still behind him. Inside the airport, Alex passed busy ticket counters. He glanced over his shoulder to make sure John was right behind. He was. Behind John swaggered five hard-faced Pakistani men. Parts of the Pakistanis' clothes protruded at sharp angles like they concealed weapons underneath. John seemed to notice the hard-faced men, too. Alex stopped to wait in a line to pass through security. The five hard-faced men congregated just inside the building entrance as if their plans didn't involve the Outcasts—Alex hoped that was true.

Alex removed his CRKT Tao pen, wallet, watch, and belt, then put them on a plastic tray. He pushed the tray onto a conveyor belt to be X-rayed by security. Alex slowly walked through the metal detector—clear. His belongings passed through the security X-ray—clear. He retrieved his stuff from the plastic tray and resumed the journey to his gate, keeping his distance behind Pancho.

Alex passed duty-free shops, bookstores, restaurants, banks, a Pakistani handicrafts shop, a prayer room, and other facilities until he reached the waiting area at the gate for Pakistan International Airlines. John arrived, too. Pancho sat nearest the gate. Alex sat in the middle of the waiting area and John took a seat farthest from the gate.

After ten minutes, Alex got up and walked to the restroom. He passed a man on his way out. Inside, the restroom appeared empty—

good, he didn't want any surprises. He stood at a urinal relieving himself when Pancho arrived at the urinal next to him.

"Did you see the five ugly bastards come into the airport after you?" Pancho asked.

"Yep."

"You think they're following us?"

"Didn't seem to but we can't be sure until we get out of here."

"Looked like they were packing."

"Just make sure we get on the plane and that plane gets airborne. We need to catch up to our friend while he's still in Paris."

Alex finished, flushed, and washed his hands. While he dried his hands with hot air, Pancho finished, flushed, and walked out. After drying his hands, Alex returned to his seat in the lobby.

The pre-boarding announcement was made in Urdu, then repeated in English with a Pakistani accent: ". . . We now invite passengers with small children, and any passengers requiring special assistance, to begin boarding at this time. Please have your boarding pass and passport ready. Thank you."

*Come on, come on, people*, Alex thought. *Get your asses on the plane.*

Shots rang out, followed by security alarms. It sounded like the hard-faced men were shooting their way through security. Gradually, the shooting became louder. They were coming.

Alex gestured to Pancho to take cover in the lobby, then he motioned for John to join him in the restroom. Pancho could pass for Pakistani, but Alex's white skin and John's dark skin stood out. John shook his head *no*. Alex took to his feet and crossed the hall. He saw that the hard-faced men had increased in number and were indiscriminately firing at men, women, children, elderly—and Alex. It was obvious that the hard-faced men weren't there to rob; they were there to terrorize. Alex took cover in the restroom. He pulled his pen out of his pocket, unscrewed the cap, then screwed the cap on the butt of the pen, exposing the sharp tip. Alex hid the butt in his right fist with his arm concealing the length and the tip of the pen. He kept his arm to his side to cover the exposed part of the pen—an assassin's grip.

Peeking out from the restroom, he saw Pancho dive to the floor before terrorist bullets tore into the passengers. Some passengers ducked, some pushed their way onto the plane, others scattered, and the remainder, sitting and standing, froze where they were.

John stood behind a wall until a terrorist with an AKS assault rifle neared him. John's left hand grabbed the terrorist's left wrist. John's right hand braced the terrorist's left elbow. Using the terrorist's elbow as a fulcrum, John spun his own body counterclockwise. The terrorist's body spun with John, but John's body spun faster and the weight of the terrorist's body snapped the terrorist's elbow. The snap sounded like the shot from a .22 rifle—the terrorist's feet left the ground and he flew headfirst into a wall. His AKS fell to the floor. John picked it up and shot the terrorist twice in the back.

Shots struck the wall next to Alex, and he ducked back inside the restroom. *Shit*. He waited a moment, then poked his head out from near the floor.

Pancho ran low and hit a terrorist from the side. It looked as if a slow-moving missile had struck the terrorist, folding him in half. The terrorist hit the ground stunned. Pancho picked up his weapon and shot him in the head.

A shot popped past Alex's ear and struck the wall behind him. *Shit!* He ducked back into the restroom. Because Alex was unarmed and didn't appear to pose a threat, it didn't seem like the terrorists were shooting at him on purpose. But the repeated shots in his direction didn't seem to be random, either. Alex wanted to get in the fight, but if he took a bullet through the skull, he wouldn't be getting in any fights. His men were getting shot at, and he wasn't doing anything about it. His frustration increased more and more. An explosion sounding like an RPG went off outside the airport. Alex hoped it wasn't their plane.

The sound of shooting increased in tempo. Either Pancho or John was getting his ass handed to him, or Pancho and John were giving the terrorists a shit sandwich. Alex expected the latter. A terrorist backed into the restroom, pressing Alex to the wall. The terrorist didn't even seem to notice Alex was behind him. Without consciously thinking, Alex shifted his grip on the pen, then raised it and drove it into the terrorist's right temple. With his adrenaline pumping and anxiousness screaming to get in the fight, Alex had driven the pen deeper than he realized. The terrorist dropped to the floor. Alex tried to pull the pen out of the terrorist's skull. In spite of the flutes and grooves on the pen for a better grip, Alex's hand slipped on the warm blood. "Screw it." He left the pen in the terrorist's head and grabbed the guy's AKS and bandolier of ammo. Alex slung the bandolier over his shoulder.

This time when Alex poked his head out of the restroom, he had a loaded AKS. Two terrorists shot up the enormous airport window. Pancho was out of sight, but his voice called out, "Reloading!" That meant Pancho could use some cover fire. John fired back, putting a hole in the upper body of each terrorist. An armed terrorist opened a secure door meant for airport personnel only and started to walk out toward the flight deck when Alex riddled his back with bullets. The terrorist's body fell, blocking the door from closing.

With terrorists' bodies littering the floor and no more in sight, Alex let out a long, slow breath, easing the tension from his muscles. He was still exhaling when an RPG slammed into the side of the plane, blowing a fiery hole into it. Passengers, their faces and clothes blackened by the explosion, stumbled off the airplane and into the lounge. Alex knew that others wouldn't be getting off the plane. His heart sank.

Pancho rose with a *what-the-hell* look on his face.

John looked out the window. "The RPG man must've run away."

"Let's find him," Alex said. "Follow me."

Alex hurried out the secure door, hopping over the corpse blocking the door open. John followed with Pancho hustling to bring up the rear. Alex descended metal stairs until he stepped onto the tarmac. "Cover me," Alex said. He climbed over a shoulder-high metal gate and covered the area in front of him while John climbed over. John would cover Pancho's ass while Pancho climbed over.

The Outcasts hurried out onto the tarmac. A terrorist with an RPG launcher jumped onto a golf cart driven by a terrorist armed with an AKS. The golf cart took off.

A refueling truck sat on the tarmac with its driver sitting petrified behind the wheel. Alex ran to it, opened the passenger door, and jumped in. John followed. Pancho tried to squeeze in, too, but he couldn't fit. "Get in the back," Alex said to Pancho as he pointed behind him.

Pancho backed out of the truck and crawled up into the box behind the truck's cab.

Alex pointed to the terrorists' golf cart and told the truck driver, "Follow that."

The driver looked at Alex as if he was crazy.

"Go!" Alex shouted. "Now!"

The driver put his refueling truck into gear and followed the golf cart.

Alex and John pressed their rifle barrels to the front windshield and blasted out firing holes. Alex aimed at the terrorist on the left, the driver. His shots missed. He knew John would take care of the terrorist on the right wielding the RPG launcher. Pancho fired, too.

The refueling truck driver chattered loudly in Urdu, but Alex and John didn't understand what he was saying. Their truck picked up speed and rammed the golf cart hard enough to give the terrorists whiplash. *Sweet*. The impact slowed the truck but sped up the cart. Alex fired and hit the terrorist driving the cart. The cart ceased accelerating.

The refueling truck driver seemed to enjoy himself as he rammed the cart again. Once again the truck slowed and the cart sped up, then the cart came to a stop. The refueling truck driver was speeding up to ram the cart again but Alex told him, "It's okay. Good job." The refueling truck driver hit the golf cart one last time anyway. Alex gestured and told him to stop the truck. He stopped.

The three SEALs unassed the truck and raced around to the cart. As they reached it, they each opened up, their bullets striking the terrorists again. If they weren't dead before, they were now.

"Where were they going?" Alex asked.

Pancho pointed ahead to a private jet and service vehicles parked on the runway. "There."

"Maybe that's how they planned to escape," Alex said. "Let's ask our friend to take us over there."

They mounted the truck again, and the driver took them across the tarmac to the private jet. When they reached within thirty yards of the plane, AK fire greeted them. The SEALs shot back. The firing ceased. Alex motioned and asked the driver to stop. The driver slammed on the brakes with enthusiasm—almost putting Alex and John's heads through the windshield. The refueling truck screeched to a halt.

The Outcasts dismounted the truck and raced to the plane. One of the terrorists lay dead on the ground. Alex climbed up an air ladder. He stepped through the door and turned aft. He quickly proceeded through a single aisle. John would secure the cockpit, and Pancho would cover their rear. An AKS fired and John called, "Tango down."

Alex moved quickly aft with his AKS aimed in front of him. A terrorist was holding the muzzle of his AKS against the back of an elderly Pakistani man wearing a well-tailored suit. The terrorist yelled, ranting and raving in Urdu.

Alex's AKS had been shooting a little high and right, so he aimed a little low and to the left of the center of the tango's face. After Alex squeezed the trigger, the tango's face sprayed a small mist of crimson, head jerking back. "Tango down," Alex said. As Alex followed through to make sure there were no more tangos hiding out aft of the plane, he felt relief that the immediate threat was removed and the hostage (called "hotel" from the military phonetic of the first letter in "hostage") was safe.

After clearing the plane, Alex checked the hotel. "You okay?"

"You saved my life," the businessman said.

"Where you flying to?" Pancho asked.

"England," the businessman said. "I work in telecommunications. I'm so glad you men were here." His English was excellent.

"We were heading to Italy, but our plane was hit by an RPG," Pancho said.

"If you like, I can take you to Italy," the businessman offered.

"I was hoping you'd say that," Pancho asked.

"It's the least I can do."

# 37

Alex, Pancho, and John flew to Italy, then rode a train to Paris, where they caught a taxi to the Hotel Le Bristol at 112 rue du Faubourg St.-Honoré. The hotel was an elegant palace nearly one hundred years old. Inside, courteous staff greeted them and helped them check into four suites. Pancho and John's suites were joined together, and across the hall, Alex and Cat's suites were also joined together.

Alex entered his spacious room, decorated in Louis XV and XVI style with original paintings. Fresh fruit on a platter and champagne had been placed on the table. The marble bathroom had a double washbasin, bidet, and separate shower. Alex stepped over to the window and saw a huge garden.

A few minutes before 2300 hours, Alex and Pancho dressed up to go out and met in John's room. "Why aren't you getting ready?" Pancho asked.

Sitting on the couch, John looked up from his Bible. "Because I'm not going."

"Why not?"

"Why should I?"

"We're going to find the Red Sheik and we need your French skills."

"Just call me when the shooting starts."

"What good are you here?"

"Cat may show up early."

"She's not going to show up early."

"What if she does?"

"There ain't nothin' new in that Bible that you didn't read the first hundred times."

"It's still useful."

"It'll be useful if I run out of toilet paper."

"Let it go," Alex said. "He can stay here and wait for Cat."

"Suit yourself," Pancho said.

Alex and Pancho finished dressing, caught a taxi to the metro, and rode the metro to the George V Station. From there they walked along the rue de Berri, near the Champs-Élysées, until they came to an entrance that read in neon light, LARRY FLYNT'S HUSTLER CLUB PARIS—OPEN.

They strolled into the spacious club, which was dimly lit, mostly red: lights, bar, floors, padded walls, and stuffed couches. Alex paid the entrance fee of thirty euros each, which included one drink apiece. A few of the areas were colored violet. From where Alex stood, he could see only three poles on the stage and one dancer shaking her assets as she removed her bikini top. The other women, about twenty-five in number and representing a variety of European types, were scattered throughout the bar. Some roamed the club, others sat with customers on the couches, and a few were giving personal table dances. Waitresses walked around serving drinks. Alex scoped the place for exits in case they had to suddenly bug out. It had become a subconscious habit when going to any new place, indoors or out: finding an escape route.

Strippers eyed Alex and Pancho as the two walked through the club. Pancho chose a violet couch in the middle of the place. There the two SEALs took a seat behind a small table with a little yellow lamp on it. Alex scanned the club for the Red Sheik, but he was nowhere to be found.

A waitress greeted them in French.

Pancho replied in English, "A martini with three olives for my friend and a Cuervo Gold for me." Alex and Pancho gave her their admission tickets. Then Pancho handed her his credit card. "Put the rest of the drinks on our tab."

"Yes," she said in English.

"What's your name?" Pancho asked.

"Suzanne," she said.

"Great."

She stepped away to bring their drinks. Pancho and Alex lit up cigars. No sooner had they taken a couple of puffs when the first two women approached their table. They were young, but they weren't the most attractive women in the room. The pair quickly asked Alex and Pancho if they wanted a table dance.

"Whoa, darling," Pancho said. "We just got here."

Alex smiled politely.

They chatted a little before the girls lost patience and left.

Suzanne brought their drinks and then three new women, more attractive than the first two, approached Alex and Pancho's table. The black-haired one gave Pancho a free table dance while the blonde sat next to him. The black-haired girl seemed equally interested in the blond beauty sitting next to Pancho. A platinum blonde chatted up Alex, but he wasn't interested in her mindless chitchat, and she migrated over to Pancho.

A girl in her early twenties with shoulder-length curly black hair appeared beside Alex, catching him by surprise. "I'm Brigitte," she said with a French accent.

"Alex."

"Is someone with you?"

He shook his head.

"May I sit?"

He smiled and gestured for her to sit.

She was more easygoing than the others. *"Merci."* Her graceful descent on the couch lit a slow burn in Alex.

"You're drinking a martini."

"Is that bad?"

*"Non.* Not many people in here drink martinis."

"Would you like a drink?"

"Cognac would be nice."

Alex flagged down the waitress and ordered a drink for Brigitte.

"You from around here?" Brigitte asked.

"Germany. How about you?"

"I live here in Paris. Why is your English so good?"

"I studied in Canada for a while."

"What did you study?"

"Business management. That's what I do now. I'm on vacation. You been working here long?"

"I'm an art student, but I ran out of money, so I started working here a year ago, so I could stay in college. Paris is expensive."

"Oh."

The waitress brought Brigitte her cognac. She took a sip. "Do you have a girlfriend?"

Alex thought about Cat, especially how she tempted him to leave the Teams. "Friend."

Brigitte smiled.

As they continued talking, Alex felt the beat of the club music pulse through his veins. Pancho strolled by with the blond- and black-haired gals. He dropped a stack of pink tickets in Alex's lap. Pancho and the girls disappeared into the back VIP room.

"I'm sorry," Brigitte said. "It's my turn to dance." She touched him on the shoulder before leaving. His eyes followed her as she glided across the club and up the stairs to the stage.

Brigitte swayed and Alex felt the air begin to heat up. As she danced, her eyes made contact with Alex's.

When she returned to her seat beside Alex, they resumed their conversation. "Do you know a girl named Colette?"

"She's pretty popular, but she hasn't been around here for a few weeks. I think she has a new boyfriend. Why do you ask?"

"A friend of mine said he knows her and she works here."

"Would you like a private dance?"

Alex hesitated. A private dance could have a variety of meanings, but he wasn't exactly sure what it meant at the Hustler Club in Paris. He nodded.

She took him by the hand and led him into the VIP room, where it was darker than the rest of the dimly lit club. Brigitte motioned for him to sit on the couch. She stood between his legs. Her legs forcefully spread his apart. The song "Porn Star Dancing" by My Darkest Days played and she slowly wrapped herself around him as she leisurely unwrapped her clothing—until the last of her clothing hit the floor. She continued to dance for him until the song ended. Watching her put her clothes back on was almost as exciting as watching her take them off.

"I'm kind of embarrassed to say this, but the dance is two pink tickets," she said.

"Sure." Alex gave her two of the pink tickets Pancho had given him.

As Brigitte and Alex left the VIP room, he spotted the blond- and black-haired girls twisted around Pancho like pretzels. It wasn't clear where their bodies ended and his began. Back at the violet couch in the club Brigitte talked some more before Alex asked, "Do you know an Arab-Pakistani man called the Red Sheik? I hear he does a lot of importing and exporting."

"I've seen him in here, but I don't talk to him," she said with distaste.

"You sound like you don't like him."

"You don't want to do business with him."

"Why is that?"

"He is not like you. He is a pig."

They talked some more, and she gave him more private dances in the VIP room. Time raced away. Then she disappeared into the restroom. When she came back, Brigitte showed him a cocktail napkin with her phone number on it. "Shh," she whispered. "We're not supposed to exchange phone numbers." She looked around for a moment, then put the cocktail napkin in his pocket. "Can I see you tonight?" Brigitte nibbled on his ear.

"I don't think that's such a good idea."

"You can come to my place. If your girlfriend doesn't know, it can't hurt her. Even if I knew her, I wouldn't tell."

"I have work to do."

"Tonight?"

"Tomorrow. I have to wake up early."

"You look strong enough to still wake up early."

"My friend isn't my girlfriend, but she's more to me than a friend."

Brigitte kissed him on the lips. "I can be more to you than a friend." Her hands caressed his body and her breaths became more rapid.

Alex could spend the night with her and still complete the mission. It wouldn't be wise, but he could. Yes, Cat irritated him with her suggestion that he leave the Teams, but Alex still had feelings for her. His body said yes to Brigitte, but his mind said no.

He tried to keep her hands away from his SIG, but eventually she found it. Alex thought she'd be scared, but it only fanned her flame. Pancho had disappeared into the VIP room again, and Alex wanted to wait for him to return, but he had no idea how much longer that would be. He stood up. "I'm sorry." He hurried to the VIP room. There a bouncer tried to prevent him from entering alone, but Alex brushed the bouncer aside.

Inside the VIP room, Alex found a shirtless Pancho buried under naked women. He called Pancho. When Pancho looked up, Alex gestured as if his parachute had failed and he was pulling his breakaway chute. Pancho jumped, bumping the girls off, and he grabbed his shirt. The girls stared at him with puzzled faces. He dropped his stack of pink tickets on the couch and followed Alex out of the VIP room.

The bouncer approached Alex again, but now that he was with Pancho, the bouncer decided against getting physical and stepped aside to let them pass. When Alex passed Brigitte, her eyes seemed sad.

Pancho had his shirt on, but he didn't bother to button it as he and Alex hurried out the front door of the club.

Outside, Pancho's hand was at the ready on his pistol, which was concealed on his hip, beneath his trousers and open shirt. Pancho scanned the area frantically. "Where's the threat?!"

"We had to get out of there," Alex explained while they put as much distance as they could between them and the club.

"Where are the bad guys?!" Pancho continued searching with his eyes.

"Brigitte was about to rape me."

"Are you serious?! That's why you gave the breakaway signal?!"

"Yes."

"Don't be a damn idiot—you should've let her rape you! She was hot! My girls were hot!"

Alex said nothing.

"What were you thinking?!" Pancho continued to swear.

Alex maintained his silence.

"Don't look now," Alex whispered. "I think we're being followed."

"By who?"

"No idea."

"Tangos, thugs, police?"

"Don't know. Follow me." Alex took Pancho down one side

street—then another. He found streets with multiple roads leading in and out. Their pursuers were forced to follow closer in order not to lose them. However, the moves were natural enough that the pursuers might not know Alex and Pancho knew they were being followed.

"Looks like there's two of them," Pancho said.

"Not very discreet, are they?"

"Should we take 'em?"

"Not tonight. Unless they corner us."

"Maybe we should let them corner us."

A lone taxi neared them on the street. Alex waved it down. The taxi stopped next to the two SEALs and they hopped into the backseat. "Take us to the nearest hotel, please," Alex said.

The taxi driver acknowledged Alex and sped away.

"Brigitte said Colette hasn't been to the club in a while," Alex said quietly. "She also knew of our man but didn't have direct contact with him."

"Well, I got this." Pancho showed him a cocktail napkin with a phone number on it.

Alex seemed puzzled.

"His cell phone number," Pancho said. He had found out the Red Sheik's number.

Alex grinned.

# 38

Damien and Mohammed boarded the New York City subway at 125th Street in East Harlem and rode south, getting off at West Thirty-Fourth Street and Sixth Avenue. From there they walked east to the Empire State Building. There Damien used his digital camera to film the skyscraper on the west, north, east, and south sides.

Mohammed asked, "Do you believe in Islam?"

"How do you come up with these questions?"

"You never talk about these things."

"No."

"What do you believe in?"

"I believe in light and darkness—me—and you. My family was always bright and cheerful. Our home was always filled with light—not just the kind you see but the feeling of light. One day as a child, I saw a bird on a fence post. I threw a rock at it and knocked it off the post. When I took a closer look, it was dead. I felt a darkness come over me that I'd never known before. I was repulsed and yet it was so beautiful. From that moment, I wanted to keep the feeling forever."

"Is that when Grandfather and Grandmother died?"

"No. Over the years they started to suspect something was *different* about me, but they didn't know what. I overheard them talk about taking me to see a psychiatrist or a priest. I worried they were going to try to change me. I even thought about killing them. But we were in a car accident, and they died. It was the first time I'd ever seen humans die before my eyes—they were so beautiful—twisted and bloody under the moonlight."

"Then you went to live with your uncle and aunt."

Damien nodded. "They fulfilled their obligation to feed, clothe, and shelter me. Other than that, they left me alone. And I left them alone."

Damien and Mohammed slipped inside the three-story lobby, where a scale model of the building stood. They rode inside a gold-colored elevator up eighty floors. After exiting the elevator, they rode another elevator that greeted them in multiple languages while they ascended to the eighty-sixth floor. There they walked outside to the observation deck and viewed the city in all four directions.

Mohammed filmed Park Avenue from the north, where he and his father would drive the explosives-filled UPS truck south until they turned right on Thirty-Third Street and rolled through the freight entrance of the Empire State Building. There they'd park underneath the building, set the explosive charges, and walk away to an SUV filled with armed men. The SUV would be backed up by another SUV filled with more armed men. If Damien, Mohammed, and their cell had to, they could fight their way out of New York City.

# 39

The next day, Alex, Pancho, and John went to visit the CIA station. As they waited in the reception room, Pancho muttered, "I hear the Paris chief is an asshole."

"He never served as a case officer or even recruited an agent," John said. "He's a desk commando."

The case officers were the heart of the CIA. They were the ones who put their lives on the line recruiting foreign agents in hot spots and armpits around the world. With their boots on the ground, not only did they gather intelligence, but they could interpret the intelligence based on the context it occurs in—something that technological gizmos, doodads, and their technicians have difficulty doing.

"The chief will see you now," the receptionist said.

Inside the office, the chief had papers spread out on his desk and a side table. Papers were stacked on his file cabinet and bulging out of binders on his shelves. He began the conversation.

"Which one of you is in charge?"

"I am, sir," Alex said.

"Then you two can wait in the reception room." The chief dismissed Pancho and John with a wave of his hand.

Pancho and John stepped out of the office, closing the door behind them.

"What is it?" the chief asked.

Alex held a paper in his hand. "I have a request I need your support on, sir."

"What kind of request?"

"I need help in finding an address in connection with a cell phone number."

"Sounds big."

"We believe a senior al Qaeda leader, known as the Red Sheik, is here in Paris. Planning an attack in the U.S."

"What about our French liaison?"

"The French have some excellent intelligence officers, but the man in charge now isn't one of them."

"I never handle this sort of thing." The chief looked down at his desk.

Alex stood staring at him in disbelief.

The chief looked up at him. "Why are you still standing there?"

"We just came from Pakistan, where our assets were killed and we barely escaped ourselves. We flew from Pakistan to Italy, then rode a train from Italy to Paris. As soon as we arrived, we went to work in gathering intel on our target. We were followed by a surveillance team last night, and we didn't return to our rooms until early morning. I got no sleep because I worked the rest of this morning writing this request. I would really be grateful if you could take a moment to look at this." Alex stepped forward and handed him the paper.

The chief stared at Alex.

Alex stared back.

The chief reluctantly took the paper and glanced over it. "Okay. I looked at it."

"He's planning an attack on American soil. Do you want to be the one responsible for what happens next?"

The chief looked at the paper again.

Alex figured he had touched a nerve in the chief, who seemed to avoid responsibility—choosing the path of least resistance.

"Things are running smoothly here, and we don't want any trouble."

"So you're saying you'll take responsibility for all American deaths that result from your inaction?"

"No. I'm saying I can't help you." He returned the paper to Alex.

"I'm sure you're good at managing budgets and personnel changes." Alex looked at all the paperwork in the office. "And paperwork. But I need help on this operation."

"I don't lead operations, I represent the director."

"After I report this, I'm sure the president will be disappointed— and if the terrorists succeed, America will mourn your inaction." Alex turned and headed for the door.

"Hey!"

Alex stopped and turned around.

"Give me that."

Alex gave him the paper.

"You'd better handle this quietly. Or you'll spend the rest of your life in a French jail—if you're lucky."

"Thank you, sir."

"If you're unlucky—well, I won't be in attendance at your funeral."


ON THE FOLLOWING DAY, Alex, Pancho, and John watched CNN in the common area of their suite. "I'm hungry," Pancho said.

"You just ate," John said.

"That was a snack. I need lunch."

A coded knock sounded at the door—two knocks followed by three. They knew who it was. Just to be safe, Alex looked through the peephole. He opened the door and she walked in with a valet pulling a cart of luggage. Cat tipped the valet. He said *merci* and left her and the guys alone.

"I heard you guys needed some ammo and other supplies, so I brought a few things with me," she said.

They thanked her.

Alex said, "We have a cell phone number for the Red Sheik. We need SIGINT to triangulate it to give us an address."

"Have you eaten lunch, Cat?" Pancho asked.

"No," she said.

Pancho smiled.

"Where should we eat?" Alex asked.

"I made reservations at the Jules Verne in the Eiffel Tower," John said. "I told Pancho it's a tourist trap, but he insisted."

"How'd you get reservations—Jules Verne is usually so packed?" Cat asked.

John grinned.

"He went in person and the lady was quite friendly," Pancho said. "Even gave him her phone number. But dumbass probably won't call her."


THE OUTCASTS ATE LUNCH 410 feet aboveground on the second level of the Eiffel Tower in the expensive Le Jules Verne restaurant. While looking at the view of Paris, they ate beef tournedos, duck foie gras, escargot, macaroons, homemade rose marshmallows, truffles, potatoes soufflé, cheese, raspberry sorbet, and red chocolate—all with a bottle of wine. Over the course of the meal, Alex's and Cat's eyes avoided each other.

After lunch, the four took the private elevator up for the view of Paris from the top of the tower. Alex and Cat continued to avoid each other.

Alex, John, and Cat voted to visit the Louvre museum, where they saw Canova's *Psyche Revived by Cupid's Kiss* among the statues. John and Pancho bugged out early.

Alex and Cat toured the museum. Alex lingered at da Vinci's *Mona Lisa*. "What are you thinking about?" Cat asked.

"I'm thinking, *what is she thinking about?* Am I strange for thinking about her so often?"

"I think it's beautiful that she has someone who cares so much. It must've been hard."

"You're the only one I can talk to about these things."

"If it helps to talk about it, I'm happy to listen."

"After she was gone, the city tore down the post office. I went by there once, but it was so empty that I couldn't stand to be near there. I had enough emptiness of my own. The townspeople argued about what to do with the space. Finally, they made a memorial park. Sarah and Grandpa would've liked that. One sunny afternoon I paid a visit. Each person's name was engraved in bronze. My mother had made sure they put Sarah's name next to Grandpa's. It was the most beautiful park I'd ever seen. More than the way it looked, it was the feeling there."

"I'm glad they built a park you liked."

"But I lost weight because I didn't feel like eating. I went to the doc to find out what was wrong with me, and he told me it was depression. It felt like plummeting into the bottom of the ocean. Little things would trigger memories. I'd see kids her age at school and remember her—every day. The first Christmas was tough. Sarah and I had always decorated the tree together. But I couldn't do it alone. Mom ended up decorating the tree that first year. No presents for Sarah. An empty chair at Christmas dinner. For years I dreaded Christmases."

"How'd you get through it?"

Alex thought for a moment. "I tried to live how she'd want me to live. One day when I visited the memorial park I scrolled through old voice messages on my cell phone. I found one from her: 'Don't be discouraged,' she said."

"Was that your key to surviving?"

"I took the first step. Then I did it again—and again. It's how I got through Hell Week—how I made it to the top of the Matter-horn. Learning to believe again is what got me through."

Alex and Cat continued through the museum and enjoyed more of the artwork.

After dinner at a small café, they went for a stroll outdoors until they found a park bench overlooking the Seine. Canoes, rowboats, dinghies, and other vessels sailed by as the sun set. There was an awkward silence between Alex and Cat.

Finally, Alex broke the silence. "When the guys and I rode the submarine to Pakistan, I thought about you. Professionally, I felt bad about not taking you with us. Personally, I missed you."

"You don't have to," she said.

"I don't know what to do."

"Neither do I."

"It's so good to see you and I have so many feelings for you, but I don't think I can give you what you want. And I don't want to mislead you into believing that I can."

"I'd rather feel the way I feel when I'm with you than the way I feel without you."

Alex put his hand on Cat's. The sun glowed orange on the Seine. She put her head on his shoulder.

When the darkness came, they walked back to the hotel and separated to their rooms. Alex wanted to sleep with her, but in his heart he knew he shouldn't. He hoped she'd crawl into his bed because he knew he didn't have the will to resist. When she didn't crawl into his bed, it saddened him, but he knew it was for the better.

Unable to sleep, he wanted to go for a swim, but the pool had closed at 2200 hours and now it was 2300. He left his room and went for a walk. Alex took the stairs down. Above the metal latticework ran a gold-colored handrail that felt warm. The stairs spiraled down around a constellation of lights.

When he reached the lobby, he saw Cat crouched on the floor, petting a fluffy white cat under a crystal chandelier supported by gold-colored supports. She looked so peaceful that he didn't want to disturb her. He thought about quietly leaving, but he couldn't take his eyes off her.

She must've sensed him standing there, because she turned and saw him.

"Where'd the cat come from?" he asked softly.

"Don't know."

"You couldn't sleep, either?"

Cat returned her gaze to the feline. "Thought I'd look around a little. Le Bristol is more than a palace—it's a work of art."

"It is."

"It is but?"

"I'm in Paris, but I haven't seen Paris."

With her head turned down, Cat's eyes looked up and sideways at him, her lips smiling innocently.

Without thinking, he asked, "Would you like to see more of the city?"

"Yes," she said without hesitation.

"Have you ridden a limousine in Paris?"

"No. Have you?"

"No. Would you like to?"

She nodded.

"I'll be right back." He left her petting the cat while he went and asked the concierge to call them a limousine. "Could you also ask the driver to prepare some chocolate and flowers for my friend?" Alex asked.

"Yes, sir," the concierge said in English with a French accent.

Alex returned to Cat, and they pet the feline's marshmallow fur until the concierge came over and told him, "Your limousine is here, sir."

Alex said to the concierge, *"Merci,"* and discreetly tipped him twenty euros. The concierge escorted Alex and Cat past golden pillars, potted flowers on a golden table, and paintings mounted in golden frames on the wall. They strolled through golden revolving doors to the outside, where the air was cold.

On the curb, the driver of a black Mercedes-Benz stretch limousine greeted them and opened the rear door. His skin was pale, and he looked dangerously thin.

Inside the limo felt warm. Alex and Cat sat close to each other on a comfortable brown leather couch. Neon lights illuminated a flat-screen TV with DVD player and sound system. Alex and Cat looked up at nearly the same time and saw themselves in the ceiling mirror. Their lips smiled with amusement and embarrassment. On a counter sat chocolates and roses, filling the limo with their fragrance.

The limousine pulled forward, and they rolled along the rue du Faubourg St.-Honoré. They passed fashionable boutiques and galleries that were closed for the evening. Alex and Cat exchanged glances. He offered her a chocolate. She accepted. Alex ate one, too. He enjoyed the bittersweet taste.

The limo turned right at the avenue de Marigny then made another right at the avenue des Champs-Élysées. Cat fed Alex chocolate. Her hair flowed wild over her shoulders. He fed her chocolate as she touched the power button on the sound system. Classical music played: cello and piano. The strings pulled him to her. Paris lights panned her skin. His lips neared hers. Hers neared his.

"This was a bad idea," he said.

"Terrible."

"We should stop."

"Right now."

The more he tried to resist, the harder the strings pulled, so he stopped resisting. Their lips touched.

His hands explored her and her hands explored him. At the edge of Alex's vision, his eyes met the driver's eyes in the rearview mirror. Then the privacy glass rose and the driver disappeared from Alex's sight.

"Did you raise the privacy glass?" Cat asked.

"No, did you?"

"No. Must've been the driver."

"He's a bad driver," Alex said.

"Terrible. What should we do?"

"I should shoot him."

"Don't shoot him."

"Why not?"

"Shoot me."

They kissed. Through the side window, the Eiffel Tower glowed in gold light, rising high among the starry buildings. The limo circled the tower once. Then twice. Round and round; soon Alex lost count.

They traveled north on avenue George V, returning to the Champs-Élysées, where their vehicle turned left and traveled northeast. Her skin smelled like apricot.

The limo passed the Charles de Gaulle–Étoile metro station. Continuing northwest, they crossed over the Seine and rode into the business district of La Défense, with its shining lights stretching up into the sky. They cruised by the Grande Arche and its golden water fountains.

Then the limousine circled the Arc de Triomphe, standing 164 feet tall and 72 feet deep, glowing gold. Around and around they circled the arch. Time melted into a blur.

Alex removed her blouse.

She opened his shirt, exposing his broad shoulders.

"Do you think you could close the curtains?" she asked.

He reached behind her and undid the clasp on her bra. "Don't you want to see Paris?"

Her warm breath touched his ear. "I don't want to see Paris; I want to feel it."

He closed the curtains.

# 40

Early the next morning, while Cat slept, Alex quietly walked into the common area of their suite—he had a terrorist to kill. Alex took a seat on the couch and checked his laptop to find an encrypted message from the Paris CIA chief: the Red Sheik's address. Alex used Google Maps for overhead views. Google was faster than going through government red tape for a current satellite photo.

After the others woke, the Outcasts ate breakfast, then in pairs rode two taxis to within four blocks of the Red Sheik's building. They walked the perimeter of the four-block square, spying toward the center, searching for any dangers, such as a countersurveillance team. When they found none, they closed in another block and surveyed the area. They continued closing in concentric squares until they had scoped out the whole area surrounding the Sheik's building.

From atop a building, while Cat kept a lookout around them, Alex peered over a low wall through pocket-sized waterproof Bushnell binoculars with antiglare coating, enhanced light transmission, and high color contrast. The Red Sheik's place was an older redbrick two-story building sandwiched between two taller buildings. On the center of the Red Sheik's first floor were mounted two security cameras aimed to the left and right.

A deliveryman brought a package to the front door of the Red

Sheik's building. From inside, a stocky man who looked like a body-guard answered the door and signed for the package. Inside the left window on the first floor, there appeared to be another bodyguard.

Through the center window on the second floor, the Red Sheik sat behind a desk looking at some papers. Alex stared past him as if the Red Sheik didn't exist. The Red Sheik looked up from his papers and out the window. Alex realized that maybe the Red Sheik sensed him, and Alex tried to unfocus his mind. The Red Sheik stood, then walked over to the window. Because fast movement might alert the Red Sheik, Alex slowly ducked behind the low wall.

The Outcasts returned to their hotel room and made sandwiches from French bread, meat, lettuce, and cheeses they'd stocked in the refrigerator. Over a late lunch, they planned their attack.

"I'm assuming we're not going to take the Red Sheik alive," John said.

"I used a cutout again to contact DGSE about possible support for a body snatch without saying who we wanted to snatch," Alex said. The Direction Générale de la Sécurité Extérieure (DGSE) was France's intelligence agency. "They promised their support, but later, someone higher up shot it down. So in other words, we're on our own. I want to first capture the Red Sheik alive, then ask him where our last target, Damien, is. More importantly, I want to find out about their attack on the U.S."

Pancho spoke with his mouthful of sandwich. "What do we do with the Red Sheik after you get the information?"

"What we always do," Alex said.

The Outcasts continued planning into the evening. The next day, after coordinating with the CIA's Technical Intelligence (TECHINT) spooks, the Outcasts chose the night for their hit.

# 41

Five minutes before 0300, Cat drove a gray van through the chilly rain on the wet black streets of Paris. As she neared the Red Sheik's building, she slowed down to five miles per hour. A light emitting from the Red Sheik's study on the second floor extinguished as TECHINT cut the building's power and phone lines. TECHINT also jammed cell phone signals.

Alex, Pancho, and John wore black assault gear: helmets, night-vision goggles, bullet-resistant vests, communications gear, sound-suppressed HK416 assault rifles, et cetera.

Out from the side of the moving van the SEALs jumped and advanced to the front door. Alex helped Pancho cover while John picked the lock. When it opened, the trio quietly slipped in.

Alex entered first, sweeping right. Pancho swept left. John came through the center of the room. Alex heard the *phht-phht-phht* of John's sound-suppressed HK416 and a heavy thud like a body hitting the floor. Alex methodically worked his way through his side of the first floor. His NVGs showed everything in 2-D green: dining room, kitchen, and bedroom. In the bedroom, a drowsy bodyguard stirred in his bed until Alex put him into a deep sleep.

By the numbers, the three SEALs worked their way up the stairs. They aimed their HK416 muzzles up, down, and 360 degrees

around. At the top of the stairs, Alex broke right and entered a bedroom, where a bodyguard reached for an AK-47 on the floor near
the bed. Alex stopped him before he reached the weapon.

A muffled scream sounded from the master bedroom on the same
floor. Pancho would be binding up Colette and keeping her quiet
and still.

When Alex entered the study, John already had the Red Sheik
knocked out cold on the Persian rug and the Sheik's hands bound.
Alex helped John bind the Red Sheik's feet. Then Alex sat behind the
Red Sheik and secured him in a light headlock.

Alex snapped at John, "Just keep watch outside."

John stepped out of the room.

The Red Sheik regained consciousness and said, "I've been expecting you."

"I came as fast as I could," Alex said.

"Why haven't you killed me?"

"I have some questions."

The Red Sheik chuckled. "Questions."

"Where's Damien?"

"Damien. Damien said a hundred ghosts can't stop him."

Alex tightened the headlock, stopping the Red Sheik's blood
from reaching his brain. The Red Sheik kicked and squirmed until
he passed out. Then Alex released his grip, allowing the blood to
flow again until the Red Sheik became conscious again. "What's so
funny?" Alex said.

"I'm sorry, little brother. I follow my own nature. Can't make a
river flow uphill."

"Where's Damien?"

"It's too late."

Alex put him to sleep again. When the Red Sheik came to, Alex
brushed his right hand through the Red Sheik's hair, like a parent
consoling a child. Then Alex put him out again. When the Red Sheik
came around, Alex said, "I just want to know where Damien is."

"I don't want to die."

"Most people don't."

"Promise not to kill me."

Alex thought for a moment. "I promise."

"New York."

"Where in New York?"

"He's going to blow up the Empire State Building."

"How?"

"I don't know."

Alex put him out again. When the Red Sheik regained conscious-ness, Alex asked, "How is he going to blow up the Empire State Building?"

"I don't know, little brother. I'm not supposed to know the details."

"When?"

"Now."

"How?!"

"I don't know."

"Don't tell me you don't know." Alex squeezed off the blood cir-culation again, knocking him out. When he came to, Alex asked, "How is Damien going to blow up the Empire State Building?!"

"If I knew, I'd tell you, but I don't know."

"Don't tell me you don't know!" Alex squeezed tight on the Red Sheik until his eyes closed. When Alex released, the Red Sheik's eyes fluttered open in slow motion.

Pancho appeared in the room and aimed his muzzle in Alex's direction. Alex raised a hand and waved Pancho off. They traded a look. Alex knew it had to be done. As the Team leader, it was his duty.

"I can take care of him, Chief," Pancho said, still keeping his weapon trained on the terrorist.

Alex began to squeeze again, cutting off the blood flow to the Red Sheik's brain. This time, when he felt the body go limp, he didn't let go, but kept up the pressure. He stayed like that for a few minutes, staring straight at Pancho. Finally, knowing it was done, he let go. The Red Sheik's body slumped to the floor.

Pancho started to say something, but Alex stood up and cut him off with a look.  It was time to move. "Take us out."

Pancho nodded and led Alex out of the study.

When they linked up with John in the hall, Alex whispered, "Six down, one to go." John followed Alex. The three patrolled down the stairs. When they hit the bottom, they moved to the front door. To Alex's left, a bodyguard with a neck like a tree trunk came out from the bedroom area firing a pistol. One shot struck Alex in the chest before Alex put him down with a burst from his HK416. *Did we miss him when we swept the first floor. Did he come in later?* Even though Alex wore a bullet-resistant vest, the shot punched hard.

Pancho cracked the front door open and waited. The waiting seemed like fifteen minutes, but it had probably been only three. Finally, Cat stopped in front with the gray van. Pancho took his partners to the van and opened the door for them. Alex piled in first, followed by John. Pancho hopped in last.

"Let's go," Pancho said.

The van pulled forward as Cat sped away. The guys stripped off their assault gear and put on civilian clothes. Alex took the passenger seat next to Cat. Police sirens wailed in the distance. The sound became louder and louder.

As Cat made a turn, the sirens faded. "Is anyone following us?" Alex asked.

"Don't think so," Cat said. "But I'll make sure." She made a series of turns to make sure they were clean. Just as she finished, a Police Nationale Renault rolled up behind them with its blue lights flashing and siren blaring. The policeman exited his vehicle. He wore a white shirt and black trousers with a pistol on his belt.

Cat looked over at Alex uneasily. The rain had stopped, so she turned off her windshield wiper. As the police officer approached her window, he looked at Alex. Then he looked into the back at Pancho and John. The police officer looked at Cat and spoke in French. Cat responded in French. He spoke again and Cat showed him her ID: a United States passport with DIPLOMATIC written across the top. He took it and looked inside. He gave it back, then spoke to Alex in French. Alex showed him his diplomatic passport. After returning Alex's passport, the policeman spoke to Pancho and John in the back. They handed him their diplomatic passports, too. The national policeman gave the two back their passports. Dispassionately the policeman spoke to Cat one more time before leaving them. He wheeled away in his police car.

Once more Cat drove a surveillance detection route (SDR) before returning to the hotel. When she was sure they weren't being followed, she parked at their hotel. The Outcasts locked their assault gear in the van. Later, the Agency would come by to take care of the van and the gear.

When the Outcasts returned to their room, Alex sat down on the couch, turned on his laptop, and typed a message.

"Who's the message for?" John asked.

"That's for Miss Pettigrew. We need our gear on a plane ready to fly us from Dam Neck to New York."

# 42

The interior of the barn was dimly lit from above. In the back of the UPS truck, Damien and Mohammed drilled boards into the floor to keep the thirteen barrels from moving around. Using plastic buckets and a weight scale, they mixed ammonium nitrate fertilizer, diesel fuel, liquid nitromethane, and Tovex in eighteen fifty-five-gallon drums. They shaped the barrels of explosives by tamping the walls of the truck with bags of ammonium nitrate fertilizer so that rather than exploding through the truck walls, the barrels would explode in the path of least resistance—upward.

"Is this going to take down the whole Empire State Building?" Mohammed asked.

"Much of it," Damien said. "If we're lucky, all of it."

"How many people will this kill?"

Damien thought about that for a moment. "Hundreds for sure. Depending on many variables, it could reach thousands. The fear it will cause, however, will be the real victory."

Mohammed nodded.

Damien watched his son closely. Mohammed was still not the cold-blooded warrior Damien hoped he would be, but perhaps this would tip the scales in his favor.

Using duct tape, they taped two brown plastic pipes, the same color as the truck, on the floor running between the driver's seat and the explosives. Then they ran two fuses through the tubes, connecting them to blasting caps, which were connected to sausages of Tovex, which would set off the barrels.

# PART THREE

*All men dream, but not equally. Those who dream by night in the dusty recesses of their minds, wake in the day to find that it was vanity: but the dreamers of the day are dangerous men, for they may act on their dreams with open eyes, to make them possible.*
—T. E. LAWRENCE

# 43

At Dam Neck, Alex visited Miss Pettigrew's office and gave her a box of chocolate bonbons. "From Paris," he said.

"They look delicious," she said, taking the box and setting it on her desk.

"I'm in a bit of a rush."

"Men," she said, pouting. "I ran a search and found there were killings near the Texas-Mexico border with a Russian OTs-38 Stechkin. Later, in Charlotte, North Carolina, there were three more killings with the same type of weapon just before a Frito-Lay truck was stolen. After that, near Albany, New York, another killing: a car painter. She was reported missing and the police found her stuffed in a paint drum. New York City is on alert, but it's tough to lock down an entire city without more data."

He thought about the Frito-Lay truck, and it didn't make sense— *was Damien trying to make some kind of statement?* Then he realized something. "Did they say what color the paint was?"

"I'm sorry?"

"Was the paint blue? Or brown. Like a U.S. mail truck or a UPS truck."

Miss Pettigrew looked at her computer screen and tapped the keyboard.

"Brown, but there were several other drums of different colors."

Alex cursed under his breath. "Tell the skipper to warn New York to be on the lookout for a delivery truck, most likely a UPS truck."

Miss Pettigrew looked at him. "There must be hundreds of those in the city. And are you sure it's UPS?"

Alex wasn't sure, but he had a gut instinct, and when all else failed, he listened. "Tell him it's almost certainly going to be filled with explosives."

"Will do." She paused. "What will you do?"

"What I always do." He turned and exited the room.

"Alex," she called.

He stopped and turned around.

"Be careful," she said. "And next time you're in Paris, bring back perfume."

ALEX WORE DARK GRAY Columbia cargo trousers—quick-drying, easy to maneuver in, and plenty of pockets. He wore a generic neutral gray, quick-drying T-shirt. Over the T-shirt, he wore an olive drab bullet-resistant vest. In a pancake holster on his hip was his SIG SAUER, holding one fifteen-round magazine. In his mag holders on both hips, he carried extra magazines for his HK416. Over his vest he wore an olive drab jacket, concealing his pistol and magazines. If he had to pass as a civilian, he could shed the HK and still be armed with his concealed pistol.

At Oceana Naval Air Station in Virginia Beach, when the Outcasts boarded a small military charter plane, their gear was already there waiting for them. Soon they were wheels up and in the air.

Alex and Cat sat on the starboard side while John and Pancho sat across from them on the port side.

Alex leaned over to John. "What do you want more than anything in the world?"

"Is that a trick question?" John asked.

"I just wonder what makes you tick."

"God's will."

"God's will?"

"That's what makes me happy—not like adrenaline kind of happy. I mean *happy* happy—the long-term kind. It's how I succeed."

"How does God's will make you succeed?"

"Because all the confidence in the world won't amount to squat if God isn't willing."

"My grandfather said there's a flow to life. When we're one with that flow, and believe in what we're doing, anything is possible. If we're not one with that flow, we set ourselves up for failure. Maybe that's what God's will is, but I don't know how to recognize it."

"Learning His teachings and following them—not perfectly, just doing our best."

"Don't let him talk you into going to Bible study with him," Pancho interrupted. "It's mostly women there, and what they're studying is John."

John ignored Pancho and said, "I believe the Bible has most of God's teachings. You believe in God?"

Alex felt uncomfortable. "I did before my sister and grandpa died."

There was an awkward silence between them.

"You said once before that you weren't sure about what we're doing," Alex said. "And now we're going after Damien."

John nodded. "Damien has to go."

"Now you sound sure."

"I've never felt so sure of anything in my life."

Alex closed his eyes and rested until their plane landed at Long Island MacArthur Airport (LIMA) in Ronkonkoma, New York. At the airport, the four rolled their black Samsonite hard-shelled luggage from the plane through the LIMA parking lot. Dark clouds released a cold drizzle. Alex and John walked behind Pancho, who followed Cat.

"I want to know," Alex said.

"Yeah?" John asked.

"About the dream."

"What dream?"

"You said you had a dream that someone on our team wasn't going to survive."

"Like you said, it was just a dream," John said, now sounding reluctant to discuss it.

"You said it felt so real. Who was it?" A little voice in Alex's head screamed at him to let it go, but he wasn't listening.

"You really want to know?" John asked.

"No, but tell me anyway."

John's eyes followed Cat.

A cold, hollow feeling filled Alex's stomach. *I shouldn't have asked.*

The Outcasts found a gray GMC Yukon idling. A woman with black hair in a ponytail sat in the driver's seat of the large SUV. She rolled her window down a crack. Alex approached her.

"Which one of you is Alex?" she said.

Alex spoke up: "That would be me."

"Sleep well?"

"Like a baby," he said.

"You good?"

"Let's do it."

She stepped out of the vehicle and opened the rear. Cat was the first to wheel her suitcase to the back. Cat waited for the woman wearing the ponytail to load her luggage.

"Is your arm broken, honey?" the woman asked.

Cat glared at the woman before loading her suitcase into the back. Pancho chuckled. The guys loaded their luggage.

Ms. Ponytail closed the back and said, "Enjoy New York." She walked over to a white sedan, hopped inside, and drove away.

Pancho and John loaded into the SUV. Before Cat could get in the vehicle, Alex pulled her aside.

"There's something I've got to tell you," Alex said.

"You have a boyfriend," she said.

Alex tried to smile.

"You can tell me about him later," she said.

Alex was serious. "I'm afraid if I don't tell you now, I may never get to tell you."

"If you're worried about something happening to you, don't. You can take Damien on your worst day." She started for the SUV, but he pulled her back. Cat turned and faced him.

"The sun is always brighter when you're around," he said. "The sea is always bluer when you're around."

She stood staring at him.

Alex wrapped his arms around her and his lips pressed against hers. He didn't want to let her go.

When Cat came up for air, she whispered in his ear, "You make me feel alive." Then she gave him a kiss on the cheek.

Pancho pounded on the door from inside the SUV. "Let's go, boss."

Cat smiled. "I won't let anything happen to you."

"Don't worry about me," Alex said. "Just take care of yourself."

Alex and Cat got in the SUV. Cat took the driver's seat and Alex rode shotgun. John sat behind Cat, with Pancho beside him. She put the vehicle into gear, drove onto Interstate 495, and traveled west to the Queens-Midtown Tunnel.

"This was the tunnel in *Men in Black*," Pancho said. "Tommy Lee Jones and Will Smith drove through here upside down in their Ford LTD."

"I hope you're not expecting the same from me," Cat said.

"I am."

"You'll have to get out to lighten the load."

John snickered through his nose.

Alex smiled.

Pancho looked at his stomach—he wasn't fat, but he was a heavyweight.

NYPD Emergency Service Unit (ESU) officers in SWAT gear monitored the Midtown Tunnel toll booth. After paying the toll, the Outcasts rolled beneath the East River and crossed over into Manhattan. They circled around the Empire State Building—it was still standing—and NYPD was in full presence. Cat drove north on Park Avenue. ESU officers in SWAT gear with portable barricades formed a checkpoint at East Ninety-Sixth Street for vehicles heading south on Park Avenue. The southbound vehicles crawled bumper-to-bumper. It looked like the skipper got the word out on the terrorist threat.

Alex turned up the volume on the police scanner installed in the SUV. He needed every bit of information he could get. Somewhere out there, someone would see something. He tried to ignore the thousand variables in that thought and focused on the chatter.

". . . truck turned on a red light and is heading south down Park Avenue," a voice on the scanner said.

"That's him, it's got to be him," Alex said.

"Chief, there are only about a thousand UPS trucks in this city. Could be a driver skirting a roadblock to make a delivery."

Alex shook his head. "Don't care. It's the first sighting and it fits. Go, Cat! If we're wrong we're still going the right way."

Cat gunned the SUV and they tore through Harlem.

"There!" John shouted, pointing to a brown truck.

"Follow it," Alex said, trying to stay calm.

Cat turned left on 129th Street.

Cat took another left, sped through a red light, and nearly hit a car as she bullied her way into traffic. She forged through the southbound lane of Park Avenue. Now the UPS truck was two blocks ahead of them, and Cat couldn't force her way any closer.

As the UPS truck neared the police checkpoint at East Ninety-Sixth Street, it turned right on Ninety-Seventh.

"It could be a coincidence, or the guy in the UPS is avoiding the police," John said.

The UPS truck could've gone south on Fifth Avenue, where there was another police checkpoint, but it continued its detour on the tree-lined street across Central Park.

# 44

Damien, wearing a brown UPS uniform, drove his truck west through Central Park on Ninety-Seventh Street. He looked in his side-view mirror for his comrades in their two large green Chevy Tahoes, but they weren't there. "Where are they?" Damien asked.

"Maybe they made a wrong turn," Mohammed said.

"They're supposed to be right behind us."

Behind the UPS truck, lights from an NYPD patrol car flashed red. Damien pulled over. He drew his Stechkin revolver and placed it under a clipboard beside him.

The patrol car parked behind the UPS truck. A police officer exited the patrol car, walked to the UPS truck, and stopped beside Damien's window. Damien was pleased to see a young police officer—inexperienced.

The police officer rapped his knuckles on Damien's window.

Damien rolled it down all the way.

"Where we heading today?" the officer asked.

"Fifth Avenue, sir," Damien replied.

"Fifth Avenue is east, but you're heading west."

"Yes, the streets were blocked."

"Not blocked. The police are letting people through."

"Oh, good. I thought they were blocked."

"Where on Fifth Avenue are you headed?"

"Am I in trouble or something?"

"Is there a problem answering my question?"

"The Empire State Building." Damien's eyes bored through him.

"Okay." The policeman paused as if to read Damien's intentions. "Mind if I take a look in the back of your truck?"

"I'm in a bit of a rush, so if I haven't broken any laws, I'd appreciate if you let me finish my work."

"It'll just take a minute."

"Yes. Of course." Damien reached for his clipboard and pulled his revolver out from under it. Then he aimed the revolver at the police officer's face and pulled the trigger. The police officer fell backward into the street. Damien put the UPS truck in gear and drove off.

# 45

The Outcasts spotted the patrol car and a moment later the body of the officer lying in the street.

"You were right, Chief, that's him!" Pancho shouted.

"The truck is just up ahead," John said.

Alex saw it. "Cat, pull up on the left side of the truck. John, Pancho, shoot out the tires," Alex commanded.

Cat stomped on the accelerator and pulled up to the left of the UPS truck. Pancho and John ripped loose with their HK416 rifles—blowing out the tires. The UPS truck's tire rims sparked as they gouged out lines in the road. A bread truck came into the Outcasts' lane, threatening a head-on collision. Cat spun the steering wheel hard and slammed the side of her SUV into the side of the UPS truck, knocking the UPS truck off the road and taking its place in the right lane, just missing the oncoming truck in the opposite lane. The UPS truck lost speed as it swerved left and right.

Cat ran off the road and rammed the side of the UPS truck again. The UPS truck crashed into an elm tree, stopping the truck dead. "Brake turn, Cat—now!" Alex shouted.

Cat pulled the handbrake, locking the wheels, and turned sharp. The SUV skidded 180 degrees around, facing the UPS truck.

The Outcasts spilled out of their SUV, using the doors as shields.

If Cat hadn't turned the vehicle 180 degrees, they'd have no shields at all.

Damien and a blond guy stumbled out of the UPS truck, and a car almost hit them as they crossed the street south and headed through the trees.

Before the Outcasts could chase them, two green SUVs arrived with tangos hanging out the windows shooting. The trucks screeched to a halt behind the UPS truck. The Outcasts returned fire, popping holes in glass and metal.

One terrorist opened his door, hopped out of the green SUV, and took a shot at the Outcasts with his AKS. The green SUVs left him, sped across the road, and stopped near the mass of trees where Damien and Blondie had run into. The now-exposed terrorist screamed and started to chase after his comrades, but John brought him down with a burst that tore open his stomach.

John ran forward toward the UPS truck, barely pausing as he put two rounds into the head of the terrorist lying on the street. "I'll take the bomb!"

Across the street, four tangos abandoned their vehicle and ran south behind Damien and Blondie.

Alex, Pancho, and Cat positioned themselves to aim at the terrorists. "Can't get a clear shot with all this traffic," Cat said. Alex and Pancho couldn't take a shot, either, without hitting innocent civilians.

A taxi screeched to a halt. Its driver got out and started running. A startled businessman hopped out of the backseat, looked around, and followed suit.

Pancho held out his hand, but traffic didn't stop for him. Alex, Pancho, and Cat waited for a lull in the traffic, then raced across the road in pursuit. As they reached the other side of the road, Alex stopped, planted his feet, aimed, and shot a running terrorist in the back of the head, toppling him to the ground. The three Outcasts hurried to the green SUVs and checked inside—empty.

The Outcasts rushed into the trees but went no faster than their eyes could search in front of them. Joggers and bicyclists snaked around to the right. The Outcasts couldn't see the terrorists. Alex wondered why the tangos were heading south. Were they still going to assault the Empire State Building? Or maybe they were trying to fool the Outcasts into thinking they were going south before they did a disappearing act and snuck out to the north.

After advancing thirty yards into the woods, the tangos appeared from behind a stand of trees and unloaded their AKSs, muzzles flashing. Bullets chewed up tree bark and spit it at Alex. So many rounds flew that it sounded like radio static. It was scary, but it was also clear to Alex that the terrorists were not proficient shooters. Their shots were flying everywhere. All the same, he stayed down, since a stray bullet was just as deadly as an aimed one.

He looked around and saw an older male-and-female couple in sweatpants and sweatshirts flat on their stomachs. A cyclist fell off his bike and after skidding along the pavement got up and started running.

As the wild fire from the terrorists slowed, Alex signaled to Pancho to cover him. The tangos were probably reloading. Alex peeked around his tree and then made a move as if he were going to stand up. A terrorist popped into the open to shoot and Pancho blew away half his face with a short burst.

When a second terrorist appeared to see what happened, Alex punched two holes in his upper body while Pancho finished him off with a single shot to the head.

Damien shouted in Arabic.

Cat translated: "Some of them are going to hit us again while the others retreat."

Sure enough, the terrorists returned fire. Although the Outcasts had to take cover behind trees, the terrorists' firepower wasn't as withering as the previous assault. When the firing started to die down this time, it immediately picked up—from farther away. The

terrorists were trying to break contact and retreat. They were probably more concerned about police or other reinforcements arriving
than they were about sticking around to kill the Outcasts. During
the next lull, Alex and Pancho returned fire, joined by Cat, but the
terrorists ran away.

The Outcasts chased after the bad guys. When the Outcasts
came to the two on the ground, Alex fired a round into one terrorist's forehead while Pancho shot the other in the side of the head.
Alex noticed that one of their AKSs was missing.

As they chased the terrorists, Alex wanted to shoot, but there
were tennis courts behind the terrorists and people were on them.
With all the shooting going on, the tennis matches had come to
halt. A squirrel scrambled up a tree.

The terrorists ran around to the right of the tennis courts, crossing small roads and paths. Damien now carried an AKS and next to
him ran Blondie, also armed with an AKS, whose appearance stood
out from the Arab terrorists. They looked like average Americans—
except for their rifles. All of the terrorists wore civilian clothes except
for Damien and the Caucasian in brown UPS uniforms.

After the Outcasts chased the terrorists past the tennis courts,
they came to the Jackie Onassis reservoir, named after the former
First Lady for her dedicated efforts to preserve the historic architecture of the city. Ducks floated on the water's surface. A trail circled
the reservoir. Joggers turned around and headed back to where they
came from, avoiding the gunfire. An artist left his painting on the
easel as he crouched to the ground to avoid being shot.

Alex wanted to stop and nail one of the terrorists, but he also
wanted to keep up with Damien. So Alex ran, weaving in and out of
trees as he charged forward. He sucked in deep breaths of oxygen.
Adrenaline surged through his veins. His vision became acute. With
Alex's mind speeding up, the terrorists and everything seemed to
move in slow motion.

Sirens squealed behind the Outcasts back where they had left their SUV. No explosion sounded—John must've succeeded in dismantling the bomb. Alex really wished he had John's gun in the fight now.

The farther south everyone ran, the more the reservoir overtook the park, until the water squeezed everyone off to a small strip of green to the west—closer to the city's streets and skyscrapers. Four of the terrorists began to straggle behind. They seemed the least physically fit of the group. Alex thought, *Damien and Blondie must understand that the gazelle doesn't have to be faster than the cheetah. It only has to be faster than the other gazelles.*

"Smoke 'em," Alex said. The Outcasts stopped and fired. Pigeons pecking on the ground took flight. The bodies of two stragglers struck the dirt. Suddenly, the other two straggling terrorists sped up to join their comrades, disappearing behind trees.

The Outcasts resumed their chase. When the tangos attempted to cross Central Park West, the traffic didn't stop until Damien and Blondie fired bursts of bullets into oncoming cars, parting a path through the vehicles. Without trees blocking Alex's field of fire, he wanted to shoot, but civilians permeated the background, and he didn't risk shooting one.

The Outcasts dodged a speeding white sedan as they crossed Central Park West and entered the Upper West Side, with its upper-class apartments rising high above the city and Central Park.

The terrorists stopped behind cars and other available cover—then they turned and blasted at the Outcasts.

Pancho ducked behind a parked truck. Cat hid to the rear at the base of a light pole. Alex used a row of metal newspaper vending machines for shelter. Pedestrians behind Alex remained standing: "Get down!" he yelled. Although the sound of the terrorists' gunfire had dissipated into the air in Central Park, now the sound had nowhere to escape, echoing off the Upper West Side skyscrapers, causing a horrible raucous. As enemy rounds cut into the buildings, particles flew. Cascades of glass erupted. Pedestrians shouted and screamed.

Sirens continued to pierce the air. Bullets banged on the vending machines that Alex hid behind. Inside his body he shuddered, but Alex quickly put that feeling in a box and closed it.

When the firing lulled, Alex and the others popped out from their cover to fire back. Alex acquired Damien moving in his sights, but there were too many civilians around, many in shock, to allow a clear shot. The tangos saw that the Outcasts didn't fire, so after reloading, they advanced toward the Outcasts, shooting as they walked.

The Outcasts took cover again. Bullets pounded the area around them.

"Get ready to peel back!" Alex called.

"Police, drop your weapons!" a voice called.

The terrorists shouted and shifted the direction of their fire, taking the pressure off the Outcasts, who came out from cover and looked for opportunities to shoot at the terrorists.

From the south two uniformed police crouched behind an NYPD patrol car parked on Columbus Avenue and fired their pistols at the terrorists. The terrorists answered the police, cutting down both police officers and a civilian woman behind them fleeing to get out of the firefight.

Alex aligned his sight with the side of a tango's head and pulled the trigger, taking him out.

More sirens sounded. The terrorists must've feared the cavalry was coming, because they fled.

The Outcasts pursued, passing vehicles pockmarked with bullet holes. They passed a high-rise before entering the back of a super-market. Inside the back of the store they passed by offices and a sink with a mop next to it and a metal bucket. The Outcasts burst through the double doors and into the main shopping area of the su-permarket, where Alex thought it smelled like oranges, but he could see no oranges.

Pancho led them past the meat and poultry section. A tango

popped out from a corner and unloaded thirty rounds at the Outcasts. They dropped to the floor. The tango shot up the display cases, then ran away, reloading in flight.

The Outcasts followed.

The fleeing terrorist grabbed a woman wearing a baby blue dress and used her as a shield. The terrorist pulled her as he backed away into the cookie aisle. She squealed until her voice hit a feverish pitch. Pancho drilled a hole above the tango's right eye. "Tango down!" Pancho called.

The woman collapsed on the floor with the tango's blood spatter on the shoulder of her dress and the side of her face.

Another tango appeared from the end of the aisle and opened fire on full auto. Pancho and Alex hit the deck—AK rounds tore through shelves, spraying the air with a rainbow of colored wrappings and cookies. The debris rained down on Alex and Pancho as rounds zipped over their heads. The tango disappeared around the end of the aisle. Pancho reached over to a split-open pack of oatmeal cookies, liberated three, and stuffed them in his mouth. Alex couldn't believe it—they were under fire and Pancho was eating—*bastard!*

When the two SEALs reached the end of the aisle near the checkout counters, Alex scanned left, looking down his sights. A rifle barrel exited the adjacent aisle and turned toward him. Alex held his breath and began to squeeze the trigger, waiting for the tango to appear in his sights before finishing the squeeze. The tango's rifle wasn't an AKS like the others, but it was moving swiftly. Alex would have to react fast. When the tango appeared he wasn't a tango. She was Cat. Alex had almost whacked her.

A tango jumped out from behind a cash register, and before he could open fire, Alex blasted through the tango's chest. The tango fell to his knees and all three Outcasts opened up on him. The tango shook like a rag doll in a hurricane.

The Outcasts proceeded through the front door, where they exited the supermarket and hounded the bad guys across Columbus Avenue, before the terrorists turned north, bobbing in, out, and around buildings between Columbus Avenue and Amsterdam Avenue.

As the terrorists neared Ninety-Seventh Street, two police officers and one ESU officer appeared. While terrorists and police engaged in a shootout, Cat stopped running and busted a cap in the back of a terrorist, who fell forward and didn't stand up again. Cat huffed and puffed as she resumed the chase. Alex and Pancho took slow, deep breaths while they ran. "How much farther can these bastards run?" Pancho asked.

The tangos continued their push north, mowing down the two police officers and ESU officer. Damien and the terrorists were crossing Ninety-Seventh Street when a gray SUV came barreling down the street, running over a terrorist and dragging him underneath the front axle before the vehicle screeched to a stop. John jumped out of the SUV.

"About time," Pancho said.

"Aren't you going to ask me about the UPS truck bomb?" John asked.

"Like I said, about time," Pancho replied.

Alex, Pancho, John, and Cat chased the terrorists into the Manhattan Valley neighborhood. They passed towering apartment buildings. Running and gunning, John tapped two bullet holes in the nearest tango's back. Alex felt energized by John's arrival and he sensed that Pancho and Cat were energized, too. Hopefully their new vitality demoralized the enemy.

The remaining tangos dodged in and out of buildings as they ran north. Damien, Blondie, and company ran onto the grounds of the Cathedral of St. John the Divine. The Outcasts followed, passing the biblical garden on the south, then the western side with its rose window on the stone façade of the Gothic cathedral standing more than two hundred feet tall.

The terrorists crossed Amsterdam Avenue, but a line of cars

blocked the Outcasts from getting to the other side. While the terrorists disappeared around the corner of Amsterdam Avenue and 114th Street, Pancho managed to stop traffic for his Teammates. The Outcasts turned the corner of Amsterdam and 114th to find the terrorists were nowhere in sight.

# 46

Alex heard a woman squeal from the direction of inside a building with a sign that read BUTLER LIBRARY. A college student came running out the front door, his neon-green backpack bouncing on his back. The Outcasts entered the library and were on the second floor. No security personnel stood present as the Outcasts proceeded through a domed lobby. A mural of Athena decorated the wall in front of them. On both sides of it were staircases. Since John was the smoothest shooter and Cat the slowest, Alex paired them up to sweep west while he and Pancho swept east.

Alex and Pancho passed under a metal sign that read COLUMBIA. Alex checked a coffee bar and lounge on the south wall—no terrorists. Next, Alex examined the computer lab. A kid with his iPod cranked up and his face in a computer monitor suddenly realized the other students had cleared out and he was alone with a man armed with an assault rifle. Alex left the computer room and checked small reading rooms on the east wall. In one room, Alex entered to discover a couple kissing heavily. Students came running downstairs from the northeast staircase. After clearing the east wall, Alex and Pancho linked up with John and Cat in a reading room that extended along most of the north wall. Then they heard a shriek that sounded like it came from the third floor. Alex motioned for Pancho to lead the four of them up the northeast staircase to the third floor.

On the third floor, they split up again. John and Cat swept from north to south on the west side while Alex and Pancho cleared north to south on the east side. Alex took the catalog room, extending along 90 percent of the east wall. He exited the room through a door to the south that led west into a reference room, covering most of the south wall. A chandelier hung from a high ceiling. When Alex exited the reference room door facing north, he linked up with Pancho, then the two hooked up with John and Cat. Across from the reference room sat the circulation desk, with a librarian cowering behind it.

"We're the good guys," whispered Alex. "Are the men with guns upstairs?"

Tears rolled down her face. She nodded.

"Go downstairs, hit the fire alarm, and get out of the building," Alex said gently but firmly. "We need to get everyone out."

She stood. Her legs wobbled, then she stumbled south to the stairs.

The Outcasts advanced through an entry to the middle of the library, where the book stacks were, surrounded by a wall that separated the center from the rest of the floor. The four cleared the area.

The Outcasts crept up another flight of stairs. On the fourth floor, Pancho and Alex crept east while John and Cat went west. Pancho covered the long east corridor in front of him and the short rows with shelves holding newspapers and periodicals to the south while Alex scanned the same corridor to the east and checked north between the long rows of shelves.

The fire alarm went off. Now the Outcasts could move faster without the sound of their footsteps betraying them to the enemy. Gunshots fired behind Alex—an HK416 followed by AKSs. Alex wanted to turn around and look. He wanted to help, but he had to trust his Teammates to handle it because if Alex failed to cover his area of responsibility, he could jeopardize the lives of his Team-mates. Three terrorists appeared in the east corridor. Alex flicked his selector from semiautomatic to automatic and unleashed his fury on the terrorists. Pancho must've been reading Alex's mind, because he unloaded on full auto, too. Empty bullet shells flew from the ejector ports of the SEALs' HK416s. The terrorists performed the *danse macabre*. Only one of the terrorists got off shots, into the ceiling, before Alex and Pancho ran out of ammo, ending the dance. The terrorists collapsed to the floor.

With the index finger of one hand, Alex pressed the button to eject his empty magazine while his other hand brought a new thirty-round magazine from a holder on the belt around his waist. He inserted the new magazine into his rifle and charged it. The whole reloading process was one fluid motion that he made without consciously thinking, because he'd done it thousands of times. Pancho reloaded, too.

The gunfire behind Alex increased in intensity as he and Pancho pressed forward. When they hit the east wall, they turned left and headed north along the last row of shelves until they reached the north wall. Then they turned left and followed the corridor west. At the far west end, the door slammed.

"Northwest door, tangos getting away!" John yelled.

Alex and Pancho ran to the door. John and Cat reached it first and disappeared. Then Alex and Pancho exited through the door.

"Northwest stairs!" John yelled.

Alex and Pancho ran through three more doors until they reached the stairs where John and Cat shot it out with the terrorists. The terrorists were gone.

The Outcasts descended to the second floor. Sirens whirred outside. Even with the added noise of the fire alarm, the Outcasts could hear the noise of terrorists shouting, which the Outcasts followed through a corridor south. John took the point, followed by Cat, Alex, and Pancho. Just before they turned the corner east, shots rang out from behind. Alex turned around to see Pancho drop a terrorist. Then Pancho dropped.

Alex felt his heart drop, too. "Pancho down! John, hold up!"

The terrorist on the floor groaned.

Alex squeezed off two rounds, quieting the terrorist. "You okay, Pancho?"

"Yeah." He tried to stand, then growled before falling down again. Blood covered his thigh.

Alex reached into the pocket on Pancho's good thigh and pulled out his first-aid kit (blowout kit). Alex took out his own knife and cut Pancho's trousers near the wound. Then he used gauze from the blowout kit to stuff in Pancho's wound. Finally he taped it in place.

Pancho stood up on his good leg, but when he tried to walk on his wounded leg he grunted and fell. Sweat drenched his face.

Pancho used Alex to support the weight that his bad leg couldn't, hopping to Room 203 in the southwest corner. Cat and John covered the area with their weapons for any unwanted visitors. Alex helped Pancho into the southwest corner of the room. "You'll have an easy view of the entrances to this room." Alex lowered Pancho to the floor.

"Over here!" John shouted to somebody outside of the room. John poked his head into the room: "Firefighters coming. Better take Pancho's rifle."

Alex looked at Pancho.

"It's okay," Pancho said. He handed his HK416 to Alex. "Still got my concealed pistol."

Alex strapped the HK416 across his back. "In here," John said.

The firefighters entered the room.

"One of the terrorists shot him in the leg," Alex said.

The firefighters began helping Pancho.

"Take care, big guy," Alex said.

Pancho's eyes seemed more pained by disappointment than physical hurt. He wanted to continue the mission. "Thanks," Pancho said.

A firefighter looked at the Outcasts' weapons and asked, "Who are you people?"

"They're on our side," Pancho said.

Alex, Cat, and John hurried out the door and exited the library. They held their HK416s down to their sides to help conceal them with the profile of their bodies.

People swarmed around the area: students, firefighters with their trucks and hoses—but no sign of the terrorists. Alex remembered the words of his grandfather as he had helped Alex and his sister track a wounded animal through the woods: "There are signs everywhere. You just have to look—and listen."

Alex crouched to the sidewalk and looked at the concrete. Between the wet residue of rain drops, he saw reddish spatter on the pavement. He touched it with his hand. "This blood is fresh. John, did you wound one of them?" Alex asked.

"No wounding," John said. "Just killing."

"I did," Cat said. "I tried to take him out, but he was too quick."

Alex looked around and saw another blood spot. "These look like more blood drops," Alex said.

John and Cat examined the spots. Then they found more leading north of the library. The Outcasts followed the blood spots through the campus until the spots ceased near 116th Street and Broadway.

"Don't focus so much on the track that you lose sight of the animal," Grandpa once warned Alex and Sarah.

Alex looked around the area and thought to himself, *If I was being hunted, where would I go?* He saw the theater—they could hide out there. *I'm tired, and I want to get away.* Then he saw the subway. "There."

From behind, a group of policemen ran toward the Outcasts. The Outcasts hurried downstairs into the subway station. They jumped the turnstile.

When Alex neared the subway platform, he saw the terrorists

board the train and move toward the lead car. Damien and Blondie were in front.

"We got cops on our tail," John warned. "And they ain't going to be pleased when they see us with our weapons."

"Those train doors are about to close," Cat added.

The Outcasts sprinted to the rear of the train and hopped on board just before the doors shut. Some of the passengers became visibly nervous when they noticed that the trio were armed. Some passengers walked forward in the car, probably to distance themselves from the Outcasts, when Alex said, "There are terrorists forward in the train. You're best off staying in this car and getting off at the next stop."

"Who are you?" a Hispanic woman with a Columbia University sweatshirt asked.

"We're the good guys," Alex said with a smile.

From the subway car in front, passengers entered the Outcasts' car. They seemed to be distancing themselves from the terrorists. One of the passengers was an athletic man in his thirties wearing a suit and tie and texting on his cell phone. He became frustrated. "Damn it." When he looked up, he noticed Alex trying to conceal an HK416 to his side with another strapped across his back. He put his cell phone away and asked, "Who are you?"

"Who are you?" Alex asked.

The man in the suit pulled back his suit jacket and exposed his badge and pistol, a Glock 9mm. "Detective Paulie Giovanni. NYPD."

The Hispanic woman with the Columbia shirt seemed relieved to hear "NYPD."

"I'm Alex."

"What I meant was, who are you working for?" Detective Giovanni said.

Alex studied him for a moment. "I'm working for the coast guard."

"Coast guard?!" the woman exclaimed.

"I don't know much about the coast guard," Detective Giovanni said. "But I served in the navy. Are the coast guard ranks the same as the navy?"

"Yes," Alex answered.

"I got out as an E-4. What rank is that in the coast guard?"

Now Alex knew that he was being tested, but that was fine. Detective Giovanni was doing his job. "Petty officer third class."

"You got a coast guard ID?"

Alex showed him.

"What brings you to New York City, Chief Alex Brown?"

"We came for some counterterrorist training, but it looks like now we're doing the real thing."

"We?"

Cat raised her hand. "Cat."

"John."

Giovanni noticed they were armed, too. "You three aren't what I imagine when I think of a recruiting poster for the coast guard," the detective said.

Alex unstrapped the HK416 from his back and said, "You know how to use one of these?"

"I was a gunner's mate."

Alex handed it to him and pointed to the selector switch. "Here is your selector switch for safe, semiauto, and full auto. You only have thirty shots."

"If we try to take them down, we're going to have a civilian bloodbath on our hands."

"I don't want that any more than you do."

Detective Giovanni typed a text message on his cell phone and sent it. "I'm giving NYPD an update on our status."

The train continued forward, making its stops along the way: 137th Street, 145th Street, and 157th Street. At each stop, Alex stuck his head out the door to see if the tangos were getting off. Except for a few people, who remained unaware of their surroundings, most of the passengers exited. The would-be passengers, who saw the terrorists and Outcasts with weapons, decided to wait for the next train. Even some people who didn't see the danger noticed the empty cars and people not boarding—warning signs that something was wrong. When the doors closed, there were no more passengers in the Outcasts' car.

Alex and his team cautiously moved forward on the train to the next car. They continued forward until they had only one car remaining between them and the terrorists. Few passengers remained—a homeless man, a woman who looked strung out on drugs, and a young lady with her earphones on as she remained absorbed in a book. Alex wanted to warn them, but the civilians were too close to the terrorists for Alex to get near.

The train rose out of the ground. The underground darkness and artificial light gave way to dark cloud-covered skies and the city. Now that the train was aboveground, Detective Giovanni could probably get cell phone reception. He made a call on his cell phone.

The train rolled past a hospital and across Broadway Bridge. Hordes of cars crawled on the bridge level below the train. Below them flowed the Harlem River.

"We should take them now," John said. "Isn't going to get much better than this."

Detective Giovanni told Alex, "ESU is going to assault the train at the Marble Hill Station."

"Which station is that?" Cat asked.

"Next," Giovanni answered.

# 47

The train slowed. Written in white on black were the words MARBLE HILL–225TH STREET. At the elevated station, ESU officers in their SWAT gear held positions behind support columns under a red roof.

The train stopped and the doors opened. The terrorists blasted through the train windows. ESU returned fire with fury. In the train, glass flew through the air, shreds of paper ads spread like confetti, holes popped into metal, and holes punched into holes. A terrorist with a square face entered the car with three passengers. The homeless man shrieked as he hobbled off the train. The woman wearing earphones tried to follow the homeless man, but Square Face entered the car and pulled her back. Then Square Face proceeded to use her as a human shield. Alex couldn't see Damien and Blondie. Maybe they had human shields, too.

Alex opened the door to the car in front, used his foot to keep the door from closing, and took aim. He squeezed the trigger. His shot struck Square Face in the side of the head. No sooner had Square Face hit the ground than the woman with earphones ran off the train. She didn't go far before another terrorist's bullet stopped her. The female junkie lay down on her seat calmly as if about to take a nap.

Tangos shot ESU officers down, and ESU officers shot terrorists down.

Alex, John, Cat, and Detective Giovanni fired through the glass doors leading to the front car. The terrorists fired back. Giovanni stood in the open, firing on full auto until his face erupted in crimson, and he fell. His eyes froze open before Alex could say anything.

Smoke erupted in the terrorists' car. It wasn't clear whether the terrorists had done it or NYPD. The smoke spread to the Outcasts' car and train platform outside.

Alex couldn't see the terrorists, if any were still alive. "Let's get to the station exit," Alex said. The smoke became so bad that he couldn't see in front of his face. He bumped into a chair as he searched for the door to exit the car. Although he found the doorway, he had difficulty finding his way off the platform. He walked into a pillar.

Shots rang out—AKS and HK416. *Cat*, he thought. Alex bumbled in the smoke until he found his way to a turnstile, where a policeman lay in a puddle of blood. "Cat!" he called. "John!"

"We're downstairs!" John yelled. "Cat's hit!"

Alex turned left. He didn't remember running down the stairs—he just found himself at the bottom. Cat lay on the sidewalk, with John next to her.

"She got ahead of me, Alex," John said, his voice tight with emotion. "Damien fired off a burst. Hit her. Two shots. I winged Blondie. They split up: Blondie went west and Damien ran into those apartments to the north." John made a 911 call on his cell phone.

Alex kneeled down next to her. John kept his hand on a pressure bandage soaked with blood on Cat's chest. There was a lot of blood. "We're going to get you to a hospital," Alex said.

Cat groaned. "No . . ."

"You're going to be okay," Alex said.

She closed her eyes.

"You're going to be okay. Don't go to sleep. Can you hear me, Cat? Don't go to sleep! Stay with me. Don't go. Please don't go."

"We both don't need to stay with her," John said. "Damien is getting away."

Black clouds packed the heavens. A siren wailed in the distance—gradually becoming louder. Alex's spirit was spent. "I lead men to their deaths. Always hated that phrase, but it's what I do."

"Each of us volunteered and each of us could've walked away at any time. This was our choice."

Alex tapped his fingers on the concrete. He watched Cat for a moment before his gaze shifted to the apartments where Damien had gone. He tapped his fingers again. Then he looked at her. Slowly he stood. His right foot took one step back away from her—then his left foot stepped back—again and again until he reached the edge of the sidewalk. He turned around. No cars were coming along the street toward him. He stepped off the curb—one foot in front of the other—again and again. Alex picked up the pace to a jog. Then a run.

# 48

Eleven buildings, with mahogany-colored brick facades, stood fourteen to fifteen stories tall and housed hundreds of apartments. Alex ran along the sidewalk between the buildings on his left and West 225th Street on his right. A scream cut the air. Alex turned left toward the noise, then dodged trees before arriving in a parking lot. To his left towered one of the apartment buildings, in front trees, and to his right another apartment. The screamer, still screaming, ran into the apartment building to the right.

Damien sat in a white station wagon among other vehicles in a parking lot. He looked like he was trying to start it. Maybe he had the wrong key or was trying to hotwire it.

Alex stopped running, planted his feet, brought his rifle to his shoulder, and leaned forward to brace for the recoil and anything else that might push against him. Damien's eyes met Alex's as he clicked off the safety. Damien ducked as Alex squeezed the trigger. It almost sounded like Alex fired on full auto, but he aimed each shot in rapid succession. The station wagon's windshield imploded on Damien, and the rear window blew out. Alex walked forward on the balls of his feet, firing, and didn't let up the heat until he'd spent all thirty rounds in his magazine. Then he took cover behind the vehicle in front of him and used it as a shield. His eyes stayed on

Damien while Alex's right index finger ejected the spent magazine and his left hand brought up a fresh one. He loaded the fresh magazine into his rifle.

Rain fell lightly. Alex popped up from behind his vehicle and fired as Damien exited his station wagon and from behind the driver's door shot at Alex. Damien moved around the door and advanced to cover behind another vehicle.

The rain poured harder. In one of the apartments, a child cried. Damien appeared and disappeared from above and beside vehicles—shooting through windows at Alex and skipping bullets off the cars' metal bodies in hopes of striking a final blow. Car alarms sounded. Alex and Damien assaulted forward. A bullet grazed the side of Alex's head—it burned and he couldn't tell if what dripped down his cheek was rain or blood. Eventually, Alex and Damien ran out of cars between them—and bullets.

The two men stood facing each other with nothing but ten yards of wet asphalt parking lot between them. Alex knew his mag was empty. Steam rolled off the barrel of his gun as he lowered it. Damien's eyes went wide for a second, and he lowered his rifle, too.

Movie scenes flashed through Alex's mind. Catchphrases and maniacal laughs played as hero and villain faced off for the final battle. It was so clichéd it made him smile.

Alex reached across his stomach with his left hand, lifted up his shirt, and pulled out the SIG from its pancake holster, clipped inside the waistband of his trousers.

Damien's eyes widened again.

A new vision entered Alex's mind. He saw the hospital room where Sarah lay. Mentally, she was no longer there. An elderly nurse walked in and spoke. "Can I talk to you for a moment?"

"Yes."

"Outside?"

They walked out into the hall.

"I've been doing this my whole life," the nurse said. "Your mother spent more time in here than anyone else—except you."

Alex nodded.

She studied his face. "You know what I'm going to tell you, don't you?"

Alex nodded.

"Sarah should've gone the day she arrived here. That was over forty-eight hours ago. I've never seen anyone suffer so much for so long."

Alex remained silent.

"You know why she hasn't gone?"

He nodded.

"You have to tell her it's okay to leave."

Alex couldn't speak—couldn't move his body. He wished it was him on the hospital bed instead of her, but wishing didn't make it so, and wishing didn't stop Sarah's suffering. The hospital seemed so white—white uniforms, white lights, white walls—like a body with the blood drained out. Somehow Alex managed to stand. Then he took the first step. After the first step, the next one became easier. He didn't remember any more steps after that. Suddenly he was at Sarah's side.

Alex put his hand on the bandaged stub that was what remained of her right arm. "I love you, Sarah." There was so much more he wanted to say, but none of it was *goodbye*. The more he thought about what he needed to say, the less he wanted to say it. Alex stopped thinking. "You'll always be in my heart. Goodbye, Sarah. It's okay to say *goodbye*."

Within a minute, her EKG went flat and Sarah departed—leaving him empty.

"Goodbye," Alex said, bringing his pistol up.

The hammer clicked back before striking the primer of a 9x19mm Parabellum bullet. The primer exploded, igniting the gunpowder, blasting the bullet forward through a corkscrew of helical grooves inside the SIG's barrel and imparting a vicious spin around its axis. The bullet cleared the barrel, followed by a thin shower of sparks and smoke. It was traveling at 1,350 feet per second when it tore through Damien's shirt just below his heart and kept going through flesh, blood, sinew, muscle, and bone before exiting out his back.

The empty shell casing ejected from Alex's pistol and bounced off the wet asphalt. It rolled around, still smoldering. A new bullet rose into the firing chamber. Alex's left hand came together with his right on the pistol grip.

Damien looked down at his chest in surprise. His rifle slipped from his hands as he brought them up to cover the wound. He swayed, then sank to his knees, his right leg buckling.

Alex walked forward, his pistol aimed squarely between Damien's eyes.

Questions remained on Damien's face. The brown discs of his eyes searched for answers that weren't there. Even then, he took his left hand away from the wound and reached for his pistol. Blood poured out over his right hand and splattered on the ground.

Alex fired. Damien's head reared up and slammed back down. His eyes continued to stare, but now saw nothing.

The cold rain continued to pour.

# 49

Morning dew on the manicured grass sparkled under the sunrise like emeralds. Alex breathed it all in. The world was saturated with colors this morning. He'd never quite noticed it before. White grave markers stood in neat rows, casting long, gentle shadows. Alex smelled the sweet fragrance of the dozen roses in his hands before he laid the flowers in front of a tombstone. He took one for himself and held it under his nose.

Next to Alex, Pancho stood with the aid of crutches. "That was a tough one."

"We knew it wouldn't be easy," Alex said.

"So what now? Desk duty?"

Alex shook his head. "Somehow, I don't think that's in our future."

A car door slammed. Alex turned around.

John helped Cat out of his black SUV and escorted her across the grass. Cat walked slowly. She carried a dozen red roses and when she reached Alex, she carefully laid them down on Sarah's grave.

"Thought you were still in the hospital," Alex said.

"She hobbled out of there without telling anyone," John said. "Head nurse was furious when she found out."

"I hate hospitals," Cat said.

"Me too," Alex said.

Pancho and John headed back to the car, leaving Alex and Cat alone.

She extended her hand.

Alex took it. "So what's going to happen now?" he asked.

"I don't know," she said. "Do you know?"

"No, I don't," he said, saying a silent goodbye to his sister, "but you know, I'm entirely okay with that."

# GLOSSARY

**ACOG:** Advance Combat Optical Gunsight. Made by Trijicon, Inc. in Wixom, Michigan. The ACOG 1.5x magnifies images to 1.5 times their normal size. Its aiming reticle glows in low-light conditions without a battery. In addition, the ACOG is waterproof to 500 feet. Sight is mounted on Picatinny rails attached to rifles such as the HK416 and M4.

**Agency:** Short for Central Intelligence Agency (CIA), which is also known as "Christians in Action."

**AK-47:** The name is a contraction of Russian: *Avtomat Kalashnikova obraztsa 1947 goda* (Kalashnikov's automatic rifle model of year 1947). This assault rifle fires a .308 (7.62x39mm) round up to an effective range of 330 yards (300 meters) and holds thirty rounds. It was developed in the Soviet Union by Mikhail Kalashnikov in two versions: the fixed-stock AK-47 and the AKS-47 (S: *Skladnoy priklad*) variant equipped with an underfolding metal shoulder stock.

**Asset:** Local personnel providing intelligence.

**AT4:** An 84mm, one-shot, light antitank rocket.

**BDU:** Battle dress uniform.

*Bedlah:* Belly-dancing costumes—fitted plunging bras and hip belts that sparkle. The beads on the fringes rattle as the girls dance.

**Blowout kit:** Medical pouch.

**Booger eater:** Generic term for *bad guys.*

**BUD/S:** Basic Underwater Demolition/SEAL training.

**Cammy, cammies:** Camouflage.

**Correct dope:** Adjust the scope to adjust for windage and distance.

**CRKT Tao pen:** CRKT stands for Columbia River Knife & Tool. Their Tao pen looks less like a tactical pen and more like a regular pen. However, the cap can be used as a blunt striking or raking weapon. Also, the butt can be applied to pressure points. In a more serious scenario, the pen point can be used as a stabbing weapon.

**Dam Neck:** Dam Neck, Virginia, home of SEAL Team Six.

**Delta:** Delta Force. The army's Tier 1 unit tasked with conducting counterterrorism and counterinsurgency.

**Dope:** *See* Correct dope.

**E&E:** Escape and evasion. Getting out of Dodge.

**Exfil:** Exfiltrate.

**Fantail:** A ship's stern overhang.

**Fast-rope:** Kick a thick rope out of the door of a helicopter. Then, wearing special gloves to prevent burning the hands, grab the rope with hands and feet while sliding down.

**Flashbang:** Stun grenade using a nonlethal flash of bright light and loud blast to disorient enemies.

**Helo:** Helicopter.

**HK416:** Assault rifle made by the German maker Heckler & Koch (HK). The HK416 has an adjustable six-position telescopic butt stock that has space inside to store items. The rifle holds 30 rounds in the magazine (with options for 20-round or 100-round magazines) and can fire .223 (5.56x45mm) ammunition at a rate of 700–900 rounds per minute. Its short-stroke gas piston operating system has fewer malfunctions, lasts longer, and is easier to clean than the M4 assault rifle. Also, SEALs can come out of the water and shoot the HK416 without having to drain it first.

**HUMINT:** Human intelligence. Intelligence gained and provided by human sources: agents, couriers, journalists, prisoners, diplomats, NGOs, refugees, etc.

**JSOC:** Joint Special Operations Command, located at Pope Air Force Base and Fort Bragg in North Carolina. After the 1980 failed attempt to rescue fifty-three American hostages at the American Embassy in Iran, it became clear that the army, navy, air force, and marines couldn't work together effectively on Special Operations missions. In 1987, the Department of Defense grafted all the military branches' Special Operations onto one tree—including Tier 1 units like SEAL Team Six and Delta. SEALs and Green Berets are truly special, but only the best make it to the top tier: Team Six and Delta. JSOC is Team Six's boss.

**KLA:** Kosovo Liberation Army.

**Knot:** One knot equals roughly 1.15 miles per hour.

**M4:** Assault rifle with retractable telescopic butt stock, firing .223 (5.56mm) rounds, and holding thirty rounds in the magazine.

*Majlis:* Sitting room.

**OIC:** Officer in charge.

**Op:** Operation.

**OP:** Observation post.

**OTs-38 Stechkin:** Russian revolver. Similar to a small .38, the double-action revolver holds only five shots. The 7.62x41.5mm SP-4 bullets make less noise and produce less flash than most sound-suppressed pistols, making for a quiet kill.

**Picatinny rail:** Named after the Picatinny Arsenal in New Jersey, where it was originally tested, this bracket attaches to a rifle

such as the HK416 or the M4. Then accessories such as a scope
or grenade launcher are added to the rail.

**PLO:** Palestine Liberation Organization. A political, paramilitary,
and terrorist organization recognized by a hundred states as
representative of the Palestinians.

**PT:** Physical training.

**RPG:** Rocket-propelled grenade.

**SATCOM:** Cryptographic (scrambled) portable satellite communication radio used by SEALs.

**SEAL:** The U.S. Navy's elite *SE*a, *A*ir, and *L*and commandos.
During World War II, the first navy frogmen were trained
to recon beaches for amphibious landings. Soon they learned
underwater demolitions in order to clear obstacles and became
known as Underwater Demolition Teams (UDTs). In the
Korean War, UDTs evolved and went farther inland, blowing
up bridges and tunnels. Years later, after observing communist
insurgency in Southeast Asia, President John F. Kennedy—who
had served in the navy during World War II—and others in the
military understood the need for unconventional warriors. The
navy created a unit that could operate from sea, air, and land—
SEALs—drawing heavily from UDTs. On January 1, 1962,
SEAL Team One and SEAL Team Two were born. By the end
of the war, the military decorated SEAL Teams One and Two
with three Medals of Honor, two Navy Crosses, forty-two
Silver Stars, 402 Bronze Stars, and numerous other awards. For
every SEAL killed, they killed two hundred. Over time, because
SEALs could do both UDT and SEAL jobs, the UDT Teams
were absorbed by the SEALs. The SEAL Teams expanded.
Currently, the odd-numbered teams—1, 3, 5, and 7—are sta-
tioned on the West Coast at Coronado, California. (Team 9
hasn't been created, but if the Teams expanded, Team 9 would
probably be next.) The even-numbered teams—2, 4, 6, 8, and
10—are located on the East Coast at Little Creek, Virginia.

**SIGINT:** Signals intelligence, which is intelligence gathered by intercepting signals between people (communications intelligence) and electronic signals (electronic intelligence) not directly involved in communication such as radar.

**SIG SAUER P226 Navy 9mm:** SIG stands for Schweizerische Industrie Gesellschaft, which is German for "Swiss Industrial Company." The P226 pistol has phosphate corrosion-resistant finish on the internal parts, contrast sights, and an anchor engraved on the slide. Holds fifteen rounds in the magazine. Designed especially for the SEALs.

**UBL:** Usama bin Laden. Abbreviation commonly used by the government.

**UDT:** Underwater Demolition Team. The frogmen, ancestors of SEALs.

**Tango:** Terrorist.

**Whiskey Tango Foxtrot:** Like other military units, SEALs often use the military phonetic alphabet "Whiskey Tango Foxtrot"—WTF—to mean "What the fuck?"

**Win Mag:** Winchester Magnum. The Win Mag is a customized Remington 700 sniper rifle that holds four rounds of .300-caliber, 190-grain match ammunition. Usually used with a Leupold 10-power scope. For evening, a KN250 night-vision scope slides over the top of the Leupold.

**WMD:** Weapon of Mass Destruction.

# FAMILIES OF FREEDOM SCHOLARSHIP FUND

The purpose of the Families of Freedom Scholarship Fund is to provide education assistance for postsecondary education study to financially needy dependents of those people killed or permanently disabled as a result of the terrorist attacks on September 11, 2001, and during the rescue activities relating to those attacks.

Established within one week of the attacks on September 11, 2001, the Families of Freedom Scholarship Fund is unprecedented in its scope. It will ultimately provide more than $100 million in postsecondary education assistance to an entire generation of financially needy dependents of those killed or permanently disabled in the 9/11 attacks and their aftermath. The fund has already provided millions of dollars in scholarship support, and will continue to provide education assistance through the year 2030.

The Lumina Foundation for Education, a private foundation that strives to help people achieve their potential by expanding access to an education beyond high school, established the fund with the foresight that the loss of a family provider to death or injury on 9/11 would put the educational futures of thousands of present and future students in jeopardy. The Lumina Foundation pledged the initial $3 million to create the fund: $1 million went directly to the fund and $2 million to a dollar-for-dollar matching grant to encourage contributions from individuals. The $2 million matching grant was met on December 18, 2001.

The first Families of Freedom scholarships were awarded in January 2002. As of the end of 2008, the fund and its subfunds had provided needed scholarships to 1,183 individuals, totaling more than $36 million; there are currently nearly 5,000 individuals registered for Families of Freedom scholarships through 2030.

The Families of Freedom Scholarship Fund is managed by Scholarship America, the nation's premier nonprofit, private sector scholarship and educational support organization. Scholarship America has administered the Families of Freedom Scholarship at cost since the inception of the fund. Scholarship America has distributed more than $2 billion to nearly two million students across the country.

**CONTACT INFORMATION:**
Families of Freedom Scholarship Fund
Scholarship America
One Scholarship Way
Saint Peter, MN 56082
www.familiesoffreedom.org
E-mail: info@familiesoffreedom.org
Toll-free phone: 1-877-862-0136

# ACKNOWLEDGMENTS

I n memory of Colonel John F. Parker—without his guidance, things may have turned out very differently for me as a young man. For Debbie, who gave me the inspiration and courage to love and live again post SEAL Teams. With thanks to the people of Wayne Co. (especially my patients), who continue to be my encouragement and give me purpose.

—*Howard E. Wasdin*

For my stepdad, Jerry Rapp, who has always supported me, I didn't realize how loud you could yell until I dropped that table on your foot. I thank my mom, Gwen. Also, I'm grateful to my yellow rose of Texas, Grandma Laura Fae Templin. Thank you to Sandi Moore, my junior high school English teacher, who always believed in me. And Lieutenant Colonel Free, Command Sergeant Major Million, Captain Bailey, Master Chief Knepper, and my SEAL instructors for teaching me about the military, how to believe, and more. Most of all, I'm grateful to Reiko, Kent, and Maria.

—*Stephen Templin*